Sir Richard Francis Bu[...] [...] [...] [...] [...],
daring explorer, prolifi[...] [...] [...] [...]
boyant celebrities of [...] [...] [...]or
unruly behavior, he joi[...] [...] [...]e
he gained a remarkab[...] [...] [...]i,
and Persian, eventual[...] [...] [...]es
and dialects. He led the famed expedition to discover the
source of the Nile and, disguised as a Muslim, made a pilgrimage to the city of Mecca, then forbidden to non-Muslims,
and penetrated the sacred city of Harare in uncharted East
Africa. Burton translated unexpurgated versions of many
Oriental texts including the *Kama Sutra* (1883) and *Arabian Nights* (1885–86), which is perhaps his most celebrated
achievement.

John Barth was born in Cambridge, Maryland, in 1930 and
educated at Johns Hopkins University. His first novel, *The
Floating Opera*, was published in 1956, followed by such
other acclaimed works of fiction as *The Sot-Weed Factor,
Giles Goat-Boy*, and *The Last Voyage of Somebody the Sailor*.
His numerous awards include the F. Scott Fitzgerald Award
for outstanding achievement in American literature and
the National Book Award (for *Chimera* [1973]).

Jack Zipes is a professor of German at the University of
Minnesota. The author of several books on fairy tales, including *Don't Bet on the Prince, Fairy Tales and the Art of
Subversion*, and *Breaking the Magic Spell*, he is also the
editor and translator of *The Complete Fairy Tales of the
Brothers Grimm* and *Beauties and Beasts and Enchantment: Classic French Fairy Tales*. And he is the editor of
the Signet Classics editions of *The Complete Fairy Tales of
Oscar Wilde*.

Arabian Nights,
Volume II

More Marvels and Wonders
of the
Thousand and One Nights

Adapted by Jack Zipes from
Sir Richard F. Burton's Unexpurgated Translation

With a New Introduction by
John Barth
and an Afterword by
Jack Zipes

SIGNET CLASSICS

SIGNET CLASSICS
Published by New American Library, a division of
Penguin Group (USA) Inc., 375 Hudson Street,
New York, New York 10014, USA
Penguin Group (Canada), 90 Eglinton Avenue East, Suite 700, Toronto,
Ontario M4P 2Y3, Canada (a division of Pearson Penguin Canada Inc.)
Penguin Books Ltd., 80 Strand, London WC2R 0RL, England
Penguin Ireland, 25 St. Stephen's Green, Dublin 2,
Ireland (a division of Penguin Books Ltd.)
Penguin Group (Australia), 250 Camberwell Road, Camberwell, Victoria 3124,
Australia (a division of Pearson Australia Group Pty. Ltd.)
Penguin Books India Pvt. Ltd., 11 Community Centre, Panchsheel Park,
New Delhi - 110 017, India
Penguin Group (NZ), 67 Apollo Drive, Rosedale, North Shore 0632,
New Zealand (a division of Pearson New Zealand Ltd.)
Penguin Books (South Africa) (Pty.) Ltd., 24 Sturdee Avenue,
Rosebank, Johannesburg 2196, South Africa

Penguin Books Ltd., Registered Offices:
80 Strand, London WC2R 0RL, England

Published by Signet Classics, an imprint of New American Library,
a division of Penguin Group (USA) Inc.

First Signet Classics Printing, November 1999
First Signet Classics Printing (Barth Introduction), February 2010

Contents

v

Introduction:
The Morning After

David Beaumont's masterful Introduction to Volume I of this two-volume Signet Classics edition of *The Arabian Nights* opens in true Scheherazadean style: "The story of the book called *The Arabian Nights*, it has been said, is a story worthy of being in *The Arabian Nights*."

To that introduction-to-an-introduction, your present introducer of Volume II—no scholarly authority like Professors Beaumont and Jack Zipes (whose Afterwords to both volumes are likewise excellent), but a longtime yarn-spinning fan of Ms. Scheherazade—cannot resist adding that "the story of the book called *The Arabian Nights*" in fact *is* in *The Arabian Nights*, or anyhow just outside it. It's the frame that frames the frame, so to speak.

I mean this literally. The stories, stories-within-stories, and stories-within-stories-within-stories that comprise the *Kitab Alf Laylah Wa Laylah*, or, as it's variously called, "The Book of a Thousand Nights and a Night" or "The Arabian Nights Entertainment," are from all over the Indian/Persian/Arabic map. Over the centuries, like old-time merchant-traders traveling the Silk Road and adding to their stash of goods along the way, the book's innumerable compilers picked up yarns from here and there and stitched them into their narrative quilt. And they're famously framed by the best story of them all: the story of their teller, the courageous, canny, beautiful, and learned young daughter of the King's Grand Vizier—a monarch so murderously deranged by his wife's infidelities that after executing her he "marries" a virgin every night and has her killed in the morning before she too can cuckold him. For the story of that story, see Beaumont's preface to Volume I—and then read the opening story in that volume, "The Story of King Shahryar and His Brother," which explains why and under what circumstances Scheherazade will spin out, by my count, no fewer than 169 "primary" tales, at least nineteen of which contain tales-within-the-tale: eighty-seven "secondary tales" in all, at least four of which contain tertiary tales-within-the-tale-within-the-tale, for a total of some 267 complete stories, plus about ten thousand lines of verse in Sir Richard Burton's original unexpurgated ten-volume translation of the *Nights* (1885–86), of which the present version is an artful two-volume abridgment. And that's before we even get to the seven volumes of Burton's later *Supplemental Nights*.

But this apparently outermost frame—the tale of King Shahryar of "the lands of India and China," his similarly cuckolded and similarly vengeful brother King Shah Zaman of Samarkand, and Scheherazade and her younger sister Dunyazade, which begins more than a thousand nights before Night 1 and winds up well after Night 1001—is itself framed, sort of, by an intriguing formulation (intriguing to some of us later storytellers, anyhow): In all versions, after the ritual invocation to Almighty Allah, the anonymous narrator-scribe declares in effect, not that "There once was a jealous king named Shahryar," et cetera, but that "There is a book called *The Book of a Thousand Nights and a Night*, in which one will find the story of King Shahryar and his brother Shah Zaman [and Scheherazade and Dunyazade], which goes like this...." A thousand-plus nights later, after that so-productive young talester—talestress?—has delivered herself not only of those several hundred stories, but also of three male children ("one walking, one crawling, one suckling") sired by her entertain-me-or-die consort, and has delivered the King as well from

his pathologically murderous, kingdom-wrecking jealousy, she successfully pleads for her life, officially weds
the father of her children and inspirer of her stories in
a regally elaborate joint ceremony with her now older
and less innocent kid sister and Shahryar's up-till-then
equally murderous kid brother, and the foursome are
declared to have lived happily thenceforth—not "ever
after," as in Western fables, but more realistically "until
the Destroyer of Delights and Severer of Societies and
Desolater of Dwelling-places came upon them": the
standard wrap-up of Scheherazade's own stories. Whereupon the successor to Shahryar's throne (One of those
three sons? We're not told) discovers in the late and
no doubt unlamented King's treasury the tales that not
only entertained him but saved his kingdom and their
teller's life, and which grateful Shahryar had therefore
obliged his scribes to record after the fact in thirty volumes for posterity (another story: imagine weary Scheherazade having to *recollect and retell* all those tales to
the royal clerks!); and said successor is so delighted with
them that he has *his* scribes recopy the whole shebang
and "spread them throughout the world."

Then comes the almost offhanded punch line: "As a
consequence," concludes this story-of-the-story-of-the-
stories, "the tales became famous, and the people called
them *The Marvels and Wonders of the Thousand and
One Nights.* This is all that we know about the origins of
this book, and Allah is omniscient. . . . FINIS."

Get it? The book that we've just finished reading is not
The Thousand and One Nights, exactly, but a book *about*
a book called *The Thousand and One Nights.* FINIS
indeed—and wow! But so lightly and engagingly does
this outermost Scheherazade, so to speak, lead us into
and out of the narrative labyrinth of tales within tales
within tales, we're scarcely aware of all this structural
complexity. Nor need we be, any more than venturers
through an amusement-park funhouse need appreciate

the intricate mechanics of its serial gee-whizzes: quite OK just to go along for the ride, at least the first time through. Closer examination has its rewards, however, and may well lead one not only through this expertly edited two-volume Signet Classics version, but on to the ten- or twelve- or thirty-volume feast of which it is a rich sampling. Ms. Scheherazade is, among other things, a storyteller's storyteller *par excellence*, whom writers as otherwise dissimilar as Johann Wolfgang von Goethe, Marcel Proust, Jorge Luis Borges, and Yours Truly have found irresistible. Goethe was impressed by the stories' mix of fantasy and realism, humor and terror, delicacy and ribaldry, even downright scatology: his journals note that the author of *The Sorrows of Young Werther* was particularly taken with Night 410, the "Tale of How Abu Hasan Farted." And as David Beaumont notes in his introduction to Volume I, Marcel Proust—whose seven-volume *Remembrance of Things Past* is itself a fiction of Scheherazadean proportions, though not of *Arabian Nights* flavor—frequently refers to her epical narrative in his. Likewise the late great Argentinian Jorge Luis Borges (who, being blind, was himself necessarily a story*teller* rather than a story writer, composing his splendid *ficciones* in his head and then, like Scheherazade after her narrative menopause, dictating them from memory for inscription), and many another storyteller from all over the globe.

That's no surprise to this one, who most certainly includes himself among the Vizier's daughter's longtime ardent admirers. As a child in the time before television, video games, and the Internet, I was charmed by a much-abridged and radically expurgated one-volume kiddie edition of the *Nights*, discreetly but handsomely illustrated by N. C. Wyeth. No gas-passing villagers in it, as in the tale that so amused Goethe (the unfortunate Abu Hasan, mortified by his accidental flatulence during a prayer service, exiles himself for years; returning finally to his village in hopes that his embarrassing faux pas has long since been forgotten, he happens to overhear a lad ask his mother how old he is, to which she replies that he's ten years old, he having been born "on the very night that Abu Hasan farted"); no lascivious sultanas cuckolding their royal spouses with ape-like "slobbering blackamoors" who swing down from the trees to service them and their handmaidens while hubby is out of town; no sad but dutiful Grand Vizier showing up at the King's court every morning, shroud over his arm, expecting royal orders to lead his daughter off to execution as he has led her thousand deflowered predecessors—but there were Aladdin and his magical lantern, Ali Baba and the forty thieves, Sinbad the Seaman and Sinbad the Landman; there were the mighty wish-granting genies/jinnees/djinns in bottles and other innocent-looking containers (even as a kid, I wondered why it never occurs to Aladdin and other wish grantees to cover their bets by wishing for *more wishes*!); there were the mermaids and dragons, the Open Sesames and other charms. . . . I was hooked.

And rehooked for keeps years later, when—as an undergraduate book filer in the Classics stacks of my university's library, reshelving cartful after cartful of tomes to help defray my tuition and eagerly perusing as I reshelved, while at the same time feeling the first stirrings of writerly Vocation—in the alcoves of what was called the "Oriental Seminary" I discovered among other marvels the ten folio volumes of Somadeva's enormous *Katha Sarit Sagara*: the eleventh-century Sanskrit "Ocean of Story" spun out by the god Shiva to his consort Parvati in reward for a particularly divine session of lovemaking. It contains not just tales within tales, but such entire *cycles* of tales-within-tales as the *Panchatantra* ("Five Principles") and the *Vetalapanchavimsati* ("25 Tales Told by a Vampire"), and is assumed to be among the antecedents of the Persian *Hazar Afsaneh* ("Book of a Thousand Tales") later translated and transmuted into the Arabic *Book of a Thousand Nights and a Night*. That too was there to be refiled, in Burton's version and others, as were (in neighboring alcoves) such frame-taled European spin-offs as Boccaccio's ten-night *Decameron*, Marguerite of Navarre's seven-night *Heptameron*, Giambattista Basile's five-night *The Tale of Tales* (also and not surpisingly known as *Pentameron*), and other more or less racy delights, none of which were included in my otherwise excellent world-lit undergrad survey courses. What wannabe fictionist wouldn't lay into such a narrative smorgasbord?

I did, for sure, and Scheherazade in particular became an important navigation-star in my own writerly adventures over the succeeding decades. While not presuming to her narrative achievement, I've found myself returning from time to time both to the Vizier's daughter herself, who shows up in several of my novels and stories, and to her appalling but endlessly fascinating situation. How can she expect to succeed where her thousand predecessors failed? Not by erotic expertise alone, for sure, although she's probably no slouch in that department: while properly virginal, she has, we're told in the frame story, "read the books, annals, and legends of former kings, and the stories, lessons, and adventures of famous men. Indeed, it was said that she had collected a thousand history books [note the number] about ancient peoples and rulers. She had perused the works of the poets and knew them by heart. She had studied philosophy and the sciences, arts, and practical things. And she was pleasant and polite, wise and witty, well read and well bred." One bets that her library included the classic Sanskrit sex manual *Kama Sutra*, and one notes that at the double wedding at stories' end, her kid sister "paced forward like the rising sun, and swayed to and fro in insolent beauty," while Scheherazade herself "came forward swaying from side to side," "shook her head and swayed her haunches," and "moved so coquettishly that she ravished the minds and hearts of all present and bewitched their eyes." So she can belly dance too! Long live the Queen!

But as I've noted elsewhere,* she has a few other things going for her as well. We're told specifically that as word of Shahryar's homicidal virgin-a-night policy spreads, so many parents flee the country with their daughters that by the time of our story there's not a maidenhead remaining for the Vizier to produce (on pain of death if he fails to) except those of his own daughters, whom Shahryar has been sparing as a political courtesy. Deranged though he is, one suspects that the King too is aware of that circumstance, and that if he kills Scheherazade the jig is up in any case. Moreover (as Scheherazade's dad will doubtless also have told her), back when the King first learned of his brother Shah Zaman's habitual cuckolding but was as yet unaware of his own, he'd vowed that if he himself were ever thus disgraced he would kill "a thousand women in revenge," despite the fact that "that way madness lies"—and now he's done so, and thus the time is ripe to rethink his modus operandi.

But hey, this is a Monarch we're dealing with, and a nutcase one at that, and so the royal Face must be saved even though the situation is staring him in it. Like, maybe, give him a little more time to come to terms with the obvious? Some sort of face-and-butt-saving interlude? How about an unobtrusively pointed *story*—or better yet, a whole *string* of stories and stories-within-stories, their delivery artfully timed to break off daily at sunrise just when the plot is really revving up, the way TV drama serials will do a thousand years later?

And so on Night One, what will become a ritual is established: Against her rueful father's wishes (whom she disarms with a couple of also-pointed stories), Scheherazade "goes in unto the King," and as he prepares to go in unto her, she pleads with him to let her sister (whom she has prepped for the role) be with her on this "last night of my life." The King consents. Dunyazade takes up her position at the foot of the royal bed, witnesses

---

*See the essay "Don't Count on It: A Note on the Number of *The 1001 Nights*," in *The Friday Book* (1984).

her sister's defloration and the couple's postcoital nap, and at midnight, on cue from Scheherazade, begs for a story to entertain all hands till dawn. Big Sis secures permission from the King (who, not surprisingly, "happened to be sleepless and restless") and obliges with the intricate "Tale of the Merchant and the Jinee," itself involving three tales-within-the-tale, all having to do with the tellers' lives being spared by their stories, and the last winding up exactly at *their* teller's appointed doom time, the crack of dawn. Dunyazade praises her sister's narrative performance; Scheherazade pooh-poohs it, declaring it to be nothing compared to what she could come up with *tomorrow* night, if only ... The King says okay ("By Allah, I won't slay her until I hear more of her wondrous stories!"), rises to go about his kingly business of "bidding and forbidding between man and man" (but neither bids the Vizier to go execute his daughter nor explains the reprieve), then returns for a second night of sex/sleep/storytelling—and the pattern is established for 999 nights thereafter, Dunyazade maintaining her rather kinky foot-of-the-royal-bed position as Primer of the Narrative Pump, Scheherazade turning out story after story (always, as each ends, immediately beginning another and then interrupting it at dawn's early light) and—so we learn on Night 1001—turning out baby after baby as well, for whose sakes she pleads on that fateful morn for her life to be thenceforth spared.

Why *then*, rather than on Night 666, say, or 777, or 1111? Why indeed *are* there 1001 nights instead of some other number? Mainly, no doubt, because just as "a thousand" is traditional shorthand for "a *lot*" (as in the *Hazar Afsaneh*'s "thousand tales" and Scheherazade's "thousand books about ancient peoples and rulers"), so 1001 is "plenty and then some," like Simon Bond's popular *101 Uses for a Dead Cat*. But think again: three sons are conceived, brought to term, and delivered over the same span of time that Shahryar previously took to fulfill his threat to "kill a thousand women" in revenge for his cuckolding. The moment is doubly auspicious, especially if it happens to coincide with Scheherazade's having ... exhausted her narrative repertory, perhaps?

Maybe, maybe not. But while numerical appropriateness is sufficient cause, and narrative exhaustion a not-impossible extra reason for Scheherazade's choosing Night 1001 to plead for the reprieve that she no doubt understands (and Shahyrar promptly acknowledges) to have been long since tacitly granted her, my imagination was piqued some decades ago to come up with yet a third possibility, an additional coincidence suggested by her sons' approximate ages: "one walking, one crawling, one suckling." For the messy details, see the aforecited essay "Don't Count on It," which half-seriously imagines that by way of additional life insurance the Vizier's cunning daughter will have timed her volunteered devirginization to coincide as closely as possible with one of her monthly ovulations, in hopes of a prompt impregnation (with her life hanging in the balance, she would most assuredly *not* want her menses to arrive early in the game!). Assuming for gee-whiz story purposes a successful conception on Night 1 (Why not? It's an Arabian Night) and working then from the arithmetical average number of days from human conception to birth (266), then the average time from delivery to first subsequent menstruation (forty-nine days), and from then to earliest *next* ovulation and possible *second* conception (fourteen days), etc., one arrives at the fascinating possibility that on that fateful 1002nd morning, when Scheherazade orders the nurses to fetch in the kids and pleads for permanent absolution on their behalf, not only will her three boys have been at the right ages for "walking" (two years + four days), "crawling" (thirteen months + ten days), and "suckling" (two and a half months), but their mom—having resumed postpartum menstruation forty-nine days after her third delivery (Night 974)—might to her own dismay on Morning 1002 have found herself, after only a normal lunar month, for the first time *re*-menstruating instead of having been reimpregnated per usual by the King! It's a circumstance of which Shahryar would have to be apprised immediately, since by Muslim law he cannot "go in unto" his wife that night, as their whole past history will have led him to anticipate doing. Having just concluded "The Tale of Ma-aruf the Cobbler and Fatimah the Turd" (her final narrative performance in the complete ten-volume Burton edition), this most resourceful of storytellers must either launch into some new one—surpassing it and Sinbad and Ali Baba combined—or else surprise her lord and master with something no less extraordinary than, so to speak, her first-ever Second Menstruation in their 1001-night history. Like, say, trotting in their offspring and saying, in effect, "Enough of this Let-Me-Entertain-You thing already: Why not come off it, marry me, and make our kids legit?"

It's a rather far-fetched bit of biological arithmetic, I'll grant, though quite within the salty parameters of the *Nights*. For details, see the essay—which it was my privilege to deliver as an open-air lecture on a warm June night in 1983 at the American School in Tangier, Morocco, under a crescent moon signaling the end of the holy month of Ramadan, while muezzins called to the faithful from the lighted minarets of nearby mosques in the city that inspired Rimsky-Korsakov's *Scheherazade Suite*: a moving experience indeed for this longtime admirer of Ms. S.

Better yet, read the book: *her* book, the one called *The Arabian Nights* or *Book of a Thousand Nights and a Night*, which this Signet Classics version (and Burton's and all the others) are books *about*.

You'll be enchanted.

—John Barth

A Note on the Text

This adaptation is based on several tales taken from Richard F. Burton's *The Book of the Thousand Nights and a Night. A Plain and Literal Translation of the Arabian Nights Entertainment*, 10 vols. (Benares: Kamashastra Society, 1885–86). It is the sequel to *Arabian Nights: The Marvels and Wonders of the Thousand and One Nights,* a Signet Classics title, which includes the frame-work story of Scheherazade and Shahryar. This well-known framework tale involves a vizier's daughter named Scheherazade, who tells tales to a crazed king to save her life and the lives of other virgins in her kingdom, and it was used by different collectors of the tales throughout the late-medieval period to connect an assortment of stories that had different origins and had not always been told or collected at the same time. In the present volume, the framework has been dropped because it was already used in the first volume of *Arabian Nights* and no longer serves a purpose here. Instead I have selected some of the most interesting tales from Burton's *Nights* to provide a cross section of his work and of the *Nights* tradition in general.

As is well known, Burton's English translation, while accurate for the most part, is convoluted and somewhat unreadable today. Therefore, I have endeavored to rework his translation into a more modern English idiom while trying to retain the flavor of his original and some of his stock phrases and mannerisms. To make his translation flow more smoothly, I have eliminated or transformed redundant elements, garrulous passages, bombastic phrases, archaic words, and inconsistent spellings. In addition, I have discarded most of the poetry, since the poems were inserted later into the tales, often without reason, and I have changed the spelling of some of the characters' names and place-names. As in the previous volume, I have chosen the tales from Burton's massive translation with an eye toward demonstrating the variety of narratives in the *Nights*: the fairy tale, the utopian story, the legend, the anecdote, the parable, the fable, the love story, the chronicle, the mystery, and even the science fiction tale. Burton used different manuscripts in composing his translation, and some were even based on French stories that have dubious Arabic origins. Of course, the origins of most of the tales are difficult to trace with exactitude. Nevertheless, they all have been connected to the *Nights*, and they have had a profound influence on both oral and literary traditions in the West.

I should like to take this opportunity to express my gratitude to Don Hymans, who took over this project at a critical time and has supervised its completion with great care. Once again, I want to thank Ted Johnson, who has done a superb job of copyediting the tales.

—Jack Zipes

Arabian Nights,
Volume II

—◆—

More Marvels and Wonders
of the
Thousand and One Nights

The Caliph's Night Adventure

One night Caliph Harun al-Rashid had trouble sleeping and lay awake until morning. When he arose, he was extremely restless. Consequently, everyone around him was troubled, because people tend to sense and react to a prince's moods. They rejoice when he is happy and are sad when he is gloomy, even though they might not know why they are affected this way. After some time had passed, the caliph sent for Masrur the eunuch, and when he arrived, Harun al-Rashid cried out, "Fetch me my vizier, Ja'afar the Barmaki, right away!"

So the eunuch went away and returned with the minister, who found the caliph alone, something that happened very rarely. As the vizier drew near, he saw that the caliph was melancholy and did not raise his eyes. Therefore he stopped still in his place until his lord recognized him. At last the prince cast his eyes upon Ja'afar but immediately turned his head away and sat as motionless as before. Since the minister did not discern anything in the demeanor of the caliph that might concern him personally, he summoned his courage and said, "Oh Commander of the Faithful, will your highness take me into your confidence and tell me what has brought upon this sadness?"

"Truly, oh vizier," responded the caliph, "I have been very upset by these recent moods, and I do not think I can get rid of them unless I hear some strange tales and verses. So, if you have not come here because of some urgent business, perhaps you will cheer me up by telling me some interesting story."

"Oh Commander of the Faithful, my position obliges me to be at your service, and thus I must remind you that this is the day appointed for informing you about the good governance of your city and the surrounding area. If God helps us, this business will distract you, and you will cast away your gloom."

"It is a good thing that you've reminded me about this matter," the caliph said. "I had totally forgotten it. Now, go and change your clothes while I do the same."

So the two men put on the garments of merchants for their disguise and left the palace through a garden door that led them into the fields. After they had skirted the city, they reached the bank of the Euphrates, which was a good distance from the gate, and they did not notice anything extraordinary. Then they crossed the river on the first ferryboat they found, and as they were making a second round on the farther side, they crossed a bridge that joined the two sides of Baghdad. Immediately, a blind beggar grabbed his hand, held it tight, and spoke: "Oh my generous friend, whoever you may be, by Allah, please do not refuse my request. I beg of you, give me a slap on my ear. It's a punishment that I deserve, if not greater."

After speaking these words, the blind man let go of the caliph's hand so that the prince could strike him. But just in case the caliph would not grant his request and would move on, he now grabbed hold of the caliph's long robe. Surprised by the blind man's words, the caliph replied, "Indeed, I shall not grant your request, nor shall I besmirch my generous deed by treating you as you want me to."

Upon saying these words, the caliph tried to get away from the blind man, but the beggar was used to such behavior and expected his benefactor's refusal. Therefore he clung to him and cried out, "My lord, forgive my audacity and my persistence. I implore you: either give me a slap on the ear or take back your alms, for I may not receive your money unless I keep a solemn oath I have sworn before Allah. And if you knew the reason, you would agree that the penalty I must pay for your generosity is in truth very light."

Then the caliph, who did not want to be delayed any longer, yielded to the blind man's demand and gave him a slight cuff on the ear. Thereupon the beggar let go of his robe, thanked him, and blessed him. When the caliph and his vizier had walked some distance from the blind man, the prince exclaimed, "This blind beggar must surely have some good reason for behaving in such a manner to people who give him alms, and I would like to know it. I want you to return to him and tell him who I am and command him to appear at my palace at midafternoon prayer time so that I may talk with him and hear what he has to say."

So Ja'afar went back to the blind man. After giving him alms and a slap on his ear, he related the caliph's command and returned immediately to his lord. Soon, when the two reached the town square, they found a vast crowd of people gazing at a handsome youth, who was mounted on a mare riding at full speed around the open space, spurring and whipping the beast so cruelly that she was covered with sweat and blood. Upon seeing this, the caliph was amazed by the young man's brutality, and he stopped to ask the bystanders whether they knew why he tortured and tormented the mare in this way. But he could learn nothing except that the young man had recently been appearing at the square every day at the same time and treating the mare in similar fashion. Puzzled by this entire matter, the caliph asked his vizier to make note of this place and to command the young man to come and see him at the same hour that was assigned for the blind man. But before the caliph could reach his palace, he saw in a street, which he had not passed through for many months, a newly built mansion that appeared to be the palace of some great lord of the land. He asked his vizier whether he knew its owner, and Ja'afar replied that he did not but that he would make inquiries. So he went over to a neighbor, who told him that the owner of the house was a man named Khwajah Hasan, also called Al-Habbal because of his craft of ropemaking. This neighbor had known Al-Habbal when he was a poor ropemaker, but he did not know how fate and fortune had graced his life; somehow Khwajah Hasan had become exceedingly wealthy so that he could pay honorably and sumptuously for all the expenses that he had incurred when he had his palace built. After hearing this, the vizier returned to the caliph and recounted what he had just heard. In turn, the prince declared, "I must see this Khwajah Hasan al-Habbal! I want you to go and tell him to come to my palace at the same time you have assigned for the other two."

The minister did his lord's bidding, and the next day, after midafternoon prayers, the caliph retired to his own apartment, and Ja'afar introduced the three men to the caliph. They all prostrated themselves at his feet, and when they arose, the Commander of the Faithful asked the blind man to tell him his name. Thereupon, the blind man said that he was called Baba Abdullah.

"Oh servant of Allah," cried the caliph, "your manner of asking alms yesterday seemed so strange to me that, if it had not been for certain considerations, I would not have granted your request. In fact, I would have prevented you from pestering the people any more. And now I have asked you here so that I may know from you yourself what impelled you to swear the rash oath that you related to me so that I may better judge whether you have done good or evil, and whether I should allow you to continue to beg in such an unsuitable way. Tell me honestly how such a mad thought entered your head, and do not conceal anything, for I want to know the truth and only the full truth."

Terrified by these words, Baba Abdullah threw himself a second time at the caliph's feet with his face to the ground, and when he rose again, he said, "Oh Commander of the Faithful, I beg pardon of your highness for the audacity that I showed you and for compelling you to do something that went against all good sense. I admit my offense, but since I did not know that it was you, your highness, at that time, I beg you to be merciful with me and to understand that I had no idea who you were. Now, with regard to my bizarre action, I readily admit that it must seem strange to most human beings, but in the eyes of Allah, it is nothing but a slight penance that I have charged myself for an enormous crime of which I am guilty. Indeed, even if all the people in the world were to give me a cuff on my ear, it would not be sufficient atonement for my crime. Your highness shall judge yourself when you hear my tale and learn about my offense."

And here he began to relate

The Story of the Blind Man, Baba Abdullah

Oh my lord, I, the humblest of your slaves, was born in Baghdad, where my father and mother died some years later within a few days of each other and left me a fortune large enough to last me throughout my lifetime. But I did not know its value, and gradually I squandered it in luxury and loose living, and I did not care anything about thrift or saving money. But when little was left, I repented my decadent ways and worked hard day and night to increase whatever money I had left from my inheritance. The old saying rings true, "After waste comes knowledge of worth." Thus, little by little, I collected eighty camels, which I hired out to merchants for their business, and I made a good profit each time I did this. In addition, I also traveled in the employ of merchants with my camels, and in this way I journeyed throughout your highness's vast domains. Briefly, I hoped before long to obtain a huge amount of gold through the hiring out of my camels.

Now, one time I had carried a merchant's materials to Bassorah so that they could be shipped to India, and as I was returning to Baghdad with my camels that were not carrying anything, I happened to pass a wonderful pasture that lay far from any village. So I stopped and unsaddled the camels which I hobbled and tethered together so that they might feed upon the luxuriant herbs and bushes and yet not go astray. Soon a dervish appeared. He was traveling by foot to Bassorah, and he

W.H.R.

sat down beside me to rest. I asked him where he was going and what the purpose of his trip was, and he asked me the same. After we had told each other our tales, we brought out our provisions and shared our food, talking about various matters as we ate.

"I know of a spot near here." said the dervish, "and

it contains a hoard of wealth that is amazingly wonderful. In fact, even if you were to load your eighty camels with great loads of golden coins and gems, the treasure would barely be diminished."

Hearing these words I rejoiced, and as I looked at his sincere face, I realized that he was not deceiving me. So, I arose right away and hugged him.

"Oh sacred man of Allah," I exclaimed, "you who care nothing for this world's goods and you who have renounced all mundane lusts and luxuries, you certainly know all there is to know about this treasure, for nothing remains hidden from holy men like you. I beg you to tell me where it may be found so that I may load my eighty camels with trunks of gold coins and jewels. I know full well that you have no desire for the wealth of this world, but I ask you to take one of my eighty camels as recompense and reward for the favor."   .

Such was my speech, but in my heart I was sad at the thought that I would have to part with even a single camel load of coins and gems. Still, I reflected that the other seventy-nine camels would be carrying loads of riches to my heart's content. As I vacillated in my mind, at one moment glad to have such great wealth and at the next instant repenting that I had to share even a camel's load, the dervish noted my greed and avarice and replied, "Not so, my brother. One camel load is not enough for me to show you this treasure hoard. I shall only tell you the place on one condition: you must agree to give me one half of the camels. With forty loads of valuable gold coins and gems, you can surely buy thousands more camels and become a wealthy man."

Seeing that refusal was impossible, I cried out, "So be it! I agree to your proposal, and I shall do as you desire."

In my heart I had mulled the matter over, and I knew full well that forty camel loads of gold and gems would be more than enough for me and many generations of my descendants. And I feared that if I did not oblige him I would repent forever that I had let so great a treasure slip out of my hands. Once we were in full agreement, I gathered together all of my beasts, and off

I went with the dervish. After traveling a short distance, we came upon a gorge between two craggy mountain walls that towered high in crescent form. The pass was so exceedingly narrow that the animals were forced to march in single file, but farther on it flared out, and we could thread it without difficulty until we arrived in a broad field below. No human being could be seen or heard anywhere in this wild land. So, we were calm and relaxed and felt nothing to fear. Once we stopped, the dervish walked a short distance from our resting place, and there he produced flint and steel and made a fire by lighting some sticks he had gotten together. Then he threw a handful of strong-smelling incense upon the flames and muttered words of incantation that I could not understand. At once a cloud of smoke arose and veiled the mountains as it spired upward. Soon the vapor cleared away, and we saw a huge rock with a pathway that led to its perpendicular face. Here the precipice showed an open door, and in the bowels of the mountain there appeared a splendid palace, which was undoubtedly the work of the jinn, for no man had the power to build anything like it. In due time, we made our way to the entrance, and once we were inside, we found an endless treasure, arranged in neat and orderly piles. Upon seeing a heap of gold coins I swept down on it as a vulture swoops upon its quarry, and I began to fill numerous sacks to my heart's content. The bags were large, but I could not fill them entirely because I had to worry about how much my camels could carry. The dervish also set to work, but he filled his sacks only with gems and jewels, advising me to do the same because they were lighter. So I cast aside the gold ducats and I filled my bags with nothing but the most precious of the rare stones. When we had finished our task, we placed the well-stuffed sacks on the backs of the camels, and we got ready to depart. But before we left the palace that housed thousands of golden vessels, exquisite in shape and workmanship, the dervish went into a hidden chamber and brought out a little golden box full of some ointment, which he showed to me, and then he placed it into his pocket. Immediately thereafter, he again threw

incense on the fire and recited his incantations, whereupon the door closed, and the rock became as it was
before. Right after this we divided the camels, he taking
one half and I the other. Then we passed through the
narrow and gloomy gorge in single file and came out
onto the open plain. Here our ways parted. He was
headed toward Bassorah, and I toward Baghdad. When
I was about to leave him, I showered thanks upon the
dervish, who had helped me obtain all this wealth and
riches worth hundreds of thousands of gold coins. I bade
him farewell with deep emotions of gratitude, and after
we embraced, we went our separate ways. But no sooner
had I said adieu to the dervish and gone some distance
from him with my string of camels than Satan tempted
me with greed of gain, and I said to myself, "This dervish is alone in the world without friends or kin, and he
is wholly cut off from mundane matters. How can these
camel loads of filthy lucre benefit him? Besides, if he
must take care of the camels and becomes consumed by
the deceitfulness of the riches, he may neglect his prayer
and worship. Therefore, it is only right for me to take
back a few of my beasts from him."

Once I reached this decision, I made my camels halt,
and after tying up their forelegs, I ran back after the
holy man and called out his name. He heard my loud
shouts and waited for me. As soon as I approached him,
I said, "After I had left you, a thought came into my
mind. It occurred to me that you are a recluse who keeps
yourself aloof from earthly things, and you are pure in
heart and concern yourself only with prayer and devotion. So, the care of these camels will only cause you
toil and trouble, and you will waste precious time. It
would be better if you gave them back to me and did
not run the risk of these disturbances and dangers."

"Oh my son," replied the dervish, "what you say is
true. The tending of these animals will bring me nothing
but a headache. So please take as many of them as you
want. I did not think about the burden and bother until
you drew my attention to it. But now I am forewarned,
and by Allah I am grateful to you."

Accordingly, I took ten animals from him, and I was

about to get on my way when it suddenly struck me, "This dervish really did not care about giving up ten camels. It would be better if I ask him for more." Therefore, I approached him again and said, "You can barely manage thirty camels. So, I think it would be best if you gave me another ten."

"Oh my son, do whatever you wish," he replied. "Take another ten camels. Twenty are more than enough for me."

I did what he said, and I added them to my forty. Then the spirit of avarice possessed me, and I kept thinking how I could get another ten camels from his share. So I retraced my steps a third time and asked him for another ten. Well, he gladly gave me these camels, plus the final ten that I managed to wheedle out of him. After all this was done, he shook out his skirts and got ready to depart, but still my accursed greed would not abandon me. To be sure, I had eighty beasts loaded with gold coins and jewels, and I could have gone away with an abundance of wealth that would have kept me happy and content for untold years to come. Yet, Satan tempted me still more and urged me to take the box of ointment, which I thought might contain something more precious than rubies.

So when I went to say farewell and embrace him once more, I paused awhile and said, "What will you do with the little box of salve that you have taken as your portion? I should like to have that as well."

The dervish did not want to part with it in any way. Therefore I desired to have it even more, and I made up my mind that if the holy man would not give it up of his free will, then I would take it from him by force. Seeing my intent, he drew the box from his breast pocket and handed it to me.

"Oh my son, if you want this box of ointment so much," the holy man said, "then I shall give it to you freely. But first it is important for you to learn the virtue of the salve that it contains."

Hearing these words, I remarked, "Now that you have done me this favor, I do request that you tell me about the ointment and the virtues that it possesses."

"The wonders of this ointment are extraordinary and rare. If you close your left eye and rub the smallest bit of the salve upon the lid, then all the treasures of the world now concealed from your gaze will appear to your sight. But if you rub some of the salve on your right eye, you will become stone blind in both eyes right away."

As soon as I learned about the powers of the salve, I wanted to test them. Therefore I placed the box in his hand and said, "I see that you fully understand how the ointment works. So now I beg you to put some of the ointment on my left eyelid with your own hand."

Thereupon the dervish closed my left eye, and with his finger he rubbed a little of the unguent on the lid. When I opened my eye and looked around, I saw the hidden hoards of the earth in countless quantities just as the dervish had told me I would see them. Then, closing my right eye, I asked him to put some of the salve on that eyelid as well.

"Oh my son," he said, "I have warned you that if you rub the salve on your right eyelid, you will become stone blind in both eyes. Put this foolish thought far from your mind! Why should you bring such evil upon yourself for no purpose?"

Indeed, he spoke the truth, but because of my accursed bad fate, I would not heed his words and thought, "If rubbing some of the salve on my left eyelid can produce such wondrous results, I am certain that the results will be even more marvelous if he rubs some on my right eyelid. This fellow is deceiving me and concealing the real truth." When I had thus made up my mind, I laughed and said to the holy man, "You are deceiving me so that I won't take advantage of the secret by rubbing the salve upon my right eyelid. Surely, you are trying to prevent me from learning about the great secret that the salve contains if it is rubbed on my right eyelid. It is impossible that such an ointment would have such an opposite effect each time it is rubbed on a different eyelid."

"Allah Almighty is my witness," replied the dervish. "The marvelous powers of the ointment are exactly as I have described them to you. Oh, dear friend, have faith in me, for I have told you nothing but the sober truth."

Still, I would not believe his words and continued to suspect that he was deceiving me and was keeping the secret of the powerful unguent from me. Obsessed by this foolish thought, I pressed him very hard and begged that he rub the ointment on my right eyelid, but he still refused and said, "You have seen how much favor I have bestowed upon you. Why should I want to bring such dire evil to your life? I'm telling you that it will surely bring you a life filled with grief and misery. Therefore, I beseech you, by Allah the Almighty, abandon your intentions and believe my words."

But the more he refused, the more I persisted, until finally, I took an oath, swore to Allah, and declared, "Oh dervish, whatever I have asked of you, you gave to me freely, and now I only have this request to make. By Allah, do not deny me, and grant me this last of your favors. I shall not hold you responsible for whatever happens to me. Let destiny decide for better or worse."

When the holy man saw that his refusal was to no avail and that I would remain persistent until the bitter end, he put the smallest bit of ointment on my right eyelid, and as I opened my eyes widely, lo and behold, both were stone blind! I could see nothing but the black darkness before them, and ever since that day I have been sightless and helpless as you found me. When I knew that I was blind, I exclaimed, "Oh dervish of ill omen, your prediction has come true."

And I began to curse him and said, "Oh, would to heaven that you had never brought me to the hoard or had given me such wealth! What can all this gold and these jewels do for me now? Take back your forty camels and restore my sight."

"What evil have I done to you? I bestowed more favors on you than any man has ever received. You would not heed my advice. Instead your heart lusted after all this wealth and you sought to pry into the hidden treasures of the earth. You were not content with what you had, and you doubted my words and thought that I was tricking you. Your condition is beyond all hope, for you will never regain your sight. No, never!"

Then, with tears and lamentations, I cried out, "Oh dervish, take all eighty camels loaded with gold and precious stones, and return to Bassorah. I absolve you from all blame. Nonetheless, I beseech you, by Allah Almighty, to restore my sight if you are able."

He did not say a word. Instead he took the eighty camels loaded with treasures and drove them to Bassorah, leaving me in a miserable plight. I cried aloud and pleaded that he take me with him out of the wilderness or put me on the path of some caravan. But he paid no attention to my cries and abandoned me there.

When the dervish departed, I almost died of grief and anger at the loss of my sight and my riches and from the pangs of thirst and hunger. The next day, thanks to a stroke of good fortune, a caravan from Bassorah passed that way, and when the merchants saw me in such a miserable condition, they had compassion on me and took me with them to Baghdad. There was nothing I could do after this but to beg for my bread in order to keep myself alive. So I became a beggar and made a vow to Allah Almighty that anyone who might take pity on me and give me alms must also give me a slap on my ear as a punishment for my unlucky greed and cursed avarice. So it was that I was so insistent and clung to you yesterday.

When the blind man had ended his story, the caliph said, "Oh Baba Abdullah, your crime was terrible. May Allah have mercy on you. Now it is your duty to tell your story to devotees and anchorites so that they may offer night prayers in your behalf. You need not concern yourself about your daily wants and needs. I have decided that you shall have an allowance of four dirhams a day from my royal treasury so that you can live according to your needs as long as you live. But you are no longer to go about my city and ask for alms."

Baba Abdullah thanked the Prince of True Believers and said, "I shall do your bidding."

Now, after the Caliph Harun al-Rashid had heard the

story of Baba Abdullah and the dervish, he turned to the young man whom he had seen riding at full speed on the mare and savagely lashing and mistreating her, and he said, "What is your name?"

"My name, oh Commander of the Faithful, is Sidi Nu'uman."

"Well, then, oh Sidi Nu'uman," responded the caliph, "listen to me. I have frequently watched the horsemen exercise their horses, and I have often done the same, but I have never seen anyone who rode so mercilessly as you rode your mare and applied both whip and spurs in the cruelest fashion. The people all stood gazing in astonishment, and against my own wishes, I, too, had to stop and ask some bystanders why you were doing this. However, nobody could explain to me why you were acting in such a cruel way. The only thing that the people could tell me was that you rode the mare in this brutal fashion every day, and such behavior puzzled me even more. So now I want you to reveal to me why you are so savage and ruthless, and make sure that you tell me the entire story and leave nothing out."

Upon hearing the order of the caliph, Sidi Nu'uman realized that the Commander of the Faithful was fully intent on knowing his whole story and would not allow him to depart until everything was explained. So the color of his countenance changed, and he stood speechless like a statue frozen by fear. Thereupon the caliph said, "Fear not, Sidi Nu'uman. Just tell me your tale. Look upon me as one of your friends. Speak freely and explain to me everything that has happened as though you were speaking to your intimate friends. Moreover, if you are afraid of revealing anything to me and fear my indignation, I hereby grant you immunity."

These comforting words of the caliph gave Sidi Nu'uman courage, and with clasped hands, he replied, "I trust that I have done nothing that goes against your highness's law and custom, and therefore I shall willingly obey your command and tell you my tale. If I have committed an offense, then I merit your punishment. It is true that I have exercised the mare every day and that I have ridden her at great speed around the square, as you saw me do. And yes, I lashed and gored her with all my might. You have compassion with the mare and think that I am cruel-hearted to treat her in this way, but when you have heard my adventure, you will admit, God willing, that this is only a trifling punishment for the mare's offense, and it is not she who deserves your pity and pardon but I! With your permission, I shall now begin my story." And the rider of the mare began in these words

The Story of Sidi Nu'uman

Oh my lord, my parents were very wealthy, and when they died, they left a great deal of money and riches to their son so that he could live a long life in the style of a nobleman of the land with ease, comfort, and delight. I—their only child—had neither care nor trouble, and when I reached the prime of manhood, I decided to wed a woman who was charming and beautiful, so that we might live together in mutual love and blessedness. But Allah Almighty did not provide me with an exemplary helpmate. Instead, destiny wedded me to grief and dire misery. I married a maiden who outwardly was a model of beauty and loveliness, but she did not have one single gracious gift of mind or soul. On the very second day after the wedding, her evil nature began to manifest itself. You are well aware, oh Prince of True Believers, that by Moslem custom no one may look at the face of his betrothed before the marriage contract, and after wedlock he is not allowed to complain even if his bride should prove to be a shrew. He must dwell with her as best he can and be grateful for his fate, be it fair or unfair.

When I first saw the face of my bride and knew how nice it was, I was overcome by happiness and gave thanks to Almighty Allah for bestowing upon me such a charming mate. That night I slept with her in joy and took great delight in love, but the next day, when the noon meal was spread for us, I did not find her at the table and sent one of the servants to summon her. After some delay, she came and sat down. I concealed my annoyance and tried to be patient so that I would not find fault with her. Yet, there were many faults to be found. It so happened that among the many dishes that were served, there was a fine rice pilaf, and according to the custom in our city, I began to eat it with a spoon. However, instead of following my example, she pulled out an ear pick from her pocket and began picking up the rice and eating it grain by grain. Seeing this strange conduct, I was greatly amazed, and fuming inwardly, I said in sweet tones, "Oh, my Aminah, how come you are eating this way? Have you learned it from your people or are you counting the grains of rice in order to make a hearty meal later? You have eaten only ten or twenty grains thus far. Or perhaps you are practicing thrift? If so, I want you to know that Allah Almighty has given me abundant provisions, and you need not worry that we shall run out of food. Just do as all women do, my darling, and eat as you see your husband eat."

I thought that she would respond with some words of thanks, but she did not utter a syllable and continued picking up grain after grain. She even sought to provoke me and cause my displeasure by pausing for a long time between each bite. Now, when the next course of cakes was served, she idly broke some bread and tossed a crumb or two into her mouth. In fact, she ate like a sparrow. I was astonished to see her so obstinate and self-willed, but I said to myself in my innocence, "Maybe she is not accustomed to eating with men, and she may be especially shy about eating too heartily in the presence of her husband. In time, she will do what other people do." I also thought that she had perhaps already broken her fast and had lost her appetite. Or perhaps it had been her habit to eat alone. So I said nothing, and after dinner, I went out for a breath of fresh air and thought nothing more of the matter. However, when we both sat down again at the next full meal, my bride ate exactly the same way as she had eaten before. Indeed, she seemed to persist in her perverse ways, and I was greatly troubled and amazed that she managed to keep herself alive without eating much food.

One night, when she thought that I was sound asleep, she arose quietly from my side. But I was wide awake. When I saw her step cautiously from the bed so that she would not disturb me, I wondered why she would rise from her sleep and leave me alone. So I decided to look into the matter. Therefore I pretended to keep sleeping and snored while watching her as I lay in the bed. Soon I saw her dress herself and leave the room. Then I sprang from the bed, threw on my robe, and slung my sword across my shoulder. Quickly I looked out the window to see where she was going, and I saw her cross the courtyard, open the street door, and disappear. In turn, I ran out through the entrance, which she had left unlocked, and then I followed her by the light of the moon until she entered a cemetery which was near our home.

When I beheld Aminah enter the cemetery, I stood outside and peered over the wall so that I could watch her but she could not see me. Then, lo and behold, I saw Aminah sitting with a ghoul. Your highness knows full well that ghouls are of the race of devils, and they are dirty spirits that terrify and destroy solitary travelers. Sometimes they seize them and feed upon their flesh. If they do not find any travelers during the day, they go to graveyards at night and dig out dead bodies and devour them. So I was tremendously amazed and terrified to see my wife sitting with a ghoul. Then the two dug up a recently buried corpse from a grave, and the ghoul and my wife tore off pieces of the flesh, which she ate. Indeed, she sat chatting with her companion and had a merry time. But since I was standing some distance away, I could not hear what they said. Just the sight of them, however, caused me to tremble with great fear. And when they had finished eating and had thrown the bones into the pit, they covered it with earth as it was before. In the meantime I left them engaged in their foul work, and I hurried home. I made sure to keep the street door half open as my wife had done. When I reached my room, I threw myself down on the bed and pretended to sleep. Soon Aminah came and took off her dress. Then she calmly lay down beside me, and I knew by her manner that she had not seen me at all or suspected that I had followed her to the cemetery. I felt greatly relieved by this even though I hated sleeping next to a cannibal and corpse eater. Despite my distaste, I lay still until the muezzin's call for dawn prayers. Then I got up and occupied myself with the Wuzu ablution and headed toward the mosque.

After saying my prayers and fulfilling my ceremonial duties, I strolled around the gardens, and during my walk, I mulled matters over in my mind and decided that I had to break up the company that my wife was keeping and wean her from the habit of devouring dead bodies. With these thoughts on my mind, I returned home at dinnertime, and when Aminah saw me enter, she ordered the servants to bring the noon meal, and we both sat down to eat. But just as before, she began to pick up the rice grain by grain, and I said to her, "Oh my wife, it irritates me very much to see you picking up each grain of rice like a hen. If this dish does not suit your taste, there are other kinds of meat before us, thanks to Allah's grace. You need only eat what pleases you. Each day the table is spread with dishes of different kinds, and if they do not suit your taste, you need only order whatever food your soul desires. Isn't there any meat on the table as rich and delicious as man's flesh that the servants can bring you and that you won't refuse to eat?"

Before I finished speaking, my wife realized that I had witnessed her nocturnal adventure. She suddenly grew mad. Her face flushed red as fire; her eyeballs seemed to pop from their sockets, and she foamed at the mouth with uncontrollable fury. The sight of her terrified me, and I was scared out of my mind. In the madness of her passion she picked up a cup of water which stood beside her, and after she dipped her fingers into the contents, she muttered some words which I could not understand. Then she sprinkled some drops over me and cried out, "You cursed thing! For your insolence and betrayal, I want you changed immediately into a dog!"

All at once I was transformed, and she picked up a stick and began to beat me mercilessly and almost killed me. I ran from room to room, but she pursued me with the stick and pounded me and whipped me with all her might until she was clean exhausted. Then she threw the street door half open, and as I made for it to save my life, she attempted to close it so as to squeeze the life out of my body. However, I saw her plan and thwarted it, leaving behind me the tip of my tail. With a great yelp, I escaped and thought myself lucky to get away from her without broken bones. When I stood in the street whining and groaning, the dogs of the quarter recognized a stranger and at once came rushing at me, barking and biting. With my tail between my legs, I tore along the marketplace and ran into the shop of a butcher who sold sheeps' and goats' heads, and there I found a hiding place and crouched low in a dark corner. Despite his scruples of conscience, which caused him to consider all dogs impure, the shopkeeper had compassion for my sorry plight and drove away the yelping and growling curs that wanted to follow me into his shop. Now that I was safe from danger, I passed the entire night hidden in my corner. Early the next morning the butcher went forth to buy his usual wares of sheeps' heads and hooves, and when he returned with a large supply, he began to lay them out for sale in the shop. Seeing that a whole pack of dogs had been attracted by the smell of flesh and gathered about the place, I also joined them. The owner noticed me among the ragged tykes and said to himself, "This dog has tasted nothing since yesterday when it ran yelping and hid in my shop." Then he threw me a fair-sized piece of meat, but I refused it and went up to him and wagged my tail to make him understand that I wanted to stay with him and be protected by his stall. However, he thought that I had eaten my fill and grabbed a stick to frighten me and chase me out of his shop. When I saw that the butcher could not understand what I wanted, I trotted off and wandered about until I came to a bakery and stood before the door from where I could see the baker eating his breakfast. Although I made no sign of wanting food, he threw me a bit of bread. Instead of snapping it up and greedily swallowing it, as is the fashion with all dogs, even the most gentle and simple of them, I approached him with it, gazed into his eyes, and wagged my tail to show my thanks. He was pleased by my well-bred behavior and smiled at me, whereupon I began to eat the bread, little by little, to humor him and to show my respect for him, even though I was not hungry. Now he was even more impressed by my manners and wanted to keep me in his shop. When I realized this was his intention, I sat by the door and looked wistfully at him, and he grasped that I desired nothing of him except his protection. Then he caressed me, took charge of me, and kept me to guard his store, but I would not enter his house until he had led the way. He also showed me where to lie during the night, and he fed me well at every meal and treated me with great hospitality. In turn, I watched his every move and always lay down or rose up whenever he desired. And each time that he left his lodging or walked anywhere, he took me with him. Sometimes, when I lay asleep and he went outside and did not find me, he would stand in the street and call out to me, crying, "Lucky! Lucky!"— this was the auspicious name that he had given me—and I would rush to him and frisk about before the door. And whenever he went out to taste the air, I would keep pace beside him, sometimes running ahead, sometimes at his heels, and always looking up at his face.

Some weeks passed, and I lived with the baker in great comfort. Then, one day it so happened that a woman came to the bakery to buy her bread, and she gave the owner several dirhams, but one of the coins was a bad one. My master tested all the silver, and when he discovered the false one, he returned it and demanded a genuine coin in exchange. But the woman wrangled and would not take it back and swore that it was real.

"The dirham is definitely worthless," said the baker. "Do you see my dog over there? He is but a beast, and yet I'm sure that he can tell you whether the coin is genuine or false."

So he called me by name—"Lucky! Lucky!"—where-

upon I sprang up and ran toward him. Then he threw all the coins onto the ground before me and said, "Here, look these dirhams over, and if there is a false coin among them, separate it from all the others."

I inspected the silver coins one by one with my nose and found the false one. Then I pushed it to one side and all the others to the other side, and I placed my paw on the false silver one, wagging what remained of my tail and looking up at my master's face. The baker was delighted by my cleverness, and the woman was also astounded by what she had witnessed. She took back her bad dirham and paid with another in exchange. After she went out of the shop, my master called together all his neighbors and relatives and told them about what had happened. So they threw some coins on the ground before me, both good and bad, in order to test me and see with their own eyes if I was as clever as my master said I was. Well, I picked out the false coin from among the genuine many times in succession without failing one time. So they all went away astonished and told everyone they saw about my feat. Thus, news of my accomplishments spread throughout the city, and from then on I spent my days testing genuine and false dirhams.

From that day on, the baker honored me even more, and all his friends and relatives laughed and said, "To be sure, you have a mighty good money changer in this dog!" Some people were jealous of my master and often tried to entice me away, but the baker kept me with him, and he would never allow me to leave his side, for my fame brought him many customers from every quarter of the town, even the farthest.

Not many days thereafter, another woman came to buy loaves of bread at our shop and paid the baker six dirhams, one of which was worthless. My master slid them over to me for a test, and right away I picked out the false one, and when I placed my paw on it, I looked up at the woman's face. When I did this, she became confused and confessed that it was a false coin and praised me for discovering her mistake. As she left the shop, this woman made a sign to me without the baker noticing it that I should follow her. Now, I had not stopped praying to Allah to help restore me to my human form, and I hoped some good follower of the Almighty would notice my miserable condition and save me. So, when the woman turned several times and looked at me, I was persuaded that she knew something about my situation. Therefore, I kept my eyes on her, and when she noticed this, she retraced her steps and beckoned me to come with her. I understood her signal and sneaked away from the baker, who happened to be busy heating his oven.

Pleased beyond measure that I was obeying her, she went straight home with me, and when she entered, she locked the door and led me into a room where a beautiful maiden in an embroidered dress was seated. I judged by her looks that she was the good woman's daughter, and since she was skilled in magic arts, the mother said to her, "Oh daughter, here is a dog that can tell good dirhams from bad dirhams. When I first heard about his marvelous accomplishments, I thought to myself that the beast must be a man whom some cruel-hearted wretch had turned into a dog. So today I decided to go and see this animal and test it while buying loaves at the shop, and behold, the dog passed the test and trial in a most admirable way. Look carefully at this dog, my daughter, and see whether it is indeed an animal or a man transformed into a beast by magic."

The young lady, who had veiled her face, looked at me attentively and soon cried out, "Oh, my mother, it's just as you say, and I shall prove this to you right away."

Upon rising from her seat, the maiden took a basin of water, dipped her hand into it, and sprinkled some drops of water on me, saying, "If you were born a dog, then remain a dog, but if you were born a man, then by virtue of this water, may you once again become a man."

Immediately I was transformed from the shape of a dog to human semblance, and I fell at the maiden's feet and kissed the ground before her. After giving her thanks and kissing the hem of her garment, I cried out, "Oh my lady, you have been exceedingly gracious and kind to a stranger! How can I find words to thank you and bless you as you deserve? Tell me, I beg you, how I may show my gratitude toward you. From this day on, you may consider me beholden to you. I am your slave."

Then I related my story and told her about Aminah's wickedness and how she had wronged me. I also paid my respects to the maiden's mother, who had brought me to her home. Upon hearing all this, the maiden said to me, "Oh Sidi Nu'uman, you need not thank me, for

I am simply glad and pleased to have been able to help
you, especially since you deserve it. I knew about your
wife, Aminah, for a long time even before you married
her. I also knew that she was skilled in witchcraft, and
she also knows about my art, for we were both taught
about science by the same mistress. We frequently met
at the Hammam bath as friends, but since she had bad
manners and a bad temper, I refused to become her
friend. Do not think that it is enough for me to have
helped you recover your human shape. Indeed, I must
take full vengeance for the wrong that she has done you.
And this I shall accomplish through you, so that you can
control her and become lord and master of your own
home. Now, I want you to wait here a while until I
come again."

Upon saying this, the maiden went into another room,
and I remained sitting and talking with her mother and
praised her kindness toward me. The old woman also
related strange and rare deeds of wonder performed by
her daughter that were always within the bounds of law
and pure in intention. Then the damsel returned with a
ewer in hand and said, "Oh Sidi Nu'uman, my magical
art tells me that Aminah is away from home at this moment, but she will return soon. In the meantime, she has
tricked the servants and pretends to mourn over your
disappearance. She has told them that when you were
eating together, you suddenly arose and went off on
some important business matter. Then a dog rushed
through the open door into the room, and she drove it
away with a stick. So, Sidi Nu'uman, I want you to return to your own house and keep this jug with you and
wait patiently until Aminah comes. As soon as she returns and sees you, she will be puzzled and will try to
escape from you. But before she leaves you, sprinkle
some drops from this jug on her and recite these spells
which I shall teach you. I need not tell you anything
more. You will see with your own eyes what will
happen."

After she said these words, the young lady taught me
magical phrases, which I memorized, and after this I
took my leave from daughter and mother. When I

reached home, everything happened just as the young magician told me it would. I was in the house but a short time when Aminah entered. I held the jug in my hand, and upon seeing me, she trembled and wanted to run away, but I quickly sprinkled some drops on her and repeated the magic words. All of a sudden, she was turned into a mare, the animal your highness noticed yesterday. I was astounded to see this transformation, and after seizing the mare's mane, I led her to the stable and secured her with a halter. After she was under my control, I reproached her for her wickedness and mean behavior, and I lashed her with a whip until my arm was tired. Then I made up my mind that I would ride her at full speed around the square every day and thus punish her in a way that she deserved.

With these words, Sidi Nu'uman held his peace, for his tale had come to an end. But soon he resumed and said, "Oh Commander of the Faithful, I trust that you are not displeased with my conduct. Perhaps you would punish such a woman even more severely than I have."

He then kissed the hem of the caliph's robe and kept silent. In the meantime, Harun al-Rashid perceived that Sidi Nu'uman had said all that he had wanted to say and exclaimed, "Indeed, your story is rare and extraordinary. Your wife's behavior has no excuse, and your punishment of her is, in my opinion, just and reasonable, but I want to ask you one thing: How long will you chastise her in this way? How long will she remain a beast? It would be a good idea now if you were to seek out the young lady whose magic enabled you to transform your wife and ask her to restore your wife's human shape. At the same time, I am somewhat fearful about recommending this course of action, for when this sorceress, this ghoul, finds herself restored to woman's form, she might resume her wicked ways and—who knows?—she might repay you with a far greater wrong than she has done before. And then you may not be able to escape."

After saying this, the Prince of True Believers decided not to urge Sidi Nu'uman to do what he recommended even though he was mild and merciful by nature. But now he turned to the third man whom the vizier had brought before him and said, "As I was walking in your neighborhood I was astonished to see your great and splendid mansion. When I asked the people in your district, they said that the palace belonged to a man called Khwajah Hasan. They added that you had at one time been very poor and desperate, but that Allah Almighty had interceded on your behalf and had sent you so much wealth that you had built the finest of mansions. Your neighbors all speak well of you, and nobody has a bad word to say against you. So, now I would like to verify all these things and hear from your own lips how you came to have this great wealth. I have summoned you before me so that I can know the full truth from you, and you need not fear anything when you tell me your tale. I desire nothing but to know your history. I want you to enjoy the opulence that Almighty Allah has bestowed on you to your heart's content. May your soul continue to enjoy destiny's favor."

Such were the words of the caliph, and the gracious words reassured the man. So, Khwajah threw himself before the Commander of the Faithful, and kissing the carpet at the foot of the throne, he exclaimed, "Oh Prince of True Believers, I shall tell you the true tale of my adventure, and Almighty Allah be my witness that I have done nothing against your laws and just commandments, and that I have obtained all my wealth through the favor and generosity of Allah alone."

Harun al-Rashid asked him once again to speak the bold truth, and the man began to recount in the following words

The Story of Khwajah Hasan al-Habbal

Oh beneficent lord, I shall now inform your highness about the means by which destiny blessed me with such wealth, but first I should like to tell you something about my two friends who live in Baghdad. The two are still alive, and both know the history which your slave shall now relate. One of them is called Sa'd and the other Sa'di. Now Sa'di was of the opinion that nobody could be happy and independent in this world without riches. Moreover, he declared that it is impossible to become wealthy without hard work, tenacity, wariness, and wisdom. But Sa'd differed and asserted that destiny, fate, and fortune determine whether one will be affluent. Sa'd was a poor man, while Sa'di was wealthy and possessed a great amount of goods. Yet, a strong friendship and affection arose between the two of them. The only thing they ever differed on was this. In sum, Sa'di relied solely on deliberation and planning, while Sa'd believed only in doom and destiny.

Now it so happened one day that as they sat talking together about this matter, Sa'di said, "A poor man is he who is either born a pauper and passes all his days in want and penury, or he who is born into a wealthy and comfortable situation but then squanders all that he has in manhood and becomes needy. Then he lacks the power to regain his riches and to live a comfortable life through his wit and industry."

But Sa'd answered, "Neither intelligence nor industry will help anyone. It is fate alone that will enable him to acquire and preserve his riches. Misery and want are nothing but accidents, and careful planning leads nowhere. Many a poor man has grown wealthy through fate, and many a rich man has been reduced to misery and beggary despite his skills and care."

"That's nonsense!" replied Sa'di. "Why don't we put the matter to a test? Let us find some craftsman who does not have much money and lives only on what he earns each day. We shall provide him with money, and he will certainly increase his stock and live in ease and comfort. Then you will be persuaded that my words are true."

Now, as the two were walking, they passed through the lane where I had my lodgings, and they saw me twisting ropes, a craft that my father, my grandfather, and many generations before me had followed. Upon regarding the condition of my home and dress, they judged that I was a needy man. So, Sa'd pointed me out to Sa'di and said, "Well, if you want to test someone, why not that man over there? He has dwelled here for years, and he earns a bare subsistence through ropemaking for himself and his family. I know all about him. He is a worthy subject for our test. So, give him some gold pieces and let us see what happens."

"I'll be glad to do it," replied Sa'di, "but first let us learn a little more about him."

So the two friends came up to me, and I put down my work and greeted them. They returned my salaam, after which Sa'di asked, "What is your name?"

"My name is Hasan," I replied, "but because of my trade of ropemaking, people call me Hasan al-Habbal."

Then Sa'di asked me, "How are you doing with your work? It seems to me that you are content with it. You have worked long and well, and no doubt you've been able to save and store a great deal of hemp and other stock. Your forebears maintained this craft for many years and must have left you a good deal of capital and property, which you have probably invested wisely and so increased your wealth."

"Oh my lord," I said, "I do not have much money in my purse to live happily or even to buy enough to eat. I spend every second of the day making ropes and have no time to rest. Still, I have great difficulty providing even dry bread for myself and my family. I have a wife and five small children who are still too young to help me in my business. It is no easy manner to provide them with what they need. How could you think that I am able to store a great deal of hemp and stock? Whatever ropes I twist every day, I sell right away. Then I spend whatever money I have earned partly on our needs and partly to buy the hemp with which I twist ropes the next day. However, may Allah be praised, despite my state of penury, He provides us with sufficient bread for our daily needs."

After I informed them about the conditions of my work, Sa'di replied, "Oh Hasan, now I know how things really stand with you, and indeed, it is different from what I had supposed. Under these conditions, I want to give you a purse of two hundred ashrafis. Certainly this will help you increase your earnings, and you will be able to live in ease and affluence. What do you say to this?"

"If you do me such a favor," I answered, "I should hope to grow richer than all my fellow craftsmen, even though Baghdad is as prosperous as it is populous."

Since Sa'di considered me honest and trustworthy, he pulled a purse of two hundred gold pieces out of his pocket and handed them to me.

"Take these coins, and use them for your business. May Allah help you. But make sure that you use this money with great care. Do not waste it in folly. I and my friend Sa'd will rejoice when we hear how well you are doing. If we come again and find you flourishing, we shall both be very satisfied."

Accordingly, oh Commander of the Faithful, I took the purse of gold with a grateful heart and with great happiness, and after putting it in my pocket, I thanked Sa'di and kissed the hem of his garment. Thereupon, the two friends departed.

In the meantime, oh Prince of True Believers, when I saw the two depart, I continued working, but I was uncertain where I should put the purse for safekeeping, for my house had neither a cupboard nor a locker. Nevertheless, I took it home and concealed the matter from my wife and children, and when I was alone, I took out ten gold coins for spending money and left the rest in the purse. Then I tied the mouth of the purse with some string and placed it in the folds of my turban and wound the cloth around my head. Soon, I went off to the market street and bought a stock of hemp, and on my way home, I bought some meat for supper, since it had been a long time since we had tasted some. But, as I trudged along the road, meat in hand, a huge bird, a hawk, came swooping down and sought to swipe the meat out of my hand. But I used my other hand to drive it away. It tried again on the other side, but again I scared it away, but while I exerted myself frantically to ward off the bird, my turban unfortunately fell to the ground. All at once the cursed hawk swooped down and flew off with it in its talons. I ran after it and pursued it, shouting aloud. Hearing my cries, the people and children at the bazaar did what they could to scare it away and make the beastly bird drop its prey, but it was all in vain. The hawk would not drop the turban and soon flew clear out of sight. I was greatly distressed and sad to lose the ashrafis, but there was nothing to do. So I went home carrying the hemp and the food that I had bought, vexed and depressed, ready to die from shame at the thought of what Sa'di would say, especially when I thought of how he would doubt my words. He certainly would not think my tale was true if I told him that a hawk had carried off my turban with the gold pieces. I was sure he would think that I wanted to deceive him and had concocted some amusing tale as an excuse. Still, I did enjoy what remained of the ten ashrafis, and for some days my family and I ate sumptuously. But when all the gold was gone and nothing remained, I became as poor and needy as I was before. Still, I was content and grateful to Almighty Allah, nor did I blame my destiny. He had sent this purse of gold to me, and I had not expected it. Now He had taken it away, and I was still grateful and satisfied, for whatever He does is always well done.

My wife, who had not known anything about the ashrafis, soon noticed that I was disturbed about something, and I had to tell her my secret if I wanted peace and quiet. Moreover, the neighbors came by to ask me what was wrong. But I was reluctant to tell them what had happened. They could not bring back what was gone, and they would have certainly laughed at my calamity. However, when they pressured me, I told them every single thing. Some thought that I was lying, and they mocked me. Others believed that I was mad and off my rocker, and that my words were the wild prating of an idiot or the drivel of dreams. The young people made fun of me and laughed to think that I, who had never in my life seen a gold coin, should tell them how I had acquired so many ashrafis and how a hawk had flown away with them. My wife, however, believed every word of my tale and wept and beat her breast with sorrow.

Thus when six months passed, the two friends, Sa'di and Sa'd, happened to come one day to my quarter of the town.

"Over there is the street where Hasan al-Habbal lives," said Sa'd to Sa'di. "Come, let us see how he has added to his stock and how much he has prospered by the two hundred ashrafis that you gave him."

"Good idea," responded Sa'di. "We have not seen him for many days. I would like to visit him, and I would be very glad to learn that he has prospered."

So the two walked toward my house, and Sa'd said to Sa'di, "If I'm not mistaken, it seems to me that he is the same, just as poor and miserable as he was before. He's wearing old and tattered garments, with the exception of his turban, which seems newer and cleaner. Look for yourself, and see if I'm not right."

Thereupon Sa'di came up closer to me, and he, too, realized that my condition was unaltered. Soon the two friends addressed me, and after the usual salutation, Sa'd asked, "Oh Hasan, how's it going with you? What's happened to your business? Have the two hundred Ashrafis helped you and your trade?"

"Oh my lords," I answered, "how can I tell you about the sad accident that I had? I dare not tell you out of shame. Yet, I cannot conceal what happened. Truthfully, something marvelous and wondrous happened to me, and when I tell you my tale, it will fill you with suspicion, and I am sure that you won't believe it. I will come off as a liar, but whether I like it or not, I must tell you the whole story."

So I recounted every single thing that happened to me, from first to last, especially the incident with the hawk. But Sa'di did not believe me and cried out, "Oh Hasan, you're joking with us, and pretending that all this happened. It is hard to believe the tale you've told. Hawks do not usually fly off with turbans, but only with things that they can eat. You want to trick us, but you are really like those who misuse their good fortune. You probably abandoned your work and wasted all your money and time by enjoying yourself. Now you've become poor again, and this is why you must eke out your living as best you can. This is definitely the case with you. You have quickly squandered our gift, and now you are as needy as you were before."

"This is not true, my lord," I cried. "I do not deserve your hard words and blame. I am totally innocent. The strange incident that happened to me is not a lie, and if you want proof that I am not lying, all the townspeople know about it. I am not trying to deceive you. You are absolutely right that hawks do not fly away with turbans, but such accidents, even if they be wondrous and marvelous, may occur to people, especially those like me who are down and out."

Then Sa'd supported me and said, "Oh Sa'di, we have often seen and heard how hawks carry off many things besides food. His tale may not be as unreasonable as it seems."

Thereupon Sa'di pulled out another purse full of gold pieces from his pocket and counted out another two hundred. When he was finished, he said, "Oh Hasan, take these ashrafis, but make sure that you keep them safe and sound, and beware! Make sure that you do not lose them like the others. Use them in such a way that you will benefit from them and prosper just like your best neighbors are prospering."

I took the money from him and poured out thanks and blessings, and when the two friends went their way, I returned to working on my ropes. Later I went straight home, and since my wife and children were not there, I again took ten gold coins from the two hundred and tied up the remainder carefully in a piece of cloth. Then I looked around to find a spot in which to hide my hoard so that my wife and children would not find it and lay their hands on it. Soon I caught sight of a large clay jar full of bran standing in a corner of the room. So I hid the cloth with the gold coins in it, and I thought that it was safely concealed from my wife and little ones. No sooner did I put the ashrafis at the bottom of the jar of bran than my wife entered, and I told her nothing about the two friends or what had happened, but I set out for the bazaar to buy hemp.

Now, as soon as I had left the house, fortune would

have it that a man who sold a kind of clay that poor
women use to wash their hair came by. My wife wanted
to buy some, but she did not have a single coin in the
house. So she quickly thought about what she could use
as payment, and it occurred to her that the jar of bran
served no special purpose, and she decided to exchange
it for the clay. The merchant agreed to this proposal,
and he left the house with the jar of bran as payment
for the clay. Soon, I came back with a load of hemp on
my head and another five on the heads of porters who
accompanied me. I helped them put down their loads,
and after storing the stuff in a room, I paid and dismissed them. Then I stretched myself out on the floor
to rest awhile, and when I glanced at the corner where
the jar of bran once stood, I found that it was gone.
Words fail me, oh Prince of True Believers, to describe
the tumultuous feelings that filled my heart. Immediately
I jumped up and called to my wife and asked her where
the jar had been taken. She replied that she had exchanged its contents for a trifle of washing clay.

Then I cried aloud, "You wretched woman! What
have you done! You have ruined me and your children!
You have given enormous wealth to that merchant!"

Then I told her everything that had happened to me,
and how I had hidden the one hundred and ninety ashrafis in the bran jar. Upon hearing this, she wept, beat
her breast, and tore her hair.

"Where can I find that merchant now?" she cried.
"That fellow is a stranger. I had never seen him before
in this quarter. And once again, you did a foolish thing
by not telling me. Otherwise, this accident would have
never happened to us. No, never!"

And she lamented and shed bitter tears. Thereupon I
said, "Don't make such a hubbub about this—otherwise
our neighbors will overhear you and learn about our
misfortune. Then they will laugh at us again and call us
fools. Our only choice is to remain content with the will
of Almighty Allah."

In the meantime, the ten ashrafis which I had taken
from the two hundred were sufficient for me to carry on
my trade and to live in more comfort for a short period

of time. But I was distressed, and I wondered what I would say to Sa'di when he came again. Since he really had not believed me the first time, I was quite sure that he would now denounce me in public as a cheat and liar. Well, some time thereafter. Sa'di and Sa'd did reappear and came strolling toward my house. They were holding a conversation, and as usual, they were arguing about me and my situation. Having noticed them from a distance, I stopped working so that I could hide myself out of the shame I felt. But they saw this and entered my shop with a salaam and asked me how things were going with me. I did not dare to raise my eyes because I was so mortified. So, with my head lowered, I returned their greeting, and when they noticed that something was bothering me, they were astonished and asked, "Are you well? How come you're behaving like this? Haven't you made use of the gold, or have you wasted your wealth in lewd living?"

"Oh my lords," I said, "let me tell you the story of what happened to the ashrafis. It begins right after your departure. I went straight home with the purse of money, and since nobody was in the house, I took out ten gold pieces, and the rest I put into a large clay jar which stood in one corner of the room. This way I intended to keep the matter a secret from my wife and children. But a merchant came by selling clay, and she needed some. Since she had nothing to pay for the clay, however, she asked him whether he would accept the clay jar with the bran. He agreed, and accordingly my wife took the clay and gave him the jar, and he took it away with him. If you were to ask me why I didn't confide in my wife and tell her that I had put the money in the jar, I would answer that you gave me strict commands to guard the money with utmost care and caution. I thought that the jar was the safest place to store the gold, and I was loath to trust my wife, fearing she would take some of the gold coins and spend them on household items. Oh, my lords, you have fully demonstrated your goodness and graciousness to me, but I fear that I have been determined for a life of poverty and penury. How then can I aspire to acquiring possessions and pros-

perity? No matter what, I shall never forget your generosity as long as I live."

"It seems," said Sa'di, "that I have spent four hundred
ashrafis for nothing. My intention in giving you the
money was not that I should obtain your praise and
thanksgiving, but that you should benefit from it."

So the two men showed me compassion and consoled
me in my unhappy fate. After showing a lead coin to
me, Sa'd said, "Do you see this lead coin? Take it, and
fate will decree what blessings it will bring you."

Upon seeing this, Sa'di laughed aloud and jested
about the matter. "What use will this be to Hasan? How
will it benefit him?"

"Pay no attention to what Sa'di says," Sa'd replied.
"Keep this with you. Let him laugh all he wants. One
day—if it is the will of Almighty Allah—it will become
the means by which you become a wealthy and magnificent man."

Well, I took the lead coin and put it into my pocket,
and the two bade me farewell and went their way. After
they departed, I continued to twist rope until nightfall.
As I undressed to go to bed, the lead coin fell out of
my pocket. So I picked it up and set it carelessly in a
small niche in the wall. Now, that very night it so happened that a fisherman, one of my neighbors, needed a
small coin to buy some twine to mend his drag net,
which he usually did during the evening so that he could
catch the fish before the dawn of day and sell his catch.
Since he was accustomed to rise when it was still night,
he asked his wife to go around to the neighbors and
borrow a coin so that he might buy the necessary twine.
The woman went from house to house, but no one
would lend her even a penny. At last, she came home
weary and disappointed.

"Have you been to Hasan al-Habbal?" the fisherman
asked her.

"No," she replied. "I haven't tried his place. It's the
farthest of all the neighbors' houses. Anyway, do you
think that if I had gone there, I would have come back
with anything?"

"You lazy hussy!" the fisherman cried. "You're nothing but excess baggage! I want you to try his place. You never know. Perhaps he has a coin to lend us."

Accordingly, the woman went off, grumbling and muttering, and when she came to my house, she knocked at the door and said, "Oh Hasan al-Habbal, my husband needs a coin to buy some twine so he can mend his nets."

I remembered the coin that Sa'd had given to me, and where I had put it. So I shouted to her, "Be patient. My wife will come and give you what you need."

Hearing all this hubbub, my wife woke from her sleep, and I told her where to find the lead coin. So she fetched it and gave it to the woman, who was very happy, and said, "You and your husband have shown great kindness to my husband. Therefore, I promise you that you will have the fish that he catches when he first throws his net tomorrow. I am certain that when my good man hears of my promise, he will give his consent."

So the woman took the money to her husband and told him about her pledge.

"You have done well and wisely," he responded, and then he bought some twine and mended all the nets before dawn. Thereupon, he hastened to the river to catch fish as was his custom. When he cast the net into the stream for the first throw and hauled it in, he discovered that it contained only one fish, and it was very large and thick. He set it aside as my portion and continued to throw his net time and again. With each cast he caught many fish small and large, but none as large as the first one that he had caught. As soon as he returned home, the fisherman came to me at once and brought the fish he had netted for me.

"My wife promised last night that you should have whatever fish would come in my first throw of the net," he said. "This fish is the only one that I caught. Here it is. Please take it as gratitude for the kindness that you showed us last night and as fulfillment of our promise. If Allah Almighty had provided me with a net full of fish with my first throw, it would have been all yours. But it is your luck that I landed only this one."

"The coin that I gave you last night was not worth

very much," I responded, "and I did not expect anything
in return." So I refused to accept the fish, but he insisted
that it was mine, and I finally agreed to keep it. Then
I gave the fish to my wife and said, "This fish is our
compensation for the coin that we gave to the fisherman,
our neighbor. Sa'd had declared that I would become
rich and prosperous because of this coin." Then I recounted to my wife how my two friends had visited me
and what they had said and had done. She was puzzled
when she saw just a single fish and asked, "How shall I
cook it? It seems to me that it would be best to cut it
up and broil it for the children, especially since we do
not have any spices and condiments with which to
dress it."

Then, as she sliced and cleaned the fish, she found a
large diamond inside its belly, and at first she thought
that it was a bit of glass or crystal. She had often heard
tell of diamonds, but she had never seen one with her
own eyes. So she gave it to one of the youngest children
for a plaything, and when the others saw it, they all
desired to have it because it was so bright and brilliant.
Each one took a turn in holding it, and when night came
and the lamp was lit, they crowded around the stone,
gazed at its beauty, and screamed and shouted with delight. When my wife spread the table, we sat down to
supper, and the eldest boy set the diamond on a tray.
As soon as we finished eating, the children fought and
scrambled to hold it just as they had done before. At
first, I paid no attention to their noise and hubbub, but
when it became so exceedingly loud and irksome, I
asked my eldest boy why they were quarreling so much
and making so much noise.

"We're all arguing over a piece of glass that produces
light as bright as a lamp," he said.

So I told him to fetch it for me, and when I glanced
at it, I was astounded by its sparkling glow and asked
my wife where she had found the crystal.

"I discovered it in the belly of the fish as I was gutting
it," she responded. "I don't think it's anything but
glass."

Then I asked my wife to put the lamp behind the

hearth, and when it was hidden from my view, the brightness of the diamond was so great that we could see perfectly well without the other light. After that I placed it on the hearth so that we could work by it, and I said to myself, "The coin that Sa'd left me has produced something beneficial. From now on we shall no longer need a lamp, and this way we can save on oil."

When the youngsters saw me put out the lamp and use the glass instead, they jumped and danced for joy and screamed and shouted with so much glee that all the neighbors could hear them, so I scolded them and sent them to bed. We also needed rest and soon fell asleep. The next day I awoke, went to work, and did not think about the piece of glass.

Now, in our vicinity there was a wealthy Jew, a jeweler, who bought and sold all kinds of precious stones, and he and his wife could not sleep that night because of all the noise that my children had made. So the next morning the jeweler's wife came to our house to complain about the hubbub. Before she could say a word, my wife, who had guessed why she had come, said to her, "Oh Rachel, I fear that my children pestered you last night with their laughing and crying. I beg your indulgence. You know how children cry and laugh at trifles. Come in and look at the cause of all their excitement."

The jeweler's wife entered and saw the piece of glass that had made our children so excited, and when she looked at the diamond, she was astounded, because she had a great deal of experience in dealing with precious stones. Then my wife told her how she had found it in the fish's belly, and the jeweler's wife said, "This piece of glass is more valuable than others of its kind. I have one just like this which I wear at times, and if you want to sell this piece, I would gladly buy it from you."

Upon hearing her words, the children began to cry and said, "Oh Mother dear, don't sell it! If you don't sell it, we promise to keep quiet."

Realizing that the children would not part with it, the women did not speak about it any more, but before the jeweler's wife left, she whispered to my wife, "Make sure that you tell nobody about this glass. If you decide to sell it, send me word at once."

Now the Jew was sitting in his shop when his wife went to him and told him about the piece of glass. "Go straight back," he said, "and offer to buy it, and say that it is for me. Begin with a small bid, then raise the amount until you get it."

Thereupon the jeweler's wife returned to my house and offered twenty ashrafis for the glass, which my wife considered to be a large sum for such a trifle. So she became suspicious and did not want to close the bargain. At that moment, I happened to leave my work and come home for my noon meal and saw the two women talking on the threshold of our house. My wife stopped me and said, "Our neighbor Rachel has offered twenty ashrafis for this piece of glass, but I have not accepted. What do you say?"

Then I remembered what Sa'd had told me about the lead coin and that it would make me wealthy and prosperous. When the jeweler's wife saw that I was hesitating, she thought that I would not consent and said, "Neighbor, if you will not agree to part with this piece of glass for twenty pieces of gold, I shall give you fifty."

When I saw that she raised her offer so quickly from twenty gold pieces to fifty, I realized that the glass had to be very valuable. So I kept silent and did not answer her until she cried out, "Very well, then take one hundred. This is its full value, but I am not so sure that my husband will consent to such a high price."

"My good woman," I finally replied, "why are you talking so foolishly? I shall not sell this diamond for less than one hundred thousand gold coins, and I am only offering it at this low price because you are our neighbor."

The jeweler's wife raised her offer to fifty thousand ashrafis and said, "Please wait until tomorrow morning, and don't sell it until then. My husband will come around and look at it then."

"All right," I consented. "By all means, have your husband drop in and inspect it."

The next day the Jew came to my house, and I produced the diamond, which glittered in the palm of my hand with light as bright as my lamp's. Now he could see that everything that his wife had told him about its luster was true. He took it in his hand, examined it, turned it around, and was amazed by its beauty.

"My wife made an offer of fifty thousand gold pieces," he said. "Now I see that it is worth another twenty thousand."

"Your wife has surely told you what price I set," I answered. "I want one hundred thousand ashrafis and nothing less. I won't come down one iota from this price."

The jeweler did all he could to buy the diamond at a cheaper price, but I kept answering, "It doesn't matter. If you don't meet my price, I shall have to sell it to another jeweler."

Finally, he consented and gave me two thousand gold pieces as a deposit. Then he said, "Tomorrow I shall bring the rest and take away my diamond."

I agreed to this bargain, and the following day he came and paid me the full sum of one hundred thousand ashrafis, which he had raised among his friends and business partners. Then I gave him the diamond, which had brought me great wealth, and I offered thanks to him and praise for Almighty Allah for this great good fortune that I had unexpectedly received. I also hoped that I could see my two friends Sa'd and Sa'di soon to thank them as well.

In the meantime, I set my house in order and gave spending money to my wife for household necessities and clothing for herself and children. In addition, I bought a fine mansion and furnished it with the best things possible. Then I said to my wife, who thought of nothing but rich clothes, good food, and a life of ease and enjoyment, "We had better not give up our trade. Indeed, I want to invest some of this money in the business and expand it."

So I went to all the ropemakers of the city, and after I had bought some places to manufacture rope, I put them all to work, and in each establishment I appointed an overseer, an intelligent and trustworthy man, so that there is not a single ward or quarter in Baghdad that does not have workshops of mine for ropemaking. Furthermore, I have warehouses in each town and every district of Irak that are under the charge of honest supervisors. And thus it is that I have amassed such great wealth. Finally, I bought another house for my own special place of business. It was a ruin with a lot of land next to it. Well, I had the shell of the house pulled down, and I constructed a new and spacious building, which your highness observed yesterday. All my workers are lodged here, and this is the place where I keep my office books and accounts. Besides my warehouse, it contains apartments equipped with furniture in simple style, sufficient for me and my family. After some time I left my old home in which Sa'd and Sa'di had seen me working, and I went to live in the new mansion. Not long after this my two friends and benefactors decided to visit me. They were puzzled when they entered my old workshop and could not find me. So they asked the neighbors, "Where does Hasan the ropemaker live? Is he still alive?"

"He is now a rich merchant," they responded. "Men no longer call him Hasan, but Master Hasan the ropemaker. He has built a splendid mansion, and he lives not too far from here."

So my two friends set out in search of me, and they rejoiced at the good news. To be sure, Sa'di was by no means convinced that my wealth had sprung from the small lead coin as Sa'd contended. Mulling the matter over in his mind, he said to his comrade, "I am delighted to hear about Hasan's good fortune, even though he deceived me twice and took four hundred gold pieces that he has probably used to acquire this wealth. It is absurd to think that it has come from the lead coin that you gave him. Nevertheless, I forgive him and bear him no grudge."

"You are mistaken," replied Sa'd. "Hasan is a good and honest man. He would not deceive you. He told you the simple truth. I am convinced that he has come upon all his wealth and fortune through the lead coin. However, we shall soon hear what he has to say."

As they conversed, they came to the street where I now dwell. Upon seeing a large and magnificent mansion that had just been built, they guessed it was mine. So they knocked, and after the porter opened, Sa'di was astonished to see such grandeur and so many people sitting inside. He was afraid at first that they might have unwittingly entered the house of some emir. Then, plucking courage, he asked the porter, "Is this the house of Khwajah Hasan al-Habbal?"

"This is indeed the house of Khwajah Hasan al-Habbal," replied the porter. "He is inside and sitting in his office. Please enter, and one of the slaves will let him know that you are here."

Thereupon the two friends walked in, and as soon as I saw them I recognized them and rose up to meet them. I ran and kissed the hems of their garments, and they would have hugged me, but in my humility I would not allow them to do so. Then I led them into a large and spacious salon and asked them to take the seats of honor. They were reluctant to take the best places, but I exclaimed, "Oh, my lords, I am no different or better than the poor ropemaker Hasan, who has always remembered your generosity and goodness and does not deserve to sit in a higher place than you."

Then they took their seats, and I sat opposite them, and Sa'di said, "My heart rejoices to see you in this condition. Indeed, Allah has given everything that you wanted. Most likely you have acquired all this wealth and fortune with the four hundred gold pieces that I gave to you. But tell me, why did you deceive me twice and tell me lies?"

Sa'd listened to these words with silent indignation, and before I could reply, he exploded and said, "Oh Sa'di, how often have I assured you that everything Hasan told us about losing the ashrafis is the truth and not a lie?"

Then they began to argue, and when I recovered from my surprise, I exclaimed, "My lords, what's the sense of all this bickering? I implore you, do not argue on my account. I have told you everything that has happened to me, and it doesn't matter to me whether you believe

my words. But now listen to the whole truth." Then I
told them the story about the lead coin that I gave to
the fisherman and how a diamond was found in the fish's
belly. In short, I told them everything that I have related
to your highness.

Upon hearing all my adventures, Sa'di remarked, "Oh
Khwajah Hasan, you say your tale is the truth, but I still
cannot believe your words, because I am convinced that
the four hundred gold pieces that I gave you have produced all this wealth."

Later, when the two arose to take their leave, I also
stood up and said, "I beseech you now to taste my food
and to stay here this night under your servant's roof. As
for tomorrow, I should like to take you along the river
to a country house that I have recently bought."

After making a few objections, the two consented to
stay. Then I gave orders for the preparation of the evening meal and showed them around the house and entertained them with pleasant conversation until a slave
came and announced that supper was to be served. So
I led them to the salon, where there were trays loaded
with many kinds of meat. Wax candles stood on all sides,
and musicians gathered before the tables and played various instruments, while in the upper part of the salon
men and women were dancing and providing lively entertainment. After we had dined, we went to bed, and
the next day, we rose early, said our morning prayers,
and soon embarked on a large boat. The rowers pro-
pelled us in the boat with the current in our favor, and
soon we arrived at my country villa. Then we strolled
around the grounds and entered the house, where I
showed them all the new additions and everything that
belonged to the house. When they saw everything, they
were amazed. Then we went to the garden and saw all
kinds of fruit trees with ripe fruit bowing down along the
rows, and they were watered from the river by means of
brick irrigation ditches. All around were shrubs with
flowers whose perfume sweetened the air. Here and
there fountains and jets of water shot high into the air.
The birds sang melodic songs on the branches covered
with green leaves. In short, all the sights filled our souls

with joy and happiness. My two friends walked about in joy and delight and thanked me repeatedly for bringing them to such a lovely site and said, "May Almighty Allah continue to grant you such a prosperous life!"

Finally I led them to the foot of a tall tree next to one of the garden walls and showed them a little summer house where I liked to relax and have refreshments. The room was furnished with cushions, divans, and pillows lined with virgin gold. Now it so happened that while we were resting in that summer house, two of my sons, whom I had sent to my country place with their tutor for a change of air, were roaming around the garden and looking for birds' nests. Soon they came across a big one at the top of a high branch and tried to climb up the trunk to snatch it, but because they were not strong enough and did not have the experience, they could not get at the nest. So they asked a slave who was always with them to climb the tree. He did as they requested, but when he looked into the nest, he was amazed to see that it was mainly made of an old turban. So he brought down the stuff and handed it to the boys. My eldest son took it from his hands and carried it to the arbor for me to see and set it at my feet.

"Father, look here!" he said gleefully. "This nest is made of cloth."

Sa'd and Sa'di were filled with wonderment at the sight, and their astonishment grew greater when I recognized it as the very turban that the hawk had snatched away from me. Then I said to my two friends, "Examine this turban yourselves, and tell me whether it is not the very same one that I wore on my head when you first honored me with your presence."

"I don't recognize it," said Sa'd.

"If you find the one hundred and ninety gold pieces in it," said Sa'di, "you will know for sure that it is your turban."

"Oh my lord," I replied, "I am sure that this is my turban." And as I held it in my hand, I found that it was heavy, and after opening the folds somewhat that were tied at the corners of the cloth, lo and behold, I found the purse of gold coins. Showing it to Sa'di, I cried, "Don't you recognize this purse?"

"I must admit," he replied, "it is the very purse of ashrafis that I gave you when we first met."

Then I opened the mouth of the purse and poured out the gold in one heap upon the carpet and asked him to count out his money. So he turned over one coin after the next until he came to the sum of one hundred and ninety ashrafis. Consequently, he became ashamed and confused. "Now I believe your words!" he exclaimed. "Nevertheless, you must admit that you earned one half of your wealth with the two hundred gold coins that I gave you after our second visit, and the other half by means of the coin that you received from Sa'd."

I refused to answer him, but my friends continued to argue about the matter. Then we sat down to eat and drink, and after we were full, we went to sleep in the cool arbor. When noon arrived, we arose and mounted horses and rode off to Baghdad with the servants following behind us. However, once we arrived at the city, we found all the shops closed and could not find grain and forage for the horses. So I sent two slave boys to look for food for the horses. One of them found a jar of bran in the shop of a corn dealer, and after paying for the provisions, he brought the grain back with the jar with the promise that he would return the jar the following day. Then he began to take out the bran by handfuls in the dark and place it before the horses. Suddenly his hand came upon a piece of cloth that was very heavy. So, he brought it to me just as he found it and said, "Isn't this the cloth that you lost? I remember your telling us about it many times."

Well, I took it and was amazed to find that it was the exact same cloth in which I had stuffed one hundred and ninety ashrafis before hiding them in the jar of bran. Then I said to my friends, "Oh my lords, it is Almighty Allah's decree that before you left me you were to witness these events and realize that everything that I told you was the truth." And I continued, addressing Sa'di, "Here you have the other sum of money that you gave me, and which I tied up in this very piece of cloth that I now recognize."

Then I sent for the jar so that they might see it, and I also had it carried to my wife so that she could testify whether it was the jar that she gave in exchange for the clay. Soon she sent word and said that it was indeed the same jar. Accordingly, Sa'di admitted that he was wrong and said to Sa'd, "Now I know that you are speaking the truth, and I am convinced that wealth does not beget wealth, but only through the grace of Almighty Allah can a poor man become a rich man."

Then he begged pardon for his mistrust, and I accepted his apology. Afterward we all retired to rest. Early the next day my two friends bade me farewell and journeyed home, convinced that I had done no wrong and had not squandered the money that they had given me.

Now, when Caliph Harun al-Rashid had heard the entire story of Khwajah Hasan, he said, "I have heard people speak about you for some time now, and they all declare that you are a good and honest man. Moreover, the diamond with which you attained your wealth is now in my treasury. Therefore, I would like to send for Sa'di right away so that he might see it with his own eyes and know for certain that men do not become rich or poor through money. Go now, and tell your tale to my treasurer so that he may write it down as a chronicle. It will be placed in the treasury together with the diamond so that people will remember your story forever."

Then the caliph dismissed Khwajah Hasan with a nod. Immediately thereafter, Sidi Nu'uman and Baba Abdullah also kissed the foot of the throne and departed.

The Porter and the Three Ladies of Baghdad

Once upon a time there was a porter in Baghdad, who was a bachelor, and who would remain unmarried. One day, when he stood on the street leaning idly on his crate, an honorable woman suddenly appeared before him. She was wearing a mantilla of Mosul silk, embroidered with gold. Her walking shoes were also lined with gold, and her hair floated in long plaits. She raised the veil on her face and revealed two beautiful black eyes fringed with jet-black lashes, and her glance was soft and languishing. Pausing a moment, she addressed the porter and said in the most smooth and finest tones, "Pick up your crate and follow me."

The porter was so dazzled that he could hardly believe that he had heard her correctly. Nevertheless, he quickly strapped the crate on his shoulders and said to himself, "Oh, this is my lucky day! May Allah be generous to me!"

The porter followed her until she stopped at the door of a house, where she knocked, and soon an old man came out. He was a Nazarene, and she gave him a gold coin and received strained wine clear as olive oil in return. Then she placed it in the porter's hamper and said, "Pick it up, and follow me."

"By Allah, this is indeed an auspicious day, a day when all the wishes of a man can be fulfilled," said the porter.

He again hoisted up the crate and followed her until she stopped at a fruit shop and she bought Shami apples, Osmani quinces, Omani peaches, Nile Valley cucumbers, Egyptian limes, and Sultani oranges and lemons. In addition she purchased Aleppine jasmine, scented myrtle berries, Damascene water lilies, flower of privet and camomile, blood-red anemones, violets, pomegranate bloom, and eglantine and narcissus, and she placed all of it in the porter's crate and commanded, "Up with it!"

So he lifted the crate and followed her until she stopped at a butcher's stand and asked for ten pounds of mutton. Then she paid the price, and the butcher wrapped it in a banana leaf, whereupon she laid it in the crate and said, "Lift it, porter." So, he hoisted and followed her as she walked on until she came to a grocer's shop, where she bought dry fruits, pistachio nuts, Tihamah raisins, shelled almonds, and all sorts of desserts. Then, once again, she said to the porter, "Lift and follow me."

So he picked up his crate and went after her until she stopped at the confectioner's shop, where she bought a clay platter and piled it with all sorts of sweetmeats, tarts, fritters scented with musk, soap cakes, lemon loaves, melon preserves, combs of honey from Zaynab, lady fingers, kazi's tidbits, and goodies of every description. All were placed in the porter's crate, and since he was a funny man, he said, "You should have told me what you were about, and I would have brought a pony or camel with me to carry all this market stuff."

She smiled, gave him a little cuff on the nape of his neck, and replied, "Keep walking, and don't talk so much. Allah willing, you will be handsomely rewarded."

Then she stopped at a perfume shop and bought ten sorts of waters, rose scent with musk, orange-flower, water lily, window flower, violet, and five other kinds. She also bought two loaves of sugar, a bottle for perfume spraying, a lump of incense, lign aloes, ambergris, and musk with candles of Alexandria wax. Then she put all of it into the crate and said, "Pick it up, porter, and follow me."

He did so and followed her until she stood before a greengrocer's stand. There she bought pickled safflower and olives in brine and oil, tarragon, and cream cheese and hard Syrian cheese, which were all placed into the porter's crate.

W.H.A

"Pick it up and follow me," she ordered once more.
And once again, he did as she said and followed her
until she came to a grand mansion with a spacious court
in front and tall fine columns to support the building.
The gate had two leaves of ebony inlaid with plates of
red gold. The lady stopped at the door and, turning her
veil sideways, she knocked softly with her knuckles while

the porter stood behind her, thinking of nothing but her beauty and loveliness. Soon the door swung back, and both sides were opened. The porter looked to see who had opened it, and behold, it was a tall lady, a model of beauty, loveliness, brilliance, and perfect grace. Her forehead was white as a flower. Her cheeks were ruddy bright like the anemone. Her eyes were similar to those of the wild heifer or gazelle, with eyebrows like the crescent moon. Her mouth was like a royal ring. Her lips were coral red, and her teeth were like a line of strung pearls or camomile petals. Her throat recalled the long graceful neck of an antelope, and her breasts were like two pomegranates of even size. Her body rose and fell in waves below her dress, like the rolls of a piece of brocade, and her navel could hold an ounce of benzoin ointment.

When the porter gazed at her, he was stunned and thought he was losing his mind. In fact he almost lost his grip of the crate. "Never in my life," he said to himself, "have I seen a more blessed day than today!"

"Come in," the magnificent hostess said to the lady whom the porter had been following, "and relieve this poor man of his load."

So they entered and walked until they reached a spacious ground-floor hall built with admirable skill and embellished with all kinds of colors and carvings. All around were upper balconies, arches, galleries, cupboards, and recesses covered by curtains. In the center there was a great basin full of water surrounding a fine fountain, and at the upper end on the raised dais was a couch of juniper wood set with gems and pearls with a canopy like mosquito curtains of red satin-silk looped with pearls as big as filberts and bigger. Sitting on this dais was a glistening lady with a brilliantly beaming brow, the dream of philosophy. Her eyes were divine, and her eyebrows were angelic arches. Her breath smelled of ambergris and perfume, and her lips had the taste of sugar. Her posture was elegant and straight, and her face put the noon sun's radiance to shame. She appeared to be a galaxy, or a dome with golden marquetry, or a bride displayed in choicest finery. Rising from the couch, she stepped forward with a graceful swaying gait until she reached the middle of the salon, then said to her sisters, "Why are you standing there? Take the crate from the poor man's shoulders!"

So they all lifted the crate from the porter's back, and after emptying it, they put everything in its place. After they had finished, they gave him two gold pieces and said, "Be on your way, porter."

But he did not go, for he stood looking at the ladies and admiring their extraordinary beauty, their pleasant manners, and kind dispositions. He also gazed wistfully at the good stock of wine, sweet-smelling flowers, fruits, and other things and was astounded to see no man in the place. Since he delayed his departure, the eldest lady asked, "What's the matter with you? Why don't you go? Have we given you too little?" And, turning to her sister, who had bought everything, she said, "Give him another dinar!"

But the porter answered, "By Allah, my lady, I don't want any more money. I always charge two dirhams. To tell you the truth, my heart and soul have been dazzled by you. I am astonished to see you all here alone without a man about and not a soul to keep you company. And as you well know, the tower of the dome would collapse if it were not held up by four pillars, and you need this fourth. Indeed, a woman without a man is short of measure. So, if you want a fourth who will be a person of good sense and prudence, smart-witted and apt to keep careful counsel, I am at your disposal."

Pleased and amused by his words, they laughed and said, "And who is to assure us of that? We are maidens, and we are fearful of entrusting our secret to someone who may not keep it, for we have read the lines of the poet Ibn al-Sumam in a certain chronicle:

"Hold fast your secret and to none unfold;
Lost is a secret when that secret's told;
If your breast fails your secret to conceal,
How can you hope another breast shall hold?"

When the porter heard their words, he responded, "By your lives! I am a sensible and discreet man who has read books and perused chronicles. I reveal only good things and conceal the foul, and I act as the poet advises:

> "None but the good a secret keep
> And good men keep it quite concealed:
> It is to me like a well-shut house
> With keyless locks, the door firmly sealed."

When the maidens heard his verse and saw his adroit use of poetry, they said to him, "You know that we have spent all our money on this place. Now tell us what you have to offer us for entertainment in return for our hospitality. Certainly you don't expect us to allow you to sit in our company and be our drinking companion and gaze upon our fair and rare faces without contributing something."

But before the porter could speak, one of the ladies added, "You will be somebody if you bring something to your plate, but there will be nothing for you to eat if nothing is what you bring."

But the lady who had bought all the goods intervened and said, "My sisters, let us stop teasing him. By Allah, he has not let us down today. If he had been someone else, he would not have had so much patience with me. So, whatever he may be, I shall bear responsibility for him."

Overjoyed, the porter kissed the ground before her and thanked her.

"By Allah," he said, "the money you gave to me are the first fruits that this day has given me."

Hearing this, they said, "Sit down. You are welcome here," and the eldest lady added, "By Allah, we shall allow you to join us on only one condition, which is: you are not to ask any questions about things that do not concern you, and you will be soundly flogged for any undue forwardness."

"I agree to this, my lady," said the porter. "You may cut off my head and my tongue if I do not keep my promise. Look, I am already dumb and have no tongue."

Then the lady who had bought everything arose and

set the table by the fountain. She put the flowers and
sweet herbs in their jars, strained the wine, arranged the
flasks in a row, and did whatever else was required. Then
she sat down with her sisters, who placed the porter in
the middle of them while he kept thinking he was in a
dream. Soon the first lady picked up the wine flagon,
poured out the first cup, and drank it down. Then she
followed it with a second and a third. After this she
filled a fourth cup, which she handed to one of her sisters. Finally she filled a goblet, passed it to the porter,
and told him to drink. In turn, he took the cup in his
hand, gave his thanks, and recited a poem. After repeating a few more couplets he kissed their hands and
drank a few cups. Soon he became drunk and sat there
swaying from side to side. Then the lady who had purchased everything gave a cup to her sister, the doorkeeper of the mansion, and she thanked her and drank.
Thereupon she poured again and passed a cup to the
eldest lady, who sat on the couch, and filled yet another
and handed it to the porter. He kissed the ground before
them, and after drinking and thanking them, he began
reciting more poetry. Then he stood up before the mistress of the house and said, "Oh lady, I am your slave,
your mameluke, your white thrall, your very bondsman."

"Drink," she replied, "and may each drink bring you
health and happiness."

So he took the cup and kissed her hand. Then the
lady took the cup and drank to her sisters' health. Indeed, they kept drinking—the porter was always in the
middle of them—dancing, laughing, reciting verses, and
singing ballads. All the time the porter was carrying on
with them, kissing, toying, biting, handling, groping, and
fingering. While one lady thrust a dainty morsel in his
mouth, another slapped him. While one threw sweet
flowers at him, another cuffed his cheeks. It was as if he
were in the very paradise of pleasure and sitting in the
seventh sphere of heaven. They continued playing like
this until the wine did something to their heads and got
the better of them. All of a sudden, the doorkeeper
stood up and took off all her clothes until she was
mother-naked. However, she let down her hair around

her body to form a shift. Then she dashed into the basin, splashed about, dived like a duck, swam up and down, swallowed some water, and spit it all over the porter. Afterward, she washed herself, first her arms and legs, between her breasts, inside her thighs, and all around her navel. Finally, she came out of the cistern, threw herself on the porter's lap, and said, "Oh my lord, oh my love, what do you call this thing here?" And she pointed to her slit, her solution of continuity.

"I call that your cleft," said the porter, and she replied, "Bad boy! Aren't you ashamed to use such a word like that?" And she grabbed him by the collar and cuffed him soundly.

"Your womb, your vulva," he said again.

And she gave him another slap and cried out, "Oh fie, fie! This is another ugly word. Don't you have any shame?"

"Your coynte," he said.

"Oh, you have no modesty at all," and she thumped and thrashed him.

"Your clitoris!" the porter exclaimed.

Just then the eldest lady came down on him with a more terrible beating and said, "No!"

The porter kept on calling the same commodity by sundry other names, but whatever he said, they beat him more and more until his neck ached and swelled with the blows he received. In this way they made him a butt and laughingstock. Finally, he turned upon them and asked, "And what do you women call this article?"

"The basil bush," said one of the ladies.

"Thank Allah for my safety," cried the porter. "Help me and please be lucky, oh basil bush!"

Then they passed around a cup for drinking until the second lady stood up, stripped off all her clothes, and jumped into the cistern as the first one had done. Then she returned and asked him what was between her legs.

"Your slit," he replied as he had done before.

"Don't you have any shame?" she responded, and she cuffed and smacked him until the salon rang with the blows. "Fie! Fie! How can you say what you said without blushing?"

"The basil bush," he suggested, but she would have none of this and said, "No! No!"

And she struck and slapped him on the back of the neck. Then he began calling out all the names he knew—"Your slit, your womb, your coynte, your clitoris"—and the maidens kept saying, "No! No!"

So he said, "I stick to the basil bush," and all three laughed until they fell on their backs and laid slaps on his neck and said, "No! No! That's not its proper name."

Thereupon he cried, "Oh my ladies, what is its name?"

"What do you say to husked sesame seed?" they answered.

Then the second lady put on her clothes, and they began carousing again, but the porter kept moaning "Oh!" and "Oh!" His neck and shoulders took a good deal of slapping while the cup passed merrily around and around again for a full hour. After that time the eldest and most beautiful of the ladies stood up and stripped off her garments, whereupon the porter took his neck in hand and rubbed and massaged it. "My neck and shoulders can only be saved by Allah!"

Then she plunged into the basin, swam, dived, splashed about, and washed her limbs. The porter looked at her naked figure as though it were a slice of the moon, while her face appeared as the full bright moon. He noted her noble stature and shape and those glorious forms that quivered as she walked naked as the day she was born.

Then the lady came out of the basin, sat down on his lap, and pointed to her genitals. "Oh, my lordling, tell me the name of this article?"

"The basil bush," he said.

"Bah, bah," she replied.

"The husked sesame seed," he said.

"Pooh, pooh," she replied.

Then he said, "Your womb."

"Fie! Fie!" she cried. "Aren't you ashamed of yourself?" And she cuffed him on the nape of the neck, and no matter what name he gave her, she beat him and cried. "No! No!" Until at last he asked, "Oh, my ladies, what is its name?"

"It is called the khan of Abu Mansur."

Thereupon, the porter exclaimed, "Oh Allah be praised for safe deliverance! Oh khan of Abu Mansur!"

Then the eldest lady got dressed. and the cup went around for a full hour. At last. the porter stood up, stripped off all his clothes, jumped into the basin, swam about, and washed under his bearded chin and armpits just as they had done. Then he came out and threw himself into the first lady's lap and rested his arms and legs upon the laps of the other two ladies. Pointing to his prickle, he said, "Oh my mistresses. what is the name of this article?"

They all laughed at his words until they fell over on their backs. Then one of them said, "Your pintle."

But he replied. "No," and gave each one of them a bite by way of penalty. Then they said, "Your pizzle!"

But he cried, "No," and gave each one of them a hug.

The ladies kept guessing and kept calling out, "Your prickle, your pintle, your pizzle." and he kept kissing, biting, and hugging until his heart was satisfied, and they laughed until they were exhausted. At last, one of the maidens asked, "Oh porter, what then is it called?"

"Don't you know?" he replied.

"No!" they said.

"Its true name," he stated, "is Mule Burst-All, which browses in the basil bush, munches the husked sesame seed, and spends the night in the khan of Abu Mansur."

Then they laughed, fell on their backs, and returned to their carousing until night began to fall.

Thereupon, they said, "In the name of Allah, it's time for our master to put on your sorry old shoes, turn your face, and depart."

"By Allah," he replied, "to part with my soul would be easier for me than parting from you. Come, let us join night to day, and tomorrow morning we shall each go our own way."

"This is fine with me," said the lady who had hired him that morning. "Let us let him stay with us so that we may laugh at him. We may live out our lives and never meet up with someone like him again. Certainly, he is a wonderful rascal and witty to boot."

So, they said, "You can only remain with us this night on the condition that you obey our commands, and that you ask no questions about whatever you see. Nor are you to ask about the cause of anything."

"All right," he replied.

And they said, "Go read the writing over the door."

So he rose and went to the entrance, and found letters written in gold: WHOEVER SPEAKS OF THINGS THAT DO NOT CONCERN HIM WILL HEAR THINGS THAT DO NOT PLEASE HIM!

"You are my witnesses," said the porter. "I swear that I shall not speak about things that do not concern me."

Then the lady who had procured all the goods arose and set food before them, and they ate. After this they changed their drinking place for another, and she lighted the lamps and candles and burned ambergris and aloes wood and set out fresh fruit and wine. Then they began carousing and talking about their lovers while eating and drinking, nibbling dry fruits and laughing and playing tricks for a full hour. Then, all of a sudden, a knock was heard at the gate. In no way did the knocking disturb the séance, but one of the ladies arose and went to see what it was. When she returned, she said, "Truly, our pleasure this night is going to be perfect."

"How is that?" the others asked.

"There are three Persian calenders at the gate. Their heads, eyebrows, and faces are completely shaven, and all three are blind in the left eye which is certainly a strange coincidence. They are foreigners from Roumland and have apparently been traveling for some time. They have just arrived in Baghdad, and since this is their first visit to the city, and since they could not find a lodging, they have knocked on our door. Indeed, one of them said to me: 'We hope the owner of this mansion will let us have the key to his stable or some old outhouse where we may spend the night.' They had not expected to arrive in the evening, and being strangers in the land, they do not know anyone who might give them shelter. And, let me tell you, my sisters, each one of them cuts a comical figure in his own fashion, and if we let them in, I am sure we shall have a lot of fun with them."

She continued talking until she persuaded her sisters, who said, "Let them in, but set the usual condition with them that they are not allowed to speak of things that do not concern them. Otherwise, they will hear things that do not please them."

The sister nodded in agreement and rejoiced that she could let the three calenders enter. She left the room to fetch them and soon returned with the three men, who bowed and stood far off by way of respect. But the three ladies rose up, welcomed them, wished them well, and asked them to sit down. The calenders looked at the room and saw that it was a pleasant place, swept cleanly and garnished with flowers. The lamps were burning, and the smoke of perfumes filled the air. And beside the desserts, fruit, and wine, there were three fair ladies who might be maidens. So, they exclaimed with one voice, "By Allah, this is good!"

Then they turned to the porter and saw that he was a cheerful fellow, even if he was by no means sober and was sore after being slapped. So they thought that he was one of them and said, "A mendicant like us! Some poor devil or a foreigner."

But when the porter heard these words, he stood up and glared at them. "Just sit down and don't talk so much!" he said. "Haven't you read what was written over the door? Surely, it is not fitting for fellows like you who come to us as paupers to wag your tongues at us."

"We beg your pardon, oh fakir!" they replied. "Our heads are in your hands."

The ladies had a good laugh at the squabble, and after making peace between the calenders and the porter, they seated the new guests, gave them meat, and ate. Then they sat together, and one of the ladies gave them something to drink. As the cup went around merrily, the porter said to the calenders, "And you, my brothers, don't you have some story or rare adventure for our amusement?"

Since the warmth of the wine had mounted to their heads, they called for musical instruments, and one of the maidens brought them a tambourine made in Mosul, a lute made in Irak, and a Persian harp. Each mendicant took one and tuned it, and soon they struck up a merry tune while the ladies sang so lustily that there was a lot of commotion. And while they were carrying on, someone suddenly knocked at the gate, and one of the ladies went to see what the matter was.

Now the cause of the knocking was no one less than the Caliph Harun al-Rashid, who had left his palace, as was his custom every now and then, to find solace in the city and to see and hear what new things were occurring. He was in merchant's garments, and he was attended by Ja'afar, his vizier, and by Masrur, his bodyguard. As they walked about the city, their way led them toward the house of the three ladies, where they heard the loud noise of musical instruments, singing, and merriment, So the caliph had said to Ja'afar, "I would like to enter this house and hear the songs and see who is singing them."

"Oh Prince of the Faithful, these folk are surely drunk with wine, and I fear that something bad might happen to us if we enter."

"But I insist on entering," replied the caliph, "and I want you to invent some pretext for our intrusion."

"To hear is to obey," said Ja'afar, and thus he knocked at the door.

When the lady came out and opened the gate, he went forward, kissed the ground before her, and said, "Oh my lady, we are merchants from Tiberias, and we arrived in Baghdad ten days ago and have been fortunate to have sold all our merchandise. Now, a certain trader invited us to an entertainment this night. So we went to his house, and he set food before us and we ate. Then we sat and drank wine with him for an hour or so when he bid us farewell. So we went out, and since we are strangers, we became lost in the darkness of the night and could not find our way back to the khan. So, we hope that you will be kind and courteous and allow us to spend the night with you. Heaven will certainly reward you!"

The lady looked them over, and seeing that they were dressed like merchants and were serious and solid, she returned to her sisters and repeated to them Ja'afar's story. In turn, they took compassion upon the strangers and said to her, "Let them enter."

She returned and opened the door to them. So the caliph entered, followed by Ja'afar and Masrur. When the maidens saw them, they stood up in respect, asked them to sit down, and looked after their wants.

"Welcome!" they greeted them. "Welcome, and may you have good cheer, with one condition."

"What is that?" they asked.

"Do not talk about things that don't concern you," one of the ladies said. "Otherwise, you will hear things that won't please you."

"We agree," they said, and sat down to their wine and began drinking.

When the caliph looked at the three calenders and realized that each of them was blind in the left eye, he was astounded. Then, he gazed at the maidens and was startled by their beauty and loveliness. They continued to carouse and converse, and one of the ladies said to the caliph, "Drink!" but he replied, "I have vowed to abstain during my pilgrimage," and he withdrew from the wine.

At this point another one of the ladies arose and spread before him a tablecloth lined with gold. Then she set a porcelain bowl on top of it and poured willow-flower water with a lump of ice and a spoonful of sugar candy into it. The caliph thanked her and said to himself, "I shall reward her tomorrow for the kind deed that she has done."

The others continued to converse and carouse, and when the wine got the better of them, the eldest lady who ruled the house rose and bowed to them. Then she took her sisters by the hand and said, "It is time that we do our duty."

"You are right," they said, and the lady who had admitted the caliph proceeded to remove the table service and the remnants of the banquet. She renewed the pastilles and cleared the middle of the salon. Then she obliged the calenders to sit on a sofa at the side of the dais, and she seated the caliph, Ja'afar, and Masrur on the other side of the salon. Then she called to the porter and said, "Show some courtesy! You are no stranger here. You are now one of the household."

So he stood up and asked, "What would you like me to do?"

"Stand in your place," she answered.

Then one of the ladies set a low chair in the middle of the salon, and after opening a closet, she cried to the porter, "Come help me."

So he went to help her and saw two black bitches with chains around their necks, and she said to him, "Take hold of them."

Then he took them and led them into the middle of the salon. All at once, the lady of the house arose, tucked up her sleeves above her wrists, and seized a whip.

"Bring forward one of the bitches," she commanded the porter.

He brought her forward, dragging her by the chain, while the bitch wept and shook her head at the lady, who began beating her with hard blows. The bitch howled, and the lady did not stop beating her until her forearm became exhausted. Then, casting the whip from her hand, she pressed the bitch to her bosom, wiped away the dog's tears with her hands, and kissed her head. Then she said to the porter, "Take her away and bring the second."

When he did this, the lady treated her just as she had done the first. Now the caliph's heart was upset by these cruel things. His chest tightened, and he was eager to know why the two bitches were beaten in this way. So he winked at Ja'afar, indicating that he wanted him to ask, but the minister turned toward him and signaled him to be silent. Then one of the other ladies said to the mistress of the house, "Oh my lady, arise and go to your place so that I, in turn, may do my duty."

"You are right," she said, and took her seat upon the couch of juniper wood, framed by gold and silver. "Now do what you have to do."

Then the other maiden went to a closet and brought out a bag of satin with green fringes and two tassels of gold. She stood up before the lady of the house and drew out a lute from the bag. After she tuned it by tightening its pegs, she began to sing an elegy. When it was done, her sister cried out, "Alas! Alas!" and she tore her garments and fell to the ground in a faint. The caliph saw scars of a rod on her back and welts of the whip, and he was most astonished. But when the company observed all this, they were troubled, for they had no inkling about the situation and did not know the story behind all this. So the caliph said to Ja'afar, "Didn't you see the scars on the damsel's body? I cannot keep silent or rest until I learn the truth about her condition and the story of this other maiden and the secret of the two black bitches."

But Ja'afar answered, "Oh my lord, they made it a condition that we are not allowed to speak of things that do not concern us, otherwise we shall hear things that do not please us."

Then the lady who had just fainted said, "By Allah, oh my sister, come to me and complete this service for me."

So the other lady, who had played the lute, replied, "With joy and delight." So she took the lute, leaned it against her breasts, swept the strings with her fingertips, and began singing. After she had finished her ode, her sister shrieked aloud again, "By Allah, it's good!" and again she tore her garments and fell to the ground in a faint. Thereupon the lute player rose, sprinkled water on her, and brought her a second change of clothes. When she recovered, she sat upright and said to her sister, "Onward and help me in my duty, for there remains but one song."

So the lute player brought out the instrument one more time and began to sing a third song. When her sister heard it, she cried aloud and tore her clothes to shreds. Once more she fainted and revealed her scars of the whip.

Then the three calenders cried out, "Would to heaven that we had never entered this house! It would have been better for us if we had spent the night on the mounds outside the city! Truly, our visit has been disturbed by these sights, which cut to the heart."

The caliph turned to them and asked, "How come?"

"Our minds are sorely troubled by this matter," they said.

"Don't you belong to this household?" asked the caliph.

"No, indeed not," they replied. "We never set our eyes on this place until an hour or so ago."

Upon hearing this, the caliph was surprised and answered, "Doesn't the man who is sitting with you know the secret of all this?"

After saying this, the caliph winked and made all sorts of signs at the porter. Then he questioned him, but the porter replied, "By Allah, I was born in Baghdad and never in my born days did I ever darken these doors until today, and the time I have spent with these ladies has been very strange."

"Indeed," said the caliph, "I took you for one of them, but now I see that you are like all of us here. Well, since we are seven men, and they are only three women without even a fourth to help them, let us ask them about their situation, and if they don't answer us, we shall then obtain the answer by force."

All of them agreed to this except Ja'afar, who said, "This does not sit right with me. Let them be, for we are guests, and as you know, they made a compact with us, which we accepted and promised to keep. Therefore, it's better that we keep silent about this matter, and since night is almost over, let us each go our own way." Then he winked at the caliph and whispered to him, "There is but one hour of darkness left, and I can bring the ladies before you tomorrow, when you can freely question them about their story."

But the caliph raised his head haughtily and cried out at him in wrath, "I can no longer be patient! Let the calenders question them this instant!"

"This is not what I would advise," said Ja'afar.

Then there was a great deal of talk, and they quarreled among themselves as to who should ask the first question. At last, they all focused on the porter. And as the discussion went on, the mistress of the house could not but notice it and asked them, "My fellows, what are you discussing so loudly?"

Then the porter stood up respectfully before her and said, "Oh my lady, this company earnestly desires that you explain the story about the two bitches and what makes you punish them so cruelly and why you wept over them and kissed them. My companions would also like to hear about your sister and why she has been whipped with palm sticks like a man. These are the questions they have asked me to put before you, and may peace be with you."

Thereupon, the mistress of the house said, "Is this true what he has said on your behalf?"

"Yes!" they all replied, except for Ja'afar, who kept silent.

When she heard these words, she cried, "By Allah, you have done us wrong. As our guests, you have committed a grievous crime. When you entered our house, we made a compact with you and set a condition that whoever speaks about things that don't concern him should hear things that don't please him. Aren't you satisfied with the fact that we took you into our house and fed you with our best food? But the fault is not so much yours as that of the lady who let you enter our house."

Then she tucked up her sleeves from her wrist, struck the floor three times with her hand, and cried out, "Come out quickly!"

Lo and behold, seven black slaves with drawn swords came out of a closet door, and she cried out, "Tie their hands behind their backs and bind them together!"

They did her bidding and then asked her, "Oh veiled and virtuous lady, would you like us to strike off their heads?"

"Let them be for now," she responded. "I want to ask them about themselves before their necks feel the sword."

"By Allah, my lady!" cried the porter. "Do not slay me for someone else's sin. All of these men have committed an offense except me, and they deserve to be punished, not me. By Allah, our night would have been charming if we had escaped the mortification of these monocular calenders who would probably transform the populous city into a howling wilderness."

Then the porter quickly recited a poem that ended with the line "Let one not suffer for the sin of another," and when he ended his verse, the lady laughed, but it did the porter no good, for she went up to the group of men and said the following: "Tell me who you are, for you have but one hour to live. If you were not men of rank and perhaps leaders of your tribes, you would not have been so insolent, and I would not have to bring about your doom."

Then the caliph said to Ja'afar, "You had better tell her who we are, otherwise we shall be slain by mistake, and speak eloquently to her before something terrible happens to us."

"This is what you deserve," replied Ja'afar.

"This is not the time for jokes," cried the caliph, "this is a time for serious work."

Then the lady approached the three calenders and asked them, "Are you brothers?"

"No, by Allah, we are nothing but fakirs and foreigners."

Then she addressed one of them and said, "Were you born blind in one eye?"

"No, by Allah," he replied. "Something marvelous happened. It was a wondrous accident that caused my eye to be torn out. Indeed, it is a tale which, if it were ever written down and engraved, it would serve as a warning to all those who need to be warned."

Then she questioned the other two calenders, and they gave the same answer as the first.

"By Allah, oh mistress," said the third, "each one of us comes from a different country, and we are all three the sons of kings, sovereign princes who rule over realms and capital cities."

Thereupon, she turned toward all the men there and said, "Let each one of you tell me his tale in due order and explain the reason for your arrival here. If your story pleases us, you may keep your head and go on your way."

The first to come forward was Hammal, the porter, who said, "Oh my lady, I am a man and a porter. Your sister hired me to carry a load and took me first to the vintner's shop, then to the butcher's booth, the fruit stand, the grocer's stall, a confectioner, and finally a perfume druggist. Afterward I was taken here, where everything that happened to me is something you already know. Such is my story, and peace be on us all!"

Upon hearing this, the lady laughed and said, "Your head is saved, and you may be on your way!"

But he cried, "By Allah, I shall not be off until I hear the stories of my companions."

Then one of the calenders came forward and began to tell her

The First Calender's Tale

You will now hear, my lady, what caused my beard to be shaved and my eye to be torn out. First, you must know that my father was a king, and he had a brother who was a king in another city. It so happened that I and my cousin, the son of my paternal uncle, were both born on the same day. Years and days passed, and as we grew up, I used to visit my uncle every now and then and spend a certain number of months with him. Now, my cousin and I became close friends, for he always treated me with great kindness. He killed the fattest sheep and strained the best of his wines for me, and we enjoyed long conversations and carousing. One day, when the wine had gotten the better of us, my cousin said to me, "I have a great service to ask of you, and I beg you not to deny whatever I ask."

"I shall gladly do whatever you ask," I replied.

Then he made me swear an oath and left me. But soon thereafter he returned leading a lady wearing a veil and dressed in rich garments with ornaments worth a large sum of money.

"Take this lady with you," he said, and he described a burial ground where I was to take the lady, lead her into a sepulcher, and wait for his arrival. The oath that I had sworn to him made me keep silent and prevented me from opposing him. So I led the woman to the cemetery, and we took our seats in the sepulcher. No sooner did we sit down than my cousin entered with a bowl of water, a bag of mortar, and a hoe. He went straight to the tomb in the middle of the sepulcher and broke it open with the hoe. Then he began to dig into the earth of the tomb until he came upon a large iron plate, the size of a wicket door. After he raised the door, I could see a winding staircase leading below. Then he turned to the lady and said, "Come now and make your final choice!"

Without hesitating she went down the staircase and disappeared. Then my cousin said to me, "Oh friend, when I have descended this staircase, I want you to close this trapdoor as your last sign of kindness. Then I want you to restore the soil to where it was. Mix this unslaked lime which is in the bag with this water in the bowl. After mounting the stones, plaster the outside so that nobody who may look upon it can say that this is a new opening in an old tomb. I have worked for a year at this place, and nobody knows about it but Allah, and this is why I need you. And may Allah never make your friends desolate and sorry by taking you away from them, my dear cousin!"

And he went down the stairs and disappeared forever. When he was out of sight, I replaced the iron plate and did all his bidding until the tomb became as it was before. I worked almost unconsciously because my head was dizzy from the wine. When I returned to the palace of my uncle, I was told that he had gone hunting. So I slept that night without seeing him, and when morning dawned, I remembered the scenes of the past evening and what had happened between me and my cousin. I repented for having obeyed him even though it was of no avail. I still thought, however, that it was a dream.

So I began asking for my cousin, but nobody knew where he was. Then I went to the graveyard and the sepulchers and looked for the tomb under which he had built the staircase, but I could not find it. I wandered from sepulcher to sepulcher and from tomb to tomb, all without success, until night set in. So, I returned to the city, but I could neither eat nor drink. My thoughts were engrossed by my cousin, because I did not know what had happened to him. I grieved a great deal and passed another sorrowful and sleepless night. Then I went to the cemetery a second time, pondering over what my cousin had done. I sorely repented that I had listened to him and went around all the tombs, but I could not find the tomb I sought. I mourned over the past and continued mourning for another seven days, while seeking the place where I had left my cousin. My scruples tortured me and grew until I almost went mad. There was no way to relieve my grief except by traveling and returning to my father. So, I set out on a journey to my home, but as I entered my father's capital, a crowd of rioters sprang upon me and tied me up. I was astonished, especially since I was the son of the sultan, and these men were my father's subjects, and some of them were my own slaves. Suddenly, I became frightened, and I said to myself, "I wish to heaven I could find out what has happened to my father!" I asked my captors why they took me prisoner, but they did not respond. However, after a while, one of them said to me (for he had been a servant in our house), "Your father has been unlucky. His troops betrayed him, and the vizier who slew him is now reigning in his stead. It was he who ordered us to lie in wait for you."

I was completely distraught and almost fainted when I heard about my father's death. Then they carried me off and took me to face the usurper. Now there happened to be an old grudge between us, and there is a story to this grudge. I had always been fond of shooting with my bow and arrow, and one day, as I was standing on the terrace roof of the palace, a bird landed on top of the vizier's house when he happened to be there. I shot at the bird and missed the mark, but I hit the vizier in the eye and knocked it out as fate and fortune decreed. Now, when I knocked out the vizier's eye, he could not say a single word, for my father was king of the city. But he hated me thereafter, and this was the dire grudge that he held against me. So, when I was brought before him, tied from hand to foot, he immediately gave orders to have me beheaded.

"For what crime will you have me put to death?" I asked.

"What crime is greater than this?" he replied, pointing to his missing eye.

"I did this by accident, not out of malicious intent," I stated.

"If you did this by accident, I shall do the same but with intention," he said. "Bring him forward!"

They brought me before him, and all at once he thrust his finger into my left eye and gouged it out so that I became one-eyed as you now see me. Then he ordered his men to put me into a chest and said to the executioner, "Take charge of this fellow and take him to the waste lands around the city, where I want you to slay him and leave his remains for the beasts and birds."

So the executioner left the city with me, and when he was in the middle of the desert, he took me out of the chest. I was still bound hand and foot, and he was about to place a bandage over my eyes before striking off my head. But I wept with such great sorrow that I made him weep with me, and as I looked at him, I recited some melancholy verse. When the executioner heard my lines—he had been in my father's employ and owed me a debt of gratitude—he cried, "Oh my lord, what can I do? I am just a slave under orders." Then he reflected, untied me, and said, "Flee for your life, and never return to this land, or they will slay both you and me!"

Hardly believing in my escape, I kissed his hand and thought the loss of my eye a small fee to pay for my escape. I arrived at my uncle's capital, and after going to see him, I told him what had happened to my father and to me. Thereupon, he wept a great deal and said, "Truly, you add grief to my grief and woe to my woe, for your cousin has been missing for many days. I don't know what has happened to him, and nobody has any news of him." And he wept until he fainted.

I remained with him to console him, and when he revived, he wanted to apply certain medicaments to my eye, but he saw that it had become like a walnut with an empty shell. Then he said, "Oh my son, better to lose your eye than to lose your life!"

So, I told him all that had happened, and he rejoiced to hear news of his son and said, "Come now, and show me the tomb."

But I replied, "By Allah, uncle, I don't know where it is. Though I searched for it carefully many times, I could not find the site."

However, my uncle and I went to the graveyard and looked all over the place until I finally recognized the tomb. Of course, we were exceedingly happy to have found it and immediately entered the sepulcher and dug around the grave. Then we lifted the trapdoor and descended some fifty steps until we came to the foot of the staircase, when we were suddenly stopped by blinding smoke. Thereupon my uncle said, "There is no majesty and there is no might except in Allah, the Glorious!" and we advanced until we came upon a salon whose floor was covered by flour, grain, and all kinds of provisions. In the midst of it stood a canopy sheltering a couch. So, my uncle went up to the couch and found his son and the lady who had entered the tomb with him, lying in each other's embrace, but the two had become as black as charred wood. It was as if they had been cast into a pit of fire. When my uncle saw this spectacle, he spat into his son's face and said, "You've received what you deserve, you pig! This is your judgment in the transitory world, but your judgment will be more severe in the world to come."

Then my uncle struck his son with his slipper as he lay there like a heap of black coal. I was astounded by his hardness of heart, and grieving for my cousin and the lady, I said, "By Allah, my uncle, please calm down. Can't you see how sorry I am for this misfortune, and how horrible it is that nothing of him remains but a black heap of charcoal? Why are you adding to my grief by hitting him with your slipper?"

"Oh son of my brother," he answered, "from the time that he was a young man, your cousin was madly in love with his own sister, and I often forbade him to see her and kept them apart. Of course, I kept saying to myself, they are but little ones. However, when they grew up, they began to sin, and although I could hardly believe it, I confined him, chided him, and threatened him with the most severe punishments. And the eunuchs and servants told him to beware of such a foul thing that none before him had ever done, and that none would ever do after him. They warned him to be careful, otherwise he would be dishonored and disgraced forever. And I added that people would gossip and spread news about this, and he had better not give them cause to talk, or I would assuredly curse him and put him to death. After that I made them live apart and had her confined to a special place in the palace. But the cursed girl loved him with such a passionate love that Satan overcame both of them and made their foul sin seem fair in their eyes. Now, after I had separated them, my son secretly built this underground apartment and furnished it with all sorts of provisions, just as you see it. When I went out hunting, he came here with his sister and hid from me. But then Allah's righteous judgment fell upon the two of them and consumed them with fire from heaven. Truly, the last judgment will deal with them in a harsher and more enduring way!"

Then he wept, and I wept with him. Finally, he looked at me and said, "You will now replace my son."

And I pondered my situation and thought about all the coincidences, how the vizier had slain my father and had taken his place and put out my eye, and how my cousin had come to his death in such a bizarre way. And I wept again, and my uncle wept with me. Then we mounted the steps and let down the iron plate and piled the earth on top of it. After restoring the tomb to its former condition, we returned to the palace. But no sooner did we sit down than we heard the beating of the kettle drum and the tantara of trumpets and clash of cymbals followed by the rattling of soldiers' lances, the clamors of assailants, the clanking of swords, and the neighing of horses. The world was covered with dense dust and clouds raised by the hoofs of horses. We were amazed at the sight and sound. Not knowing what could be the matter, we asked some people, and they told us that the vizier who had usurped my father's kingdom had sent an army and a host of wild Arabs, and they had come down upon us with powerful troops. It was impossible to tell their number, and impossible to prevail against them. They attacked the city without warning, and the inhabitants surrendered the place without a fight. My uncle was slain, and I escaped to the surrounding area. "If I should fall into the villain's hands," I said to myself, "he will surely kill me." So now all my troubles began again. I thought about what had happened to my father and uncle, and I didn't know what to do. If some people from the city or some of my father's troops were to recognize me, they were sure to try to win the vizier's favor by destroying me. I could think of no way to escape except by shaving off my beard and eyebrows. So I shaved them, exchanged my fine clothes for a calender's rags, and left my uncle's capital in the direction of this city. I had hoped that someone might assist me in obtaining an audience with the caliph, Prince of the Faithful, who is the vice-regent of Allah upon earth. Indeed, this is the reason why I have come here—to tell him my tale and lay my case before him. I arrived here this very night, and I was wandering about not knowing where to go when suddenly I saw this other calender. So I bowed to him and said, "I am a stranger."

"I, too, am a stranger," he answered.

And, as we were conversing, our companion, the third calender, suddenly appeared and greeted us by saying, "I am a stranger."

And we answered, "So are we!"

Then the three of us walked on together until darkness overtook us, and destiny drew us to your house. Such, then, is the reason why I have shaved my beard, mustache, and eyebrows. Now you also know how I lost my left eye.

Everyone was astounded by this tale, and the caliph said to Ja'afar, "By Allah, I have never seen nor heard such a tale as this before!"

"You may keep your head and go your way," said the lady of the house.

But he replied, "I shall not go until I hear the story of the two others."

Thereupon the second calender came forward, and after kissing the ground, he began to tell

The Second Calender's Tale

I should like you to know, my lady, that I was not born with one eye, and my story is a strange one. Indeed, it is a tale which, if it were ever written down and engraved, would serve as a warning to all those who need to be warned. I am a king, the son of a king, and was brought up like a prince. I learned how to read the Koran according to seven schools, and I read all kinds of books and discussed their contents with doctors and men of science. Moreover I studied astrology, the fair sayings of the poets, and all fields of learning until I surpassed the people of my time. My skill in calligraphy exceeded that of all the scribes. My fame was spread abroad throughout the world, and all the kings became familiar with my name. Among them was the king of Hind, who asked my father to send me to his court and offered presents and rare items that were fit for kings. So my father prepared six ships for me and my people, and we spent a full month at sea until we arrived at our destination. Then we brought out the horses that were with us in the ships, and after loading the camels with our presents for the king, we began our inland journey. But we had traveled only a little way when all of a sudden a dust storm arose, and it grew until we could no longer see the horizon. After an hour or so, the veil lifted, and we discovered fifty horsemen in bright armor, who looked like rapacious lions. When we could distinguish who they were, we realized they were wild Arab highwaymen. And when they saw that we had only a meager force with us and had ten camels carrying presents, they attacked us with their lances. We signaled to them with our fingers to indicate that we were messengers of the great king of Hind and they had better not harm us. But they answered that they were not from his realm and thus not subject to his laws. So they set upon us, killed some of my slaves, and put my guards to flight. After I was wounded, I, too, fled the scene, while the Arabs took the money and the presents. My only choice was to wander, not knowing where I was going, and I walked until I came to the crest of a mountain, where I took shelter for the night in a cave. The next morning I set out again, and I continued journeying this way until I arrived at a fair city with many people. Now it was springtime, and the trees were blooming, and the streams were flowing, and the birds were singing sweetly. I was happy to have arrived at a city, because I was exhausted, weak, and starving. My plight was pitiable, and I did not know where to turn. So I approached a tailor sitting in his little shop and greeted him. He returned my greeting and welcomed me. Then he wished me well and asked me where I came from and why. I told him all about my past from first to last, and he was very concerned about me and said, "My young man, do not tell anyone who you are. The king of this city is your father's greatest enemy, and there is bad blood between them. You have every reason to fear for your life."

Then he set meat and drink before me, and I ate and drank with him, and we conversed freely until nightfall, when he cleared a space for me in a corner of his shop and brought me a carpet and a coverlet. I stayed with him for three days, and at the end of this time, he said to me, "Do you know of any vocation that will enable you to earn a living?"

"I am learned in the law," I replied, "and a doctor of doctrine. I am also adept in art, science, math, and orthography."

"Your expertise will not help you much in our city," the tailor said. "No one understands science or writing. Most of the people know something about making money."

"By Allah," I replied, "the only things I know how to do are the things I have already mentioned."

"Put a belt around your waist and take a hatchet and cord," he advised. "Then go and chop wood for your daily bread, until Allah sends you some relief. Tell nobody who you are. Otherwise, they may slay you."

So the tailor bought me an ax and rope and introduced me to some woodcutters, who took charge of me. Then I went into the forest with them, where I cut wood the entire day, and came back in the evening bearing my bundle on my head. I sold it for half a dinar, and then I bought some provisions with part of it and put the rest aside. I spent a whole year doing this kind of work, and one day I went into the wilderness, as was my custom, and wandered away from my companions. All of a sudden I came across some dense lowlands in which there was a great deal of wood. So I entered and found the gnarled stump of a large tree and loosened the ground around it by shoveling away the dirt. Soon my hatchet rang upon a copper ring. So I cleared away the soil, and lo and behold, the ring was attached to a wooden trapdoor, which I raised, and I found that there was a staircase, which I descended to the bottom. Then I came upon a door, which I opened, and found myself in a noble hall that was beautifully built. When I looked around, I was astounded to see a damsel like a precious pearl who banished all trouble and care from my heart, and whose soft speech healed the soul in despair and captivated the wise. She was about five feet in height. Her breasts were firm and upright; her face gleamed like dawn through curly tresses which gloomed like night. Above the snows of her bosom glittered pearl-white teeth. After my first glance at her, I prostrated myself before Him who had created her and gave thanks for the beauty and loveliness that He had shaped in her, and she looked at me and said, "Are you man or jinnee?"

"I am a man," I answered.

"And who brought you to this place where I have dwelled for twenty-five years without ever seeing a man in it?" she asked.

Her words were wonderfully sweet, and my heart was melted to the core by them, but I managed to respond, "Oh my lady, my good fortune led me here to ease my troubles."

And I went on to relate to her all my misfortunes from beginning to end, and my story seemed so sorrowful to her that she wept and said, "I shall tell you my story in turn. I am the daughter of King Ifitamus, lord of the Islands of Abnus, who married me to my cousin, the son of my paternal uncle. However, on my wedding night an ifrit named Jirjis bin Rajmus, the first cousin of Iblis, the foul fiend, snatched me and flew away with me like a bird. He set me down in this place, where he carried all the things I needed, such as fine stuffs, clothes, jewels, furniture, meat, and drink. Once in every ten days he comes here and spends one night with me. Then he goes on his way, for he took me without the consent of his family, and he has agreed with me that if I ever need him night or day, I only have to pass my hand over those two lines engraved upon the alcove, and he will appear to me before my finger finishes touching the lines. Four days have passed since he was here, and since there are six days before he comes again, I would like you to spend five days with me and then go the day before he arrives."

"Gladly," I replied. "Of course I will! It all seems to be a dream."

She was very glad that I consented and sprang to her feet. She seized my hand and led me through an arched doorway to a Hammam bath in a splendid hall that was richly decorated. I took off my clothes, and she took off hers, and we bathed. Then she washed me, and when this was done, we left the bath, and she seated me by her side upon a high divan and brought me sherbet scented with musk. When we were relaxed after the bath, she placed food before me, and we ate and conversed. But soon she said to me, "Lie down and get some rest. Surely you must be tired."

So I thanked her, lay down, slept soundly, and forgot all that had happened to me. When I awoke, I found her rubbing and shampooing my feet. So again I thanked her and blessed her, and we talked for a while.

"By Allah," she said, "I have been very sad, for I have lived alone twenty-five years in this underground palace. Praise be to Allah for sending someone to me with whom I can converse." Then she asked, "Would you like some wine, my young man?"

"As you will," I responded.

Thereupon she went to a cupboard and took out a sealed flask of old wine and set the table with flowers and scented herbs. She recited some poetry, and when she was finished, I thanked her. Indeed, I was overcome by love, and my grief and anguish were gone. We sat conversing and carousing until nightfall, and then I spent the night with her—and I have never spent a night like that in my entire life! The next day, delight followed delight until noon, by which time I had drunk wine so freely that I had lost control of my senses. I stood up, staggered to the right and to the left, and said, "Come, oh my charmer, and I shall carry you from this underground vault and rescue you from the spell of your jinnee."

She laughed and replied, "Be content, and don't say anything more. The ifrit has only one of ten days, and you have the other nine."

But the alcohol had gotten the better of me, and I declared, "I shall break down the alcove where his words are engraved this very instant, and I shall summon the ifrit so I can slay him, for it is a practice of mine to slay ifrits!"

When she heard my words, she turned pale and cried out, "By Allah, don't do this!"

But I paid no attention to her words. I raised my foot and gave the supports of the alcove a mighty kick. Then all at once the air became thick and dark. There was thunder and lightning. The earth trembled and quaked, and the world became invisible. My head became clear, and I cried to her, "What's going on?"

"The ifrit is coming!" she replied. "Didn't I warn you this would happen? By Allah, you have brought about my destruction. Flee for your life, and go up the way you came!"

So I fled up the staircase, but in my fright, I forgot my sandals and hatchet. And when I mounted two steps, I turned to look for them, and lo! I saw the earth split in two, and a most hideous monster appeared. It was the ifrit, and he said to the damsel, "What terrible thing has happened here that has caused you to disturb me? What has happened to you?"

"Nothing has happened to me," she answered. "I was feeling lonely and sad. So I took some wine to cheer me up. After drinking a fair amount, I rose to obey a call of nature. But the wine had gotten the best of me, and I fell against the alcove."

"You're lying! You whore!" shrieked the ifrit, and he looked around the hall right and left until he caught sight of my ax and sandals and said to her, "Whose things are these? They must belong to some mortal who's been keeping you company!"

"I have never set eyes on them until this moment," she responded. "They must have been dragged along by you."

"You're being absurd, you harlot!" he cried.

Then he stripped her stark naked and stretched her upon the floor. He bound her hands and feet to four stakes as if she were crucified. Then he began torturing her to make her confess. I could not bear to stand and listen to her cries and groans. So I climbed to the top of the stairs in great fear, and when I reached the top, I replaced the trapdoor and covered it with earth. Then I repented what I had done and thought of the lady and her beauty and loveliness and the tortures she was suffering at the hands of the cursed jinnee after her quiet life of twenty-five years. All that was now happening was caused by me. Then I thought about my father and his kingly estate and how I had become a woodcutter and how my world had turned turbulent again after a short serene time. So I wept bitter tears and walked until I reached the home of my friend the tailor, who had become extremely anxious about my disappearance. Indeed, as the saying goes, he was sitting on coals and fire because of me. And when he saw me, he said, "All night long I have had a heavy heart because I was afraid that some wild beasts had killed you, or that something else terrible had happened to you."

I thanked him for his friendly concern, and after retiring to my corner, I sat pondering and musing about what had happened to me. I blamed and chided myself for my folly and for carelessly kicking down the alcove. I was in the process of blaming myself when, al! at once, the tailor came to me and said, "There is an old man, a Persian, in the shop, and he is looking for you. He has your hatchet and sandals, which he had taken to the woodcutters. He told them that he had gone out to begin the call to dawn prayer when he happened to come upon these things. Then he asked the woodcutters to direct him to their owner. The woodcutters recognized your hatchet and sandals and sent him here. He is sitting in my shop. So go out to him, thank him, and take back your hatchet and sandals."

When I heard these words, I turned yellow with fear and felt stunned, as if I had been hit by a blow. Before I could recover, the floor of my room suddenly split in two, and out of it arose the Persian, who was the ifrit. He had submitted the lady to all kinds of torture, but she had confessed to nothing. So he had taken the hatchet and sandals and said to her, "As surely as I am Jirjis of the seed of Iblis, I shall bring you back the owner of this hatchet and the sandals!" Then he had gone to the woodcutters with his pretense, and when he had reached the shop, and his intuition had been confirmed, he suddenly snatched me as a hawk snatches a mouse and flew high in the air. But soon he descended and plunged down into the earth with me—I was unconscious during the whole time. Finally, he set me down in the subterranean palace in which I had spent that blissful night. There I saw the lady stripped to the skin, her limbs bound to four stakes and blood dripping from her sides. My eyes filled with tears at the sight, but the ifrit covered her body and said, "Oh wanton woman, isn't this the man you love?"

She looked at me and replied, "I don't know him, nor have I ever seen him until this moment!"

"What!" cried the ifrit. "All this torture and no confession!"

"I never saw this man in my entire life, and it is not lawful in Allah's sight to tell lies about him."

"If you don't know him," said the ifrit, "then take this sword, and strike off his head."

The ifrit untied her, and she took the sword in her hand and came close to me. I signaled to her with my eyebrows while tears were flowing down my cheeks. She understood me and answered me through signs, "How could you bring all this evil upon me?" and I replied in the same way, indicating, "This is the time for mercy and forgiveness." Then my lady threw away the sword and said, "How can I strike the neck of someone whom I don't know, and who has not caused me any evil? Such a deed is not legal according to my law."

"You would grieve too much if you were to kill your lover!" said the ifrit. "Just because he has lain with you, you've endured all these torments and obstinately refuse to confess. After this it is clear to me that you only care for your own kind." Then he turned to me and said, "Oh man, most likely you don't know this woman."

"I don't have the faintest idea," I said. "I never saw her in my life until this moment."

"Then take the sword," he said, "and strike off her head, and I shall believe that you do not know her and shall let you go free."

"I shall do as you command," I replied, and I picked up the sword, moved forward, and had raised the sword to strike her when she signaled to me with her eyebrows, "Is this the way you repay me for the love I've shown you?" And I understood what her looks meant and answered her with a glance of my eye, "I shall sacrifice my soul for you." Then my eyes filled with tears, and I threw the sword onto the floor and said to the jinnee, "Oh mighty ifrit, if a woman who lacks sense and faith considers it unlawful to strike off my head, how can it be lawful for me, a man, to cut off her head, a person whom I had never seen in my entire life? I cannot do such a misdeed though it may mean my death."

"You two have a good mutual understanding," replied the ifrit, "but I shall let you see where such things end."

He took the sword and struck off the lady's hands and feet with four strokes. And while I looked on and saw her die, she bid me farewell with dying eyes.

"You whore!" cried the jinnee. "This is what you get for making a cuckold out of me!" And he struck her so hard that her head went flying.

Then he turned to me and said, "Oh mortal, our laws permit us to slay our wives when they commit adultery. With regard to this damsel, I snatched her away on her wedding night, when she was a girl of twelve, and she knew nobody but myself. I used to come to her once every ten days and lie with her during the night under the guise of a man, a Persian. But once I found out that she cuckolded me, she had to die. With regard to you, I am not totally convinced that you are the one who slept with her. Nevertheless, I cannot let you go unharmed. But you may ask me one favor, and I shall grant it."

So I rejoiced and said, "What favor may I ask of you?"

"Ask me what I shall turn you into, a dog, an ass, or an ape," replied the ifrit.

I had hoped that the jinnee might show me some mercy and spare me, and so I cried out, "By Allah, spare me, and Allah will spare you for sparing a Moslem and a man who never did you any wrong." And I humbled myself before him and said, "I am entirely at your disposal."

"Stop bothering me with all this talk," said the jinnee. "I have the power to slay you, and here I am giving you a choice."

"Oh ifrit," I stated, "it would suit you better if you pardoned me just as the envied pardoned the envier."

"And how did that happen?" he asked, and I began to tell him

The Tale of the Envier and the Envied

It is said that there were two men who lived in a certain city and dwelled in adjoining houses. They shared a common wall, and one of them envied the other and regarded him with an evil eye and did his utmost to harm him. He was so jealous of his neighbor that his malice grew and he could hardly eat or enjoy the sweet pleasures of sleep. But the envied man did nothing but prosper, and the more the other sought to harm him, the more wealthy he grew and flourished. Gradually, he learned about his neighbor's jealousy and his intention to harm him, and he said, "By Allah! God's earth is large enough for all people." So he left the neighborhood and went to another city, where he bought some land that contained a dried-up well in terrible condition. Here he built an oratory, furnished it with a few necessities, and made it his home, where he devoted himself to prayer and worshiping Allah Almighty. Fakirs and holy mendicants flocked to him from all parts of the world, and his fame spread throughout the city and countryside. Soon the news reached his envious neighbor, who learned what good fortune he had and how the city notables had become his disciples. So he traveled to the place and presented himself at the holy man's hermitage, where he was met by the envied and welcomed with honor.

"I have a word to say to you," said the envier, "and this is the reason for my journey here. I want to give you a piece of good news. So come to my cell with me."

Thereupon the envied arose and took the envier by the hand, and they went to the innermost part of the hermitage. But the envier said, "Tell your fakirs to retire to their cells, for I shall not tell you what I have to say except in secret where no one can hear us."

Accordingly, the envied said to his fakirs, "Please retire to your private cells." And when all had done as he had requested, he set out with his visitor and walked some way until the two reached the ruined well. As they stood at the brink, the envier gave the envied a push which sent him headlong down into the well, and nobody witnessed this treacherous act. Consequently, the envier left the place and went his way, thinking that he had slain the holy man. Now this well happened to be haunted by the jinn, who helped him reach the bottom of the well without hurting himself. After seating him upon a large stone, one of them asked his companions, "Does anyone know this man?"

"No," they answered.

"This man," continued the speaker, "is called the envied, who fled from his envier to dwell in our city, and here he founded this holy house, and he has edified us through his litanies and readings of the Koran. But the envier sought him out and cunningly contrived to deceive him and cast him down into this well where we are now. But the fame of this good man has this very night come to the attention of the sultan in our city, who plans to visit him tomorrow on account of his daughter."

"What's wrong with his daughter?" asked one.

"She is possessed by a spirit. Maymun, son of Damdam, is madly in love with her, but if this pious man knew the remedy, her cure would be as easy as could be."

"What is the medicine?" one of them inquired.

The speaker replied, "The black tomcat which is with him in the oratory has a white spot on the end of his tail, the size of a dirham. Let him pluck seven white hairs from the spot and then let him fumigate with it, and the marid will flee from her and never return. Then she will be sane for the rest of her life."

All this took place, oh ifrit, within earshot of the envied, who listened intently, and when dawn broke and morning arose in splendor, the fakirs went looking for the holy man and found him climbing up the wall of the well, and this made a great impression on them.

The holy man was now full aware that he had to pluck seven hairs from the white spot of the tomcat, and he went and did this as soon as he returned to his house.

No sooner had the sun risen than the sultan entered the hermitage with the great lords of his realm. The holy man gave him a hearty welcome, and after seating the sultan by his side, he asked, "Shall I tell you why you have come to see me?"

"Yes," the king answered.

"You have come under the pretext of a mere visit," the holy man said, "but you really have come to seek some advice about your daughter."

"You're absolutely right," replied the sultan.

And the envied continued, "Send for her, for I believe that I shall be able to heal her right away, if such is the will of Allah!"

The king rejoiced and sent for his daughter, who was tied and bound so she could be controlled. They brought her to the holy man, who made her sit down behind a curtain, where he began taking out the hairs and fumigating her. No sooner had he done this than the voice which was in her head cried out and departed. The maiden was at once restored to her right mind, and veiling her face, she said, "What has happened, and who has brought me here?"

The sultan was beside himself with joy. He kissed his daughter's eyes and the holy man's hands. Then, turning to his great lords, he asked, "What do you say to this? What fee does this man deserve after he has made my daughter whole?"

"He deserves to have her as his wife," they all said.

And the king said, "You speak the truth!"

So he married her to him, and the envied became the king's son-in-law. After some time passed, the vizier died, and the king said, "Whom can I now appoint to be my new minister?"

"Your son-in-law," replied his courtiers.

So the envied became a vizier, and after a while the sultan also died, and the lieges asked, "Whom shall we make king?"

And all cried, "The vizier!"

So the vizier was made sultan right away, and he became a true ruler of men as king.

One day, when he had mounted his horse and was

flourishing as king, he rode among his emirs, viziers, and nobles, and he happened to glance at his old neighbor, the envier, who was on foot nearby. So he turned to one of his ministers and said, "Bring me that man over there, but do not frighten him."

The vizier brought him, and the king said, "Give him a thousand gold coins from the treasury, and load ten camels with merchandise for trade. Then give him an escort and send him to his own town."

Then he said farewell to his enemy, set him on his way, and refused to punish him for the many and great evils he had done.

"Do you see, oh ifrit, the mercy of the envied to the envier, who had hated him from the beginning and had borne him such bitter hate and always tried to cause him trouble. Indeed, he had driven him from house and home and had traveled for the sole purpose of taking his life by throwing him down the well. Nevertheless, the holy man did not take revenge, but he forgave him and was generous to him."

Then I wept before the jinnee, and never did anyone weep more bitter tears than mine. But the ifrit said, "Do not bother to speak so long. As to my slaying you, don't worry, and as to my pardoning you, there is no hope. I shall definitely bewitch you."

Then he tore me from the ground, which closed under my feet, and he flew high into the sky with me until I saw the earth as a large white cloud or a saucer in the midst of waters. Soon he set me down on a mountain, and after taking a little dust, over which he muttered some magic words, he sprinkled me and said, "Leave your present shape, and take on the shape of an ape!"

All at once I became an ape, a tailless baboon. Now after he had left me and I saw myself in this ugly and hateful shape, I wept for myself, but I resigned myself to the tyranny of time and circumstance, knowing full well that fortune is fair and constant to no man. I descended the mountain and found a long, broad, and plain desert over which I traveled for a month until I arrived at the brink of a briny sea. After standing there awhile,

I noticed a ship on the point of landing at the port. I hid myself behind a rock on the beach and waited until the ship drew near. Then I leapt on board.

I found the ship full of merchants and passengers, and one of them cried, "Oh captain, this cursed brute will bring us bad luck!"

"Throw the beast overboard," said another.

"Let us kill it!" replied the captain.

"Slay it with a sword," a third person cried.

"Drown it!" yelled a fourth.

"Shoot it with an arrow."

But I sprang up and grabbed hold of the captain's pants, and he took pity on me and said, "Oh merchants, this ape has appealed to me for protection, and I shall protect him. From here on in, he is under my care. Nobody is to harm or hurt him, otherwise there will be bad blood between us."

Then he treated me kindly, and whatever he said, I understood and attended to his every need and was like a servant. To be sure my tongue would not obey my wishes. But he came to love me. The vessel sailed on, and the wind was fair for the next fifty days. At the end of our journey we cast anchor under the walls of a large city where there were huge amounts of people, especially learned men, so many that it was impossible to tell their number. No sooner did we arrive than we were visited by some mameluke officials from the king of that city. After boarding the ship, they greeted the merchants and said, "Our king welcomes you and sends you this roll of paper. Each one of you must write a line on it, for you know that the king's minister, a famous calligrapher, is dead, and the king has sworn a solemn oath that he will only appoint a new vizier who can write as well as his former minister."

Then one of the mamelukes gave us a scroll that was ten feet long, and each and every one of the merchants who knew how to write wrote a little on the scroll. Then I stood up—still in the form of an ape—and snatched the scroll from their hands. They were afraid that I might tear it or throw it overboard. So they tried to grab me and scare me, but I signaled to them that I could write, and they were all astounded.

"We never saw an ape who could write!" they exclaimed.

"Let him write," the captain said, "and if he scribbles, we shall kick him out and kill him. But if he writes correctly, I shall adopt him as my son, for surely I have never seen a more intelligent and well-mannered monkey than this one. If only my own real son were his match in morals and manners!"

So I took the reed, stretched out my paw, dipped it in ink, and wrote several couplets in different languages. Then I gave the scroll to the officials, and after we had all written lines, they carried the scroll to the king. When he saw the paper, only my writing pleased him, and he said to the courtiers around him, "Go and seek the writer of these lines. Dress him in a splendid robe of honor. Then mount him on a mule. Let a band of music precede him, and bring him to me."

Upon hearing these words, they smiled, and the king became angry with them and cried, "You cursed people! I gave you an order, and you laugh at me?"

"Oh king," they replied, "If we are laughing, it is not at you and not without a reason."

"Well, what is it?" he asked.

"Oh king, you ordered us to bring you the man who wrote these lines," they replied. "But the truth is that he who wrote them is not a son of Adam, but an ape, a tailless baboon, who belongs to the captain of the ship."

"Is this true what you are saying?" he asked.

"Yes," they said. "With all due respect to your majesty."

The king was astonished by their words and shook with mirth. "I have a mind to buy the captain's ape," he said, and he sent messengers to the ship with a mule, a dress, an escort, and the state drums, commanding that the ape should be clothed in the robe of honor, mounted on the mule, escorted by the guards, and preceded by the band of music.

Well, they came to the ship, took me from the captain, dressed me in the robe of honor, and mounted me on the mule. Then they led me in state procession through the streets, while the people were amazed and amused. The people could not believe their eyes and said to one another, "Is our sultan about to make an ape his minister?"

They all came in crowds to gaze at me. The city was astir and turned topsy-turvy because of me. When they brought me to the king and set me down in his presence, I kissed the ground before him three times and one time before the high chamberlain and great nobles. The king told me to sit down, and I squatted respectfully on shins and knees, and all who were present were astounded by my fine manners, and the king most of all. Thereupon, he ordered his lords to retire, and when nobody remained except for the king, the eunuch on duty, and a little white slave, he commanded them to set a table of food before me that contained all kinds of birds such as quail and sand grouse. Then he signaled me to eat with him. So, I rose and kissed the ground before him, sat down, and ate with him. And when the table was removed, I washed my hands in seven waters. Then I took the reed case and reed, and wrote some poems for the king. Afterward I rose and seated myself at a respectful distance while the king read what I had written. Stunned, he cried out, "What a miracle that an ape should be gifted with this graceful style and this power of penmanship! By Allah, it is a miracle of miracles!"

Soon they brought choice wines to the king, and after he had a drink, he passed on the cup to me. I kissed the ground, drank, and wrote some more verses. The king read them and said with a sigh, "Were these gifts in a man, he would be superior to all the people in his time!" Then he called for a chessboard and said, "Nod 'yes' if you will play with me."

I nodded my head "yes," and then I came forward, ordered the pieces, and played two games with him, both of which I won. He was speechless with surprise. So, I took the pen again and indicated to him in a poem that two hosts were fighting over my soul and destiny. The king read these lines with wonder and delight and said to his eunuch, "Go to your mistress, Sitt al-Husnm, and tell her that I want her to come here and regard this wondrous ape."

So the eunuch left and soon returned with the lady, who veiled her face when she saw me and said, "Oh Father, have you lost all sense of honor? Why have you sent for me? You know I'm not allowed to show myself to strange men."

"Oh Sitt al-Husnm," he replied, "no man is here except this little foot page and the eunuch who raised you, and I, your father. Why then are you veiling your face?"

"The animal whom you think is an ape is really a young man," she answered. "He is a clever, polite, wise, and learned son of a king. But he is enchanted. The ifrit Jirjis cast a spell on him after slaying his own wife, the daughter of King Ifitamus, lord of the Islands of Abnus."

The king was astounded by his daughter's words, and he turned to me and said, "Is this true what my daughter has said?"

And I nodded my head "yes" and began to weep bitter tears.

"Oh my dear Papa, when I was a child, there was an old woman, a wily and wise witch, who taught me all about magic and its practice. I wrote down notes and became perfect in the art of magic. I memorized one hundred and seventy chapters of egromantic formulas so that I could transport the stones of your city behind the Mountain Kaf or transform its site into a sea and all the people into fish."

"Oh my daughter," said her father, "I beg you to disenchant this young man so that I may make him my vizier and have him wed you, for he is indeed an ingenious fellow and deeply learned."

"Gladly, my father," the princess replied, and she picked up a knife on which the name of Allah was inscribed in Hebrew letters, and she drew a wide circle in the middle of the palace hall. Then she wrote mysterious names and talismans in Cufic letters. After this, she uttered words and muttered charms, some of which we understood, and others were incomprehensible. Soon the world turned dark before our eyes until we thought the sky was falling upon our heads. All of a sudden the ifrit appeared in his own shape and aspect. His hands were like multipronged pitchforks, his legs like the masts of great ships, and his eyes like the cressets of gleaming fire. We were extremely frightened by him, but the king's daughter cried at him, "No welcome to you, and no greetings, you dog!"

Thereupon he turned into a lion and said, "Oh traitoress, why have you broken the oath that we each swore never to oppose one another?"

"Oh cursed one," she answered, "how could there be a compact between me and the likes of you?"

Then he said, "Well, you will pay for what you have said!" And he opened his jaws and rushed at her, but she was too quick for him. She plucked a hair from her head, waved it in the air, and when she muttered something, it became a trenchant sword, with which she struck the lion and cut him in two. Then the two halves flew away into the air, and the head changed to a scorpion, and the princess became a huge serpent and set upon the cursed scorpion. The two fought a stiff fight for at least an hour, coiling and recoiling, until the scorpion changed into a vulture, and the serpent became an eagle that attacked the vulture and pursued him for an hour until he became a tomcat which mewed, grinned, and spat. Thereupon the eagle changed into a wolf and battled the cat in the place for a long time until the cat changed into a worm and crept into a red pomegranate which lay beside the fountain in the middle of the palace. Then the pomegranate swelled to the size of a watermelon in the air, but it fell upon the marble pavement of the palace and broke to pieces, and all the seeds fell out and were scattered all over the floor. Then the wolf shook himself and became a snow-white cock that began picking up the seeds with the intention not to leave a single one on the floor. Unfortunately, one seed rolled to the edge of the fountain, and when the cock ran to pick it up, it sprang into the water, became a fish, and dived to the bottom of the basin. In turn, the cock changed to a big fish, plunged in after the other fish, and the two disappeared for a while and lo! we heard loud shrieks and cries of pain, which made us tremble. After this the ifrit rose out of the water, and he appeared to be a burning flame, spurting fire and smoke from his mouth, eyes, and nostrils. Immediately, the princess came out of the basin, and she appeared to be a flaming coal. Again the two of them battled for an hour until their fires were entirely extinguished and their thick smoke filled the palace. As for us, we panted for breath, for we almost suffocated, and we longed to jump into the water for fear that we might burn up and become utterly destroyed. The king cried out, "There is no majesty and there is no might except for Allah the Glorious the Great! Truly, we belong to Allah, and it is to him that we are returning! If only I had not urged my daughter to attempt to disenchant the ape! I have imposed on her a terrible task of fighting the cursed ifrit against whom all the jinnees in the world could not prevail. If only I had never seen this ape! Allah should not bless the day of his coming! I thought I would do a good deed before the face of Allah by releasing him from his enchantment, and now I have only brought trouble to my heart."

Suddenly, before we were aware of anything, the ifrit yelled out from under the flames, came up to us as we stood on the dais, and blew fire in our faces. The maiden overtook him and breathed blasts of fire at his face, and the sparks from her and from him rained down upon us. Her sparks did us no harm, but one of his sparks landed on my eye and destroyed it, making me a monocular ape. Another fell on the king's face, scorching the lower half, burning off his beard and mustache and causing his lower teeth to fall out. A third spark landed on the castrato's breast, killing him on the spot. So, we became desperate and got ready for death, then all of a sudden we heard a voice cry out, "Allah is God Almighty! Allah is God Almighty! May help and victory be granted to all who believe in the truth, and disappointment and grace be given to all who do not believe in the religion of Mohammed, the moon of faith."

Then she came up to us and said, "Give me a cup of water."

We gave it to her, and she spoke some words over it

that we could not understand, and after sprinkling the water over me, she cried, "By virtue of the truth and by the greatest name Allah, I charge you to return to your former shape."

And all of a sudden I shook and became a man as I was before except that I had utterly lost an eye. Then she cried out, "The fire! The fire! Oh my dear Papa, an arrow from the cursed jinnee has wounded me to death, for I am not used to fighting with the jinn. If he had been a man, I would have slain him right away. I had no trouble with him until the pomegranate burst and the seeds scattered, but I overlooked the seed that contained the very life of the jinnee. If I had picked it up, he would have died right on the spot, but as fate and fortune decreed, I did not see it. So he caught me unaware, and we had a fierce struggle under the earth, high in the air, and in the water. As often as I thought I had the advantage, he changed forms and finally opened the gate of fire, and few are saved when the fire strikes. But destiny demanded that my cunning prevail over his cunning, and I burned him to death after I vainly exhorted him to embrace the religion of Al-Islam. As for me, I am a dead woman. May Allah replace me!"

Then she called upon heaven for help and did not stop imploring for relief from the fire. Then, all at once, a black spark shot up from her robed feet to her thighs. Then it flew to her bosom and to her face. When it reached her face, she wept and said, "I testify that there is no god but *the* God and that Mohammed is the Apostle of God!"

And we looked at her and saw nothing but a heap of ashes next to the heap that had been the ifrit. We mourned for her, and I wished I had been in her place and wished that I had never seen her lovely face, especially after she had done me so much good. But there is no denying the will of Allah.

When the king saw his daughter's terrible death, he plucked out what was left of his beard, beat his face, and tore his garments. And I did the same, and we both wept over her. Then the chamberlains and lords entered and were amazed to find two heaps of ashes and the sultan about to faint. So they stood around him until he revived and told them what had happened to his daughter in her fight against the ifrit. Of course, their grief was enormous, and the women and slave girls shrieked and wept, and they continued to lament for seven days. The king ordered a vast vaulted tomb over his daughter's ashes, and wax candles and sepulchral lamps were burned inside. As for the ifrit's ashes, they were scattered in the winds and sent to be cursed by Allah. Then the sultan became so sick that he almost died, but after a month he recovered. When his health returned and his beard grew back and he had been converted to Al-Islam by the mercy of Allah, he sent for me and said, "Oh young man, fate had decreed the happiest of times for us, and we were safe from all the changes and accidents of time until you appeared. Then our troubles began. If only we had never seen you and your foul face! But we took pity on you, and as a result, we have lost everything. Because of you I have lost my daughter, who was worth more than a hundred men. I have suffered from the fire and lost my teeth. My eunuch was also slain. I don't blame you, because you had no power to prevent this. Allah's doom was cast on you as well as on us, and thanks to the Almighty, my daughter was able to rescue you, even though she lost her own life! Go forth now, my son. Leave this city. You have done enough. Go forth in peace, and if I ever see you again, I shall certainly slay you."

And as I left, he cried out at me. Then I began weeping and could hardly believe in my escape and had no idea where I should go. I recalled all that had happened to me, my meeting with the tailor, my love for the maiden in the subterranean palace, my narrow escape from the ifrit, my transformation into an ape, and my departure as a man. Then I expressed my thanks to Allah and said, "My eye and not my life!" So, right before I left the city, I entered the bath, shaved my beard, mustache, and eyebrows, cast ashes on my head, and put on the coarse black woolen robe of a calender. Then I wandered forth, my lady, and every day I pondered all the calamities that had happened to me, and I wept and repeated some verses. So I continued journeying through many regions and saw many a city. My destination was Baghdad to seek an audience with the Commander of the Faithful and tell him about everything that had happened to me. I arrived here this very night and found my brother in Allah, this first calender, standing around and looking somewhat lost. So, I saluted him with "Peace be with you," and began conversing with him. Soon our brother the third calender arrived and said, "Peace be with you. I am a stranger."

"We are strangers, too," we responded, "and have just arrived."

So we walked on together, none of us aware of the other's history, until destiny drove us to this door, and we entered. Such then is my story of how I lost my eye, and the reason for shaving my beard and mustache.

"Your story is a rare one, indeed," said the mistress of the house. "So, you may keep your head, and go your way."

But he replied, "I shall not budge until I hear my companions' stories."

Then the third calender came forward and said, "Oh illustrious lady, my story is not like those of my comrades, but it is actually more wondrous and far more marvelous. In their case, fate and fortune came down on them unexpectedly, but I drew destiny upon me and brought sorrow to my own soul, and I shaved my own beard and lost my own eye. And now I shall tell you

The Third Calender's Tale

My lady, I, too, am a king and the son of a king, and my name is Ajib son of Khazib. When my father died, I succeeded him, and I ruled justly and dealt fairly with all my lords and subjects. I delighted in trips by sea, for my capital stood on the shore, before which the ocean

stretched far and wide. Nearby there were many great
islands with garrisons. My fleet numbered fifty mer-
chantmen, and I had as many yachts for pleasure, and
one hundred and fifty ships outfitted for holy war with
the unbelievers. It so happened that I decided to enjoy
myself on the islands I just mentioned, and I departed
with my people in ten ships with a month's supplies of
food. But one night a headwind struck us, and the sea
rose against us with huge waves. Darkness descended on
us as we were battered by a storm. We gave ourselves
up for lost, and I said, "Those who give up the ship
deserve no praise!" Then we prayed to Allah and asked
him to come to our aid. But the storm continued and
the winds knocked us about until dawn broke, and then
the gale. fell, the seas became still, and the sun shone
upon us with kindness. Soon we landed on an island and
were able to cook food. So we ate heartily and rested
for a couple of days. After that we set out again and
sailed another twenty days. Soon the current ran against
us, and we found ourselves in strange waters, where the
captain became wholly bewildered. So we told the lookout man, "Climb up to the masthead and keep your
eyes open!"

So he scampered up the mast, looked out, and cried
aloud, "Oh king, I see something on the starboard side,
something dark like a fish floating on top of the sea."

When the captain heard the lookout's words, he threw
his turban on the deck, plucked out his beard, and beat
his face. "This is not good news at all!" he exclaimed.

"Captain," I said, "tell us what the lookout saw."

"Oh my king," replied the captain, "you know that
we lost our course on the night of the storm, and we
have continued to go astray ever since. Tomorrow, by
the end of the day, we shall come to a mountain of black
stone called the Magnet Mountain, for all currents will
carry us there willy-nilly. As soon as we are under its
sway, the ships' sides will open, and every nail in the
planks will fly out and stick to the mountain. Almighty
Allah has. endowed the lodestone with a mysterious virtue and a love for iron so that anything made of iron
travels toward it. There is a great deal of iron on this

mountain, and nobody but Allah knows how much. Most of it comes from the many vessels that have been lost there in times past. The bright spot on its summit is a dome of yellow from Andalusia set upon ten columns. On its peak is a horseman who sits upon a horse of brass and holds a lance of brass in his hand. On his bosom there is a tablet of lead engraved with names and talismans. This rider destroys people, and his magic power cannot be destroyed until he falls from his horse."

Then the captain wept bitter tears, and we all prepared to die, and each one of us said farewell to his friend and put him in charge of his last will and testament in case the friend should survive. No one slept that night, and in the morning we found ourselves closer to the Magnet Mountain. The waters kept driving us there with violent currents. When the ships fell entirely under its sway, they opened up. Nails flew out, and all the iron in the ships went flying toward the Magnet Mountain and stuck to it so that by the end of the day we were all struggling in the waves around the mountain. Some of us were saved, but most drowned, and even those who escaped could no longer recognize each other because they were so stunned by the beating of the billows and the raving winds. As for me, Allah preserved my life so that I might suffer whatever hardship, misfortune, and calamity He had in store for me. Thanks to a plank from one of the ships, I was able to make it to the foot of the mountain, where I found a path with steps carved out of the rock that led to the summit. After calling upon Allah and beseeching Him passionately, I took courage and began climbing the mountain little by little. Since the Lord silenced the wind and helped me in the ascent, I succeeded in reaching the peak. But I did not find a resting place there, only the dome, which I entered with joy and celebrated my escape by making Wuzu ablution and thanking God for my salvation. Then I fell asleep under the dome and heard a mysterious voice in my dream that said, "Oh son of Khazib, when you wake from your sleep, dig beneath your feet, and you will find a bow of brass and three leaden arrows engraved with talismans and characters. Take the bow and shoot the arrows at the horseman on top of the dome and free mankind from his tyranny. After you shoot him, he will fall into the sea, and the horse will also drop at your feet. Then bury it in the place of the bow. When this has been done, the ocean will swell and rise until it reaches the level of the mountain head. Another man of brass will appear in a skiff, and he will be holding a pair of paddles in his hand. He will come to you, and you will embark with him. But beware of saying 'Praise the Lord' or mentioning Allah Almighty in any way. He will row you for ten days until he brings you to the Island of Safety. From there you will easily reach a port and find your way back to your native land. All this will happen as I said, so you need not call on the name of Allah."

Then I woke from my sleep in joy, and I hastened to do the bidding of the mysterious voice. I found the bow and arrows and shot the horseman, who tumbled into the ocean while the horse dropped to my feet. So I took it and buried it. Soon the sea surged up and rose until it reached the top of the mountain. Fortunately, I did not have to wait long before I saw a skiff coming toward me. I gave thanks to Allah, and when the skiff came up to me, I saw a man of brass in it with a tablet of lead on his breast that was engraved with talismans and characters. I embarked without saying a word. For the next ten days, the boatman rowed in silence until I caught sight of the Island of Safety whereupon I exclaimed with joy, "Allah be praised! There is no god but *the* God, and Allah is almighty."

All of a sudden the skiff turned over and threw me into the sea. Then it righted itself and sank into the depths. Now I am a good swimmer. So I swam the entire day until nightfall, when my arms and shoulders were numbed with fatigue, and I thought I was going to die. So I prepared myself for death. The sea was still surging because of heavy winds, and soon a wave came and swept me up and sent me flying onto dry land so that His will might be fulfilled. I crawled on the beach, took off my garments, and wrung them out to dry in the sunshine. Then I lay down and slept the whole night. As soon as it was day, I put on my clothes, rose, and began walking. When I came to a group of trees and walked around them, I could see that I was on an island. "As soon as I'm saved from one predicament," I said to myself, "I find myself in a new one!" But while I was pondering my situation and longing for death, I saw a ship that was heading toward the island. So I climbed a tree and hid myself among the branches. Soon the ship took anchor, and ten slaves landed carrying iron hoes and baskets. They walked until they reached the middle of the island, where they dug deep into the ground and uncovered a plate of metal, which they lifted. Then they descended through a trapdoor and after a short time returned to the ship, from which they carried forth bread, flour, honey, fruits, butter, leather bottles with different kinds of liquor, household supplies, furniture, mirrors, rugs, and carpets. In fact, they carried everything one needed to furnish a dwelling, and they went back and forth until they had taken everything from the ship to the underground hiding place. After this the slaves went on board once more and brought back garments and an old, old man who looked as though he were about to die. All that remained of him was a live skeleton wrapped in a rag of blue stuff through which the east and west winds whistled. At his side was a young man who was perfectly elegant and graceful. He was so handsome that poems should have memorialized him. All of them, the slaves, the old man, and the youth, went down through the trapdoor and did not reappear for an hour or more. Then the slaves and old man came up without the young man, and after replacing the metal plate and carefully closing the door, they returned to the ship, set sail, and were soon out of sight. So I climbed down the tree and went to the place that they had uncovered, and I scraped and removed the dirt and found the trapdoor. When I lifted it up, I discovered a winding stone staircase, and I descended the steps until I found a splendid hall filled with various kinds of carpets and silk stuff. The young man was sitting on a raised couch and leaning back on a round cushion with a fan in his hand and nosegays and posies of sweet-scented herbs and flowers before him. He was alone, not a soul near him in the vault. When he saw me, he turned pale, but I greeted him courteously and said, "Don't worry. There is no need to fear. I am a man like yourself and the son of a king to boot. Destiny has sent me to keep you company and cheer you in your loneliness. But now, tell me your story. Why do you have to dwell here all by yourself?"

When he was assured that I was of his kind and not a jinnee, he rejoiced, and the color returned to his face. Signaling me to draw near, he said, "Oh my brother, my story is a strange one. My father is a wealthy merchant who deals in jewels. He has many white and black slaves who travel in ships and on camels and trade for him in distant cities. But he never was blessed with a child, not even one. Now, one night he dreamed that he would be favored with a son, who would not live very long. So, when morning arrived, my father wept and was steeped in sorrow. On the following night, my mother conceived, and my father noted down the date of her becoming pregnant. When nine months passed and she gave birth to me, my father rejoiced and celebrated with banquets. He called together the neighbors and fed the fakirs and the poor, because he had finally been blessed with a son near the end of his days. Then he assembled the astrologers and astronomers and all the wizards and wise men of our time who knew the movements of the stars, and they drew my chart and said to my father, 'Your son will live to be fifteen years old, but in his fifteenth year, something sinister will happen. If he can safely survive this period, he will reach a great age. The threat to his life will be this. In the Sea of Peril there is a mountain called Mount Magnet. On top of it is a horseman made of yellow brass. He is seated on a horse, also made of brass, and he bears a tablet of lead on his breast. Fifty days after this rider falls from his steed, your son will die, and his slayer will be the man who shoots down the horseman. He is a prince named Ajib son of King Khazib.' Well, my father was overcome with grief when he heard these words, but he reared me in the most tender fashion and gave me an excellent education until

I was fifteen. Ten days ago news came to him that the horseman had fallen into the sea, and the man who shot him was Ajib son of King Khazib. Therefore, my father wept bitter tears, because he knew he had to part with me, and he seemed to be possessed by a jinnee. Since he was afraid that something might happen to me, he built me this underground place and stocked it with all that I would need for the days left in the prophecy. Then he transported me in a ship and left me here. Ten days have already passed, and when the forty have gone by without danger to me, he will come and take me home, for he has done all this only in fear of Prince Ajib. Such, then, is my story and the cause of my loneliness."

When I heard his story, I was astonished and said to myself, "I am the Prince Ajib, who shot the horseman, but as Allah is my witness, I shall not slay him!" So I said to him, "Oh my lord, you are free of harm. May Allah protect you so that you need not worry. I shall stay with you and be your servant. After keeping you company for forty days, I shall go with you to your home, where you will provide me with an escort of mamelukes who will accompany me back to my native city. This way you will repay me for my services."

He was very glad to hear these words. So I arose, lit some wax candles, and set meat, drink, and sweetmeats on the table. We ate, drank, and talked about various matters·until most of the night was gone. When he lay down to rest, I covered him and went to sleep myself. The next morning I arose and warmed some water. After waking him gently, I brought him the warm water, with which he washed his face, and he said, "May heaven repay you with many blessings! By Allah, if I manage to survive this danger and am saved from the man named Ajib bin Khazib, I shall make my father reward you and send you home healthy and wealthy. Even if I die, my blessings will go with you."

"May the day never dawn when evil strikes you," I answered. "May Allah take me away before you!"

Then I set some food before him, and we ate. Afterward I fumigated the hall with perfumes, and this pleased him. After I had changed his clothes, we played and ate sweetmeats, and then we played again and amused ourselves until nightfall, when I rose, lit the lamps, and set something to eat before him. Then I told him stories until late into the night, when he lay down to rest, and I covered him and went to sleep as well. I continued to do this for days and nights, and my affection for him grew deeper. Therefore, my sorrow abated, and I said to myself, "The astrologers lied when they predicted that he would be slain by Ajib bin Khazib. By Allah, I shall not slay him."

Thirty-nine days went by, and I did not stop serving him. We entertained ourselves in conversation, and I told him all kinds of tales. On the fortieth night, the young man rejoiced and said, "Oh my brother, praise be to Allah, who has saved me from death, and may you also be blessed for coming to me. And I pray to God that he enable you to return to your native land. But now, my brother, I would like you to warm some water for the Ghusl ablution, and I would appreciate it if you would bathe me and change my clothes."

"Gladly," I replied. So I heated plenty of water, carried it to him, and washed his body all over. Then I rubbed him well and changed his clothes. Afterward he was drowsy and lay down on a high bed and said, "Oh my brother, please cut me some watermelon and sweeten it with a little sugar candy."

So I went to the pantry and brought out a fine watermelon on a platter and laid it before him.

"Oh master," I asked, "don't you have a knife?"

"Here it is," he answered, "over my head on the high shelf."

So I quickly got up and drew the knife from its sheath, but my foot slipped when I stepped down, and I fell on top of the young man holding the knife in my hand and buried the knife in his heart. And so I hastened to fulfill what had been written on the day that decided the destinies of man. He died instantaneously, and when I saw that he was slain, I uttered a loud and bitter cry, beat my face, and tore my garments. "Verily we belong to Allah," I cried. "And we shall return to Him. Only one day remained for this boy. If only I had not tried to cut the watermelon! What dire disaster this is! I have no choice, but I must bear it. What an affliction! What a disaster! Oh Allah, please pardon me, and declare me innocent. But God's will must be done."

When it was perfectly clear that the boy was dead, I arose and went up·the stairs. I replaced the trapdoor and covered it with dirt as it was before. Then I looked toward the sea and saw the ship heading toward the island. Filled with fear I said, "The moment they come and see the dead boy, they will know it was I who killed him, and they will slay me right away." So I climbed high up a tree and concealed myself among the leaves. No sooner had I done this than the ship anchored and the slaves landed with the ancient man, the young boy's father, and they headed directly for the place they had carried the boy. When they removed the dirt, they were surprised to see that it had been touched. Then they lifted the trapdoor and went down and found the dead boy stretched out in new garments with a knife deep in his heart. Upon seeing him, they shrieked, wept, and beat their faces. While they were loudly cursing the murderer, the sheikh fainted so that they thought he was dead, unable to survive his son.

Finally they wrapped the slain boy in his clothes, carried him up the stairs, and laid him on the ground, where they covered him with a shroud of silk. While they were walking to the ship, the old man revived, and when he gazed at his son, he fell to the ground, spread dust over his head, struck his face, and plucked out his beard. Again he began weeping at the thought of his murdered son, and he fainted once more. After a while a slave went and fetched a strip of silk upon which they placed the old man, and they sat down at his head.

All this took place beneath my tree, and I watched everything that was happening. My heart became heavy and my hair turned gray all because of my hard luck and the distress and anguish that I had suffered. In the meantime the old man did not recover from his swoon until near sunset, and when he came to himself and looked upon his dead son, he recalled what had happened and how what he had dreaded had turned out to be true. After reciting some verses, he sobbed a single sob, and his soul fled his flesh. The slaves shrieked, "Alas, our lord!" They showered dust on their heads and continued weeping and wailing. Soon they carried their dead master to the ship side by side with his dead son, and after they transported all the stuff from the underground dwelling to the ship, they set sail and disappeared from my eyes.

So now I climbed down the tree and ran over to the trapdoor. Then I descended the stairs into the underground dwelling, where everything reminded me of the young boy, and I mourned his loss. Then I went back up the stairs, and every day I used to wander around the island, and every night I returned to the underground hall. I lived this way for about a month, until, at last, I observed that every day the tide ebbed on the western side of the island and left shallow enough water, so that I could head for dry land. When I realized this, I rejoiced and soon made for the mainland, where I saw some fire burning in the distance.

When I drew near, I saw that it was actually a palace with gates of copper burnished red, which glistened when the rising sun shone upon it. This is why I had thought it was a fire. I was overcome with joy by the sight and sat down against the gate, but I had barely sat down when I encountered ten young men clothed in sumptuous garments, and they were all blind in the left eye, as if their eyes had been plucked out. They were accompanied by a sheikh, an old, old man, and I was astounded by the appearance, especially since they were all blind in the same eye. When they saw me, they greeted me and asked me about myself and what had led me to this place. Thereupon I told them about what had happened to me and about my misfortunes.

Astonished by my tale, they took me into the mansion, where I saw ten blue couches arranged around a hall and a smaller one in the middle. As we entered, each of the young men took his seat on his own couch, and the old man seated himself on the small one in the middle. "Young man," he said to me, "sit down on the floor and don't ask about our condition or how we lost our eyes." Soon he stood up and set meat and drink before each young man, and he treated me the same. After that they sat and asked me about my adventures and what had happened to me, and I continued telling them my tale until the early hours of the morning. Then the young men said, "Oh sheikh, please set the usual before us. The time has come."

"Gladly," he said and stood up. Then he disappeared into a closet and soon returned carrying ten trays on his head each covered with a strip of blue stuff. He set a tray before each young man and lit ten wax candles. Then he drew off the covers, but there was nothing beneath them but ashes, powdered charcoal, and soot. Then all the young men tucked up their sleeves to the elbows and began to weep and wail. They blackened their faces, smeared their clothes, struck their brows, and beat their breasts. "We were sitting and relaxing," they cried out, "but our boldness brought us unrest!" They continued doing this until dawn drew near. Then the old man rose and heated water for them so they could wash their faces and put on clean clothes.

Now, when I saw this, I was completely stunned and almost lost my wits. In fact, I forgot all that had happened to me and felt that I had to speak and ask them about the strange things that I had just witnessed. So I said to them, "How come you have done all this after we have been so open and cheerful? By Allah, you are all sound and sane, but your actions before this are those that only madmen or those possessed by an evil spirit would do. I beg you, please tell me your story and why you lost your eyes and why you blacken your faces with ashes and soot."

Thereupon they turned to me and said, "Young man, do not listen to the curious mind of youth, and do not ask us any questions!"

Then they slept, and I, too, went to bed. When they awoke, the old man brought us some food. After we had eaten and the plates and goblets were removed, they sat conversing until nightfall, when the old man rose, lit the wax candles and lamps, and set meat and food before us. After we had eaten and drunk, we sat conversing and carousing until midnight, when they said to the old man, "Bring us the usual, for the hour of sleep is at hand."

So he arose and brought them the trays of soot and ashes, and they did as they had done on the previous night, no more, nor less. I lived with them for one more month, and during this time they used to blacken their faces with ashes every night. Then they washed and changed their clothes when dawn fell. My astonishment grew, and my scruples and curiosity increased to such an extent that I stopped eating and drinking. At last, I lost control of myself, for my heart was on fire with unquenchable inquisitiveness, and I said, "Young men, I beg you to tell me why you blacken your faces and what you mean when you say, 'We were sitting and relaxing but our boldness brought us unrest.' "

"It would be better to keep these things secret," they said.

Still, I was bewildered by their actions and on the point of losing my patience. So I said, "I can't stand it anymore! You must tell me why you are doing what you are doing!"

"We are keeping our secret only for your good," they replied. "If we grant your request, evil things will happen to you, and you will lose your left eye."

"I can't stand it anymore," I repeated myself. "If you won't tell me, let me leave you and return to my own people. I can't bear to watch you anymore."

Thereupon they said to me, "Remember, young man, that if evil should happen to you, we shall not offer you refuge or allow you to stay with us."

Then they fetched a ram, slaughtered it, and skinned it. After doing this, they gave me a knife and said, "Take this skin, wrap it around you, and we will sew it together. Soon a bird called Rukh will come and pick you up in its claws. Then it will fly away with you and set you down on a mountain. When you feel he is no longer flying, rip open the pelt with this blade, and come out of it. The bird will be scared and fly away. After this you are to travel for half a day, and you will come to a wondrous beautiful palace towering high in the air and built of lign aloes and sandalwood and plated with red gold and studded with all kinds of emeralds and costly gems. You are to enter this palace, and there you will find the answer to your wish, for we have all entered that palace. This is why we lost our eyes and why we blacken our faces. If we were to tell you our stories now, it would take too long, for each one of us lost his left eye on a different adventure."

I rejoiced at their words, and they did exactly as they said they would. Then the Rukh carried me to the mountain, and I came out of the skin and walked until I reached the palace. The door stood open as I entered, and I found myself in a spacious and beautiful hall that was as wide as a racetrack for horses, and around it there were a hundred chambers with doors of sandalwood and aloes wood, plated with red gold and furnished with silver rings as knockers. At the upper end of the hall I saw forty damsels sumptuously dressed, each one bright as the moon. They were the most beautiful women I had ever seen, and even the most ascetic man in the world would have become their slave and obeyed their will on first sight. When they saw me the whole group came up to me and said, "Welcome, and may you be content with us, my lord! We have been expecting you for a month. Praise be Allah who has sent us one who is worthy of us, just as we are worthy of you!" Then they made me sit down on a high divan and continued, "You are our lord and master this day, and we are your servants and handmaids. So give us any orders you desire."

They were a wonder to behold, and soon one of them rose and set meat before me. I ate, and they ate with me. Then some of them warmed water and washed my hands and feet and changed my clothes. Others prepared sherbets and provided us with something to drink. All of them gathered around me full of joy and happy about my arrival. Then they sat down and held conversations with me until nightfall, when five of them arose, laid the trays, spread them with flowers, fragrant herbs, and fruits, fresh and dried, and confections in profusion. At last they brought out a fine wine service with rich old wine, and we sat down to drink. Some sang songs, and others played the lute, recorders, and other instruments, and the bowl went merrily around. As a result, I was glad and forgot the sorrows of the world and said, "This is life! How sad that it is fleeting!" I enjoyed their company until the time came for us to rest. Our heads were all warm with wine, when they said, "Oh lord, choose among us who will be your bedfellow this night, and she will not lie with you again until forty days have passed."

So I chose a girl who had a beautiful face, with a perfect figure, and coal-black eyes. Her hair was long and jet-black, and she had slightly parted teeth and eyebrows that joined together. It was as if she were some limber graceful branch or the slender stalk of sweet basil. Indeed, her beauty was amazing. So I lay with her that night, and I had never enjoyed a night like that. When morning arrived, the damsels carried me to the Hammam bath, where they bathed me and dressed me in the fairest garments. Then they served food, and we ate and drank. The cup went around until nightfall, when I chose a soft and graceful maiden from among them. Then I spent a splendid night with her, and to be brief, my lady, I stayed with them eating and drinking to my heart's content. We conversed and caroused, and each night I lay with a different maiden. But at the beginning of the new year they came to me in tears and wished me farewell. As they were weeping and clinging to me, I wondered what was happening, and I asked, "What's the matter? You're breaking my heart."

"If only we had never met you!" they exclaimed. "Though we have spent time with many men, none have been more pleasant or more courteous than you." And they continued weeping.

"But explain to me more clearly," I said. "Why are you weeping? You are breaking my heart."

"Oh our lord and master, it is the separation that is making us weep," they said. "And only you are the cause of our tears. If you listen to us, we need never part, and if you do not listen to us, we shall never see each other again. But our heart tells us that you won't listen to our words, and this is why we are crying."

"Tell me your story and what I must do," I demanded.

"You must know, oh lord," they responded, "that we are the daughters of kings, who have met here and have lived together for years. Once every year we are absent for forty days, and afterward we return and dwell here for the rest of the twelve months, eating, drinking, taking our pleasure, and enjoying ourselves. We are about to depart according to our custom, and we fear that you will not obey our instructions and charge while we are gone. We are going to give you the keys of the palace which contains forty chambers, and you may open thirty-nine, but beware—and we beg you by Allah and by our own lives—do not open the fortieth door, because there is something in there that could cause us to separate forever."

"You can rest assured that I shall not open it," I said.

Then one of them came up to me, embraced me, and recited a poem. Afterward, when I saw her weeping, I said, "By Allah, I shall never open that fortieth door. Never ever."

I said farewell to her, and thereupon they all departed, flying away like birds, and they signaled farewell with their hands as they left me alone in the palace. When evening drew near, I opened the door of the first chamber, and after entering it, I found myself in a place like paradise. It was a garden with trees of the freshest green and ripe fruits that glistened in the sun. Birds were singing, and their clear songs rang through the fair terrain. The sights and sounds brought solace to my spirit. As I walked among the trees and smelled the flowers in the breeze, I heard the birds sing the praise of the Almighty, and I took in the beauty of all the fruits. When I left the place and locked the door, everything was as it had been before. The next day, I opened the second door, and when I entered, I found myself on a spacious plain set with tall palm trees and watered by a running stream whose banks were lined with bushes of rose and jasmine, while violets, lilies, and other flowers carpeted the borders. The breath of the breeze swept over these sweet-smelling plants, and their delicious odors spread throughout the place, perfuming the world and filling my soul with delight. After taking my pleasure there for a while, I left and closed the door, and everything was as it had been before. Then I opened the third door, and I saw a high open hall with walls and floors made out of marble and other precious stones. Cages made of sandalwood were hanging about the place, and they were full of birds which made sweet music as if a thousand voices were singing. My heart was filled with pleasure, and I forgot my grief, and I slept in the aviary until dawn. Then I unlocked the door of the fourth chamber and found a grand salon with forty smaller chambers leading off it. All their doors stood open, and I entered and found them full of pearls, jacinths, beryls, emeralds, corals, carbuncles, and many other precious gems and jewels that were indescribably beautiful. I was stunned by the sight and said to myself, "All these things together could only be found among the treasures of a king of kings. I don't think that all the monarchs of the world could have collected the likes of these things!" My heart expanded, and my sorrows ceased. "Verily," I said, "I am now the monarch of these times, since, by Allah's grace, this enormous wealth is mine, and I have forty damsels under my charge, and nobody claims them except myself." Then I continued opening door after door until thirty-nine days had passed. During that time I entered every chamber except the one that the princesses had charged me not to open. But my thoughts kept returning to the forbidden fortieth door, and Satan urged me to open it for my own undoing, and I did not have the patience to withstand the temptation, even though there was only one day left of my trial. So I went to the fortieth door, and after a moment's hesitation, I opened the gold-plated door and entered. I was met by a perfume that I had never smelled before, and so sharp and subtle was the odor that I felt as if I were drunk with wine. Consequently, I fell to the floor in a faint, which lasted a full hour. When I came to myself, I took heart and continued on my way until I found myself in a chamber with a floor spread with saffron and blazing with light from golden candelabras and lamps with precious oils which gave off a scent of musk and ambergris.

Soon I noticed a noble steed, black as night, already
saddled and bridled. It was standing before two mangers,
one of clear crystal that contained husked sesame and
the other, also made of crystal, that contained water with
a rose and musk scent. When I saw this, I was astounded
and said to myself, "There must be some wondrous mystery about this animal." Since Satan enticed me, I led
the horse outside the palace and mounted it, but the
horse would not stir from its place. I kicked its sides
with my heels, but it would not move, and then I took
the whip and struck it hard. When the horse felt the
blow, it neighed with a sound that was like deafening
thunder, and it opened a pair of wings and flew with me
into the heavens far beyond the eyesight of any man.
After a full hour of flight the horse descended and
landed on a terrace roof, and after shaking me off its
back, it lashed me on the face with its tail and gouged
out my left eye, causing it to roll along my cheek. Then
it flew away.

I went down from the terrace and found myself again
among the ten one-eyed young men sitting upon their
ten couches with blue covers, and they cried out when
they saw me, "No welcome to you, nor do we wish you
good cheer. We all lived the happiest of lives, and we
ate and drank the best. We took our rest on beds of
gold brocade, and we slept with our heads on the breasts
of beautiful women. But we could not wait one day to
gain the delights of one year."

"Behold!" I exclaimed. "I have become one with you,
and now I want you to bring me a tray of soot so I can
blacken my face and you can accept me into your
society."

"No, by Allah," they answered, "you will not stay
with us. You're to leave right now!"

So they drove me away, and seeing how hard they
rejected me, I realized that things were going to get
worse, and I remembered the many miseries that destiny
had written on my forehead. So I went on my way with a
heavy heart and tears in my eyes, repeating the following
words to myself: "I was sitting and relaxing, but my
boldness brought me unrest." Then I shaved my beard,

mustache, and eyebrows off, renounced the world, and
wandered the earth in the clothes of a calender, and the
Almighty kept me safe until I arrived at Baghdad, which
was this very evening, when I met these other two calenders, who were standing so bewildered. So I greeted
them, saying, "I am a stranger." And they answered,
"We, too, are strangers!" By a freak of fortune, we were
all alike, three one-eyed men all blind in the left eye.
Such, my lady, is the reason why I shaved my beard and
lost my eye.

"You may keep your head," said the lady, "and be
on your way."
"By Allah," he said, "I shall not go until I hear the
stories of these other men."
Then the lady turned toward the caliph, Ja'afar, and
Masrur and said to them, "It is now your turn to give
an account of yourselves!"
Thereupon Ja'afar stepped forward and told her what
he had told the lady who had admitted them at the door,
and when the mistress of the house heard this story and
that they were merchants and good Moslems, who had
lost their way, she said, "I grant you your lives, and now
be on your way, all of you!"
So they all went out, and when they were in the street,
the caliph said to the calenders, "Oh my friends, where
are you going to go now? Dawn has yet to break."
"By Allah," they said, "we have no idea where we
should go."
"Come and spend the rest of the night with us," said
the caliph, and turning to Ja'afar, he ordered, "Take
them home with you, and tomorrow bring them to me
so that we can write a chronicle about their adventures."
Ja'afar did as the caliph ordered, and the Commander
of the Faithful returned to his palace, but he could not
fall asleep. In fact, he lay awake thinking about the
adventures of the three calender princes, and he was
eager to learn all about the history of the ladies and the
two black bitches. No sooner did morning dawn than he
went forth and sat upon his throne. After his nobles and
lords had gathered, he turned to Ja'afar and said, "Bring

me the three ladies, the two bitches, and the three calenders."

So Ja'afar went out and returned with them all. To be sure, the ladies were all veiled. Then the minister turned to them and said in the caliph's name, "We pardon the poor way you treated us last night, considering the fact that you showed us courtesy and kindness in the beginning. And, of course, you did not know who we were. Now, however, I want you to know that you stand in the presence of the fifth of the sons of Abbas, Harun al-Rashid, brother of Caliph Musa al-Hadi, son of Al-Mansur; son of Mohammed the brother of Al-Saffah bin Mohammed, who was the first of the royal house. You are now to tell him the truth and nothing but the whole truth!"

When the ladies heard Ja'afar's words about the Commander of the Faithful, the eldest lady came forward and said, "Oh Prince of True Believers, my story is one, if it were ever written down and engraved, that would serve as a warning and an example for those who need it. Indeed, my tale is a strange one, and you may call it

The Eldest Sister's Tale

You see those two black bitches over there, oh Commander of the Faithful. Well, they are my eldest sisters by one mother and father, and these two others, the maiden who has stripes on her back and the other who went shopping, are my sisters by another mother. When my father died, each took her share of the heritage, and after a while, my mother also passed away, leaving me and my sisters three thousand dinars. So each daughter received her portion of a thousand dinars. In due course of time my sisters married with the usual festivities, and they lived with their husbands, who bought merchandise with the money of their wives and went traveling with their wives. Thus, I became separated from them. My brothers-in-law and their wives were absent for five years, during which time they spent all the money they had and became bankrupt. Moreover, the two men deserted my sisters in a foreign country, and after five years my eldest sister returned to me and appeared like a beggar in rags and tatters and a dirty old mantilla. Truly, she was in a most sorrowful plight, and at first glance I did not know my own sister, but soon I recognized her and said, "What's become of you?"

"Oh, my sister," she replied, "words cannot undo what has been done, and destiny has carried out what Allah decreed."

Then I sent her to the bath and dressed her in my clothes. After that I made a bouillon, gave her good wine, and said, "My sister, you are the eldest and have taken our parents' place. As for the inheritance I received, Allah has blessed it and enabled me to increase it. My circumstances are comfortable now, because I have made a great deal of money by spinning and cleaning silk. So, you and I shall share my wealth."

I treated her with kindness, and she lived with me for a whole year, during which time our thoughts were always with our other sister. Soon, she, too, came home in even worse condition than my eldest sister. Once again, I treated her as honorably as I did the first, and each of them had a share of my wealth. After some time had passed, they said to me, "Oh sister, we desire to marry again. We have no patience to spend our days without husbands and to lead the lives of bewitched widows."

"By Allah!" I cried. "You have not done very well in marriage, and nowadays good and honest men are very hard to find. I really don't think it is advisable for you to marry, especially since your first tries ended in disasters."

But they would not accept my advice and married without my consent. Nevertheless, I provided them with dowries out of my money, and they went away with their mates. Soon thereafter, however, their husbands deceived them and took whatever they could get their hands on and left them in the lurch. Thereupon, they came back to me and were ashamed about what had happened. They were abject and made excuses to me. "Pardon our fault," they said, "and do not be angry with us, for though you are younger than we are, you are also wiser. So let us come live with you as your handmaidens so we may have something to eat."

"I welcome you, my sisters," I replied. "Nothing is dearer to me than you."

So, I took them in and was even more kind to them than I had been before. We continued to live in a caring relationship for a full year, when I decided to sell my wares abroad. So I hired a large ship and equipped it with all the necessities and merchandise for my voyage. Then I asked my sisters, "Do you want to stay at home while I travel, or would you like to accompany me?"

"We shall travel with you," they answered, "for we cannot bear to be separated from you."

So I divided my money into two parts, one that I was going to take with me, and the other part was left in charge of a trustworthy person, because, as I said to myself, if some accident happened to the ship and we survived, we would find some money on our return that would stand us in good stead.

So I took my sisters, and we set sail. But the captain was careless, and the ship went off course so that we entered a strange sea. For a while we were not even aware of this, and the wind was favorable for ten days when the lookout man climbed the masthead and cried out, "Good news!" Then he came down and was as happy as a lark. "I've spotted a city in the distance," he reported.

Upon hearing this news, we rejoiced, and before an hour had passed, the buildings of the city could clearly be seen, and we asked the captain, "What is the name of this city?"

"By Allah," he replied. "I don't know. I never saw it before, and I never sailed these seas in my life. But since our troubles have ended in safety, all you have to do is to land there with your merchandise, and if you find that you can sell your things profitably, then you should sell. If not, we shall rest here two days, obtain provisions, and go on our way."

So we entered the port, and the captain went into town and was absent for a while. When he returned, he said to us, "Go into the city, and you will be astounded by what Allah has done, and you had better pray to be preserved from his righteous wrath!"

So we went into the city and saw men holding staves in their hands, but when we drew near them, they were suddenly transformed into stones by the anger of Allah. Then we entered the city and found everyone in it changed into black stones. No one was alive in any of the houses, and we were awed by the sight and threaded through the market streets, where we found all the goods and gold and silver lying in their places. We were happy to find things as they were and said, "Doubtless there is some mystery to all this."

Then we spread out and went through the streets, and each one of us busily picked up money, rich materials, and other things without paying much attention to friend or comrade. Upon entering the king's castle through a gate of golden red, I found the king himself seated in the midst of his chamberlains, nabobs, emirs, and viziers, all clad in unique and wonderful garments, I drew nearer and saw him sitting on a throne inlaid with pearls and gems. His robes were made of gold cloth adorned with all kinds of jewels, each one flashing like a star. Around him stood fifty mamelukes, white slaves, clad in different kinds of silk and holding their drawn swords in their hands. But when I drew near to them, they were suddenly turned into black stones. I was totally confused by this, but I walked on and entered the great hall of the harem, whose walls I found hung with tapestries of gold-striped silk and spread with silken carpets embroidered with golden flowers. Here I saw the queen lying at full length arrayed in robes purled with fresh young pearls. On her head was a diadem set with many sorts of gems, and there were necklaces around her neck. All her garments and ornaments were in a natural state, but she had been turned into a black stone because of Allah's wrath. So I walked up and came upon a place lined with marble and gold carpets and tapestry hung all around. At the far end of one of the walls there was an alcove whose curtains were strung with pearls. They were let down, and I saw a light issuing from there. So I drew near and perceived that the light came from a precious stone as big as an ostrich egg set at the upper end of the alcove upon a little chryselephantine couch made of ivory and gold. Blazing like the sun, this jewel cast its rays far and wide. The couch was also spread with all kinds of silken stuffs whose richness and beauty would amaze any viewer. I was dazzled by all this, especially when I saw that the candles had already been lit, and I said to myself, "Someone must have lit these candles." Then I went forth to the kitchen, and I eventually made my way to the king's treasure chambers. I continued to explore the palace and went from place to place. I forgot myself in my awe and marveled at what I saw, and I was drowned in thought when night set in, and I would have left the palace, but I did not know how to find the exit. In fact, I lost my way and had to return to the alcove. The candles showed me the way, and I sat down on a couch and wrapped myself in a cover. After I repeated some passages from the Koran, I wanted to sleep, but I was unable to because I was so restless. When midnight arrived, I heard a voice chanting the Koran in the sweetest tones. So I arose, glad to hear the silence broken, and followed the sounds until I reached a closet whose door stood ajar. Then, peeping through the slit, I saw an oratory with a niche for praying. In it were two wax candles and lamps hanging from the ceiling. On the floor was a handsome young man sitting on a carpet and reading from the Koran. I was astonished to see him alone and alive among the people of the city. So I entered and greeted him with a salaam. Thereupon, he raised his eyes and returned my salaam. Then I said to him, "By all that is holy and truthful in Allah's book, I beg you to answer my question."

He looked at me with a smile and replied, "Oh hand-maid of Allah, first tell me why you have come here, and I shall tell you what has happened to me and the people of this city, and how I escaped their doom."

So, I told him my story, which he found astonishing, and I asked him about the people of his city, and he

responded, "Have patience with me for a while." Then
he reverently closed the holy book, put it into a satin
bag, and sat me by his side. When I looked at him,
he was like the full moon, a handsome face, and well-
proportioned, bright cheeks. He was dressed in eloquent
clothes, and as I glanced at him I sighed a thousand
times, and my heart was completely captivated by him.

"Oh my lord and my love," I asked him, "please respond to my question."

"To hear is to obey," he said. "Let me begin by telling
you that this city was the capital of my father, who is
the king you saw transformed by Allah's wrath into a
black stone, and the queen you found in the alcove is
my mother. They and all the people of the city were
Magians, who worshiped fire instead of the Omnipotent
Lord, and they tended to make oaths by calling on the
sun and the moon. My father did not have a son until
he was blessed with me in the latter part of his life, and
he educated me until I grew up and was faced with a
prosperous future. Now it so happened there was an old
woman, a Moslem, who lived with us. She believed
deeply in Allah, but she did not show it. Instead, she
outwardly conformed to the religion of my people. Indeed, my father placed complete confidence in her, for
he thought she was trustworthy and virtuous, and he
treated her with increasing kindness and thought that
she shared his convictions. So when I was almost finished
with my education, my father placed me under her care
and said, 'Take him and educate him and teach him the
laws of our faith. Let him have the best instruction, and
keep him under your protection and care.' So she took
me and taught me the tenets of Al-Islam with the divine
ordinances of the Wuzu ablution and the five daily prayers, and she made me learn the Koran by heart, often
repeating, 'Serve no one but Allah Almighty!' When I
mastered all this knowledge, she said to me, 'Oh my
son, keep all this concealed from your father, and reveal
nothing to him. Otherwise, he might slay you!' So I hid
it from him, and I had lived this way for ten days when
the old woman died. In the meantime, the people of the

city became even more impious, arrogant, and erred in their ways.

"One day, as they went about their usual affairs, they suddenly heard a loud and terrible sound, and a voice as loud as roaring thunder exclaimed so that everyone could hear from far and near, 'Oh people of this city, stop your fire worship, and adore Allah, the compassionate king!'

"Upon hearing this, fear and terror fell upon the citizens of the city, and they rushed to my father the king and asked, 'What is this terrifying voice we have just heard? We are totally confused and frightened.'

" 'Do not let a voice frighten you,' answered the king. 'Do not let it shake your steadfast spirits or turn you away from your rightful faith.'

"Their hearts were swayed by his words, and they did not stop worshiping the fire. Indeed, they persisted in rebellion for a full year after they had first heard the voice and even after they heard it the following two years. They continued their malpractices until one day at the break of dawn, judgment and the wrath of heaven descended upon them without warning. Allah brought about their transformation into black stones and their beasts and cattle as well. Nobody was saved except me, for I was engaged in devotion to Allah at the time. From that day until now I have been doing what you saw— praying, fasting, and reading and reciting the Koran. But I have, indeed, grown exhausted and bored because there has been nobody to keep me company."

Then I said to him (for, in truth, he had won my heart and was the lord of my life and soul), "Young man, will you travel with me to Baghdad and visit the holy men and the men who are learned in law and divinity? This way your understanding of theology will increase. And I want to assure you that the lady who stands before you will be your handmaid, even though I am the head of my family and mistress over men, eunuchs, servants, and slaves. Indeed, I had no life until I met you. I have a ship here that is loaded with merchandise, and in truth, destiny drove me to this city so that I might become acquainted with your situation. Fate decided that we should meet." And I continued to try to persuade him and spoke with great art until he consented.

That night I slept at his feet, and I hardly knew where I was because I was so happy. As soon as dawn arrived, I arose, and we entered the treasuries and took as many valuable things as we could carry. Then we went down from the castle to the city, where we were met by the captain, my sisters, and slaves who had been searching for me. When they saw me coming, they rejoiced and asked what had kept me, and I told them all that I had seen and related the story of the young prince and why the people had all been transformed into black stones. Thereupon they were all astonished, but when my two sisters saw me by the side of my young lover, they became jealous, and in their anger, they decided to plot some mischief against me. We waited for a fair wind and went onboard rejoicing and ready to travel because we had all found treasures, but my most important treasure was the young man. We waited awhile until the wind turned fair, and then we set sail. Now, as we sat talking, my sisters asked me, "And what will you do with this handsome young man?"

"I plan to make him my husband," I responded, and then I turned to him and said, "Oh my lord, I want to make you a proposition, and I hope that you will not be cross with me. When we reach Baghdad, my native city, I shall offer you my life as handmaiden in holy matrimony, and you will become my baron, and I shall be your femme."

He answered, "I hear and obey. You are my lady and my mistress, and whatever you want is my desire."

Then I turned to my sisters and said, "This is my gain, and I am content with this young man, and those who have obtained some of my property, I propose that you keep it as a sign of my goodwill."

"You have spoken and done well," my two sisters responded, but they kept planning to trick me.

We kept sailing with the fair wind, until we moved from the sea of peril to the sea of safety, and a few days later, we landed in Bassorah, whose buildings loomed clear before us as evening fell. But after we had retired to rest and were sound asleep, my sisters arose, carried me, bed and all, to the deck of the ship, and threw me, bed and all, overboard. They did the same thing with the young prince, who, since he could not swim, sank and was drowned, and Allah enrolled him in the noble army of martyrs. As for me, I only wish to heaven that I had drowned with him, but Allah decided that I should be saved. So, when I awoke, I found myself in the sea and saw the ship making off like a flash of lightning, but Allah threw a piece of wood in my way, and I climbed onto it. The waves tossed me back and forth until they cast me on an island coast that was uninhabited. I landed and walked around the island during the rest of the night, and when morning arrived, I saw a rough track barely fit for a child to tread. But it led to what proved to be a shallow ford that connected the island with the mainland. As soon as the sun had risen, I spread my garments out to dry in its rays, and I ate some fruit and drank water. Then I set out along the track and continued walking until I reached the mainland. Now, just when I was about two hours away from the major city, a huge serpent appeared all at once. It was the size of a palm tree and came toward me in great haste, gliding from right to left until it was almost on top of me. Its tongue rolled along the ground and swept the dust as it ran. It was being pursued by a dragon who was no longer than two lances and built like a slender spear. Although the serpent was so frightened that it moved faster than it normally would, and although it kept wriggling from side to side, the dragon overtook it and seized the serpent by the tail. Tears streamed down, and its tongue was thrust out in agony. I took pity on the serpent, and therefore I picked up a stone and called upon Allah for help. Then I threw the stone at the dragon's head and hit it with such force that it died on the spot. Meanwhile, the serpent opened a pair of wings, flew into the air, and disappeared before my eyes. I sat down and was astounded by that adventure, but I was weary and overcome by sleep. When I awoke, I found a jet-black damsel sitting by my feet and shampooing them. By her side stood two black bitches, who were my sisters, oh Commander of the Faithful. I was ashamed, and after I sat up, I asked her, "Oh my lady, who and what are you?"

"How soon you have forgotten me!" she responded. "I am the creature you saved through your good deed, for I am the serpent whom through Allah's intervention you saved from the dragon. I am a jinniyah, and he was a jinnee who hated me. No one could have saved my life but you. Well, as soon you freed me from him, I flew on the wind to the ship from which your sisters threw you. I removed everything in the ship to your house, and then I ordered my attending marids to sink the ship. Meanwhile, I transformed your two sisters into these black bitches, for I know everything that has happened between you. As for the young man, he has unfortunately drowned."

Upon saying this, she flew with me and the two bitches to the terrace roof of my house, in which I found all my property from the ship, and not a single thing was missing.

"Now," continued the jinniyah, "I swear by the ring of Solomon that unless you give these bitches three hundred blows with the whip every day, I shall come and imprison you beneath the earth forever."

"To hear is to obey," I responded, and away she flew. But before she departed, she cried out, "I swear by him who made the two seas flow that if you do not follow my orders, I shall come and transform you like your sisters."

Since then, oh Commander of the Faithful, I have beaten them every day with three hundred blows until their blood flows with my tears. Indeed, I pity them all the time, and they know full well that their whipping is no fault of mine, and they accept my apologies. Such is my tale and my story.

And the caliph was astounded by her adventures and then signaled to Ja'afar, who said to the second lady, the doorkeeper, "And how did you manage to get the welts and scratches on your body?"

So she began

The Doorkeeper's Tale

You should know, oh Commander of the Faithful, that I once had a father, who left me a great deal of money after his death. I remained single for a short time, but then married one of the richest men in the city. I lived with him for a year, when he, too, died, and my share of his property amounted to eighty thousand dinars in gold. Thus I became extremely rich, and my reputation spread far and wide, for I had ten sets of clothes made for me, each worth a thousand dinars. One day, as I was sitting at home, an old woman suddenly appeared with jaws like lanterns, hollow cheeks, scant eyebrows, a bald head, broken teeth, a crooked and bent back, a blotched face, and hair like a black-and-white speckled snake. She was a veritable fright, and when the old woman entered, she bowed, kissed the ground before me, and said, "I am a widow, and my only daughter is to be wed tonight. We are poor folk and strangers in this city, and since we do not know a soul, we are broken-hearted. So, if you would like to do a good deed and earn a reward in heaven, we would appreciate it if you would attend her display. When the ladies of this city hear that you will be present at this event, they will also present themselves. This way you will comfort her, for she is low in spirits, and she has no one to look after her except Allah the Most High." When she broke down into tears, I took pity and said, "Hearing is consenting, and if it pleases Allah, I shall do something more for her. I declare that she will be shown to her bridegroom only in my clothes, ornaments, and jewelry."

Upon hearing this the old woman rejoiced, bowed her head to my feet, and kissed them. "May Allah reward you with wealth, and may He comfort your heart in the same way that you have comforted mine. But, my lady, you need not do me this favor right away. If you are ready by suppertime, then I shall come and fetch you."

Then she kissed my hand and went her way, while I set about stringing my pearls, putting on my brocades, and making my toilette. Little did I know what fortune had in store for me. Before I knew it, the old woman stood before me, simpering and smiling, until she showed every tooth stump in her mouth.

"Oh my mistress, all the ladies of the city have arrived, and when I informed them that you would be present, they were very glad, and they are now awaiting you and looking forward to your arrival and the honor of meeting you."

So I threw on my mantilla, and making the old crone walk in front of me and my handmaidens behind me, I strode forth until we came to a street that had been recently cleaned, and the breeze blew cool and sweet. Here we were stopped by an arched gate leading to a palace whose walls rose tall and proud and whose pinnacle was crowned by the clouds. The old woman knocked at the gate, and after it was opened, we entered and found a vestibule, spread with carpets. Lamps were hung all around, and wax candles were in the candelabra adorned with pendants of precious gems and gold. We passed through this place and entered a salon that was incomparable in its beauty and grandeur. There was silk on the walls and the floors, and it was illuminated with branches and tapers arranged in a double row that formed an avenue leading to the end of the salon, where a couch of juniper wood was standing that was encrusted with pearls and gems and surrounded by mosquito curtains of satin.

No sooner had we taken notice of this when a young girl came forward, and she had a face and form more perfect than the moon when it is its fullest. The beautiful young girl came down from the estrade and said to me, "Welcome and good cheer to my sister, the dearly beloved and illustrious lady!" After she sat down with me, she continued speaking and said, "Oh my sister, I have a brother, who has noticed you at various wedding feasts and festivities. He is a handsome young man, and he has fallen desperately in love with you, for destiny has provided you with perfection and great beauty. So he paid the old woman in silver to visit you and find some way to bring you and him together. He has heard that you are one of the noble ladies in this city, and he is no less than you. Since he would like to wed you in accordance with Allah and His Apostle, he has set up this meeting so I could talk to you. Certainly, there is no shame in doing what is lawful and right."

When I heard these words and saw myself somewhat entrapped in this house, I said, "I am at your disposal."

She was delighted at hearing this and clapped her hands, whereupon a door opened, and out came a young man in the prime of his life, exquisitely dressed, a model of handsomeness, symmetry, grace, and gentleness. He had gentle winning manners and bewitching eyes. As soon as I looked at him, I was captivated by him and fell in love. Then he sat by my side and talked with me for a while. When the young lady came again and clapped her hands, a side door opened, and out came the kazi with his four assessors as witnesses. After greeting us and sitting down, they drew up and wrote down the marriage contract between me and the young man. Then they retired, and the young man turned to me and said, "May we have a pleasant and blessed night, but I do have a condition to place on you."

"What is it, my lord?" I asked.

Thereupon he rose and fetched a copy of the Holy Book and presented it to me, saying, "Swear on this book that you will never look at another man other than me nor give your body or heart to him."

I willingly swore this oath, and he was very happy and embraced me, while I was totally overcome by love for him. Then the servants set out the table before us, and we ate and drank until we were satisfied, and I longed for night to come. When night finally did arrive, he led me to the bridal chamber and slept with me on the bed and continued to kiss and embrace me until morning. Never had I ever imagined such a night in my wildest dreams! I lived in happiness and delight with him for a full month, and at the end of this time, I asked for his permission to go on foot to the bazaar where I wanted to buy some special material, and he gave me the permission. So I put on my mantilla and took the old woman and a slave girl with me. I went straight to the khan of the silk merchants, where I sat down in the front of the shop with a young merchant whom the old woman had recommended. "This young man's father died when he was a boy," she said, "and he left him a great store of wealth. He has a fine stock of goods, and you will find what you want in his shop, for there is none better in the bazaar." Then she said to him, "Show this lady your most costly stuff."

"I am at your service," he replied.

Then she whispered to me, "Say a civil word to him."

But I replied, "I have pledged not to address any man except my husband."

And as the old woman began to sound the praise of the young merchant, I was sharp with her and said, "I want none of your sweet speeches. I have come here to buy whatever I need and then to return home."

So he brought me all that I wanted, and I offered him his money, but he refused to take it, saying, "Let this be a gift for my guest today!"

Then I said to the old woman, "If he will not take the money, give him back his stuff!"

"By Allah," he cried, "I shall not take a thing from you. I shall not sell it to you for gold or silver, but only for a single kiss. A kiss is more precious to me than everything in my shop."

The old woman turned to me and said, "What do you have to lose? You've heard what this young man said. What harm will it do you if he gets a kiss from you and you get what you want at that price?"

"May Allah protect me," I replied. "Don't you realize that I am bound by an oath?"

But she answered, "Just let him have one kiss, and don't speak to him or lean over. This way you will have kept your oath and your silver, and you will not be harmed in any way whatsoever."

And she continued to persuade me and plead with me and make light of the matter until evil entered my mind and I finally consented. So I veiled my eyes and held up the edge of my mantilla between me and the people who were passing, and he put his mouth to my cheek, under the veil. But while kissing me, he bit me so hard that it tore flesh from my cheek, and blood streamed down my cheek, causing me to faint. The old woman caught me in her arms, and when I came to myself, I found the shop was shut and that she was grieving over me. "Thank heaven for averting what might have been worse!" she said. "Come take heart and let us go home before the matter becomes public and you are dishonored. And when you are safe inside the house, you are to pretend to be sick. Lie down and cover yourself, and I shall bring you powders and plasters to cure this bite. Your wound will heal in three days at the latest."

So, after a while, I arose and was extremely distressed and terrified. But I walked on little by little until I reached the house. Then I feigned sickness and said that I had to lie down. When night came, my husband came in and said, "What has happened to you during your excursion, my darling?"

"I'm not well," I replied. "I have a very bad headache."

Then he lit a candle, drew near to me, looked closely, and said, "What is the wound that I see on your cheek?"

"When I left with your permission to buy some material, a camel loaded with firewood jostled me, and one of the pieces of wood tore my veil and wounded my cheek, as you can see. Indeed, the alleys and streets of this city are very narrow."

"Tomorrow," he stated, "I shall go and complain to the governor so that he punishes all the wood merchants in Baghdad."

"By Allah," I answered, "do not go to such trouble for such a minor thing as this. The fact is, I was riding on an ass, and it stumbled and threw me to the ground. My cheek hit a stick, or perhaps it was a piece of glass, and I got this wound."

"Then tomorrow I shall go to Ja'afar the Barmaki," my husband said, "and I shall tell him the story so that he will kill every donkey boy in Baghdad."

"Would you have all the donkey boys in Baghdad

killed just because of my wound?" I asked. "After all.
it was Allah's will that I was wounded."

But he answered, "This is the way it must be," and
he jumped up and kept asking so many questions that I
became confused and frightened. I stuttered and stam-
mered, and I said, "This was merely an accident, and it
was Allah's will." Then, oh Commander of the Faithful,
he guessed the truth and said, "You have not kept
your oath."

Upon saying this, he cried loudly, and a door opened.
In came seven black slaves, whom he commanded to
drag me from my bed and throw me into the middle of
the room. Furthermore, he ordered one of them to hold
my elbows down and to squat on my head. A second
sat on my knees and held my feet. Then he drew his
sword, gave it to a third slave, and said, "Strike her, oh
Sa'ad, and cut her in two. Afterward you are to take
both parts and throw them into the river so that the fish
may eat her. Such is the retribution due to those who
violate their vows and are unfaithful to their husbands."
Then he repeated to the slave. "Strike her. oh Sa'ad!"

When the slave who was sitting on me made sure of
the command he bent down to me and said, "Oh my
mistress. repeat the profession of faith and think whether
there is anything you want done, for truly this is the last
hour of your life."

"Oh good slave," said I, "wait a moment and get off
my head so that I can tell you my last wishes."

Then I raised my head and realized how disgraceful
my situation was, and I knew that I had brought my
punishment on myself by my own sin. Tears streamed
down from my eyes, and I wept, but my husband looked
at me with fury in his eyes, and my weeping only added
to his fury. I begged for his pardon and humbled myself
before him and spoke softly, saying to myself, "If only
I can find the right words so that he will perhaps refuse
to slay me, even if he takes all that I have." So I recited
some couplets about my sufferings, and when I ended
my verse, I wept again, and he looked at me, reviled me
in abusive language, and cried out to the slave, "Cut her
in half so that we are rid of her! She is of no use to us!"

So the slave drew close to me, oh Commander of the Faithful, and I stopped speaking and prepared myself for death, when all of a sudden the old woman rushed in and threw herself at my husband's feet. She began kissing them and weeping. "Oh my son," she cried, "by rights of my bearing you and serving you all these years, I beg you to pardon this lady. She has done nothing to deserve this doom. You are a very young man, and I am afraid that you may be making a mistake, for it is said, 'Whoever slays will be slain.' As for this wanton woman, drive her from your doors, from your love, and from your heart." And she continued begging, imploring, and weeping until he relented and said, "I shall pardon her, but I want to set my mark on her that will be with her for the rest of her life."

Then he ordered the slaves to drag me along the ground and stretch me out at full length and to strip off my clothes. When the slaves had sat on me so that I could not move, he fetched a rod and began beating me on the back and sides until I lost consciousness from all the pain, and I thought I was going to die. Then he commanded the slaves to take me away as soon as it was dark. The old woman was to go with them and show them the way to the house in which I lived before my marriage. Then they did their lord's bidding and delivered me to my old home and went their way. I did not revive from my fainting spell until dawn, when I tended to my wounds with ointments and other medicaments. Nevertheless, my sides and ribs still showed signs of the rod, as you have seen. I was very weak and lay in bed for four months before I was able to rise and regain my health. At the end of that time I went to the house where all this had happened and found it a ruin. The street had been destroyed, and there was nothing but heaps of rubbish where the building had once stood, and I could not learn how all this had come about. So I went on my way and decided to go to my sister on my father's side, and I found her with these two black bitches. I greeted her and told her what had happened to me and my entire story, and she said, "Oh sister, who is ever safe from the spite of time? Be grateful to Allah, who has brought you to safety." Then she told me her story, what had happened to her and her two sisters, and how things had ended.

So we decided to live together, and the subject of marriage was never mentioned during these years. After a while we were joined by our other sister, who goes out every morning to buy all that we need for day and night. And we continued to live this way until last night. In the morning our sister went out to the market as usual, and then we invited the porter inside as well as the three calenders. We treated them kindly and honorably. Some time later, three grave and respectable merchants from Mosul joined us and told us about their adventures. We sat talking with them, but we also set one condition, which they violated. Therefore we treated them as they deserved and made them repeat the stories of their lives. They did as we asked, and so we forgave their offense. Then they departed from us, and this morning we were unexpectedly summoned to appear before you. Such is our story!

The caliph was astounded by her words and ordered her tale to be written down as a chronicle and stored in the royal archives. Then he asked the eldest lady, "Do you know the whereabouts of the ifritah who cast a spell over your sisters?"

"Oh Commander of the Faithful," the lady replied, "she gave me a ringlet of her hair and told me, 'Whenever you want to see me, burn a couple of these hairs, and I shall be with you instantaneously, even if it were somewhere beyond the Caucasian Mountains.'"

"Bring the ringlet here," commanded the caliph.

So she brought it and threw the whole lock onto the fire. As soon as the odor of the burning hair had permeated the room, the palace shook and trembled, and everyone present heard a rumbling and rolling of thunder and a noise like wings. All of a sudden, the jinniyah, who had once been a serpent, stood in the caliph's presence. Since she was a Moslem, she saluted him and said, "Peace be with you, oh Vicar of Allah."

"May peace also be with you," he replied, "and may you have the mercy and blessing of Allah."

"You know, of course," she continued, "that this lady did me a kind deed, and I cannot thank her enough, for she saved me from my death and destroyed my enemy. Since I had seen how her sisters had dealt with her, I felt myself bound to avenge her by transforming her sisters into bitches. But if you desire their release, oh Commander of the Faithful, I shall release them to please you and her, for I am of the Moslem faith."

"Release them, and afterward we shall look into the affair of the beaten lady and examine her case carefully. If we can get to the truth of her story, I shall want to retaliate against the man who has wronged her."

"Oh Commander of the Faithful," said the ifritah, "I shall release the two sisters right away, and I shall reveal the man who wronged this lady and took her property, for he is the nearest of all men to you!"

Upon saying this she took a cup of water, muttered a spell over it, and uttered words that could not be understood. Then she sprinkled some of the water over the faces of the two bitches and said, "Return to your former human shape!"

All at once they were restored to their natural forms and fell to their knees in praise of the Creator. Then the ifritah said, "Oh Commander of the Faithful, if the truth must be known, the man who whipped this lady with a rod is your son Al-Amin, brother of Al-Maamun, for he had heard of the beauty and loveliness of this woman, and he tricked her into marriage through a lover's stratagem. Then he committed the crime of whipping her. Yet, he is not to be blamed, for he did set a condition on her, and she swore by a solemn oath not to do a certain thing."

When the caliph heard the words of the ifritah and knew who had beaten the damsel, he was astonished and said, "Praise be to Allah the Almighty, who has shown great mercy toward me, enabling me to rescue these two ladies from sorcery and torture, and allowing me to know the secret of this lady's history. And now, by

Allah, I shall perform a deed that will be recorded for history and will be known long after we are gone."

Then he summoned his son Al-Amin and questioned him in private about the second lady, and his son told the whole truth. Then the caliph commanded that the kazis, their witnesses, the three calenders, and the first lady with her three sisters be brought into his presence. Then he married the three sisters to the three calenders, whom he knew were princes and sons of kings, and he appointed them as his chamberlains with appropriate salaries and allowances, and they were lodged in his palace at Baghdad. He returned the beaten lady to his son, Al-Amin, and renewed the marriage contract between them, returned the great wealth, and commanded that the house be rebuilt and made even fairer than it was before. As for himself, he wed the last lady and lay with her that night. The next day he had an apartment set up for her in his seraglio and placed handmaidens at her disposal and gave her a fixed daily allowance. And the people marveled at their caliph's generosity, his natural beneficence and royal wisdom. Nor did he forget to have all the stories recorded in his annals.

The Sleeper and the Waker

There was once a merchant in Baghdad who had a son named Abu al-Hasan al-Khali'a. When the merchant died, he left a great deal of wealth to his son, who divided it into two equal parts. One half was put away for safekeeping, and the other half was spent. He fell into some bad company, sons of other merchants, and he drank and attended feasts until all his wealth was wasted. So he went to his friends and drinking companions and explained to them that he had lost all his money. But none of them paid attention to him or even deigned to answer him. Consequently, he returned to his mother with a broken heart and told her what had happened to him and how his friends had treated him in such a thoughtless and indifferent manner.

"Oh Abu al-Hasan, this is the way such men are in these times," she responded. "If you have money, they are your friends, but if you have nothing, they shun you."

And she went on to console him, while he bemoaned his fate. His tears flowed, and he repeated these lines: "When my wealth diminishes, nobody is there to help me. When my wealth grows, everyone is friendly. I have all the friends I need when I am wealthy, and when my wealth vanishes, my friends all turn into foes!"

Then he rose and went to the place where he had stored the other half of his inheritance. He took it and began living well again, and he swore that he would never again mingle with a single one of those young men he had known. He decided that he would share his company only with a stranger and spend only one evening of entertainment with him, and afterward he would

W.H.R.

never want to see him again. In keeping with his resolution he began sitting every evening on the bridge of the Tigris and gazing at everyone who would pass by him. If he saw the man was a stranger, he made friends with him and took him to his house, where he conversed and caroused with him all night until morning. Then he would bid him farewell and never greet him again with the salaam. Nor would he ever approach or invite him again. He continued to act this way for a full year until one day, while he sat on the bridge in his usual way and waited for a stranger with whom he might spend the night, lo and behold, who should come by but the Caliph Al-Rashid and Masrur, his bodyguard, disguised as merchants as was their custom. So Abu al-Hasan looked at them, and rising to greet them because he did not know them, said, "What do you say? Would you like to come with me to my home so that you may eat and drink with me? Whatever I have is at your disposal, and I have freshly baked bread in a platter, cooked meat, and strained wine."

The caliph refused this invitation, but Abu al-Hasan would not take no for an answer and said, "May Allah go with you, my lord. Do come with me and be my guest for the night. Please do not disappoint me!"

And he insisted and kept cajoling until the caliph consented, whereupon Abu al-Hasan rejoiced. As he walked in front of the caliph, he kept talking until they came to his house, and he led the caliph into the salon. Al-Rashid entered a hall, which was filled with marvelous things and had a fountain encased with gold in the center. The caliph ordered his guard to wait at the door, and as soon as he was seated, the host brought him something to eat. So he ate, and Abu al-Hasan ate with him to make sure that the food would be to his liking. Then he removed the tray, and after they had washed their hands, the caliph sat down again. Now Abu al-Hasan set out the drinking cups and seated himself by the caliph's side, pouring him wine and entertaining him with conversation. When they had drunk a sufficient amount, the host called for a slave girl as slender as a branch of Ban, and she took a lute and sang two couplets. Abu al-Hasan's hospitality and courteous manners pleased the caliph, and he said to him, "Who are you, young man? Tell me something about yourself so that I may repay your kindness."

But Abu al-Hasan smiled and said, "Oh my lord, it's not possible. Alas, what has passed is past. After this evening we will not be able to enjoy each other's company again."

"Why not?" asked the caliph. "Why won't you tell me something about yourself?"

"My story is strange, my lord," answered Abu al-Hasan, "and there is a reason for my acting the way I do."

"And what is the cause?" said the caliph.

"The cause has a tail."

The caliph laughed at his words, and Abu al-Hasan said, "I shall explain this to you by telling you the tale of the scoundrel and the cook. So listen, my lord, to

The Story of the Scoundrel and the Cook

One fine morning a ne'er-do-well found himself without anything in the world, and since there was nothing for him to do, he lost his patience and lay down to sleep. He continued slumbering until the sun stung him and foam came out his mouth. Thereupon he got up and began walking without a penny in his pocket. He did not even have so much as a single dirham. Soon he arrived at the shop of a cook, who had set his pots and pans over the fire, washed his saucers, wiped his scales, swept his shop, and sprinkled it. Indeed, his fats and oils were clear and his spices fragrant. He himself stood behind his cooking pots ready to serve his customers. So the scoundrel, whose wits had been sharpened by hunger, went to the cook's shop, greeted him, and said, "I would like half a dirham's worth of meat and a quarter of a dirham's worth of boiled grain as well as bread."

So the cook measured everything, and the scoundrel entered the shop. Then the cook set the food before him, and he ate until he had gobbled up everything and licked the saucers and sat there wondering how he should pay the cook for everything that he had eaten. He turned his eyes on everything in the shop, and as he looked, he caught sight of a clay pan lying upside down on its mouth. So he lifted it from the ground and found a horse's tail beneath it, freshly cut and blood oozing from it. Immediately he realized that the cook adulterated his meat with horsemeat. When he discovered this fraud, he was joyfully relieved, and after washing his hands, he bowed his head and went out of the shop. When the cook saw that he was leaving without paying, he cried out, "Stop, you pest! You thief!"

So the scoundrel stopped and said to him, "How dare you cry out to me and call me those words, oh cuckold!"

The cook, who was running from his shop, became even angrier and said, "What do you mean by this, you parasite? You eat meat, millet, and bread and then leave with 'peace be with you,' as if you had not had a thing to eat and did not have to pay for it. Who do you think you are?"

"You're lying," said the ne'er do well. "You cursed son of a cuckold!" -

Thereupon the cook cried out, grabbed hold of the scoundrel's collar, and said, "Oh Moslems, this fellow was my first customer today, and he ate my food and gave me nothing."

So the people gathered around them and started accusing the thief and yelling, "Pay him what you owe!"

"I gave him a dirham before I entered the shop," replied the crook.

"May everything I sell this day be forbidden if he gave me so much as the name of a coin," said the cook. "By Allah, he gave me nothing but ate my food and would have left without paying anything."

"I gave him a dirham," the scoundrel insisted, and he cursed the cook, who returned his abuse, and they started a fight, gripping, grabbing, and throttling each other. When the people saw them fighting, they came up to them and asked them, "Why are you fighting? There's no reason to do this."

Then the scoundrel answered, "By Allah, there is a reason, and the reason has a tail."

Thereupon the cook cried out, "Yes, by Allah, now that I think about it, you did give me a dirham! Yes, he gave me a dirham, and he only spent a quarter of it. Come back and eat whatever I still owe you."

Indeed, the cook understood what he had to do when the scoundrel mentioned the tail.

* * *

"And I, my brother," added Abu al-Hasan, "I, too, have a story that has a cause, which I'll tell you."

The caliph laughed and said, "By Allah, this has been a most delightful tale! Now tell me your story and the cause."

"With pleasure, my lord," said the host. "My name is Abu al-Hasan al-Khali'a, and my father died and left me a great deal of money, which I divided in two. Then I put away one part in safekeeping, and the other I took to enjoy the pleasure of company and friendship and to amuse myself with good companions and the sons of merchants. As soon as I left one friend, I would meet another and carouse with him, and he with me. I did this for some time until I had lavished all my money on comrades and entertainment, and nothing remained. So I went to my friends and companions on whom I had spent a fortune to ask for assistance. But when I visited them, I found that they would not grace me with their help. In fact, they wouldn't even give me a crumb. So I wept and returned to my mother and told her all about my situation. 'Such are friends,' she said. 'If you have plenty, they will frequent your home and eat with you, but if you have nothing, they will cast you off and chase you away.' Then I took out the other half of my money and swore an oath that I would entertain a guest only for a single night. After that I would never again greet him or pay him any attention. This is why I said to you, 'It won't be possible. Alas, what has passed is past. We shall not be able to enjoy each other's company again.'"

When the caliph heard this, he laughed a loud laugh and said, "By Allah, my brother, you are indeed excused, now that I know your reason, and that the cause has a tail. Nevertheless, by Allah, I shall not part company."

"Oh my guest," Abu al-Hasan replied, "didn't I say to you, 'It won't be possible. Alas, what has passed is past'? Indeed, I shall never come together with you again!"

Then the caliph rose, and the host set a dish of roast goose and unleavened bread in front of him. Then they sat down, and Abu al-Hasan cut off morsels and gave them to his guest. They did not stop eating until they were full, whereupon Abu al-Hasan brought a basin, ewer, and potash, and they washed their hands. Then he lit three wax candles and spread a drinking cloth for the strained wine that was clear, old, and fragrant with a scent of virgin musk. He filled the first cup and said, "Oh my friend, let us cast ceremony aside, if you permit! I am your slave, and I shall not regret your loss!" Upon saying these words, he drank the cup and filled another, which he handed to the caliph with due reverence. His behavior and words pleased the caliph, who said to himself, "By Allah, I shall certainly repay his hospitality!"

Then Abu al-Hasan filled the cup again and handed it to the caliph, reciting these two couplets:

"If we had known of your visit, we would as sacrifice
Have poured out the blood of our heart, darkened
   our eyes;
Ay, and we would have opened our bosoms to pave
   your way
So that your feet would glide and your soul would
   rise."

When the caliph heard these verses, he took the cup from his hand and kissed it. Then he drank the wine and returned it to Abu al-Hasan, who bowed to him, filled the cup, and drank. Once again he filled it and kissed the cup three times while reciting these lines:

"Your presence honors the base,
And we confess the deed of grace;
When you absent yourself from us,
We shall find no one to fill your place."

Then he gave the cup to the caliph and said, "Drink it in good health! It will do away with sickness, bring remedies, and let the funnels of health flow free."

Thus they continued carousing and conversing until midnight, when the caliph said to his host, "Oh my brother, is there anything in your heart's desire that you would like to accomplish or something that you would like to avert?"

"By Allah," replied Abu al-Hasan, "I have no regrets about my life, although I would not mind being in a position to command and forbid so I could manage what I have on my mind!"

"By Allah," said the caliph, "tell me what is on your mind."

"I pray to heaven that I might be caliph one day," replied Abu al-Hasan, "so that I could take vengeance on my neighbors. You see, there is a mosque in the vicinity of my house, and there are four sheikhs there who consider it grievous when a guest comes to me. They trouble me with their talk and threaten that they will complain about me to the caliph. Indeed, they are always oppressing me, and I implore Allah that I might have the power for one day to beat each one of them with four hundred lashes, including the imam of the mosque, and parade them around the city of Baghdad. Then I would cry out, 'This is the reward and the least reward of those who talk too much and irritate people and poison their joy.' This is what I wish and no more."

"May Allah grant you what you seek!" said the caliph. "Now let us drink one more cup before the rise of dawn, and tomorrow night I shall be with you again."

"It won't be possible!" said Abu al-Hasan.

The caliph drank his cup and quickly placed a piece of Cretan bhang in it. Then he gave it to his host and said, "I pledge my life to you, my brother. Drink this cup from my hand!"

"Ay, I shall drink to your life from your hand."

So Abu al-Hasan took the cup and drank, but the drink had hardly settled in his stomach when he fell head over heels to the ground as if he had been slain. Thereupon the caliph went outside and said to his slave Masrur, "Go inside to the young man, and carry him to me at the palace. When you leave, make sure that you shut the door."

Upon saying this, the caliph went away, while Masrur entered the house. When he reached Abu al-Hasan, he picked him up, carried him outside, shut the door, and carried him to the palace as the night drew to an end and the cocks began crowing. Once inside the palace, he set the young man down before the caliph, who laughed at Abu al-Hasan. Then he sent for Ja'afar the Barmaki, and when the latter arrived, the caliph said, "Take a good look at that young man over there. Well, when you see him tomorrow seated on my throne and clad in my royal clothing, I want you to attend him and to command the emirs, nobles, officers, and my entire household to serve him and obey all his commands no matter what he says. If he asks you for anything, you are to listen to him and carry out all his wishes during this coming day."

"I hear and obey, your majesty," Ja'afar acknowledged the orders and withdrew, while the caliph called for the palace women and pointed to Abu al-Hasan, saying, "When this sleeper awakes later this morning, I want you to kiss the ground between his hands. You are to wait upon him, gather around him, and dress him in royal garments. You are to serve him as if he were the caliph, and you are to address him that way."

Then he taught them what they should say to him and how they should treat him. Afterward he retired to a separate room, let down a curtain before himself, and slept.

So much for the caliph, but Abu al-Hasan kept snoring in his sleep until daybreak and the rising sun drew near. Then a woman in waiting came up to him and said, "Oh our lord, the morning prayer!"

Hearing these words, he laughed, and when he opened his eyes and glanced around the palace, he saw that he was in an apartment whose walls were painted with gold and lapis lazuli, and its ceiling was dotted and starred with red gold. Around it were sleeping chambers with silk curtains embroidered in gold let down over their doors, and all around were vessels of gold and porcelain. There were also crystal, furniture, and carpets spread about and lamps burning before the niche where men prayed. There were also slave girls, eunuchs, mamelukes, slaves, boys, pages, and attendants. When he saw all this, he was bewildered and said, "By Allah, either I am dreaming, or this is paradise!"

And he shut his eyes and would have slept again, but one of the eunuchs cried out, "Oh my lord, this is not what you usually do."

Then handmaids of the palace came up to him and lifted him in a sitting position on a mattress stuffed with floss silk that was about a foot off the ground. They propped his elbow with a pillow, and he looked at the vast apartment and saw eunuchs and slave girls attending him and standing around him. Thereupon he laughed at himself and said, "By Allah, I don't seem to be awake, and yet I am not asleep!"

Totally confused, he bowed his chin toward his chest and then opened his eyes, little by little, smiling and saying, "What's happening to me?"

Then he lifted his head and sat up while the damsels laughed at him privately. Out of bewilderment he bit his finger, and when he felt the pain, he cried out, "Oh!" and was irritated. While he was doing this, the caliph watched him from a concealed place and laughed.

Now Abu al-Hasan called a damsel who was standing nearby, and she answered, "At your service, oh Prince of True Believers, my caliph."

"What is your name?" he asked.

"Shjarat al-Durr."

Then he said to her, "I grant you the protection of Allah, oh damsel. Now tell me the truth—am I really the caliph?"

She replied, "Yes, indeed, by protection of Allah, you are the caliph at this time."

"By Allah," he said, "you're nothing but a liar, you miserable whore!"

Then he glanced at the chief eunuch and called to him. When the eunuch approached, he kissed the ground before Abu al-Hasan and said, "Yes, oh Commander of the Faithful."

"Who is the caliph?" asked Abu al-Hasan.

"You," responded the eunuch.

"You're nothing but a liar, you miserable wretch!" cried Abu al-Hasan and turned to another eunuch and asked him, "Oh my good man, by the protection of Allah, am I the Prince of True Believers?"

"By Allah, my lord," said the eunuch, "you are the caliph at this time."

Abu al-Hasan laughed at himself and thought he was going insane. He was totally confused by what he saw and said, "Is it possible that I could become caliph in one night? Yesterday I was Abu al-Hasan the wag, and today I am Commander of the Faithful."

Then the chief eunuch came up to him and said, "Oh Prince of True Believers, you are indeed Commander of the Faithful and Vice-Regent of the Lord of the Three Worlds!"

And the slave girls and eunuchs flocked around him until he arose and kept wondering about what was happening. The eunuch brought him a pair of sandals made out of raw silk and green silk and purled with red gold. Abu al-Hasan took them, and after examining them, put them in his sleeve, whereupon the castrato cried out, "Allah! Allah! Oh my lord, these are sandals for your feet so you may walk to the wardrobe."

Abu al-Hasan was confounded, and shaking the sandals from his sleeve, he put them on his feet, while the caliph was dying of laughter. The slave went ahead of him to the bathroom, where Abu al-Hasan relieved himself and returned to the chamber. The slave girls brought him a basin of gold and a ewer of silver and poured water on his hands, and he made the Wuzu ablution. Then they spread out a carpet before him, and he prayed. But he was so confused that he forgot how to pray and did much more than the four normal inclinations, bowing and prostrating himself twenty times. Meanwhile he pondered his situation and said to himself, "By Allah, I think I really am the caliph! This is certainly no dream. Things like this do not happen in a dream." And he was soon convinced that he was Prince of True Believers. So he pronounced the salutation to the guardian angels and finished his prayers, whereupon the mamelukes and slave girls came around him and dressed him in the silken garments of the caliph and placed the royal dagger in his hand. Then the chief eunuch approached and said, "Oh Prince of True Believers, the chamberlain is at the door begging permission to enter."

"Let him enter," said Abu al-Hasan.

When the chamberlain entered, he kissed the ground and offered his greetings: "Peace be with you, oh Commander of the Faithful!"

Then Abu al-Hasan rose and descended from his couch, whereupon the official exclaimed, "Allah! Allah! Oh Prince of True Believers, don't you know that all men are your liege lords and under your rule and that it is not fitting for the caliph to rise to any man?"

Soon after this, the eunuch went out ahead of him, and the little slaves behind him. They all led Abu al-Hasan to the hall of judgment and the throne room of the caliphate. There he saw the curtains and the forty doors, and Al-'Ijli and Al-Rakashi the poets, and 'Ibdan, Jadim, and Abu Ishak the cup companions. He also beheld the drawn swords and the warriors encompassing the throne just as the white of the eye encircles the black. Before him were Ajams, Arabs, Turks, and Daylamites, and emirs, viziers, captains, nobles, lords of the land, men of war in bands, and all sorts of people. In truth, the might of the house of Abbas and the majesty of the Prophet's family were there. So he sat down upon the throne and set the dagger on his lap, whereupon all those present came up to kiss the ground between his hands and wished him a long life and fortune. Then Ja'afar the Barmaki came forward, and after kissing the ground, he said, "May the wide world of Allah be your treading place and may paradise be your abode and the fire the home of your foes! May your neighbors never defy you, nor the lights of fire die out for you, oh caliph of all cities and ruler of all countries!"

Thereupon Abu al-Hasan cried out, "Oh dog of the sons of Barmak, I want you and the chief of police to go straight to the street where the mother of Abu al-Hasan the wag lives. You are to offer her my greetings and deliver a hundred dinars of gold to her. Then you are to go to the nearby mosque and take the four sheikhs and the imam and whip each of them with four hundred lashes. After this you are to mount them on beasts, their faces to the tails, and parade them around the city and banish them to some other city. Finally, you are to command the crier to proclaim the following words: 'This is the reward and the least of the reward to those who spread nasty gossip, molest their neighbors, spoil their amusement, and interfere with their drinking and eating!' "

Ja'afar listened to the instructions and answered, "Your words are my command."

Then he went to the city and did all he had been ordered to do. Meanwhile, Abu al-Hasan spent the day in the caliphate, where he took and gave gifts, issued orders and prohibitions, until the end of the day, when he gave permission to everyone to withdraw. So the emirs and the officers of state departed to take care of their business, and Abu al-Hasan looked at the chamberlain and the rest of the attendants, and said, "Away with you!"

Then the eunuchs came to him and wished him long life and fortune. They escorted him to the pavilion of the harem, where he found candles and lamps burning and singing women playing instruments, and ten slave girls with nice bosoms. When he saw all this, he was astounded and said to himself, "By Allah, I am indeed Commander of the Faithful!" and he added, "Or perhaps these women are of the jinn, and my guest the other night was one of their kings, who saw no way to repay me except by commanding his ifrits to address me as Prince of True Believers. But if these are women of the jinn, may Allah protect me from their mischief!"

As soon as he appeared, the slave girls rose and carried him up on to the dais, where they brought him a great tray spread with the richest meat. So he ate heartily until he was full and then called one of the handmaids and said to her, "What is your name?"

"My name is Miskah," she answered.

And he said to another, "What is your name?"

"My name is Tarkah."

Then he asked a third, "What is your name?"

"My name is Tohfah."

He went on to ask the names of all the damsels, one

after another, until he had learned the ten names. Afterward he left that place and went to the wine chamber. He found it complete in every way and saw ten trays covered with all sorts of fruits, cakes, and sweetmeats. So he sat down and ate, and as he enjoyed himself, he was amazed to find three groups of singing girls and ordered them to eat. Then he sat with the singers, while the slaves, eunuchs, pages, and boys stood. Some of the slave girls also stood, while some sat. The damsels sang all kinds of melodies, and the place rang with the sweetness of the songs, while the pipes and lutes joined in harmony until it seemed to Abu al-Hasan that he was in paradise and his heart was bursting with joy. So he amused himself and bestowed robes of honor on the damsels. He sported with one girl, kissed another, and teased a third. Together they drank wine and ate the food until nightfall. While all this took place, the caliph amused himself by watching Abu al-Hasan and laughing. When it became very late, he told one of the slave girls to drop a piece of bhang into a cup and give it to Abu al-Hasan to drink. So she followed his order and gave Abu al-Hasan the cup. No sooner did he take a sip than he fell down unconscious. Thereupon the caliph came out from behind the curtain, laughing and calling to his bodyguard, who had brought Abu al-Hasan to the palace, and said to him, "Carry this man to his own place."

So Masrur picked him up, carried him to his own house, and set him down in the salon. Then he went away, shut the door, and returned to the caliph, who slept until the next day. As for Abu al-Hasan, he, too, continued to slumber until the morning, when he recovered from the drug. As soon as he awoke, he cried out, "Ho, Tuffahah! Rhahat al-Kulub! Miskah! Tohfah!" And he continued to call out the names of the palace handmaids until his mother heard him summoning strange damsels. She quickly got up and rushed to him and said, "In Allah's name, what has come over you? Get up, my son, oh Abu al-Hasan! You're dreaming."

So he opened his eyes, and finding an old woman at his head, he raised his eyes to her and said, "Who are you?"

"I am your mother," she said.

"You're lying," he replied. "I am the Commander of the Faithful, Vice-Regent of Allah."

Consequently, his mother shrieked loudly and said, "Heaven preserve your sanity! Be quiet, my son. Otherwise we shall be sentenced to death and shall lose all our money. If anyone hears your ranting, they will certainly tell the caliph."

So he got up, and when he saw that he was in his own salon with his mother beside him, he thought he was going out of his mind.

"By Allah, Mother," he said, "I saw myself in a dream in a palace with slave girls and mamelukes attending me. I sat upon the throne of the caliphate and ruled. I swear to you in Allah's name, Mother, this is what I saw, and indeed, it was not a dream!" Then he pondered everything for a while and said, "No, to tell the truth, I am Abu al-Hasan al-Khali'a, and what I saw was only a dream. I did not issue orders and commands as caliph." Then he thought about everything again and said, "No, it wasn't a dream, and I am none other than the caliph. Indeed, I did give gifts and bestow robes of honor on people."

"Oh my son," said his mother, "you're playing tricks with your mind. You'll be sent to the madhouse and make a spectacle out of yourself. Truly, all that you've seen was concocted by the demon. It was only an imbroglio of dreams, for Satan sometimes toys with men in all sorts of ways. Tell me, my son, was there anyone with you last night?"

And he reflected and said, "Yes, someone spent the night with me, and I told him all about my past. Undoubtedly, he was some kind of a demon, and I am truly Abu al-Hasan al-Khali'a, just as you say, Mother."

"Oh my son," she responded, "now you can rejoice in the good news that I have for you. Yesterday, the vizier Ja'afar the Barmaki and his guards came and beat the sheikhs of the mosque and the imam. Each received four hundred lashes, and afterward they paraded them around the city and proclaimed, 'This is the reward and the least of the reward of those who are not kind to their neigh bors and trouble their lives!' And he banished them from Baghdad. Moreover, the caliph sent me his greetings and one hundred dinars."

Upon hearing this, Abu al-Hasan cried out, "You cursed crone, how dare you contradict me and tell me that I'm not the Prince of True Believers? It was I who commanded Ja'afar the Barmaki to beat the sheikhs and parade them around the city with the proclamation. It was I who sent you a greeting and the hundred dinars. You unfortunate creature, I am truly the Commander of the Faithful, and you are a liar who wants to make an idiot out of me."

After saying all this, he attacked her and began beating her with a wood stick until she cried out, "Help, help! Help me somebody!"

And he kept beating her until the neighbors heard her cries and came to her. They found Abu al-Hasan bashing his mother and saying, "Oh old woman of misfortune, tell me the truth! Aren't I the Commander of the Faithful? You've cast a spell on me!"

When the people heard his words, they said, "This man is raving mad!"

So they came in, seized him, tied him up, and carried him to the madhouse.

"What's the matter with this young man?" the director asked.

"He's a madman," they said. "The jinn have gotten to him."

"By Allah," Abu al-Hasan cried, "they're lying. I'm not a madman, but the Commander of the Faithful."

And the director answered, "Nobody is lying but you, oh foul mouth. The jinn have driven you mad!"

Then he stripped Abu al-Hasan of his clothes, clapped a heavy chain on his neck, bound him to a high lattice, and beat him twice a day and twice a night. He continued doing this for the next ten days. Finally, his mother came to him and said, "Oh my son, Abu al-Hasan, please become reasonable again. The devil is responsible for your suffering."

"You are right, Mother," he responded, "and I would like you to bear witness that I repent all my crazy talk and actions. Please free me from this place, otherwise I shall certainly die."

Accordingly, his mother went to the director and procured his release, and he returned to his own house. Now this was at the beginning of the month, and when it ended, Abu al-Hasan longed to drink some liquor and return to his former habits. Therefore he furnished his salon with good food and wine. Afterward, he went to the bridge and waited for someone with whom he could converse and carouse as was his custom. But while he was sitting there, lo and behold, the caliph and Masrur came by. However, Abu al-Hasan did not greet them. Instead, he said to Al-Rashid, "No friendly welcome for you, oh king of the jinn!"

"What have I done to you?" asked the caliph.

"What more could you have done to me than what was done to me, oh foulest of the jinn? I have been beaten and thrown into the madhouse because everyone believed me to be driven crazy by the jinn, and I know you caused it all. Indeed, I brought you to my house and fed you with nothing but the best food. Afterward you empowered your demons and marids to play tricks with my mind from morning till evening. So make off with you, and never let me see you again!"

The caliph smiled and sat down by his side and said, "Oh my brother, didn't I tell you that I would return to you?"

"I have no need of you," said Abu al-Hasan. "As the old verse goes,

"My friend, it would be better and wiser to part.
What the eye doesn't see cannot grieve the heart.

"And indeed, my brother, the night you came to me and we conversed and caroused together, it was as if the devil had come to me and caused all sorts of trouble."

"And who is the devil?" asked the caliph.

"He is none other than you yourself," answered Abu al-Hasan.

Upon hearing this, the caliph laughed and teased him

some more by saying, "My brother, when I left you, I forgot to close the door. Perhaps Satan came in after I left."

"Don't ask me to tell you what happened to me," said Abu al-Hasan. "Why in heaven's name did you forget to close the door? You allowed the devil to come in and play all sorts of tricks on me."

And he told the caliph everything that had happened to him, from the first thing to the last. Meanwhile the caliph did his best to keep himself from laughing. Then he said to Abu al-Hasan, "Praise be to Allah, who has got rid of whatever was troubling you. I am glad to see you so well!"

And Abu al-Hasan replied, "Never again shall I take you to my house for drink and conversation, for the proverb says: 'He who stumbles on a stone and returns to it will bear the blame for his own faults.' So you see, my brother, I shall never entertain you again, for you have not brought me good fortune."

But the caliph teased him and said, "I have the means to help you get revenge on the imam and the sheikhs."

"You do?" replied Abu al-Hasan.

"And perhaps something more shall happen to you that will make you rejoice," Al-Rashid continued.

"What do I need to do?"

"I want to be your guest," the Commander of the Faithful said. "Do not reject me."

"On the condition," Abu al-Hasan stated, "that you swear to me on the seal of Solomon, David's son, that you will not let your ifrits make fun of me."

"Your word is my command," the caliph replied.

Thereupon Abu al-Hasan brought him to his home and set food before him and entertained him with friendly conversation. When the young man told the caliph about everything that had happened to him, the caliph almost died stifling his laughter. After Abu al-Hasan took away the tray of food, he brought the wine, filled a cup, and then gave it to the caliph and said, "Do not be annoyed with me, and I don't want you to annoy me." And he recited the following verses:

"Let me wish you well and tell you that lips shall bless
Only those who drink and through drinking transgress.
I shall not stop until the night falls dark
And I lower my forehead to its mark:
In wine like liquid is my delight
Which clears all care and makes all seem right."

When the caliph heard these verses and saw how apt
he was at couplets, he was very pleased and took the
cup and drank it down, and the two continued conversing and carousing until the wine rose to their heads.
Then Abu al-Hasan said to the caliph, "My good friend,
to tell the truth, I am still somewhat confused about
everything that happened to me. It seemed to me that I
was Commander of the Faithful and ruled with generosity. I'm convinced it wasn't a dream."

"Those were the imbroglios of sleep," replied the caliph as he crumbled a bit of bhang into the cup. "Do
me the honor and drink this cup."

"I shall certainly drink it from your hand."

Then Abu al-Hasan took the cup and drank it down.
No sooner had the drink settled in his stomach than he
fell head over heels. Since his manners and frankness
had once again pleased the caliph, he said to himself, "I
shall certainly make him my drinking and conversation
partner." So he got up and told Masrur, "Take him with
us." And they returned to the palace. Once there the
bodyguard set him down before Al-Rashid, who told the
slaves and the slave girls to gather around him while he
hid in a place where Abu al-Hasan could not see him.
Then he commanded one of the handmaidens to take
the lute and play it over the young man's head, while
the rest of them also played their instruments. So they
played and sang, until Abu al-Hasan awoke at the rise
of dawn and heard the concert of lutes and tambourines
and the sound of the flutes and the singing of the slave
girls. When he opened his eyes and found himself in the
palace with the handmaids and eunuchs around him, he
exclaimed, "Glory be to Allah, whose power is great!
Please help me this night, for I fear it may be worse
than the other one. Truly, I am afraid of the madhouse

and all that I suffered the first time, and I am positive that the devil has come again to trouble me. Oh Allah, my Lord, put Satan to shame!"

Then he shut his eyes and covered his head with his sleeve. At times he laughed softly and raised his head, but he still found that the apartment was all lit up and the girls were singing. Soon one of the eunuchs sat down at his head and said to him, "Sit up, oh Prince of the True Believers, and look at your palace and slave girls."

"By Allah, am I truly the Commander of the Faithful?" he asked. "You're lying, aren't you? There is no way that I rode out and ruled the land. Rather I drank and slept, and now this eunuch comes to me and makes me rise."

Then he sat up and recalled everything that had happened to him with his mother and how he had beaten her and was taken to the madhouse. Indeed, he saw the marks of the whip with which the director had beaten him, and he was bewildered by all this and remarked, "I have no idea how all this happened and what's happening to me!" Then, gazing at the scene around him, he said to himself, "All these are jinn in human shape, and I can only trust in Allah." Then he turned to one of the damsels and asked her, "Who am I?"

"You are the Commander of the Faithful," she said.

"You lie," he responded, "and I hope all those who have anything to do with you are struck with calamity! If I am indeed the Commander of the Faithful, come and bite my finger."

So she approached him and bit his finger with all her might, and he said to her, "That's enough!" Then he asked the chief eunuch, "Who am I?"

"You are the Commander of the Faithful," he responded.

Abu al-Hasan left him and still felt perplexed. So he turned to a little slave and said to him, "Bite my ear."

And he bent down to him and put his ear to his mouth. Now the mameluke was young and was not particularly bright. So he bit Abu al-Hasan's ear as hard as he could and nearly severed it. Since he did not know Arabic, he kept biting, because whenever Abu al-Hasan said, "That's enough," the boy thought he heard "Bite the stuff," and he would bite harder. Meanwhile the damsels did not pay attention because they were diverted by the singing girls, and Abu al-Hasan cried out for someone to save him from the biting boy and the caliph almost fell over from laughing so hard. Finally, Abu al-Hasan smacked the boy, and he let go of his ear, whereupon everyone present fell over with laughter and said to the little mameluke, "Are you crazy? Why did you bite the caliph's ear so hard?"

And Abu al-Hasan cried out to them, "Isn't what has happened to me enough for you, you wretched jinnees? But the fault is not yours. It is your chief who has transformed you from jinnees to mortals. I shall seek protection from you this night by the chapter of sincerity in the Koran!"

After saying this, he took off his clothes until he was stark naked. Then he danced among the slave girls, and they bound his hands. As he wriggled among them, they split their sides with laughter, as did the caliph, who finally came out from behind the curtain and said to Abu al-Hasan, "Stop all this, Abu al-Hasan. You're slaying me with laughter!"

"By Allah," said Abu al-Hasan, who recognized the caliph, "it's you who are slaying me and my mother. It's you who took care of the sheikhs and the imam of the mosque!"

After saying all this, he kissed the ground before him and wished him prosperity and immortality. The caliph had him clothed at once in a rich robe and gave him a thousand dinars. Soon he bestowed special favors on him by having him wed and giving him a good deal of money. He had Abu al-Hasan lodged in the palace and made him chief of his drinking companions. Indeed, he promoted him above all the others, who were ten in number. Indeed, Abu al-Hasan received the highest honors from the caliph and sat with him and the Lady Zubaydah bint al-Kasim, whose treasure was given to him in marriage.

After this Abu al-Hasan dwelled with his wife in eating, drinking, and all the delights of life until they began running out of money. So he went to his wife and said to her, "Listen to me, oh Nuzhat al-Fuad! I have in mind to play a trick on the caliph, and we will take from them two hundred dinars and two pieces of silk to begin with."

"As you wish," she replied. "But what are you thinking of doing?"

"We shall pretend to be dead," he said, "and here is how we shall do it. I shall die before you and lay myself out. You will spread a silken sheet over me, loosen my turban, tie my shoes, place a knife on my stomach, and a little salt. Then let down your hair, and go to your mistress Zubaydah, tearing your dress, slapping your face, and crying out. She will ask you what's the matter, and you'll answer her that you hope she outlives Abu al-Hasan, for he is dead. She will mourn for me and weep. Moreover, she will order her new treasurer to give you a hundred dinars and a piece of silk and will say to you, 'Go, lay him out, and carry him forth.' So, you are to take the hundred dinars and come back, and when you return to me, I shall get up and you will lie down in my place. I shall go to the caliph and say to him, 'I hope you outlive Nuzhat al-Fuad,' and I shall tear my garments and rip out my beard. He will mourn for you and say to his treasurer, 'Give Abu al-Hasan a hundred dinars and a piece of silk.' Then he will say to me, 'Go and lay her out and carry her forth.' And I shall come back to you."

Upon hearing all this, Nuzhat al-Fuad rejoiced and said, "This is indeed an excellent plan."

Then Abu al-Hasan stretched himself out, and she shut his eyes, tied his feet, covered him with the sheet, and did whatever her lord told her to do. Afterward, she tore her garments, let her hair down, and went to the Lady Zubaydah, weeping and crying out. When the princess saw her in this state, she asked, "What terrible thing has happened? Tell me why you are weeping."

And Nuzhat al-Fuad answered with a loud moan, "Oh my lady, may you live longer than Abu al-Hasan, for he is dead."

The Lady Zubaydah mourned for him and said, "Alas for poor Abu al-Hasan!" and she shed tears for him awhile. Then she told her treasurer to give Nuzhat al-

Fuad a hundred dinars and a piece of silk and said to
her, "Oh Nuzhat al Fuad, go, lay him out, and carry
him forth."

So she took the hundred dinars and the piece of silk
and returned to her dwelling with joy. After she entered
she told her husband what had happened, whereupon he
got up, rejoiced, girdled his middle, danced, took the
hundred dinars and the piece of silk, and stored them
away. Then he laid out Nuzhat al-Fuad and arranged
her exactly the same way as she had done with him.
Afterward he tore his clothes, ripped out his beard, un-
rolled his turban, and ran to the caliph, who was sitting
in the judgment hall. Once there, Abu al-Hasan began
beating his breast, and the caliph asked, "What's wrong
with you, Abu al-Hasan?"

Weeping, he answered, "I wish I had never been created and that this hour had never come!"

"Tell me what has happened," the caliph insisted.

"Oh my lord," exclaimed Abu al-Hasan, "may you
long outlive Nuzhat al-Fuad!"

"There is no god but God," the caliph responded and
clasped his hands. Then he comforted Abu al-Hasan and
said to him, "Don't grieve, for I shall soon find you
another woman to wed." And he ordered the treasurer
to give him a hundred dinars and a piece of silk. The
treasurer did what he ordered, and the caliph said to
Abu al-Hasan, "Go, lay her out, carry her forth, and
give her a beautiful funeral."

So Abu al-Hasan took the money and the silk and
returned happily to Nuzhat al-Fuad and said to her,
"Arise, for our plan has worked!"

Thereupon she got up, and he laid the hundred ducats
and the piece of silk before her. She was delighted by
their success, and they added the gold to the gold and
the silk to the silk and sat talking and laughing. Meanwhile, after Abu al-Hasan had left the caliph, the Commander of the Faithful mourned for her, and after he
left the divan, escorted by Masrur, and went to the Lady
Zubaydah to console her for the loss of her handmaid.
He found her sitting and weeping, and she seemed to
expect his visit so that she could console him for the loss

of his companion Abu al-Hasan. As he approached, he said, "May you outlive your slave girl Nuzhat al-Fuad!"

"Oh my lord," she responded, "may Allah preserve my slave girl. May you long outlive your companion Abu al-Hasan, for he is dead."

The caliph smiled and said to his eunuch, "Oh Masrur, women are so foolish. By Allah, tell me, wasn't Abu al-Hasan just with me a moment ago?"

"Please don't jest now," replied the Lady Zubaydah, full of anger. "It's enough that Abu al-Hasan is dead, but you must also insinuate that my slave girl is also dead, do away with the two of them, and make me appear a fool!"

"Indeed, it is Nuzhat al-Fuad who is dead," the caliph answered.

"On the contrary," maintained the Lady Zubaydah, "he wasn't with you, and you haven't seen him. In fact, Nuzhat al-Fuad was just with me, and she was weeping in deep sorrow and with her clothes torn to tatters. I calmed her down and gave her a hundred dinars and a piece of silk. Then I waited for your visit so that I might console you for the loss of your drinking companion Abu al-Hasan and was about to send for you."

The caliph laughed and said, "Nobody is dead except Nuzhat al-Fuad."

"No, no, my good lord," she insisted, "nobody is dead except your companion Abu al-Hasan."

With this the caliph became mad. His veins started to throb in his eyes, and he cried out to Masrur, "Go to the house of Abu al-Hasan and see which one of them is dead."

So Masrur went running, and the caliph said to the Lady Zubaydah, "Do you want to make a wager with me?"

"Yes," she replied, "I shall make a wager, and I say that Abu al-Hasan is dead."

"And I wager that nobody is dead except Nuzhat al-Fuad," her husband stated, "and the stakes will be my garden of pleasure against your palace and the pavilion of pictures."

After they agreed to the bet, they sat waiting for Masrur's return with the news. As for the eunuch, he ran until he came to the street where the home of Abu al-Hasan was located. Now the young man happened to be comfortably seated and leaning against the window when he saw Masrur running down the street. Quickly he said to Nuzhat al-Fuad, "It seems that the caliph has gone to the Lady Zubaydah to console her, and she has probably consoled him for the loss of Abu al-Hasan! They have probably had an argument about who is dead and made some sort of a wager, because they have sent Masrur to us. Therefore, it's best if you lie down so he may see you and go and tell the caliph that what I said was true."

So Nuzhat al-Fuad stretched herself out, and Abu al-Hasan covered her with her mantilla and sat weeping at her head. Soon Masrur the eunuch came in and greeted him. Upon seeing Nuzhat al-Fuad stretched out, he uncovered her face and said, "There is no god but God! Our sister Nuzhat al-Fuad is dead indeed! How sudden was the stroke of destiny! May Allah have pity on you and bless you!"

Then he returned and began relating what he had seen to the caliph and Lady Zubaydah, laughing as he spoke.

"You cur," said the caliph. "This is no time for laughter! Tell us which one is dead."

"By Allah, my lord," he replied, "Abu al-Hasan is well, and nobody is dead except Nuzhat al-Fuad."

The caliph then turned to Lady Zubaydah and said, "You've lost your pavilion, my dear," and he jeered at her and said, "Oh Masrur, tell her what you saw."

"Truly, my lady," said the eunuch, "I ran without stopping until I came to Abu al-Hasan's house and found Nuzhat al-Fuad lying dead and Abu al-Hasan sitting with tears at her head. I greeted him and gave him my condolences. Then I sat down by his side and uncovered the face of Nuzhat al-Fuad and saw her dead and her face swollen. So I said to him, 'Carry her to her grave so that we may pray over her.' He replied, 'As you say.' And I left him to prepare the funeral and came here so that I could tell you the news."

The caliph laughed and said, "Tell it again and again to your Lady Little-Wit!"

When the Lady Zubaydah heard Masrur's words and those of the caliph, she exploded with anger and said, "Nobody has a little wit except somebody who believes a slave!"

And she cursed Masrur, while the Commander of the Faithful laughed. The eunuch was irritated by all of this and said to the caliph, "Whoever said women possess no wit at all and lack religion spoke the truth."

Then the Lady Zubaydah said to the caliph, "You are playing and jesting with me, and this slave has hoodwinked me just to please you. Now I want to send someone whom I trust to see which one of them is dead."

And he answered, "Send whomever you want to see which one of them is dead."

So the lady cried out to an old duenna and said to her, "I want you to go quickly to the house of Nuzhat al-Fuad and see who is dead. And don't tarry!"

And she was so fierce with her words that the old woman ran out, while the caliph and Masrur laughed. Indeed, the duenna kept running until she came to the street where Abu al-Hasan lived, but he saw her and recognized her right away. So he said to his wife, "Oh Nuzhat al-Fuad, it seems that the Lady Zubaydah has sent an old woman to us to see who is dead because she does not believe Masrur's report of your death. So I had better lie down dead in my turn so that your credit with Lady Zubaydah will be good."

Thereupon he lay down and stretched himself out, and she covered him, bound his eyes and feet, and sat in tears at this head. Soon the old woman entered and saw her sitting at Abu al-Hasan's head, weeping and recounting his fine qualities. When Nuzhat al-Fuad saw the old woman, she cried out, "See what has happened to me! Indeed, Abu al-Hasan is dead and has left me alone and forlorn!" Then she shrieked, tore her garments, and said to the woman, "Oh my mother, how very good he was to me!"

"Indeed," said the duenna, "you are excused, for you treated him well, and he you."

Then she pondered what Masrur had reported to the caliph and the Lady Zubaydah and said to her, "Indeed,

Masrur is trying to cause trouble between the caliph and the Lady Zubaydah, for he gave them news that you were dead and that Abu al-Hasan was well."

Nuzhat al-Fuad said to her, "My dear woman, I was just with my lady, and she gave me a hundred dinars and a piece of silk. You now see what my situation is and what has happened to me! Indeed, I am falling apart. What shall I do now that I am alone and forlorn? I pray to heaven that I should have died and not him!"

Then she wept, and after the old woman went up to Abu al-Hasan, uncovered his face, and saw his eyes bound and swollen because of the swathing, she wept with her. Soon after she covered him again and said, "Indeed, oh Nuzhat al-Fuad, I am sorry that the loss of Abu al-Hasan has caused you so much suffering."

After offering her condolence, the old woman ran out and returned to the Lady Zubaydah and related what she had witnessed. Thereupon the princess, who broke into laughter, said, "Tell it over again to the caliph, who believes I have neither brains nor religion, and who would rather believe his cursed liar of a slave than me."

"This old woman lies," said Masrur. "I saw Abu al-Hasan alive and well, and it was Nuzhat al-Fuad who was dead."

"It's you who is the liar," answered the duenna. "You want to cause trouble between the caliph and the Lady Zubaydah."

"Nobody is lying but you, you evil witch!" screamed Masrur. "If your lady believes you, she must be senile."

Upon hearing this the Lady Zubaydah yelled at him, and indeed, she was enraged by his words and broke into tears. Then the caliph said to her, "I am lying, and my eunuch is lying. You are lying, and your waiting woman is lying. So, my advice is that all four of us go together so that we can see who is telling the truth."

"Come," said Masrur, "let us go so that I may put this old woman to shame and give her a sound drubbing for her lying."

And the duenna answered him, "You nitwit, you think you're smarter than I am, but you have no more brains in your head than a witless hen."

Masrur was incensed by her words and would have given her a good beating right there and then, but the Lady Zubaydah pushed him away from her and said, "We shall soon find out who's been telling the truth and who's to blame for all the lies that have been spread."

Then all four arose and placed bets with one another as they walked from the palace until they came to the street where Abu al-Hasan lived. He saw them and said to his wife, Nuzhat al-Fuad, "Truly, it's not just pancakes that are sticky, nor does the crock escape the shock every time. It seems that the old woman has gone and told her lady what has happened and has had an argument with Masrur. They've probably laid wagers with each other about our death. All four have come to see us."

When Nuzhat al-Fuad heard this, she jumped up from her outstretched position and asked, "What shall we do?"

"We shall both pretend to be dead together and stretch ourselves out and hold our breath," he answered.

So she did what he said, and they both lay down on the place where they usually spent the siesta, and they bound their feet, shut their eyes, covered themselves, and held their breath. Soon the caliph, Lady Zubaydah, Masrur, and the old woman entered and found Abu al-Hasan and his wife stretched out as if they were dead. When the Lady Zubaydah saw this, she wept and said, "Now I know the bad news of her death is true. She must have died out of grief over Abu al-Hasan's death."

"Don't fool me with your prattle," said the caliph. "She certainly died before Abu al-Hasan. He came to me with torn clothes and his beard ripped out beating his breast with bricks. And I gave him a hundred dinars and a piece of silk and said to him, 'Go and bury her, and I shall make sure that you will be wed with another woman, even more beautiful than she was.' But it would appear that her death was no light matter to him, and he died of grief for her loss. So it is I who have won the wager."

The Lady Zubaydah did not agree, and the argument between them grew even more heated than it was before. At last the caliph sat down at the heads of the pair and said, "By Allah and the graves of my fathers and forefathers, I shall gladly give a thousand dinars to whoever tells me which one died before the other!"

When Abu al-Hasan heard the caliph's words, he sprang up quickly and said, "I died first, oh Commander of the Faithful! So give me the thousand dinars that you swore you would give by your oath."

Nuzhat al-Fuad also stood up before the caliph and Lady Zubaydah, who both rejoiced in seeing them alive and well, but the princess chided her slave girl. Both the caliph and Lady Zubaydah showed them how glad they were that they were alive and they knew that this death was a trick to get the gold.

"You should have asked me for what you needed," said the Lady Zubaydah to Nuzhat al-Fuad. "You didn't have to go about everything this way. You've tortured my heart."

"Truly, my lady," replied the slave girl, "I was too ashamed to ask."

As for the caliph, he was doubled over with laughter and said, "Oh Abu al-Hasan, you'll always be a rascal and never stop surprising me with your clever antics."

"Oh Commander of the Faithful," replied Abu al-Hasan, "I played this trick on you because the money you had given me was exhausted, and I was ashamed to ask you for more. When I was single, I could never keep track of my money. Then, ever since you married me to this damsel, I've spent even more money until none was left. Therefore, I thought up this trick so I could get a hundred dinars and a piece of silk. But now give me the thousand dinars and make good your promise!"

The caliph and the Lady Zubaydah laughed, and they all returned to the palace, where the Commander of the Faithful gave Abu al-Hasan the thousand dinars and said, "Take this money as a gratuity or my thanks that you did not die," while Lady Zubaydah did the same with Nuzhat al-Fuad, honoring her with the same words. Moreover, the caliph increased Abu al-Hasan's wages and supplies, and he and his wife continued to live in joy and contentment until the Destroyer of Delights came and took them away.

The Craft and Malice of Women, or the Tale of the King, His Son, His Concubine, and the Seven Viziers

In days of old there was a powerful king among the kings of China, and he ruled over many vassals and soldiers with wisdom, justice, might, and majesty. He was fair and generous to his nobles and dearly beloved by the people. He was as wealthy as he was powerful, but he had grown old without being blessed with a son, and this situation caused him a great deal of grief. Indeed, he brooded and was depressed because he had no heir to carry on his name, and he felt that his realm would probably pass into a stranger's hands. So he secluded himself in his palace and never left. He did this for such a long time that his liege lords had no news of him and were worried and puzzled.

"He's dead," some said.

"No, he's not," others replied.

But they all resolved to find a ruler who would reign over them and carry out the duties of government. In the meantime, the king, who had become utterly desperate, sought the intercession of Allah Almighty and asked Him to grant him a son to be the heir of the kingdom. Then he rose, went to his salon, and sent for his wife, who was the daughter of his uncle. Now, this queen was unsurpassable in beauty and loveliness, and she was the dearest and fairest of all his wives. Moreover, she was a witty and judicious woman. She found the king dejected and sorrowful with tears in his eyes and a heavy heart. So she kissed the ground between his hands and said, "Oh my king, may my life ransom your life! May time never prove to be your enemy, nor the tides of fortune ever go against you! May Allah grant you a joyful life and ward off your troubles! Why do I find you brooding and so tormented?"

"You know very well," he replied, "that I am getting on in years, and that I have never been blessed with a son who would bring joy to my eyes. So I know that my kingdom will be passed on to a stranger, and oblivion will bury my name and memory. This is why I am so depressed and tormented."

"May Allah do away with all your sorrows," she answered. "I, too, have been thinking about this and longing for a child as you have. Well, one night I had a dream, and a voice said to me, 'The king, your husband, pines for progeny. If a daughter is born, she will be the ruin of his realm. If a son is born, this boy will have many troubling experiences, but he will manage to survive. Such a son can be conceived by you and only you, and the destined time is when the moon meets with Gemini!' I awoke from my dream, but after hearing that voice and the prophecy, I refused to bear children."

"I must have a son—God willing!" exclaimed the king. Thereupon she soothed and consoled him until he forgot his sorrows. Soon he returned to his nobles and sat among them as he used to do. And they all rejoiced to see him once more. Now, when the moon and Gemini were in the right constellation, the king went and slept with his wife, and thanks to Allah, she became pregnant. As soon as she knew, she announced the good news to her husband and led her usual life until the nine months were completed and she gave birth to a male child whose face was as round as the moon. The nobles of the realm were pleased by this event, and the king brought together an assembly of his philosophers, astrologers, and horoscopists and spoke as follows: "I want you to tell my son's fortune and to determine his chart and reveal to me all that you can find about his birth and destiny."

They agreed to do this to the best of their ability, and after determining the constellation and drawing his chart, they went to the king and said, "The stars are favorable, and he will have a long life. But there is danger ahead for the boy."

Upon hearing this, the king was distressed, but they

added, "Oh king, he will escape this danger, and he will not be injured."

So the king was greatly relieved, and he bestowed great honors upon the astrologers and philosophers. Then he resigned himself to the will of heaven, for he knew that the decrees of destiny cannot be countered. He placed wet nurses, handmaids, and eunuchs in charge of his son and let him grow and mature in the harem until he reached the age of seven. Then he sent letters to all his viceroys and governors throughout his realm, and he called together an assembly of these men along with his liege lords, philosophers, and doctors of law and religion from all countries. When they were all in his presence—and there were well over three hundred—he asked them to relax while he sent for food and drink, and they ate and drank as much as they wanted. When the banquet ended, and everyone had taken his seat according to his rank, the king asked them, "Do you know why I have gathered you together?"

"We do not know, oh king," they answered.

"It is my wish," he continued, "that you select fifty men from among you, and then from those fifty, ten, and from those ten one, who will teach my son all there is to know. Only when I see the boy perfect in all sciences shall I share my rank with the prince and make him my partner in everything that I own."

"We can tell you right now, oh king," they replied, "that there is no one among us who is more learned and wise than Al-Sindibad, also called the sage, who lives in your capital under your protection. Given your intention, we urge you to summon him, and he will do as you like."

The king acted upon their advice, and when the sage arrived and expressed his loyal sentiments to the king, the sovereign asked him to draw near and raised him in rank by saying, "I want you to know, oh sage, that I summoned this assembly of learned men and asked them to choose a man to teach my son about all the sciences, and they selected you without dissent. If you feel capable of doing this, I want you to undertake this task, but I also want you to know that a man's son and heir is the very fruit of his vitals and core of his heart. My only desire is that you instruct him well and that Allah help you achieve the best results."

The king then sent for his son and placed Al-Sindibad in charge of him and commanded the sage to finish his task in three years. Well, Al-Sindibad did as the king requested, but at the end of that time, the young prince had learned nothing, since his mind was wholly occupied with amusements and sport. When summoned and examined by his father, his knowledge was zero. Thereupon the king called another assembly of learned men and nobles and asked them again to elect a tutor for his son. But they asked, "And what has his teacher Al-Sindibad been doing?"

"He has taught my son nothing." the king answered.

Then the olema, philosophers, and high officers summoned the tutor to appear in front of the king and said to him, "Oh sage, what has prevented you from teaching the king's son during the past three years?"

"Oh wise men," he replied, "the prince's mind is wholly occupied by amusements and sport. But if the king will grant me three conditions, I shall teach the boy in seven months what he would not learn in seven years."

"I am listening," said the king, "and I shall abide by the conditions that you set."

"Then listen carefully, sire," replied Al-Sindibad, "and bear in mind these three sayings. First, do not do to others what you would not like done to you. Second, do nothing hastily without consulting the experienced. Third, where you have power show pity. If I am to continue teaching your son, I ask you to accept these three principles and to adhere to them."

"I ask all those who are gathered here," declared the king, "to be my witness that I shall stand firmly behind these principles." Then he had a written account of what he had sworn to be drawn up, and he signed it in front of his courtiers.

Thereupon the sage took the prince's hand and led him to this place, and the king sent them all the provisions such as kitchen utensils, carpets, and other furniture that they needed. Moreover, the tutor had a house built whose walls were lined with the whitest stucco, and on the walls he wrote all the subjects that he proposed to teach his pupil. When the place was duly furnished, he took the boy's hand and installed him in the apartment, and then he left and locked the door with seven padlocks. From then on he visited the prince every third day when he taught him the knowledge that was to be gained from one of the pictures on the walls and when he replenished the provisions of food and drink. Then he would leave the prince alone. So whenever the prince was bored by the solitude and felt lonely, there was nothing he could do but study, and soon he began to master his lessons. When the sage saw this, he began to teach him the inner meanings of external things, and in a short time, his pupil learned all there was to know. Then the sage took him outside the house and taught him how to ride horseback, swordplay, and archery. When the prince had learned all of this, the sage sent a message to the king and informed him that the prince was perfect in everything that was demanded for a person of his rank. Upon hearing this, the king rejoiced, and he summoned his viziers and noblemen to be present at the examination. When the king commanded the sage to send his son to him, Al-Sindibad consulted his pupil's horoscope and found there was a bad constellation that would last seven days. So, in fear for the boy's life, he went to him and told him to look at his chart. When the prince did this, he, too, recognized the bad omen and became afraid.

"What do you advise me to do?" he asked the sage.

"You will have to be silent for the next seven days," he replied, "even though your sire threatens you with a whipping. If you can make it through this period safely, you will succeed your father and become a king. If things go wrong, only Allah can determine your fate."

"You are the one to blame, oh teacher," said the prince. "You should have looked at my horoscope before sending a message to the king. You were too hasty. If you had delayed everything one week, then there would be no danger."

"Oh my son," replied the sage. "what has happened was bound to happen. If there was a fault, then it was my delight in your scholarship. But now, be firm in your determination. Rely on Allah Almighty and be prepared not to utter a single word."

Thereupon the prince got ready for the audience with his father and was met by the viziers, who led him to his father. When the king addressed him, he did not answer. Then his father continued to urge him to speak, but the boy did not say a word. Consequently, the courtiers were astounded, and the monarch was troubled by his son and sent for Al-Sindibad. But the tutor had hidden himself so that nobody could find a trace of him. People began to spread rumors and said that the sage was ashamed to appear before the king and his courtiers. While rumors were flying, the king heard some of those present saying, "Send the boy to the seraglio, where he will talk with the women and forget his bashfulness."

The king thought that this was a good idea. So he gave orders for the prince to be led into the palace that was encompassed by a stream whose banks were planted with eleven kinds of fruit trees and sweet-smelling flowers. Moreover, in this palace there were forty chambers, and in each chamber were ten slave girls, each skilled in some musical instrument so that when one of them played, the palace danced to her melodic strains. Here the prince passed one night, and on the following morning, the king's favorite concubine happened to cast her eyes on his handsome face and figure and perfect grace. Before he knew it, she was ravished by his charms and fell in love with him. So she went up to him and threw herself on him, but he made no response. Still, she was so dazzled by his handsome qualities that she cried out to him and pleaded with him to give of himself to her. Once again she threw herself upon him and pulled him to her bosom, kissing him and saying, "Oh king's son, grant me your favors, and you will replace your father. I shall give your father poison so that he will die, and you will enjoy his realm and his wealth."

When the prince heard these words, he was terribly enraged and said to her by signs, "Oh cursed one, if

Allah wills, I shall certainly punish you for such a deed as soon as I can speak, for I shall go straight to my father and tell him, and he will kill you."

After signaling to her what he felt, he arose in rage and left her chamber. Now she was in a state of fear. So she ripped her clothes, scratched her face, tore her hair, and ran to the king. When she arrived, she threw herself at his feet, weeping and wailing. When the king saw her in this pitiful state, he was concerned and asked her, "What's the matter, my dear? What's happening with my son? Isn't he well?"

"Oh king," she cried, "your son, whom your courtiers believe to be speechless, tried to force himself upon me, and I resisted him. So he beat me and treated me as you can well see. He would have slain me, but I fled from him. Nor shall I ever return to him or to the palace again. No, never again!"

When the king heard this, he became tremendously angry and called his seven viziers and ordered them to put his son to death. However, they said to one another, "If we do as the king commands, he will surely repent of having ordered his son's death, for the boy is most dear to him, and he was at the brink of despair until his son was born. Indeed, he will blame us and ask us why we did not try to dissuade him from slaying his son."

So they took counsel together to try to avert a catastrophe, and the chief vizier said, "I shall manage to save us this first day."

Then he went to the king, and after prostrating himself before his majesty, he asked permission to speak. After the king granted it, he said, "Oh king, even if you had a thousand sons, it would not be a light matter to put even one of them to death simply due to the story of a woman, whether it be true or false. Indeed, oh king, I have heard many stories that tell about the malice, craft, and perfidy of women."

"Well then," said the king, "tell me about something that has reached your ears."

And the vizier answered and said, "Oh king, I have heard a tale entitled

The King and His Vizier's Wife

There was once a powerful and proud king who was devoted to the love of women, and one day, when he was in his palace, he noticed a beautiful woman on the terrace roof of her house and could not restrain himself from falling totally in love with her. He asked his servants to whom the house and lady belonged, and they said, "This is the dwelling of your well-known vizier, and she is his wife."

So he called the minister in question and sent him on a mission to a distant part of the kingdom, where he was to collect some information and return some time in the future. As soon as he was gone, the king managed to use a trick to gain entrance to his house and to his wife. When the vizier's wife saw him, she recognized him, stood up, kissed his hands and feet, and welcomed him. Then she moved away from him to prepare to serve him.

"My lord," she said, "why is it that you have come here? I did not expect nor do I deserve such an honor."

"The reason I have come," he stated bluntly, "is that I have fallen in love with you and my desire has caused me to take this step."

Thereupon she kissed the ground before him a second time and said, "By Allah, oh my lord, I am not worthy to be your handmaid. How is it that I have the good fortune to have won this honor and your favor?"

Then the king stretched his hand toward her, intending to enjoy her, but she said, "Let us not be so hasty. We have time, my king. I ask you to stay with me the entire day so that I may prepare something to eat and drink for you."

So the king sat down on his minister's couch, and she quickly ran and brought him a book to read, while she prepared the food. He took the book, and as he read, he found moral examples and exhortations that restrained him from adultery and broke his courage to commit adultery. After a while, she returned and set some ninety different dishes before him, and he ate a mouthful of each one but found that the taste was always the same. He was astounded by this and said to the vizier's wife, "Oh lady, you have placed numerous kinds of meat before me, but the taste of each is simple and the same."

"May Allah bring prosperity to the king," she replied. "This is a parable I have set before you so that you might be admonished by it."

"And what is the meaning?" he asked.

"May Allah help the king to mend his ways," she answered. "There are ninety concubines of various kinds in your palace, but their taste is one and the same."

When the king heard this, he was ashamed, and, after rising hastily, he went out without insulting her and returned to his palace. But in his haste and confusion, he forgot his signet ring and left it under the cushion where he had been sitting. Even though he remembered it, he was ashamed to send for it.

Now, no sooner had he reached home than the vizier returned and appeared before the king, and gave him his report about the state of the province in question. Then he returned to his own home, sat down on his couch, and happened to put his hand under the cushion, when, behold, he found the king's seal ring. Since he recognized it, he realized what had happened and took the affair to heart. In his grief he kept away from his wife for a whole year, never sleeping or speaking with her, while she was unaware of the reason for his anger. Finally, frustrated and exhausted by the long neglect, she asked her father to come to her, and she told him what was bothering her.

"I shall complain to the king about him," her father said, "at a time when he is in the king's presence."

So one day he went to the king, and upon finding the vizier and the kazi of the army with the king, he remarked, "Almighty Allah, please lend your powers to the king so that he might help me. I had a fair flower garden which I planted with my own hands and spent my money and time until it bore fruit. When the fruit was ripe for plucking, I gave it to your vizier, who ate whatever seemed good to him. Then he abandoned it and did not water it so that its bloom has wilted and withered. Its shine has vanished, and its state has changed."

Then the vizier said, "Oh my king, this man speaks the truth. I did indeed care for and guard the garden and kept it in good condition. I ate a great deal from this garden until one day I went there, and I saw the trail of the lion. Fearing for my life, I withdrew from the garden and haven't returned."

The king understood that the trail of the lion meant his own seal ring, which he had forgotten in the vizier's house. So he said, "Return, oh vizier, to your flower garden and fear nothing. The truth is that the lion never came near it. I know that he went there, but by the honor of my forefathers, he did no damage to it."

"Hearing is obeying," answered the minister, and he returned home, sent for his wife, and made his peace with her. From then on he placed his faith in her chastity.

"I tell this to you, oh king," continued the vizier, "for no other purpose except to let you know how great women's craft is and how haste produces waste and repentance. And I have also heard the story of

The Confectioner, His Wife, and the Parrot

Once upon a time there was a confectioner, who lived in Egypt, and a wife, famous for her beauty and her loveliness. He also had a parrot which, depending on the occasion, served as a watchman, guard, bell, and spy, and she would flap her wings if she but heard a fly buzzing around the sugar. The parrot was extremely trouble-some for the wife because she always told the husband what took place during his absence.

Now, one evening, before going out to visit certain friends, the confectioner gave the bird strict instructions to watch all night and told his wife to lock everything up tightly because he would not return until morning. No sooner did he leave the house than the woman went to fetch her old lover, who returned with her, and they passed the night together in mirth and merriment, while the parrot observed everything. Sometime in the morning, the lover left, and when the husband returned, the parrot informed him about what had taken place. So the confectioner rushed to his wife's room and gave her a terrible beating. Then she thought to herself, "Who could have informed against me?" and she asked a woman with whom she was intimate whether it had been her. The woman protested and swore that she had not betrayed her mistress, but she did reveal that on the morning of her husband's return home, he had stood some time in front of the parrot's cage and had listened to her talk. When the wife heard this, she decided to bring about the destruction of the bird.

Some days after, the husband was once again invited to the house of a friend, where he was to spend the night. Before leaving, he gave the parrot the same instructions as before, and his mind was set at ease because he had his spy at home. But the wife and her confidante began to plan how they could undermine the credit of the parrot with the master. As part of their plan, they created a fake storm over the parrot's head by grinding a hand mill, pouring water on a piece of hide, and waving a fan over a candle. In this way they made it seem that there was a tempest of rain and light-ning, and the parrot was drenched and half drowned in a deluge. The thunder rolled, and the lightning flashed from the hand mill and the candle. The parrot thought to herself, "In truth, this is a flood that is perhaps greater than the one that Noah had witnessed." Upon saying this, she buried her head under her wing, a prey to ter-ror. On his return, the husband went directly to the parrot to ask what had happened during his absence, and the bird answered that she found it impossible to describe the deluge and tempest of the past night, and that years would be required to explain the uproar of the hurricane and storm. When the shopkeeper heard the parrot talk of last night's deluge, he said, "Certainly, oh bird, you've gone clean out of your mind! There wasn't the slightest drop of rain or flash of lightning last night. You have utterly ruined the ancient reputation of my house and family. My wife is the most virtuous woman living today, and all your accusations concerning her are false."

In his fury he threw the cage onto the ground, tore off the parrot's head, and threw it out the window. Soon his friend, who had come to pay a visit, arrived and saw the parrot with her head torn off and without wings and feathers. When he was informed about what had happened, he suspected some trick on the part of the woman and said to the husband, "When your wife leaves home to go to the Hammam bath, compel her confidante to disclose her secret."

So as soon as the wife went out, the husband entered his harem and insisted that the woman tell him the truth. She recounted the whole story, and the husband now bitterly repented having killed the parrot, because now he had clear proof of the bird's innocence.

"I tell you all this, oh king," continued the vizier, "so that you may know how great are the craft and the malice of women and that to act in haste will cause you to repent later on."

So the king delayed the slaying of his son, but the next day, his favorite concubine came to him, kissed the ground before him, and said, "Oh king, why are you delaying the execution of justice for me? Indeed, the people have heard that you command one thing, and your vizier counter-commands it. Now, every subject is required to obey his king's commandments, and everyone knows how just and fair you are. So I want justice done for me in the case of the prince. I have also heard a tale concerning

The Fuller and His Son

There was once a man who was a fuller, and he used to go to the bank of the Tigris every day to clean clothes. His son usually went with him so that he could swim while his father was cleaning clothes. One day, as the boy was swimming, he suffered a cramp in his forearms and began drowning. Immediately, the fuller plunged into the water and caught hold of him, but the boy clung to him and pulled him down. So both the father and the son were drowned.

"Thus it is with you, oh king," the concubine stated. "Unless you prevent your son from clinging to you and do me justice, you and he may sink together. Moreover, if you want an example of the malice of men, I have heard a tale concerning

The Rake's Trick Against the Chaste Wife

A certain man loved a beautiful and lovely woman, a model of charm and grace, who was married to a man whom she loved and who loved her. Moreover, she was virtuous and chaste as I am, and the rake, who wanted her, could find no way to get to her. So when he ran out of patience, he conceived a plan to gain the object of his desire.

Now, the husband had a young man, whom he had brought up in his house, and who was in a position of high trust as steward. So the rake approached the young man and continually tried to win his favor through presents, fair words, and deeds, until the young man obeyed his every desire and did whatever the rake ordered him to do.

One day the rake said to him, "Listen, I would very much appreciate it if you would bring me into your house when the lady has gone out."

The young steward agreed, and when his master was at the shop and his lady had gone out to the Hammam, he took his friend by the hand, brought him into the house, and showed him the sitting rooms and everything in them. Now the rake was determined to play a trick on the woman. So he took the white of an egg which he had brought with him in a vessel and spilt it on the merchant's bed when the steward was not looking. Afterward he thanked the young man and departed.

In an hour or so, the merchant came home, and when he went to bed to rest, he found something wet on it. He picked it up in his hand, looked at it, and was convinced that it was some man's semen. Therefore, he glared at the young man in anger and asked, "Where is my mistress?"

"She has gone to the Hammam," he answered, "and she will return as soon as she has done her ablutions."

When the man heard this, his suspicion concerning the semen was confirmed, and he grew furious and said, "Go at once and bring her back."

Accordingly, the steward fetched her, and when she stood before her husband, he jumped on her and gave her a horrendous beating. Then he tied her arms behind her and threatened to cut her throat with a knife, but she cried out to the neighbors, who came to her aid.

"This man has beaten me unjustly and without reason!" she cried. "He has threatened to kill me, even though I do not know how I have offended him."

So the people asked him, "Why have you treated her like this?"

"I consider her divorced," he said.

"You have no right to treat her this way," they declared. "Either divorce her properly or treat her kindly, for we have always known her as a prudent, pure, and chaste woman. Indeed, she has been our neighbor for a long time, and we have never heard one bad word about her."

"When I returned home today," he said, "I found something wet on my bed like semen, and I don't know what to make of this."

Upon hearing this, a little boy who was present came forward and said, "Show it to me, uncle."

When he saw it, he smelt it and called for fire and a frying pan. He took the white of the egg and cooked it so that it became solid. Then he ate some of it and asked the husband and the others to taste it, and they became convinced that it was the white of an egg. So the husband realized that he had sinned against his innocent wife, and the neighbors brought about peace between the two. He begged her pardon and gave her a present of one hundred gold pieces. So the wicked rake's cunning trick came to nothing.

"This, then, oh king, is a good example of the malice of men," the concubine concluded.

When the king heard this, he commanded that his son be slain, but on the next day the second vizier came forward to intercede and kissed the ground in prostration. Whereupon the king said, "Raise your head. You are to prostrate yourself only before Allah Almighty."

So the minister rose before him and said, "Oh king, do not be too hasty to slay your son, for he was granted to his mother only after you were in great despair. Nor did you expect such great luck. We hope that he will live to become the heir of your realm and a guardian of all your goods. Please, have patience, oh king. I am sure that he will be able to explain everything. If you are too hasty and have him slain, you will surely repent just as the merchant repented."

"And what happened with the merchant?" the king asked.

"Oh king," said the vizier, "I have heard a tale of

The Miser and the Loaves of Bread

There was once a merchant who was very miserly when it came to eating and drinking. One day he went on a journey to a certain town, and as he walked through the market streets, he met an old woman with two scones of bread that looked very enticing. So he asked her, "Are these for sale?"

When she answered, "Yes," he bargained with her and bought them at the lowest possible price. Then he took them home, where he ate them that day. The next day he returned to the same place, and upon finding the woman there with two other scones, he bought these as well, and he continued to do this for the next twenty-five days until the old woman disappeared. He asked after her, but he could not obtain any news of her until, one day, as he was walking around the streets, he happened to come upon her. So he approached her, and after the usual salutation and with much praise and politeness, he asked why she had disappeared from the market and had stopped supplying him with the two scones. At first she tried to evade him, but he implored her to explain her absence until she said, "My lord, I was attending a man who had a corroding ulcer on his spine, and his doctor asked us to knead flour with butter into a plaster and lay it on the place of pain, where it stayed all night. In the morning, I used to take that flour, turn it into dough, and make it into two scones, which I baked and sold to you or someone else. But when the man died, I was no longer in a position to make the scones."

When the man heard this, he repented, but his repentance did not help. "Truly, we are Allah's," he said. "Truly, we shall return to Him. We bring about all the evil that happens to us." And he vomited and repented, but it did him no good.

"Moreover, oh king," the vizier continued, "I have another example of the malice of women in the tale of

The Lady and Her Two Lovers

Once upon a time there was a man who was the sword-bearer to one of the kings, and he loved a maiden from the lower classes. One day he sent his page to her with a message as he usually did, and the young man sat down with her and began playing with her. She leaned over to him, pressed him to her breast, embraced him, and kissed him. He was so aroused that he wanted to make love to her, and she consented. But as the two were about to make love, the page's master knocked at the door. So she pushed the page through a trapdoor into an underground chamber and opened the door to the sword-bearer, who entered with his sword in hand and sat down on her bed. Then she came up to him and began playing and toying with him. She kissed him and pressed him to her bosom, and he took her and lay with her. Soon her husband knocked at the door, and the sword-bearer asked her, "Who is that?"

"My husband," she replied.

"What shall I do?" he said.

"Draw your sword," she responded, "and stand in the vestibule. Then abuse me and revile me. When my husband comes in, you leave and go your way."

He did as she told him, and when the husband entered, he saw the king's sword-bearer standing with his sword in hand, abusing and threatening his wife. As soon as the sword-bearer saw the husband, he became ashamed, sheathed his scimitar, and left the house.

"What is the meaning of this?" asked the husband.

"Oh husband!" she cried. "What a blessing that you arrived when you did! You have saved a true believer from slaughter. I was spinning on the house terrace when all of a sudden a young man came up to me. He was distracted and panting out of fear for death. Indeed, he was fleeing from that man you just saw, who had followed with a drawn sword. The young man fell down before me, kissed my hands and feet, and said, 'Oh lady, have mercy on me! Save me from this man who wants to slay me unjustly.' So, I hid him in that underground chamber of ours, and soon the man with the sword entered and demanded the young man. But I refused. So he began to abuse me and threaten me just as you saw. Praise be to Allah for sending you to me at the right moment, for I was distraught and had no one to save me."

"You have done well!" said the husband. "Your reward is with Allah Almighty, and may He reward you abundantly for your good deed!"

Then he went to the trapdoor and called the page: "Come out and do not fear. No harm shall be done to you."

So he came out, trembling with fear, and the husband said, "Don't worry. Nobody will hurt you."

The husband sympathized with him, and the page was grateful. Then they both went forth, and neither one of them, neither the cuckold nor the page, realized how the woman had cunningly saved the day for herself.

"This, then, oh king," said the vizier, "is one of the tricks of women. So beware and do not trust their words."

The king was persuaded and delayed putting his son to death. But on the third day, his favorite concubine came to him, kissed the ground before him, and said, "Oh king, I should like justice. Please do not be turned away from doing your duty by your ministers' nonsensical talk, for there is nothing good in wicked viziers, and don't be like the king of Baghdad, who relied on the word of a certain wicked counselor."

"And how was that?" asked the king.

"Oh benevolent king," she responded, "I have heard the tale of

The King's Son and the Ogress

A certain king had a son, whom he loved and favored over all his other children, and this son said to him one day, "Oh my father, I would like to go out and hunt today."

So the king had him properly equipped and commanded one of his viziers to keep him company and provide him with all the service he needed during his trip. Accordingly, the minister took everything that was necessary for the journey, and they set out with a retinue of eunuchs and officers. As they proceeded, they played various games along the way until they came to a green pasture with water and game. Here the prince turned to the minister and told him that the place pleased him, and he wanted to halt there. They were very happy about all this and stayed there some days enjoying themselves. Then the king's son gave the signal for departure, but as they went along, a beautiful gazelle with glistening horns that had strayed from her mate sprang in front of the prince. So taken was he by the gazelle that he longed to capture her. Therefore he said to the vizier, "I want to follow that gazelle."

"Do what you like," the minister replied.

Thereupon the prince rode off by himself and pursued the gazelle until he lost sight of his companions and chased her all that day until dusk, when she took refuge in a bit of rocky ground, and darkness overtook him. "Only the Almighty Allah can save me now!" he said.

Well, he sat on his mare all night until morning arrived, and he went in quest of relief but found none. As the day went on, he roamed randomly and became fearful, famished, and thirsty, and he did not know where to turn until it was noon and the sun beat down on him with burning heat. By that time he came in sight of a great city with a massive fortress and bulwarks. However, it was ruined and desolate, and the only living things were owls and ravens. As he stood among the buildings, marveling at their condition, his eyes fell on a young, beautiful, and lovely maiden sitting under one of the city walls weeping copious tears. So he approached her and asked, "Who are you, and who brought you here?"

"I am called Bint al-Tamimah, daughter of Al-Tiyakh, king of the Gray Country," she answered. "I went out one day to obey a call of nature and an ifrit of the jinn snatched me and soared with me between heaven and earth. But as he flew, he was struck by a shooting star in the form of a flame of fire that burned him, and I dropped here, where I have spent the last three days dying of hunger and thirst. However, as soon as I saw you, I longed for life."

When the prince heard these words, he felt sorry for her and had great compassion for her. So he lifted her up on his saddle and said, "Cheer up, and don't weep. If Allah restores me to my people, I shall send you back to your folk."

Then he rode on, and soon the maiden said to him, "Oh prince, please set me down, for I should like to go over there near the wall."

The prince stopped the horse, and she got down. He waited for a long time as she went behind the wall. When she came out, she had the foulest smell and looked so terrible that his hair stood on end. Indeed, he trembled for fear of her and turned deadly pale. Then she sprang up on his steed, right behind him, and had a loathsome aspect.

"My prince," she said, "what's the matter? You seem to be troubled, and your mood has changed."

"I know what troubles me."

"Then seek the aid of your father's troops and warriors."

"He whom I fear is not afraid of troops or warriors."

"Then seek the aid of your father's money and gold."

"He whom I fear will not be satisfied with wealth."

"You maintain that you have a God in heaven who sees and is not seen and is omnipotent and omniscient."

"Yes, we have none but Him."

"Then pray to Him, and perhaps he will save you from your enemy!"

So the king's son raised his eyes toward heaven and began to pray with his whole heart:

"Oh my God, I beg of you. Please send me help against that which is troubling me!"

Then he pointed to her with his hand, and she fell to the ground, burnt black as charcoal. Thereupon he thanked Allah and praised Him and continued on his way. The Almighty made his way easy and guided him onto the right road so that he reached his own country and arrived at his father's capital after he had despaired of living. Now all this happened because of the deceitful vizier, who had traveled with him and wanted the prince to perish. But Almighty Allah saved him.

"I have told you this story, oh king," continued the concubine, "so that you will know that wicked viziers do not deal honestly and do not give honest advice. So beware of them in this matter."

The king listened to her speech and ordered his son to be put to death, but the third vizier came in and said to his fellow ministers, "I shall protect you from the king's mischief today," and when he went to the king, he kissed the ground between his hands and said, "Oh king, I am your true counselor and care about you and your state. Indeed, I always give you the best advice, and now I should like to warn you not to slay your son, for his sin is but a slight slip which this lady has exaggerated. Indeed, I have heard tell that the people of two villages once destroyed one another because of a drop of honey."

"How was that?" asked the king.

"Oh king," the vizier replied, "this story is called

The Drop of Honey

A certain hunter used to chase wild beasts in the woods, and one day he came upon a grotto in the mountains, where he found a hollow full of bees' honey. So he took some of it in a water skin that he had with him, and after throwing it over his shoulder, he carried it to the city, followed by a hunting dog that was dear to him. He stopped at the shop of an oilman and offered to sell him the honey, which he bought. Then the oilman emptied it out of the skin so that he might see it, and while he was doing this, a drop fell to the ground. All at once the flies flocked to it, and a bird swooped down upon the flies. Now the oilman had a cat, which sprang upon the bird, and the hunter's dog, upon seeing the cat, sprang upon it and killed it. In turn, the oilman sprang upon the dog and killed it, causing the hunter to spring upon the oilman and kill him. Now the oilman belonged to one village, and the hunter to another. When the people of the two places learned what had happened, they took up arms and weapons and attacked each other in fury. The two sides met, and they did not drop their swords until numerous people had died, so many that only Allah Almighty knows the exact number.

"But let me also tell you another story about the malice of women," continued the vizier. "I have heard one concerning

The Woman Who Made Her Husband Sift Dirt

A man once gave his wife a dirham to buy some rice. So she took it and went to the rice seller, who gave her the rice and began to jest with her and ogle her, for she was beautiful and lovely.

"Rice is only good with sugar," he said, "and if you would like some, come into my shop with me for an hour."

"Well then," she responded, "give me some sugar."

So she went into his shop, and he won his will with her and said to his slave, "Give her a dirham's worth of sugar."

But he signaled to the slave on the sly, and when the boy took the napkin which held the rice, he emptied it out and put in earth and dust instead. Then he stuck in stones in place of sugar, tied a knot around the napkin, and placed it by the woman's side. The shopkeeper's purpose in having his slave do this was to have her come to the shop a second time. So when she left, he gave her the napkin, and she took it, assuming that it contained rice and sugar. But when she returned home and set it before her husband, she went looking for a pot while he found the earth and stones in the napkin. So as soon as she came back with the pot, he said to her, "Did I tell you that I was building something? Is this why you have brought me earth and stones?"

When she saw this, she knew that the rice seller's slave had tricked her, and she said to her husband, "Oh, I've been so upset today that I went to fetch the sieve and brought the cooking pot."

"What's upsetting you?" he asked.

"Oh husband," she moaned, "I dropped the dirham you gave me in the market street and was ashamed to search for it in front of all the people. But I also felt bad about losing the silver. So I gathered the dirt from the place where it fell and brought it home, where I wanted to sift it. This is why I went to fetch the sieve but brought the pot instead."

Then she fetched the sieve and gave it to her husband and said, "Why don't you sift for it? Your eyes are sharper than mine."

Accordingly, he sat, sifting the dirt, until his face and beard were covered with dust, and he did not discover her trick or what had happened to her.

"This, then, oh king," continued the vizier, "is an example of the malice of women. Remember the saying of Allah Almighty: 'Surely, the cunning of women is great!' Or, 'Indeed, the malice of Satan is weak in comparison with the malice of women.'"

The King listened to his vizier's speech and was persuaded by it. He liked what the vizier had quoted from Allah, and the vizier's good counsel made him realize how foolish it would be to have his son slain. But on the fourth day, his favorite concubine came in weeping and wailing, and she kissed the ground before him.

"Oh beneficent king," she said, "I have made very clear to you what my grievance is, and you have dealt unjustly with me. Indeed, you refuse to revenge me against the man who has wronged me just because he is your son and your favorite. But Allah will soon help me against him just as he helped the king's son against his father's vizier."

"And how was that?" the king asked.

Then she answered, "Oh king, I have heard tell of a tale of

The Enchanted Spring

In olden days there was once a king who had only one son, and when the prince had grown up, the king signed a contract to have him marry another king's daughter. Now, this maiden was a model of beauty and grace, and her uncle's son had wanted to marry her, but she had not wanted him. So when he found out that she was to be married to another, he was overcome by envy and jealousy. Therefore he decided to send a noble present and a goodly treasure to the vizier of the bridegroom's father in order to recruit him to kill the prince or to make him abandon his intention of marrying her.

"Oh vizier," he wrote, "it is great jealousy that has prompted me to act this way."

The vizier accepted the present and sent him an answer: "Do not fret, and keep a cool head, for I shall do everything that you wish."

Soon the bride's father wrote to the prince and invited him to the capital so that he might visit his daughter. Thereupon his father gave him permission to go, and he sent the bribed vizier with him along with a thousand horses, presents, litters, tents, and pavilions. During the journey the minister was plotting against the prince, and when they reached the desert, he recalled a certain spring of running water in the mountains called Al-Zahara, and it was said that whenever a man drank from it he became a woman. So he called the troops to halt near the fountain, and then he himself remounted his steed and asked the prince if he would like to go with him and look at a spring of water nearby. Not knowing what would happen to him, the prince mounted, and they rode on without any guards until they came to the spring. Since he was thirsty, the prince said to the vizier, "Oh minister, I'm very thirsty."

"Well," said the vizier, "get down and drink some water from this spring."

So they stopped, and the prince got down, washed his hands, and drank. All of a sudden, he became a woman, and as soon as he realized this, he fainted. The vizier went up to him as if to find out what had happened to him and cried, "What's the matter?"

The prince quickly recovered from his fainting spell and told him what had happened. The minister pretended to feel sorry for him and wept.

"May Allah Almighty help you!" the minister sighed. "How did this calamity happen? This is certainly your misfortune. Here we are, taking you with joy and happiness to the king's daughter, and this happens! Truly, I do not know whether we should go to her. It is your decision. I shall do what you command me to do."

"Go back to my father and tell him what has happened," the prince said. "I shall not stir from this spot until I can do something about my condition. If I can't change things, I'll die out of shame."

So he wrote a letter to his father, telling him what had happened, and the vizier took it and returned to the city, leaving the troops with the prince and inwardly rejoicing at the success of his plot. As soon as he reached the king's capital, he went to him and delivered the letter. The king mourned for his son and sent for the wise men and masters of esoteric science so that they might explain what had happened to his son, but none could provide him with an answer. Then the vizier wrote to the lady's cousin to tell him the good news of the prince's misfortune. When this rival prince read the letter, he was exceedingly happy and thought that he could now marry the princess. He sent the minister more rich presents and precious jewels from his treasury in thanks for his deed.

Meanwhile, the prince dwelled three days and nights by the spring, and he did not eat or drink. He placed his fate in the hands of Allah, who does not disappoint those who rely on him. On the fourth night, a cavalier arrived on a bright bay steed. He had a crown on his head as if he were a son of a king, and he asked, "Who brought you here, young man?"

The prince told him about his misfortune, and as he spoke, his speech was broken by tears. After hearing his story, the horseman pitied him and said, "It was your father's vizier who caused this predicament. He is the only man alive who knows about this spring. Now, I want you to mount behind me and come with me to my dwelling, for you are my guest tonight."

"Please tell me who you are before I go away with you," the prince requested.

"I am a prince of the jinn," said the horseman, "just as you are the prince of a human king. So, cheer up and don't weep, for I shall certainly change things for you. It is easy for me to do."

So the prince mounted behind the stranger, and they rode off, leaving the troops behind them, for the entire day until midnight, when the jinnee asked the prince, "Do you know how many days' march we have accomplished?"

The prince replied, "No."

"We have done a full year's journey!"

The prince was astonished upon hearing this and said, "But how shall I return to my people?"

"That is not your affair, but my business," the jinnee said. "As soon as I rid you of your present form, you will return to your people in less than the twinkling of an eye. It is an easy matter for me."

When the prince heard these words, he was beyond himself with joy. It seemed to him that he was in a dream, and he exclaimed, "Glory be to Him who has the power to restore the unhappy to happiness!"

So they continued their journey until the next morning, when they found themselves in a verdant country full of tall trees, birds, fruit, high palaces, streams, and flowers. Here the jinnee dismounted and told the prince to do the same. He took him by the hand and led him into one of the palaces, where he met a great king and powerful sultan. The prince stayed with him all that day eating and drinking until nightfall. Then the jinnee mounted his horse and lifted the prince up behind him. They journeyed through darkness until morning, when they found themselves in a bleak land, a desert full of black rocks and stones as if it were a part of hell. The prince asked the jinnee, "What is the name of this land?"

"It is called the Black Country and belongs to one of the kings of the jinn, named Zu'l Janahayn, who is omnipotent. Nobody may enter his dominions except by his consent. So wait here while I go ask his permission."

Upon saying this, the jinnee went away and soon returned. Then they continued their journey until they came to a spring of water that sprouted from a black rock, and the jinnee said to the prince, "Get down!"

The prince dismounted, and the jinnee cried, "Drink the water!"

So he drank water from the spring, and no sooner had he done so than he became as man as he was before by the grace of Allah. Consequently, he burst with joy and asked the jinnee, "Oh my brother, what is the name of this spring?"

"It is called the Women's Spring," he replied. "If a woman drinks here, she becomes a man right away. So now praise Allah and thank him for restoring you to your former condition. Then let us mount and be on our way."

So the prince prostrated himself in gratitude to the Almighty. After that he mounted, and they traveled all day until they reached the jinnee's home, where the prince passed the night in solace. They spent the next day in eating and drinking until nightfall, when the jinnee asked the prince, "Would you like to return to your people this very night?"

"Yes," he answered, "for I have missed them."

Then the jinnee called one of his father's slaves named

Rajiz and said to him, "Take this young man, place him on your shoulders, and do not let the day dawn until he is with his father-in-law and wife."

"I am at your service," replied the slave. "This I shall do willingly and with love and care!"

The slave withdrew for a moment and then reappeared as an ifrit. When the prince saw this, he was scared out of his mind, but the jinnee said to him, "Don't be afraid. No harm will come to you. Mount your horse, and let him jump onto the ifrit's shoulders."

"No," the prince answered, "I shall leave my horse with you, and get on his shoulders by myself."

So he sprang onto the ifrit's shoulders, and the jinnee cried, "Close your eyes, my lord, and don't be a coward!"

The prince plucked up his courage and shut his eyes. Thereupon the ifrit arose with him into the air and did not stop flying between heaven and earth while the prince was unconscious. Indeed, it took three days before the ifrit finally set him down on the terrace roof of his father-in-law's palace. Then the ifrit said, "Dismount and open your eyes, for this is the palace of your father-in-law and his daughter."

So the prince got down, and the ifrit flew away, leaving him on the roof of the palace. When dawn arrived and the prince recovered from his dangerous flight, he descended into the palace, and his father-in-law caught sight of him and was astonished to see him descend from the roof of the palace.

"We generally see people enter through doors," he said, "but you have come from the sky."

"Whatever Allah decrees," said the prince, "this is the way it will be done."

And the prince told him all that happened to him from first to last, and the king was amazed and very glad that he had arrived safely in his palace. As soon as the sun rose, he ordered his vizier to prepare splendid wedding feasts. Once everything was arranged, they held the marriage celebration, and the prince went in and slept with his bride and stayed with her for two months. Then he departed with her for his father's capital. As for the lady's cousin, he died right away from envy and jealousy. When the prince and his bride drew near his father's city, the king came out to meet them with his troops and ministers, and so Allah enabled the prince to triumph over his bride's cousin and his father's vizier.

*   *   *

"And pray to the Almighty," the concubine added, "that He will aid you against your viziers, oh king! I beseech you to do me justice against your son!"

When the king heard this, he ordered his son to be put to death. Now, this was the fourth day, and so the fourth vizier entered, and after kissing the ground before the king, he said, "May Allah protect your majesty! Oh king, I implore you to be careful about your actions, for the wise man does nothing until he considers every aspect of the situation. There is a proverb that says, 'He who does not understand the consequences of his actions will not have a friend in the world,' and he who acts without consideration for others will experience what the Hammam-keeper experienced with his wife."

"And what happened to him?" asked the king.

And the vizier replied, "I have heard tell, oh king, of

The Vizier's Son and the Hammam-Keeper's Wife

There was once a bath-keeper whose Hammam was frequented by all the notables and chiefs of the city, and one day a handsome young man appeared. He was the son of a vizier and was fat and husky. So the bath-keeper attended him, and when the young man took off his clothes, he did not see his yardstick that was hidden between his thighs because of the man's excessive fat. When the bath-keeper noticed that something was missing, he lamented and wrung his hands. But the young man saw this and asked, "What's the matter, bath-keeper? Why are you lamenting so?"

"Oh my lord," said the bath-keeper, "I am lamenting for you because of your present condition. Despite all your good fortune and handsome qualities, I see that you have nothing to gain and receive pleasure like other men."

"You speak the truth," said the young man, "but you remind me of something that I had forgotten."

"What is that?" asked the bath-keeper.

And the young man answered, "Take this gold piece and fetch me a pretty woman so that I can prove my nature on her."

So he took the money and went to his wife and said, "There is a young man in the baths, a son of a vizier, who is as handsome as the full moon, but he doesn't have a prickle like other men, and the only thing I could see was some small thing like a little nut. I lamented about his condition, and the young man gave me this dinar and asked me to fetch him a woman with whom he could have some pleasure. Now, why don't you take this money, for no harm will come to you, and I shall protect you. All you have to do is sit with him awhile, laugh at him, and take this dinar."

So the good wife took the dinar, got up, and put on her richest clothes and looked like the most beautiful woman of her time. Then she went out with her husband, and he took her to the vizier's son in a private place. When she entered, she found him extremely handsome and was taken by his attractive features. Similarly, his heart and soul were captivated by the first sight of her and her smile. So he arose right away and locked the door. He took the lady into his arms and pressed her into his bosom, and they embraced, causing the young man's yardstick to swell and rise erect as a rod, and he rode on her and futtered her, while she sobbed, sighed, writhed, and wriggled under him. Now the bath-keeper was standing behind the door waiting for his wife, and he called out to her, "Oh Abdillah, enough! Come out. You've been there for quite some time, and your baby boy needs you."

"Go to your boy," the vizier's son said to the woman, "and then return to me later."

But she answered, "If I leave you, my soul will leave my body. As far as the child is concerned, he will either have to die of weeping or be reared an orphan without a mother."

So she stayed with him until he took his pleasure of

her ten times while her husband stood at the door calling her, crying out, weeping, and calling for help. But nobody came to his aid, and he continued to cry out until he finally sighed, "I shall kill myself if you don't come out!"

But she did not come out, and since he heard her sighing, murmuring, and breathing hard under the young man, he became distraught with rage and jealousy. Therefore, he went to the top of the bathhouse and jumped into the street and died.

"Moreover, oh king," continued the vizier, "I have another story for you about

The Wife's Plan to Cheat Her Husband

There was once a woman who had no equal in her day when it came to beauty, loveliness, and grace. One day, a certain obscene and lewd young man set his eyes on her and fell passionately in love with her, but she was chaste and not inclined to adultery.

Soon after he saw her, it so happened that her husband had to take a journey to a certain town, and the young man kept sending her messages and presents many times during the day, but she did not reply. At last, he found an old woman who lived nearby, and after greeting her, he sat down and told her how much he was suffering because of his love and longing for this woman.

"I can help you end your suffering," said the old woman. "I shall make sure that you get what you desire, Allah willing."

Upon hearing these words, he gave her a dinar and went his way. When morning came, she appeared before the woman, and after renewing her acquaintance with her, she began visiting her daily, eating meals with her, and carrying food away for her children. Moreover, she began to play and jest with her until the wife became so

used to her that she could not endure an hour without
her company. Now, when the old woman left the lady's
house, she was accustomed to take bread and fat with
which she mixed a little pepper, and she fed a dog that
was in that quarter. She kept doing this every day until
the dog became fond of her and followed her wherever
she went. One day she took a cake of dough and put an
overdose of pepper in it. Then she gave it to the dog to

eat, and the animal's eyes began to shed tears because of the hot pepper, and the weeping dog followed the woman. When the lady saw this, she was amazed and asked the old woman, "Oh mother, what's the matter with this dog?"

"It's a strange story, my heart's love," said the old woman. "This bitch was once a close friend of mine, a lovely and accomplished young lady, a model of beauty and perfect grace. Well, a young Nazarene fell in love with her, and his passion and pining increased until he could no longer get out of bed. He sent many messages to her, begging her to have compassion on him and show him mercy, but she refused, even though I gave her good advice, saying, 'Oh my daughter, have pity on him and be kind and consent to all that he desires.' She paid no attention to my advice, causing the young man to complain to one of his friends, who cast a spell on her so that she was changed into a dog. When she saw how she had been transformed and nobody pitied her except me, she came to my house and began to fawn, kiss my hands and feet, whine, and shed tears. Finally, I recognized her and said, 'Didn't I warn you many times? Now see what has happened!' Nevertheless, my daughter, I had pity on her and have kept her by me. Now, whenever she thinks about her former condition, she weeps in pity for herself."

When the lady heard this, she was greatly alarmed and said, "Oh my mother, by Allah, you frighten me with this story."

"Why so?" asked the old woman.

"Because a certain handsome young man fell in love with me and has sent messages and presents to me many times, but I have repelled him. Now I'm afraid that something might happen to me like what happened to this bitch."

"Oh my daughter," responded the old woman, "here is what I advise, and make sure that you do as I say, for I am afraid about your fate. If you do not know where he lives, describe him to me so that I may take him to you and so that no one will get angry at you."

So the lady described him to her, and the old woman

pretended not to know him and said, "When I go out, I shall ask after him."

But when she left the lady, she went straight to the young man and said to him, "Cheer up. I have played some tricks on the lady's mind. So, tomorrow noon wait at the head of the street until I come and fetch you to her house, where you may relax with her for the entire day and night."

The young man was exceedingly happy when he heard this news and gave her two dinars.

"When I have taken my pleasure with her," he said, "I shall give you ten gold pieces."

Then she returned to the lady and said, "I have seen him and talked to him about this matter. I found him very angry with you and about to cause you some harm. But I persuaded him with fair words until he agreed to come tomorrow at the time of noon prayer."

When the lady heard this, she was very happy and said, "Oh mother, if he keeps his promise, I shall give you ten dinars."

"I shall make sure that he comes," she said.

The next day the old woman said to the lady, "Prepare a grand meal and make sure that you do not forget the wine. Put on your richest dress and jewels while I go fetch him."

So she clad herself in her finest garments and prepared food while the old woman went out to look for the young man, who did not arrive. So she went around searching for him, but she could not obtain any news of him. "What is to be done?" she said to herself. "Shall all the food and drink be wasted and I lose the gold pieces that she has promised me? Indeed, I shall not allow my cunning and plans to come to nothing. I'll look for another man and take him to her." So she continued walking around the streets until she noticed a handsome fellow, young and distinguished-looking, to whom people bowed. From his face, it seemed that he had just been traveling. So, she went up to him and saluted him, "Would you like to have a good meal, something to drink, and a prim and pretty lady?"

"Where may I find all this?" he asked.

"At home in my house," she responded and took him to his own house and knocked at the door. The lady opened the door and quickly ran back to the toilet to finish her dressing and perfuming. In the meantime, the wicked old woman brought the man, who was the lady's own husband, into the salon and had him sit down, congratulating herself on her cunning deception. Soon the lady entered the salon, and as soon as she set eyes on her husband sitting by the old trot, she recognized him and guessed at how things stood. Nevertheless, she was not taken aback, and she immediately thought of a plan to hoodwink him. So she pulled off her outer boot and cried at her husband, "Is this how you want our relationship to be? How can you betray me and treat me like this? I want to tell you that when I heard of your coming, I sent this old woman to test you, and she has made you fall into my trap. So now I know that you have other relationships and have broken my trust in you. I thought that you were faithful and pure until I saw you with my own eyes in this old woman's company. Now I know that you prefer loose living!"

Upon saying all this, she began to beat him on his head with her slipper, crying out, "Divorce me! Divorce me!"

He tried desperately to excuse himself and swore to her by Allah the Most High that he had never in his life been untrue to her, nor had he ever done anything wrong before this. But she wept and screamed and bashed him. "Come to my help, oh Moslems!" she cried. Finally, he had to place his hand over her mouth, and she bit it. Then he got down on his hands and knees and kissed her hands and feet, but she was not satisfied and continued to cuff him. At last, the lady winked at the old woman to come and hold her hands so she wouldn't hit him anymore. So the old woman came up to her, kissed her hands and feet, and made peace between them. Thereupon they sat down together, and the husband began to kiss her hands and say, "May Allah Almighty reward you for saving me from temptation!"

In the end, it was the old woman who was completely

astonished and impressed by the wife's cunning and quick wit.

"This, then, oh king," continued the vizier, "is one of the many examples of the craft, malice, and perfidy of women."

When the king heard this story, he was persuaded by it and decided not to have his son slain. But on the fifth day, the concubine entered with a bowl of poison in her hand. She called upon heaven to help her and slapped her cheeks and face and said to him, "Oh king, either you will do justice and avenge me on your son, or I shall drink this cup with poison and die. The sin of my blood will be on your head at the Day of Doom. Your ministers accuse me of malice and perfidy, but none in the world are more perfidious than men. Have you never heard of the story of

The Goldsmith and the Cashmere Singing Girl

There was once a goldsmith who lived in a city of Persia, and he delighted in women and wine. One day he was at the house of a friend, and he saw the figure of a lutanist, a beautiful maiden, painted on the wall, and never before had he ever beheld such a lovely damsel. He looked at the picture time and again and marveled at her beauty. Soon he fell so desperately in love with the maiden in the picture that he was close to dying.

Now it so happened that one of his friends came to visit him, and after he sat down by his side, he asked him why he was so sick, whereupon the goldsmith replied, "Oh brother, I am sick because of love, and it is all due to a picture of a woman painted on the house wall of our friend Abdul."

Upon hearing this, the goldsmith's friend said, "Have

you lost your mind? How could you fall in love with a painted figure on a wall when this figure can neither harm you nor benefit you, neither sees nor hears, and neither takes nor withholds?"

But the goldsmith replied, "Whoever painted that picture could not have done so without basing it on the human likeness of an enchanting woman."

"Most likely he painted it from his imagination," rejoined his friend.

"In any case," said the goldsmith, "here I am dying out of love for the picture, and if there is an original in the world somewhere, may Allah grant me the opportunity to see her before I die."

When his friend left, he went about and asked whether anyone knew about the painter of the picture, and when he learned that the painter had moved to another town, he wrote him a letter and informed him of the goldsmith's condition. He also asked whether he had drawn the figure from his own imagination or based it on a living model. The painter wrote back that he had used a singing girl as his model, and she belonged to one of the viziers in the city of Cashmere in the land of Hind. When the goldsmith learned about this, he left Persia for Cashmere, where he arrived after many trials and tribulations. After he was there awhile, he formed an acquaintance with a druggist, who was a keen, witty, and crafty fellow. One evening he asked the druggist about their king and his politics, and he responded, "Our king is just and righteous, fair to all his liege lords and beneficent to the common people. He abhors nothing in the world except for sorcerers. So whenever a sorcerer or sorceress falls into his hands, he throws them into a pit outside the city and leaves them there to die."

Then the goldsmith asked him about the king's viziers, and the druggist told him about each minister until the talk touched on the singing girl, and he revealed which vizier was her master. The goldsmith took note of the minister's dwelling and waited a few days until he concocted a plan to win his desire. Well, one rainy and stormy night, he took some thieves' tackle and went to the house of the vizier who owned the damsel. Here he threw a rope ladder with grappling irons onto the battlements and climbed up to the terrace room of the palace. Then he descended into the inner court and made his way to the harem, where he found all the slave girls lying asleep, each on her own couch. Among them was the damsel in the picture, but here she was reclining on a couch of alabaster and was covered with a coverlet of cloth of gold and shone like the half-moon. At her head stood a candle of ambergris, and at her feet another candle, each in a candlestick of glittering gold. Yet her brilliant beauty made them appear dim in comparison. Under her pillow lay a casket of silver that contained her jewels. He raised the coverlet, and drawing near her, he examined her up close and recognized the lutanist whom he desired. So he took out a knife and wounded her in the back parts, whereupon she awoke in terror. But when she saw him, she was afraid to cry out, thinking that he had come to steal her possessions. So she said to him, "Take the box and all that it contains, but please don't slay me, for I am in your hands and my death will not bring you any profit."

So he took the box and left. When morning arrived, he put on some clothes that are worn by men of learning and doctors, and he took the jewel case to the king of the city. When he was before the king, he kissed the ground and said to him, "Oh king, I am a devout man and wish you well. I have come here as a pilgrim to your court from the land of Khorasan, attracted by the report of your just government and fair treatment of your subjects, and I should like to be under your protection. I reached this city last night, and finding the gate locked and barred, I lay down to sleep outside your walls. But as I was about to fall asleep, I saw four women appear: one was riding on a broomstick, another on a wine jar, a third on an oven peel, and a fourth on a black bitch, and I knew that they were witches heading for your city. One of them came up to me and kicked me with her foot and beat me with a fox's tail. She hurt me so badly that I became mad and attacked her with a knife that I had with me, and I managed to wound her on her back parts as she turned to flee. But as she flew away, she dropped this casket, which I picked up and opened, and I found these precious jewels. So, please take them, for I don't need them. I am merely a wanderer in the mountains who has rejected the world and renounced everything worldly, seeking only the face of Allah the Most High."

Then the goldsmith set the casket before the king and went away. The king opened the box and emptied out all the trinkets. As he began turning them over in his hand, he came upon a necklace which he had presented to the vizier who was the master of the singing girl. Upon seeing this, he called the minister in question and asked him, "Is this the necklace that I had given to you?"

He recognized it immediately and answered, "It is. I gave it to my singing girl."

"Fetch the girl here right away," ordered the king.

So the vizier fetched the girl, and the king said, "Uncover her back parts and see if there is a wound."

The vizier did as he said and found a knife wound there.

"Yes, my lord," he replied, "there is a wound."

Then the king said, "This is the witch about whom the pilgrim told me, and there can be no doubt about it."

So he ordered her to be cast into the witches' pit, and they carried her there at once. As soon as it was night and the goldsmith knew that his plot had succeeded, he went to the pit, taking with him a purse of a thousand dinars. Once there he began a conversation with one of the guards and sat talking with him until a third of the night had passed, when he broached the matter of the singing girl with him. "You know, my brother," he said, "this girl is innocent of the charge brought against her, and it was really me who brought her into this predicament." Then he told him the whole story from first to last and added, "Please take this purse of a thousand dinars and give me the maiden so that I can take her to my country. These gold pieces will benefit you more than if you were to keep her in prison. Moreover, Allah will reward you for your compassion and we shall pray for your safety and prosperity."

When the guard heard this story, he was impressed by the goldsmith's cunning plan and its success. Then he took the money and delivered the girl to the goldsmith with the condition that he had to leave the city with her immediately. Consequently, the goldsmith took the girl and traveled without stopping until he reached his own country. This was the way that he managed to fulfill his wish.

"So, you see, oh majesty," continued the concubine, "just how devious and malicious men are. And now you know why your viziers are preventing you from doing justice to me. But tomorrow, you and I shall both stand before the just Judge, and He shall give me justice, oh king."

When the king heard this, he commanded his son to be put to death, but the fifth vizier came to him, kissed the ground, and said, "Oh mighty king, do not be rash. Haste will often bring about repentance, and I am afraid that you might suffer and repent just as the man who never laughed for the rest of his days."

"And how was that?" the king asked.

"Oh king," the vizier replied, "I have heard this tale concerning

The Man Who Never Laughed During the Rest of His Days

There was once a man who was very rich and owned a great deal of land, houses, money, goods, eunuchs, and slaves, but he died and left everything to a young son, who indulged himself in feasting, carousing, music, singing, and the loud laughter of parasites. Indeed, he wasted his inheritance in gifts and loose living until he had squandered everything he had owned. Consequently, he was reduced to poverty and had to work for his living as a day laborer. He lived this way for one year, and one day he was sitting under a wall waiting for someone to hire him when an old man, who was dressed in fine clothes and had handsome features, came up and saluted him.

"My lord," asked the young man, "have we met before?"

"Not that I know of," replied the gentleman. "We've never met, but I see a trace of gentle breeding in you despite your present condition."

"My lord," said the young man, "fate and fortune have had their way, but tell me, would you like to hire me to do some work for you?"

"I wish, my son," the old man responded, "to employ you in a slight matter. We are eleven old men in one house, but we have no one to serve us. So, if you will come and serve us, you will have as much food and clothing as you want to your heart's content in addition to a salary and tips. Perhaps Allah will help you this way, and fortune will be restored to you."

"I am at your disposal," said the young man.

"But I have one condition to impose on you," added the old man.

"What is that?"

"Oh my son," replied the old man, "you must keep our secret. You must not tell anyone about what you see, and if you see us weep, you may not question us about the cause of our weeping."

"I agree."

"Come with me, my son, and may Allah Almighty bless you."

So the young man followed him to the bath, where the old man had him clean his body of the crusted dirt, and afterward he sent some one to fetch linen garments for the young man. Then he took him to the home where he and his company of men lived. The young man found a lofty and spacious house with a solid foundation, and inside there were sitting chambers facing one another. In each of the salons there was a fountain of water with the birds warbling over it, and there were windows on every side that looked upon a magnificent garden. The old man brought him into one of the parlors with walls of marble in various colors. The ceiling was decorated with ultramarine and glowing gold, and the floor was covered with silken carpets. Here he found ten sheikhs in mourning garments seated opposite one another, weeping and wailing. He was curious and astounded by their behavior and was about to ask why they were mourning when he remembered the condition of his work and held his peace. Then the man who had brought him to the house took him to a chest containing thirty thousand dinars and said to him, "Oh my son, spend freely from this chest for our entertainment and yours. Just be faithful and remember the condition with which I hired you."

"I hear and obey," said the young man, and he served them night and day until one of them died, whereupon his friends washed him, shrouded him, and buried him in a garden behind the house. Then death came and took them one by one until only the sheikh who had hired the young man remained. Then the two men, old and young, dwelled together in that house alone for years and years, and there was never a third in the house except for Allah Almighty. Finally, the elder man fell sick, and the younger one despaired for his life. So he went to him and showed how sad he was and said, "Oh my lord, I have served you for twelve years and have never failed to carry out my duties, and I have always been loyal to you."

"Yes, my son," answered the old man. "You have served us well while all my comrades have gone to the mercy of Allah, and I, too, must die."

"Oh my lord," said the younger man, "before you die, I would like you to tell me why you have wept and wailed and mourned all these years."

"My son," said the old man, "this does not concern you. So please do not request me to tell you something I cannot do, for I have sworn to Almighty Allah that I would tell nobody about this. If I do, you will be afflicted with what happened to me and my comrades. If you want to be spared the suffering that I and my comrades have experienced, do not open that door over there."

And he pointed to a certain part of the house. "But if you want to suffer what we have suffered, then open it, and you will learn the reason why we have mourned all these years. And when you know it, you will repent what you have done."

Then the old man became sicker and died soon thereafter. The young man washed him with his own hands, shrouded him, and buried him by the side of his comrades. After this he lived alone in the place and took possession of everything. Still, he was uneasy and troubled by the history of these old men until, one day, as he sat pondering the words of his dead master and his warning not to open the door, he suddenly decided to go and look for it. So he rose up and went to the spot where the dead man had pointed and searched until he found a little door in a dark unfrequented corner over which a spider had spun her webs and which was locked with four padlocks of steel. Upon seeing this he recalled the old man's warning and restrained himself and went away. He kept his distance from the door for seven days, while his heart kept prompting him to open it. On the eighth day his curiosity got the better of him, and he said, "Come what may, I must open the door and see what will happen to me. Nothing can stop what is ordained and determined by Allah Almighty. Nor does anything happen except by His will."

Upon saying this he rose and broke the padlocks, and after opening the door, he saw a narrow passage, which he followed for some three hours, when, all of a sudden, he came out on the shore of a vast ocean and went along the beach, marveling at the great ocean about which he had known nothing. He turned to the right and to the left, and soon a huge eagle swooped down on him, seized him in its talons, and flew away with him into the sky, until it came to an island in the midst of the sea, where it cast him down and flew away. The young man was dazed and did not know where he should go, but after a few days, as he sat pondering his situation, he caught sight of the sails of a ship in the middle of the ocean, as if it were a star in the sky. His heart jumped, for he hoped rescue was near at hand. He kept gazing at the ship until it drew near, and then he saw that it was built of ivory and ebony with inlays of gold and oars of sandalwood and lign aloes. In it were ten maidens all as beautiful as the moon, and when they saw him, they came ashore and kissed his hands.

"You are the king, the bridegroom!" they said. Then a young lady, who looked as if she were the sun shining in the serene sky, came up to him bearing a royal robe and crown of gold set with all kinds of rubies and pearls. She threw the robe over him and set the crown on his head, after which the maidens carried him on their arms to the ship, where he found all kinds of silk carpets and hangings of various colors. Then they spread the sails and headed for midocean. It seemed to the young man that he was in a dream, and he did not know where they were going with him. Soon they drew near land, and he saw the shore full of a vast number of troops all magnificently arrayed and clad in solid steel. As soon as the ship arrived at the port, they brought him five noble horses with saddles of gold and jewels. He chose one of them and mounted it, while they led the other four behind him. Then they raised the banners and standards over his head, while the troops arranged themselves to the right and left as they set out. Drums beat, and cymbals clashed, and they rode on while he kept wondering whether he was asleep or awake, and they kept going until they drew near a green meadow full of palaces, gardens, trees, streams, blossoms, and birds chanting the praises of Allah the Victorious. All of a sudden, an army sallied forth from the palaces and gardens like a torrent, and the soldiers overflowed the meadow. These troops halted some distance from him, and soon a king rode forth, preceded by his chief officers on foot. When he came up to the young man, he dismounted, and the two saluted each other in a courteous fashion. Then the king said, "Come with me, for you are my guest."

So they both mounted their horses again and rode on in a great and stately procession, conversing as they rode, until they came to the royal palace, where they dismounted together. Then the king took the young man by the hand, led him into a dome room followed by his suite, and made him sit down on a throne of gold next to himself. Then he untied the swathe from his lower face, and behold the king was a young lady as splendid as the sun shining in the blue sky, perfect in beauty, loveliness, brilliance, grace, and pride. The young man looked at this magnificent blessing and was totally captivated by her charms and the splendor and affluence that he saw around him.

"I want you to know, oh king," she said, "that I am queen of this land, and that all the troops that you have seen are women. There is no man among them. In this state the men farm the fields, build the towns, and occupy themselves with mechanical crafts and other useful arts, while the women govern and fill the offices of state and bear arms."

The young man was astounded by this, and as they were talking, in came the vizier. who was a tall gray-haired old woman of venerable appearance and majestic aspect, and he was told that this was the queen's minister.

"Bring us the kazi and the witnesses," the queen commanded her.

So she went out to do this, and the queen continued conversing with him in a friendly fashion and tried to make him feel at ease. "Are you content to become my husband and accept me as your wife?"

Thereupon he arose and would have kissed the ground between her hands, but she forbade him. and he replied, "Oh my lady, I am your slave."

"Do you see all these servants, soldiers, riches, and treasures?" she asked. "They are at your command, and you may dispose of them as you see fit." Then she pointed to a closed door and said, "All these things are at your disposal, except that door over there. You are not to open it, and if you do open it. you will repent it, and your repentance will bring you nothing. So beware! And I repeat this—beware!"

No sooner did she conclude her speech than the female vizier entered followed by the kazi and witnesses, all old women with a reverent and majestic appearance and their hair streaming over their shoulders. The queen ordered them to draw up the marriage contract between herself and the young man. Accordingly they performed the marriage ceremony, and the queen celebrated with a great feast to which she invited all her troops. After they had eaten and drunk some wine, he went and slept with his bride, who was a virgin. So he did away with her hymen and stayed with her for seven years in joy and solace until one day he thought about the forbidden door and said to himself, "The only reason she may have forbidden me from entering is that there are greater treasures in that room, perhaps grander than I have ever seen." So he rose and opened the door, when, lo and behold, he encountered the very bird that had brought him from the seashore to the island, and it said to him, "No welcome to a face that will never prosper!"

When he saw it and heard what it had said, he fled from it, but the eagle followed him and seized him in its talons, flew with him into the sky, and after an hour, the bird set him down on the shore where he had first found him and flew away. When the young man came to his senses, he remembered his former great estate that was so grand and glorious. He recalled the troops that rode before him and his lordly rule and all the honor and fair fortune he had lost, and he began weeping and wailing. He remained on the seashore for two months, hoping to return to his wife, until, one night, while he was mourning and musing, he heard someone invisible speaking and saying, "How great were the delights! Alas, you will never again see the wonders that you experienced!"

When he heard this, he regretted his actions even more and despaired of ever recovering his wife and fair estate. So, he returned, weary and broken-hearted, to the house where he had dwelt with the old men and knew that the same thing had happened to them and that this was the reason for their shedding tears and lamenting. Consequently, he understood them all too well. Then, since he was overcome with sorrow, he went to his chamber and began mourning and lamenting. He did not stop crying and moaning and abandoned eating, drinking, and merry times. Nor did he ever laugh again, and when he died, they buried him next to the sheikhs.

* * *

"You see, then, oh king," continued the vizier, "what happens when one is too precipitate. Truly, it is not praiseworthy, and it will make you repent your actions. Believe me, I am trying to give you true advice and loyal counsel."

When the king heard his story, he canceled the slaying of his son, but on the sixth day, his favorite concubine appeared carrying a knife in her hand and said to him, "I want you to know, my lord, that unless you listen to my complaint and protect my honor against these ministers who have banded together against me, I shall kill myself with this knife, and my blood will testify against you on the Day of Doom. Indeed, they pretend that women are full of tricks and malice and perfidy, but they plan to defeat me and prevent the king from doing justice. Still, I shall prove to you that men are more perfidious than women with this story about a king and how he gained access to the wife of a merchant."

"And how did this come about?" asked the king.

And she answered, "I have heard tell, oh king, a tale of

The King's Son and the Merchant's Wife

A certain merchant, who was very jealous, had a wife, who was a model of beauty and loveliness. But since he was so fearful and jealous, he would not live with her in any town. Rather, he built her a pavilion outside the city, separate from all other buildings. It was a tall building with sturdy doors that had strange locks. When he had to go to town on occasion, he locked the doors and hung the keys around his neck.

One day, when the merchant was out, the king's son of that city went into the country to enjoy the solace of nature outside the walls. When he saw the solitary pavilion, he examined it for a long time. Finally, he caught sight of a charming lady looking and leaning out one of the windows, and since he was captivated by her charms and grace, he searched for some way to get to her, but he could not find anything. So he called to one of his pages, who brought him ink and paper, and wrote her a letter telling her how he had fallen passionately in love with her. Then he set the letter on the point of an arrow and shot it into the pavilion, where it fell into the garden. It just so happened that the lady was walking there with her maidens, and she said to one of the girls, "Quick, go and pick up that letter," for she could read writing, and when she had read it and understood what the prince revealed of his love, passion, yearning, and longing, she wrote him a merciful reply and confessed that her desire for him was just as fierce if not fiercer. Then she threw the letter down to him from one of the windows of the pavilion. When he saw her, he picked up the reply, and after reading it, he came under the window and said to her, "Send down a piece of thread so that I may attach this key to it that I want you to keep."

So she let down some thread, and he tied the key to it. Then he went away and sought out one of his father's viziers and revealed his passion for the lady and told him that he could not live without her.

"And what would you like me to do?" asked the vizier.

"I want you to put me into a chest," said the prince, "and send it to the merchant, pretending that it is yours and requesting that he keep it for you in his country house for some days. This way I shall be able to get his wife, and then later, you are to ask him to return the chest."

"I'll be glad to do this," answered the vizier.

So the prince returned to his palace, and after placing a lock, to which the lady had a key, on a certain chest, he got inside, and the vizier locked it. Then he set it on a mule and carried it to the merchant's pavilion. When the merchant saw him, he came forth, kissed his hands, and said, "It is nice to see my lord. Do you need something or have some business that I may have the pleasure and honor of doing for you?"

"I would appreciate it," said the vizier, "if you would place this chest in the safest and best place inside your house until I come for it again."

So the merchant had the porters carry it inside and set it down in one of the large storage closets. Then the merchant went off on some business. As soon as he was gone, his wife arose, went up to the chest, and unlocked it with the key of the king's son. All at once, he appeared bright and handsome as the moon. When she saw him, she put on her richest garments and took him to her sitting salon, where they stayed seven days, eating and drinking and making merry. Whenever her husband came home, she put the prince back into the chest and locked him inside. One day the king asked for his son, and the vizier hurried off to the merchant's place of business and asked him to return the chest. So the merchant hastily returned to his pavilion and knocked at the door. When his wife realized who was at the door, she quickly led the prince back into the chest, but in her confusion, she forgot to lock it. The merchant ordered the porters to pick up the chest and take it to his house in town. So they picked it up by the lid, which flew open, and lo and behold, the prince was found lying in it. When the merchant saw him and recognized him as the prince, he went to the vizier and said, "You must go in and take the king's son, for none of us may lay hands on him."

So the vizier went in and took the prince away with him. As soon as they were gone, the merchant got rid of his wife and swore that he would never marry again.

"And," continued the concubine, "I have also heard tell, oh king, of

The Page Who Pretended to Know the Speech of Birds

A nobleman once entered the slave market and saw a page being offered for sale. So he bought him, took him home, and said to his wife, "Take good care of him."

The boy lived there for some time, until, one day, the man said to his wife, "Go to the garden tomorrow and amuse yourself."

"With pleasure," she replied.

Now, when the page heard this, he secretly prepared meat, drink, fruits, and dessert and took them to the garden that night. He placed the meat under one tree, the wine under another, and the fruit and conserves under a third. Since his mistress would have to pass by these trees, she would have to see everything. When morning arrived, the husband ordered him to accompany the lady to the garden and to carry all the provisions that were needed for the day. So she mounted a horse and rode to the garden with the page. When they dismounted and entered, they began walking about, and a crow croaked, and the page said, "That's very true."

Thereupon his mistress asked him, "Do you know what the crow said?"

"Oh yes, my lady," he replied. "It said that we would find meat under the tree over there, and we should go and eat it."

So she said, "Let's see if you really do understand them."

Then she went up to the tree, and after finding a dish of meat, she was sure that the young man told the truth and was astounded. They ate the meat and then began walking around awhile, taking their pleasure in the garden, until the crow croaked a second time, and the page replied, "That's very true!"

"What did he say?" asked the lady.

"Oh lady," responded the page, "he said that there is some water flavored with musk and a pitcher of wine under that tree over there."

So she went up with him to the tree, and after finding the water and wine there, her amazement increased, and she was enormously impressed by the page. They sat down and drank, then arose and walked in another part of the garden. Soon the crow croaked again, and the page said, "That's very true!"

"What did he say?" asked the lady.

"He said," replied the page, "that there are fresh and dried fruit under that tree over there."

So they went to the tree and found everything as the crow said and sat down and ate. Then they walked about until the crow croaked a fourth time, whereupon the page took a stone and threw it at him.

"What did he say," asked the lady, "that caused you to throw a stone at him?"

"Oh my lady," he responded, "he said something that I cannot reveal to you."

"Tell me," she insisted, "and do not be shy in my presence, for there should be no secrets between you and me."

But he refused to talk, and she continued to press him until at last she implored him to tell her, and he answered, "The crow said to me that I should do with my lady what her husband does with her."

When she heard his words, she laughed until she fell backward and said, "This is not a serious matter, and I cannot refuse you."

Upon saying this, she went to a tree, spread the carpet beneath it, lay down, and called him to come and do her need, when all of a sudden her husband, who had followed them unawares, cried out to the page, "Listen boy! What's the matter with your mistress? Why is she lying there?"

"Oh my lord," he quickly responded, "she fell off the tree and was nearly killed. Thanks to Allah, she is still alive. She decided to lie down awhile to recover from the shock."

When the lady saw her husband standing by her head, she arose and pretended to be weak and in pain. "Oh my back!" she cried. "Oh my sides! Come help me, my friends. I shall never survive this."

So her husband was deceived and said to the page, "Fetch your mistress's horse, and set her on it."

Then he led her home, the boy holding one stirrup and the man the other.

"May Allah grant you a quick recovery!" the man said to his wife.

*   *   *

"These examples, oh king," said the concubine, "are instances of the craft and devious nature of men. So, do not let your viziers turn you away from helping me and doing justice."

Then she wept, and when the king saw her weeping, he once again ordered his son to be put to death. But the sixth minister entered, kissed the ground before him, and said, "May the Almighty advance the king! You know how loyal I have been to you, and now, I, too, advise you to deal deliberately with your son. Falsehood is a smoke, and fact is built on a solid foundation that cannot be destroyed. The light of truth pierces the night of lies. You must know how perfidious women are, just as it is written in Allah's holy book, 'Truly the malice of women is great.' Indeed, I have a tale to tell you about a woman who fooled the chiefs of state in a way that they had never been fooled before."

"And how was that?" asked the king.

And the vizier answered, "Oh king, I have heard tell a tale about

The Lady and Her Five Suitors

There was once a merchant's daughter who was married to a man who was a great traveler. One day he set out for a far country, and he was absent so long that his wife, out of pure boredom, fell in love with a handsome young merchant, and they became passionately attached to one another. But this young man happened to quarrel with another man, who filed a complaint against him with the chief of police, and consequently he was thrown into jail. When the news reached his mistress, she almost went out of her mind. Then she arose, put on her richest clothes, and went directly to the house of the chief of police. She saluted him and presented a written petition stating that the man he had put in jail was her brother and that the people who had testified against him had borne false witness. The petition went on to say that the young man had been wrongly imprisoned and asked for his release. After the magistrate had read the paper, he cast his eyes on her and fell right in love with her. So he said to her, "Come into my house until I get him from the prison. Then you can take him home with you."

"Oh my lord," she replied, "I have no one to protect me except Almighty Allah. I am a stranger and am not allowed to enter any man's dwelling."

"I will not let him go unless you come into my home," said the wali, "and unless you let me have my way with you."

"If this is the way it must be," she replied, "then you must come to my lodging, and you must sit, sleep the siesta, and rest the whole day there."

"And where are your lodgings?" he asked.

Then she told him and set a time for him to come. When she left him, she took his heart with her. Next she went to the kazi of the city, to whom she said, "Oh my lord, I would like you to look into a certain matter for me, and Allah Almighty will reward you for your help."

"Who has wronged you?" he asked.

"Oh my lord," she sighed, "I have a brother, and he is my only one, and it is on his account that I have come to you. The wali has imprisoned him for a crime that he did not do. Some men have borne false witness against him, and I implore you to intercede on his behalf with the chief of police."

When the kazi looked at her, he fell right in love with her and said, "Come into my house and rest awhile with my handmaids while I send a message telling the wali to release your brother. If I knew the amount of the fine levied against him, I would pay it out of my own pocket so I might have my way with you, for you please me with your sweet speech."

"If you, my lord, do things this way," she said, "we must not blame others."

"If you will not come in," he replied, "then be on your way."

"If this is the way you want it, my lord," she remarked,

"it will be more private and better in my place than yours, for there are slave girls, eunuchs, and people who come in and out. Indeed, I am a woman who does not live this way, but I am being compelled out of need."

"Where is your house?" he asked.

And she told him and set an appointment to see him the same time as the chief of police. Then she left him and went directly to the vizier, to whom she showed her petition for the release of her brother, but he, too, fell in love with her and wanted her. "If you will let me have my way with you," he said, "I shall set your brother free."

"If this is the way it must be," she responded, "let it be at my house, because it will be more private for you and me. It is not very far from here, and you know that women like to clean themselves a certain way and adorn themselves for a special occasion."

"Where is your house?" he asked.

She told him where she was lodging and set an appointment the exact same time as the others, and then she went directly to the king of the city and told him her story and sought her brother's release.

"Who imprisoned him?" he enquired.

"It was your chief of police."

When the king heard her speech, his heart was pierced by the arrows of love, and he asked her to enter the palace with him so that he might send the kazi to have her brother released.

"Oh king," she said, "this thing is easy for you whether I want to or not, and if the king wants to have his way with me, it is my good fortune, but if he comes to my house, he will do me more honor."

"I shall not disappoint you," said the king.

So she set an appointment with him that was the same as the three others and told him where her house was. When she left him, she went to a carpenter and said to him. "I would like you to make a cabinet with four compartments one above each other, and each with a door. Let me know your price, and I shall give it to you."

"My price will be four dinars," he replied. "but, oh

noble lady, if you will do me a favor and let me have my way with you, I shall ask nothing."

"If that is the way it must be," she answered, "then it will have to be this way. So, make five compartments with padlocks for the doors."

And she told him where she lived and set an appointment on the day that the others had set theirs.

"Fine, my lady," he said. "I shall make it for you right away, and afterward, I shall come to you at your convenience."

So she sat down by him while he went to work on the cabinet, and when he finished it, she looked at it, took it home with the help of porters, and set it up in the sitting chamber. Then she took four gowns and carried them to the dyer, who dyed them each a different color. After that she began preparing the meat, drink, fruits, flowers, and perfumes. Now, when the appointed time arrived, she put on her most expensive dress and adorned herself with her most precious jewels and sprayed perfume all over. Then she spread the sitting room with various kinds of rich carpets and sat down to await her first guest.

Behold, the kazi was the first to appear before the others, and when she saw him, she rose to her feet, kissed the ground before him, and took him by the hand. She made him sit down by her on the couch, lay down, and began to jest and toy with him. He soon wanted to fulfill his desire with her, but she said, "Oh my lord, take off your clothes and turban, and put on this yellow cassock and handkerchief, while I bring you meat and drink. After that, you will have your way."

Upon saying this, she took his clothes and turban and clothed him in the cassock and the kerchief, but no sooner did she do this than there was a knocking at the door.

"Who is that knocking at the door?" he asked.

"My husband," she responded.

"What should I do? Where can I hide?" he cried.

"Fear nothing," she assured him. "I shall hide you in this cabinet."

"Do whatever you think best."

So she took him by the hand and pushed him into the lowest compartment and locked the door. Then she went to the entrance of the house, where she found the wali. So she kissed the ground before him, took his hand, and led him into the salon, where she made him sit down and said to him, "Oh lord, this house is your house. This place is your place, and I am your handmaid. You will spend the day with me. So take off your clothes and put on this red gown, for it is a sleeping gown."

So she took away his clothes and had him put on the red gown and placed an old patched rag on his head. Then she sat down next to him on the divan, and she began to play with him awhile, while he toyed with her until he desired her completely. But she said to him, "Oh lord, this day is your day, and nobody will share it with you. First, however, please write me an order for my brother's release from jail so that my heart will be set at ease."

"I'm at your disposal," he said, "and I swear that everything will be as you like."

So he wrote a letter to his treasurer telling him to release the lady's lover as soon as he received the document. Then he sealed it, and after she took it from him, she resumed playing with him on the divan, when suddenly somebody knocked on the door, and he asked, "Who is that?"

"My husband," she answered.

"What shall I do?"

"Enter this cabinet until I send him away."

So she sent him into the second compartment from the bottom and locked the door. Meanwhile the kazi had heard everything they had said. Then she went to the entrance of the house and opened it. In walked the vizier, and she kissed the ground before him and said, "My lord, you honor my house by coming here. May Allah never deprive me of the light of your countenance!" Then she seated him on the divan and said, "My lord, take off your heavy dress and turban and put on these lighter garments."

So she took off his clothes and turban and clad him in a blue cassock and a tall red bonnet and said to him.

"This light gown is better suited for fun, play, and sleep." Thereupon she began to play with him, and he with her, and when he wanted to take his full desire of her, she put him off by saying, "Oh my lord, be patient."

As they were talking, there was a knock at the door, and the vizier asked her, "Who is that?"

"My husband," she said.

"What shall I do?"

"Enter this cabinet until I get rid of him and come back to you. Don't be afraid."

So she put him in the third compartment and locked the door. After that she went out and opened the house door, and in came the king. As soon as she saw him, she kissed the ground before him, took him by the hand, led him into the salon, and seated him on the divan. Then she said to him, "Truly, oh king, you do me a high honor, and even if I were given the most precious gift in the world, it would not be worth the step that you have taken toward me. Now, please give me permission to say one word to you."

"Say what you will," he answered.

"Oh my lord," she said, "relax and take off your garments and turban."

Now his clothes were worth a thousand dinars, and when he took them off, she clad him in a patched gown worth ten dirhams at the most. Then she began talking and jesting with him, while the other men in the cabinet heard everything that was going on but did not dare to say a word. Soon, when the king sought to have his full desire with her, she said, "Have patience, my lord. I promised myself first to entertain you in this sitting chamber, and I have something that will make you very happy."

Now, as they were speaking, someone knocked on the door, and he asked her, "Who is that?"

"My husband," she said.

"Make him go away," he said, "or I shall come out and send him away by force."

"Oh no, my good lord," she replied. "Have patience until I use a trick to send him away."

"But what shall I do?"

Thereupon she took him by the hand and made him enter the fourth compartment of the cabinet and locked the door behind him. Then she went out and opened the house door, and the carpenter entered and saluted her.

"What kind of cabinet did you make?" she said, complaining.

"What's the matter, my lady?" he asked.

"The top compartment is too narrow," she answered.

"It can't be," he said.

"Go look for yourself," she insisted. "See if it is wide enough for you."

"It should be wide enough for four," he maintained, and as he entered the fifth compartment, she slammed the door and locked it. Then she took the letter of the chief of police and carried it to the treasurer, who read it and set her lover free.

When she told her lover all that she had done, he said, "But what shall we do now?"

"We shall go to another city," she said. "After all that I've accomplished here, we don't have much time to lose and had better leave as soon as possible."

So the two packed their possessions, and after loading them on camels, they set out for another city. Meanwhile the five men lived in their compartments of the cabinet without eating or drinking for three whole days. During this time they held their water until the carpenter could not retain his any longer. So he let loose a waterfall on the king's head, and the king urinated on the vizier's head, and vizier piddled on the wali, and the wali pissed on the head of the kazi, whereupon the judge cried out, "How nasty can you get? It's bad enough that we are in this lousy situation, but do you have to urinate on me?"

The chief of police recognized the kazi's voice and answered, "May Allah pay you even more, oh kazi!"

When the kazi heard him, he knew it was the wali. Then the chief of police raised his voice and said, "What's the meaning of all this nastiness?"

And the vizier answered, "May Allah pay you even more, wali."

As a result, he knew that it was the minister speaking.

Then the vizier raised his voice: "What's the meaning of this nastiness?"

But when the king heard and recognized his vizier's voice, he kept silent and concealed his situation. Then the vizier said, "May God damn this woman for treating us like this. She has managed to bring together all the chief officers of the state except the king."

"Hold your peace," cried the king, "for I was the first to fall into the trap of this lewd strumpet."

Thereupon the carpenter intervened and said, "And I, what have I done? I made her a cabinet for four gold pieces, and when I came to seek my pay, she tricked me into entering this compartment and locked the door on me."

They began talking with one another and tried to distract the king from his sorrow. Soon the neighbors heard the noise and went to the house. Seeing it deserted, one of them said, "Somebody used to live here, but now it seems empty. Let's break open the door and see what has happened. If we don't investigate, the wali or king may think we have done something wrong and throw us into prison."

So they broke open the door and entered the salon, where they saw a large wooden cabinet and heard men groaning for water and food. Then one of the neighbors said, "Is there a jinnee in this cabinet?"

"We had better spread some fuel around it and burn it down," said another.

When the kazi heard this, he bawled out to them, "Don't do it!!"

And they said to one another, "Truly, the jinnees are making believe they are mortals and are speaking with men's voices."

Thereupon the kazi repeated some verses from the Koran and said to the neighbors, "Draw near the cabinet where we are."

So they came closer, and he said, "I am the kazi, and I know you very well." And the kazi told them where they lived and something about themselves.

"Who brought you here?" they asked.

And he told them the entire story from beginning to

end. Thereupon they fetched a carpenter, who opened
the five doors and let out the kazi, vizier, wali, king, and
carpenter, in their strange outfits. Each one of them
burst into laughter when they caught sight of the others.
Now, since she had taken away all their clothes, each
one of them had to send to their people for fresh garments. Then they put them on and sneaked off to avoid
the notice of the folk.

"Just think, oh king," continued the vizier, "how deceitful this woman was! And I have also heard tell a
tale of

The Three Wishes, or the Man Who Longed to See the Night of Power

There was once a man who had longed his entire life
to look at the Night of Power, and one night he happened to be gazing at the sky when he saw the angels
and heaven's gates thrown open, and many creatures
prostrating themselves before the Lord. So he said to
his wife, "Listen to me! Allah has finally shown me the
Night of Power, and I know from the invisible world
that three wishes will be granted to me. So I want to
ask your advice about what I should ask."

"Oh husband," she replied, "man's perfection and delight are in his prickle. So why don't you pray to Allah
to enlarge and magnify your yardstick."

So he lifted his hands to heaven and said, "Oh Allah,
please enlarge and magnify my yardstick."

No sooner did he speak than his tool became as big
as a column, and he could neither sit, stand, move about,
or even stir from his place. When he wanted to have
intercourse with his wife, she fled from him from place
to place. So he said to her, "Oh cursed woman, what's
to be done? All this has happened because of your lust."

"No, by Allah," she responded. "I did not ask for this length and huge bulk. Even the gate of a street would be too narrow for this prickle. Pray to heaven to make it less."

So he raised his eyes to heaven and said, "Oh Allah, get rid of this thing for me and save me."

And immediately his prickle disappeared altogether, and he was totally smooth in his genital area. When his wife saw this, she said, "I have no use for you now that you've become as pegless as a eunuch all shaven and shorn."

"All this comes from your bad advice and imbecilic judgment," he answered. "Allah granted me three wishes, and I could have used them to better myself both in this world and the next. Now two have been wasted because you are so lewd, and only one remains."

"Pray to Allah to restore your yardstick to its former shape."

So he prayed to the Lord, and his prickle was restored to its former state. Thus the man lost his three wishes because of the bad advice and the stupidity of his wife.

"And I have told you this tale, oh king," continued the vizier, "so that you may realize how thoughtless women are and what results from their foolishness and how dangerous it is to listen to their advice. Therefore do not be persuaded by a woman to slay your son, who will live to make your deeds known for posterity."

The king listened to his minister's words and decided once again to postpone his son's death. But on the seventh day, the concubine entered and started shrieking. After lighting a fire in front of the king, she made it seem that she would throw herself on the fire, but the king's guards grabbed her and brought her before him.

"Why have you done this?" he asked.

"Unless you do me justice," she responded, "I shall throw myself into this fire and accuse you on the Day of Resurrection, for I am tired of my life. Before I came to see you, I wrote my last will and testament and gave away all my possessions to the poor. And you will sorely repent your actions just as the king who punished the pious woman who attended the Hammam."

"How did that happen?" the king asked.

"I have heard tell, oh king," she said, "this tale concerning

The Stolen Necklace

There was once a woman who devoted herself so much to religion that she became a recluse. Now she used to go to a certain king's palace whose inhabitants were blessed by her presence, and she was held in high esteem. One day, she entered that palace as was her custom and sat down beside the king's wife. At one point the queen gave her a necklace worth a thousand dinars and said, "Please keep this for me, while I go to the Hammam."

So the queen went to the bath, which was in the palace, and the pious woman remained in the chamber where the queen had been, and while waiting for her to return, she placed the necklace on the prayer carpet and stood up to pray. As she was praying, a magpie swooped down, snatched the necklace, and carried it off. Then it hid the necklace inside a crevice in the corner of the palace walls. When the queen returned from the bath, she asked for the necklace from the recluse, who looked for it but could not find it. There was no trace of the necklace whatsoever. So she said to the king's wife, "By Allah, my daughter, nobody has been with me. When you gave me the necklace, I placed it on the prayer carpet. Perhaps one of the servants saw it and took it while I was engaged in prayer. Only Allah Almighty knows what has happened to it."

When the king heard what had happened, he told his queen to interrogate the recluse with fire and beatings. So they tortured her in many different ways, but they could not bring her to confess or accuse anyone. Then the king commanded her to be thrown into prison and placed in chains, and they did as he said. Some time later, as the king sat in the inner court of his palace with the queen by his side and water flowing all around him, he saw the magpie fly into a crevice in the corner of the wall and pull out the necklace. Immediately he cried to a servant, and she caught the bird and took the necklace from it. When the king recognized the necklace, the king knew that the pious recluse had been wronged, and he repented for what he had done with her. So he sent for her and began kissing her head and sought her pardon with many tears. Moreover, he commanded a good deal of his treasure to be given to her, but she refused and would have none of it. However, she forgave him and went away, swearing never again to enter anyone's house. She started wandering in the mountains and valleys and worshiped God until she died, and Almighty Allah have mercy on her!

"Now let me also tell you, oh King, an example of the malice of the male sex," continued the concubine. "I have heard tell this tale of

The Two Pigeons

A pair of pigeons once stored up wheat and barley in their nest during the winter, and when the summer came, the grain shriveled and was soon diminished in quantity. So the male pigeon said to his wife, "You've eaten some of the grain."

"No, by Allah," she answered. "I have never touched it."

But he did not believe her words and beat her with his wings and pecked her so hard with his bill that he killed her. When the cold season returned, the corn swelled and became as plentiful as it was before. Then he knew that he had been wrong and wicked in slaying his wife. Though he repented, his repentance brought him nothing. Then he lay down by her side and began mourning and weeping over her. Finally, he stopped eating and drinking until he fell sick and died.

"Now you see the malice of men, oh king," continued the concubine, "and how poorly they treat their women. As for me, I shall not stop insisting on justice until I die."

So the king gave the order to put his son to death, but the seventh vizier entered, kissed the ground before him, and said, "Oh king, have patience with me while I offer you words of good advice. Let me begin by reminding you that many are the men who are slow and patient who attain their heart's desire, while those who are precipitate and fast fall into a shameful state. Now I have witnessed how this lady has reprehensibly upset and excited the king by her horrible lies. But I, his mameluke, whom you have overwhelmed with favors and rewards, I shall offer you honest and loyal advice. Truthfully, I know more about the malice of women than anyone, and in particular, I have heard a story on this subject about the old woman and the son of a merchant who were involved in a terrible conflict."

"What happened between them?" asked the king.

And the seventh vizier said, "I have heard tell, oh king, the tale of

The House with the Belvedere

A wealthy merchant had a son who was very dear to him, and this son came to him one day and said, "Oh my father, I have a favor to ask of you."

"Oh my son," answered the merchant, "what might I give you or bring you to make you happy?"

"Give me money so that I may journey with the merchants to the city of Baghdad and see its sights, sail on the Tigris, and look at the palace of the caliphs. Indeed, the other sons of merchants have described these things to me, and I long to see them for myself."

"Oh my son, how can I bear to part with you?"

But the young man replied, "I've told you what I wanted, and I feel I must journey to Baghdad with or without your consent. I have such a great longing to see the sights there that it can only be fulfilled by journeying there."

Now, when the father saw that there was nothing he could do about it, he provided his son with goods that were worth thirty thousand gold pieces and sent some merchants with him whom he trusted and placed them in charge of his son. Then he took leave of the young man, who journeyed with the merchants until they reached Baghdad, where he entered the market and sought to rent a house that was so beautiful, spacious, and elegant that he almost went out of his mind when he saw it. Inside were pavilions facing one another with floors of colored marble and ceilings inlaid with gold and lapis lazuli, and its gardens were full of warbling birds. So he asked the doorkeeper what was the monthly rent, and the man replied, "Ten dinars."

"Are you speaking the truth," the young merchant asked, "or are you jesting with me?"

"By Allah," said the doorkeeper, "I speak nothing but the truth, for nobody lives in this house for more than a week or two."

"And how is that?" said the young merchant.

"Oh my son," he replied, "whoever dwells in this house does not leave it without being sick or dead. This is well known by all the folk of Baghdad, so nobody wants to inhabit it. This is the reason why the rent is so low."

Upon hearing this, the young merchant was amazed and said, "There must be some reason why people become sick and perish." After thinking about it for a while and calling upon Allah for counsel, he decided to rent the house and set up his lodgings there. Then he dismissed from his mind any fears that he might have and set about his business of buying and selling. Some days passed without anything bad happening to him as the doorkeeper had mentioned.

One day, as he sat on the bench before his door, an old crone who looked like a speckled black-and-white snake came by, and she cried out the name of Allah in great praise very loudly. At the same time she moved stones and other obstacles from the path. Upon seeing the young man sitting on the bench, she stared at him in astonishment, whereupon the young man said, "Old woman, do you know me, or do I resemble someone you know?"

When she heard him speak, she wobbled over toward him, saluted him with the salaam, and asked, "How long have you lived in this house?"

"Two months, my mother," he answered.

"I was astonished, my son," she said, "not because I know you or because you resemble someone I know. I was astonished because you are the first who has set up lodging in this house without turning sick or perishing. Certainly, my son, you have placed your young life in danger. But I suppose that you have not climbed up to the upper story or looked out from the belvedere there."

After saying this, she went her way, and he began pondering her words and said to himself, "I have not gone up to the top of the house, nor did I know that there was a belvedere there."

Then he rose right away and went into the house. He looked around the courtyard until he saw a narrow door in the corner of the wall among the trees. A spider had woven her web over the door, and he said to himself, "I hope that the spider has not woven a web over the door because death and doom are inside." However, he plucked up his courage with the saying of God the Most High—"Nothing will ever happen except what Allah has written for us"—and he opened the door and climbed a narrow flight of stairs until he came to the terrace roof, where he found a belvedere, in which he sat down to rest and content himself with the view. Soon he caught sight of a fine house that was nearby, and it had a lofty belvedere overlooking the entire city of Baghdad. Inside was a maiden as fair as a nymph. Her beauty swept his heart away and sent him out of his mind so that he felt like the suffering Job and the weeping Jacob. As he looked at her and studied all her wonderful features, he became lovesick and a fire was lit in his vitals. "People say that whoever lives in this house becomes sick or dies. If this is the case, then the maiden over there is certainly the cause. Heaven help me to get out of this predicament, for I've gone out of my mind!"

Then he descended the terrace, pondered his situation, and sat down in the house. But since he was unable to rest, he went outside and took his seat at the door, absorbed in melancholy thoughts. All of a sudden, the old woman reappeared, praising Allah as she went. When he saw her, he rose and approached her with a courteous salaam and wishes for long life and prosperity.

"Oh my mother," he said, "I was healthy and happy until you mentioned the door leading to the belvedere. So I opened it and climbed to the top of the house, and then I saw a maiden who stole my senses. Now I think I'm a lost man, and I know no physician who can cure me except you yourself."

When she heard this, she laughed and said, "Nothing bad will happen to you, Allah willing!"

Thereupon he arose, went into the house, and returned with a hundred dinars in his hand.

"Here, take this," he said. "Treat me as a lord treats a slave and help me. If I die, there will be a claim for your blood on Doomsday."

"I shall take this money gladly," she replied. "But, my son, I expect you to help me in a small matter, and your wish will depend on it."

"What would you like me to do, oh mother?" he asked.

"Go to the silk market and ask for the shop of Abu al-Fath bin Kaydam," she said. "Sit down at his counter, greet him, and say, 'Let me see the face veil lined with gold,' for this is the most beautiful thing that he has in his shop. Then buy it from him, my son, no matter how expensive it is, and keep it until I come to you tomorrow, Allah willing."

After saying all this, she went away, and he passed

the night as if he were sitting on live coals. The next morning he put a thousand ducats in his pocket and went to the silk market, and after finding the shop of Abu al-Fath, he encountered a distinguished man, surrounded by pages, eunuchs, and attendants, for he was a merchant of great wealth and considered a friend of the caliph. Among the blessings that Allah Almighty had bestowed on him was the maiden who had ravished the young man's heart. She was his wife, and no woman could match her beauty, nor did any of the kings have a wife as beautiful as she was. The young man saluted him, and Abu al-Fath returned his salaam and asked him to be seated. So he sat down and said, "Oh merchant, I would like to look at the face veil lined with gold."

Thereupon the merchant ordered his slave to bring him a bundle of silk from inside the shop, and after opening it, he brought out a number of veils whose beauty amazed the young man. Among them was the veil he sought, and he bought it for fifty pieces of gold and took it home with him, very pleased with himself. No sooner did he reach the house than the old woman appeared. He rose and gave her the veil, and then she told him to bring some live coals, which she used to burn a corner of the veil. Afterward she folded it up as it was before and went to Abu al-Fath's house and knocked at the door. Since the maiden knew her as a friend of her mother, she let her enter and asked, "Tell me why you have come. My mother has left and gone to her own house."

"Oh my daughter," she replied, "I know your mother is not with you, for I have been with her in her home, and I've come to you because I want to make my Wuzu ablution with you, for you are clean and your house is pure."

Then the old woman took the pitcher and went to the washhouse and prayed there. Soon she came out and said to the young lady, "Oh my daughter, I suspect that your handmaidens have been in that place and defiled it. So please show me another place where I may pray, for the prayer that I have prayed is now null and void."

So the maiden took her by the hand and said to her,

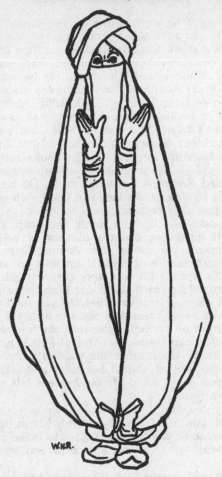

W.H.R.

"Oh my mother, come and pray on my carpet where my
husband sits."

So she stood there and prayed and bowed and prostrated herself, and when the young woman wasn't looking, she slipped the veil underneath the cushion. Then
she blessed her and went her way. Now, when the day

came to an end, Abu al-Fath came home and sat down on the carpet, while his wife brought him some food, and he ate it until he was full and washed his hands. Afterward, he leaned back upon the cushion and soon caught sight of a corner of the veil protruding from under the cushion. So he pulled it out and examined it carefully. When he recognized it as the veil that he had sold to the young man, he immediately suspected his wife of being unfaithful, and called her to him.

"Where did you get this veil?" he asked.

And she swore to him that nobody had come to see her that day except him. The merchant was silent, fearing a scandal, and he said to himself, "If I open this can of worms, I shall be put to shame before everyone in Baghdad." Since he was one of the caliph's intimate friends, he thought it would best to hold his peace. So he asked no questions but said to his wife, whose name was Mahziyah, "I have heard that your mother has a bad heart and is sick and all the women are with her, weeping over her. So I order you to go and visit her."

So she went to her mother's house and found her in the best of health. Indeed, her mother was surprised to see her and asked, "What brings you here this hour?"

Then she told her what her husband had said and sat there awhile. All of a sudden, porters arrived with her clothes from her husband's house, and they transported all her paraphernalia and deposited everything in her mother's lodging. When her mother saw this, she said to her daughter, "Tell me what has happened between you and your husband that has caused him to ship all your possessions to me."

Her daughter swore that she did not know the reason and that nothing had happened between them to have caused him to behave this way.

"There must be some reason," her mother insisted.

"I really do not know of any," the daughter responded.

Then her mother began weeping and lamenting her daughter's separation from this distinguished man because of his rank, dignity, and wealth. And this is how things remained for the next several days, when the

cursed old woman named Miryam the Koranist paid a
visit to Mahziyah in her mother's house. After saluting
her cordially, she said, "What's bothering you, my
daughter, my darling? Indeed, I'm concerned about
you." Then she went to her mother and said, "Oh my
sister, what's going on between your daughter and her
husband? I have heard that he has divorced her! What
has she done to cause him to take such a step?"

"Maybe her husband will return to her through the
blessed influence of your prayers, oh Hafizah. So please
pray for her, my sister, for you fast by day and pray
at night."

Then the three women began talking among themselves, and the old woman said to Mahziyah, "Do not
grieve. Allah willing, I shall make peace between you
and your husband before long."

Then she left them and went to the young merchant.

"I want you to arrange for some wonderful entertainment, for I shall bring her to you this very night," she
said.

Immediately he jumped up and began ordering all the
food and drink that was appropriate for such an occasion, while the old woman returned to the girl's mother
and said, "Oh my sister, we have a splendid bridal feast
tonight. So let your daughter come with me so she can
take her mind off things and have some fun. This way
she can discard all her cares and forget how her home
has been ruined. I shall bring her back to you safe and
sound."

The mother dressed her daughter in her finest dress
and most expensive jewels and accompanied her to the
door, where she placed her in the old woman's charge.

"Make sure that nobody recognizes her," she said.
"You know her husband's position with the caliph. And
don't stay too long. I want you to bring her back to me
as soon as possible."

The old woman took the maiden to the young man's
house, and Mahziyah thought it was the place where the
wedding was to be held, but as soon as she entered the
sitting salon, the young man jumped up, flung his arms
around her neck, and kissed her hands and feet. She was

confounded by his passion, and she was impressed by the beauty of the place, the large amounts of meat, drink, flowers, and perfumes. Indeed, she thought she was in a dream. When the old woman saw her amazement, she said to her, "May Allah bless you, my daughter. Don't be afraid. I am here with you and won't leave you for a moment. You are worthy of him, and he is worthy of you."

So the maiden sat down in shame and in great confusion. But the young man jested and toyed with her and entertained her with humorous stories and beautiful poems until she relaxed. Then she ate and drank, and since the wine went to her head, she took the lute and sang some beautiful songs addressed to him. When the youth realized that she was attracted to him, he became somewhat drunk without wine, and his love for her transcended his concern for his own life. Soon the old woman went out and left them alone to enjoy their lovemaking until the next morning, when she went back, wished them good day, and asked the maiden, "How was last night, my lady?"

"Wonderful," she responded, "thanks to your adroit actions and experience as a go-between."

Then the old woman said, "Let's get up and go back to your mother."

At these words the young man pulled out a hundred sequins and gave them to her.

"Take this and leave her with me tonight."

So she left them and returned to the girl's mother and said, "Your daughter sends her greetings, and the bride's mother has asked her to stay with her tonight."

"Oh my sister," said the mother, "return my greetings to her. If it pleases and amuses the girl, there is no harm in her staying one more night. So let her do this and amuse herself and come back to me at her leisure, for I fear that she is still upset by her angry husband."

The old woman continued to make excuse after excuse to the girl's mother until Mahziyah had spent seven days with the young man. Meanwhile the old woman took a hundred dinars each day for herself while he was blissful and enjoyed lovemaking with the young woman. But at the end of the week, the girl's mother said, "Bring my daughter back to me right away, for I am worried about her. She has been away too long, and I suspect that something's wrong."

So the old woman went out and cried, "Woe to you! How dare you speak this way to me!"

She went straight to the young man's house, grabbed the girl by the hand, and took her away, for the young man was asleep on the bed after having drunk a large quantity of wine. Her mother welcomed her with pleasure, and upon seeing her more beautiful than ever, she rejoiced and said, "Oh my daughter, my heart was troubled because of your long absence, and because of my troubled heart, I insulted my sister the Koranist and hurt her."

"Arise and kiss her hands and feet," Mahziyah said, "for she has been a servant to me in my hour of need, and if you don't apologize, you are not my mother, and I am not your daughter."

So the mother stood up at once and made peace with the old woman. Meanwhile the young man recovered from his drunkenness and missed the young lady, but he congratulated himself on having enjoyed his desire. Soon Miryam, the old Koranist, came to him and greeted him.

"What do you think of my accomplishments?" she asked.

"You've done superbly," he remarked.

"Well then," she said. "Let us now mend what we have marred and restore this girl to her husband, for we have been the cause of their separation, and this is not right."

"What shall I do?" he asked.

"Go to Abu al-Fath's shop," she said, "salute him, and sit down next to him until you see me pass by. Then I want you to jump up, catch hold of my dress, and warn me that I had better return the veil to you. Then turn to the merchant and say, 'You know the veil that I had bought from you, oh lord? Well, it so happened that my handmaid put it on and burned a corner of it by accident. So she gave it to this old woman, who took it because she promised to repair and return it. But the old woman departed and I have not seen her again until today.' "

"I'd be glad to do all this," said the young man. So he got up right away, walked to the shop of the silk merchant, and as he was sitting with him, the old woman passed by. When he saw her, he sprang up and began to scold her, whereupon she replied, "It was not my fault!"

So the people of the bazaar flocked around the two and asked, "What's the matter? What's going on here?"

And the young merchant cried out, "I bought a veil for fifty dinars from this merchant and gave it to my slave girl, who wore it awhile. When she sat down to spray perfume on it, a spark flew from the censer and burned a hole in it. So we gave it to this pestilent old woman to mend it and return it to us. But from that time on we never set eyes on her again until this moment."

"This young man speaks the truth," the old woman answered. "I took the veil from him, but I took it to a friend's house on a visit and forgot it there. Now I don't know where I left it. And since I am a poor woman, I was afraid of what the owner would do to me, and I didn't dare to return."

Now the young woman's husband was listening to all that they said, and when he heard the tale which the old woman had concocted with the young man, he rose to his feet and said, "Allah Almighty! I beg pardon of the Omniscient One for my sins and for what my heart suspected!"

And he praised the Lord for revealing the truth to him. Then he approached the old woman and said to her, "Didn't you use to visit us?"

"Oh my son," she replied, "I do visit you and others to ask for alms. But from the day I lost the veil, I have had no news from anyone about it."

"Did you ask at my house?" the merchant continued.

"Oh my lord," she stated, "I did indeed go to your house and ask, but they told me that the lady of the house had been divorced by the merchant. So I went away and didn't ask any more questions. Nor have I asked anyone else about it until today."

Thereupon the merchant turned to the young man and

said, "Let the old woman go her way, for the veil is with me."

In fact, he went into the shop and brought it out and gave it to the young man. Afterward he went to his wife, gave her some money, and took her back into the house after begging her pardon because he had not known what the old woman had done.

"This, then, oh king," continued the vizier, "is a good example of the malice of women, and for another one that is similar, I have heard tell of the following tale called

The Prince and the Ifrit's Mistress

There was once a prince who was walking alone for his pleasure when he came to a green meadow filled with trees that were covered by fruit and birds singing on the boughs, and there was a glistening stream running alongside it. The place pleased him. So he sat down, took out some dried fruits, and began to eat, when all of a sudden he saw some smoke rising in the sky. He became so scared that he climbed up a tree and hid himself among the branches. Then he saw an ifrit rise out of the middle of a stream, and on his head was a chest of marble secured by a padlock. He set the chest down on the meadow and opened it, and out came a maiden like the sun shining in a bright blue sky. After seating her, he gazed upon her to his heart's content. Then he laid his head in her lap and fell asleep. When this happened, she lifted up his head, laid it on the chest, rose, and walked about. At one point, she happened to raise her eyes to the tree in which the prince was hiding, and upon seeing him, she signaled him to come down. He refused, but she cried out, "If you don't come down and do as I say, I shall wake the ifrit and point you out to him, and he will kill you right away."

Since the prince feared that she would do as she warned, he came down to her, and she began kissing his hands and feet, and she soon seduced him. When he had satisfied her desires, she said to him, "Give me this seal ring that I see on your finger."

So he gave her his signet, and she placed it in a silk kerchief in which she had more than eighty others. When the prince saw this, he asked her, "What do you do with all these rings?"

"Well, if you want to know the truth," she replied, "this ifrit took me away from my father's palace and shut me in this box, which he carries around on his head wherever he goes, and he keeps the keys on him. He very rarely leaves me alone because he is so jealous, and he prevents me from fulfilling my desires. When I experienced this, I swore that I would never deny my favors to any man, and these rings that you see are gifts from all the men who have had me. After intercourse I have always taken a signet and placed it in this handkerchief. Now go your way so that I can look for another man for myself. The ifrit will not wake for some time."

The prince could hardly believe his ears, and he returned to his father's palace and did not tell his father what had happened. The king knew nothing about the lady's malice. Indeed, she was not afraid of anyone and did not care about the consequences of her actions. So when the king saw that his son had lost his ring, he ordered him to be put to death. Then he rose from his throne and entered his palace. But his viziers came to him and prevailed upon him to change his mind. The same night, the king thanked them for having dissuaded him from slaying his son, and the prince also thanked them and said, "By Allah, I am most grateful that you advised my father to let me live, and I shall reward you in ample fashion."

Then he recounted to them how he had lost the ring, and they offered prayers for his long life and prosperity.

* * *

"You see, then, oh king," continued the vizier, "how malicious women can be and what they do to men."

The king listened to the minister's counsel and again decided not to have his son slain. Next morning, which was the eighth day, the king was sitting in his audience chamber amid his nobles, emirs, viziers, and olema, when the prince entered with his hand in that of his teacher, Al-Sindibad, and praised his father, ministers, lords, and priests in the most eloquent words and thanked them for having saved his life. All those who were present were astonished by his eloquence and fluent speech. His father rejoiced and told him to approach, whereupon he kissed him between the eyes. Then he called his tutor, Al-Sindibad, and asked him why his son had remained silent these past seven days.

"Oh Lord," he replied, "the truth is that it was I who instructed him to do this, for I feared that he might die. I knew this from the day of his birth, and when I read his charts, I found written in the stars that if he were to speak during this period, he would surely die. But now the danger is over, and it is the king's good fortune."

Upon hearing this the king was most happy and said to his viziers, "If I had killed my son, would the fault have been mine, my concubine's, or the tutor's?"

But all those present refused to answer, and Al-Sindibad said to the prince, "Answer him, my son."

The prince replied, "I have heard tell that when a merchant received some guests at his house one day, he sent his slave girl to the market to buy a jar of fresh milk So she bought it and set out on her return home. But on the way a hawk flew over her and was holding and squeezing a serpent in its claws, and a drop of the serpent's venom fell into the milk jar, unknown to the girl. So when she came back, the merchant took the milk from her and shared it with his guests. No sooner had the milk settled in their stomachs, however, than they all died. Now think about this, oh king, who was to blame for their deaths?"

Some of the people present offered their views first and said, "It was the fault of the men who drank the milk without examining it."

Others maintained, "The girl is to blame because she did not cover the jar."

But Al-Sindibad asked the prince, "What do you say, my son?"

"I say that you are all wrong," responded the prince. "Neither the girl nor the men are to blame because their appointed hour had come. Their time was up, and Allah had foreordained that they were to die in this manner."

When the courtiers heard this, they were impressed and raised their voices in praise of the king's son.

"Young prince," they said, "you have replied without fear, and you are the sagest man in your day without reproach."

"I am not a sage," asserted the prince. "The blind sheikh and his son of three and son of five were all wiser than I."

"Oh prince," said the courtiers, "tell us the story of these three who were wiser than you."

"Gladly," responded the prince. "I have heard this tale concerning

The Sandalwood Merchant and the Thieves

There once was a very rich merchant who was a great traveler and visited all sorts of places. One day he decided to journey to a particular city, and he asked those who were familiar with it, "What are the most profitable goods to bring there?"

They answered, "Sandalwood, because it sells for a high price."

So he invested a lot of his money in sandalwood and set out for that city. When he arrived at dusk, he met an old woman driving her sheep.

"Who are you, stranger?" she asked.

"I am a merchant," he responded.

"Well, then," she warned, "beware of the townsfolk, for they are cheats, rascals, and robbers, who love nothing more than taking advantage of a foreigner. Take care that you heed my advice."

Then she left him, and the next day one of the citizens of the city greeted him and said, "Oh my lord, where are you coming from?"

The merchant named his city, and the man continued, "What merchandise have you brought with you?"

"Sandalwood," the merchant said, "because I heard that its price was high."

"Well, whoever told you that was a blundering fool," the citizen responded. "We just use sandalwood for firewood, and it is not worth a great deal here."

When the merchant heard this, he sighed and was unsure whether he should believe him. Then he arrived at one of the khans of the city, and when it was night, he saw a merchant make fire with chander wood under his cooking pot. Now this man was the one who had spoken with him earlier in the day, and the merchant realized that he had been trying to trick him. When the townsman saw the merchant looking at him, he asked, "I'll buy some of your sandalwood at your asking price."

"Yes, I'll sell it to you at my asking price," answered the merchant, and the buyer transported all the wood to his own house and stored it there. Meanwhile, the merchant received an equal quantity of gold for it.

The next morning the merchant, who was a blue-eyed man, went out to walk in the city, but as he went along, one of the townsfolk, who was blue-eyed and one-eyed to boot, grabbed hold of him and said, "You're the one who stole my eye, and I'll never let you go."

The merchant denied this and said, "I never stole it. Such a thing is impossible!"

In the meantime the folk gathered around them and persuaded the one-eyed man to grant the merchant until the next day to give him the price of his eye. But the merchant had to hire a man to guarantee that he would return to the one-eyed man, and they let him go. Now his sandal had been torn in the conflict with the one-eyed man. So he stopped at a cobbler's stall and gave it to him.

"Please mend it, and I shall pay whatever you want," said the merchant. Then he went on until he came to some people sitting and playing, and he sat down with them to take his mind off his troubles. A gambler invited him to play with them, and he did. But the gambler cheated him, and, after winning, he offered the merchant a choice either to drink up the sea or give them all the money he had.

"Be patient with me until tomorrow," the merchant said, and the gambler granted him a reprieve, and he went away, troubled by what had happened to him and not knowing what he should do. When he came to an isolated place he sat down with a heavy heart and sad thoughts. All of a sudden the old woman passed by, and when she noticed how troubled he was, she said, "I see that the townsfolk have gotten the better of you. Tell me your troubles and what has happened to you."

So he told her all that had occurred from first to last, and she said, "With regard to the price of the sandalwood, you should know that it is worth ten gold pieces a pound. But now I shall give you some advice to save yourself. Go to the town gate, and nearby you will find the home of a blind sheikh, a cripple, who is wise as a wizard and has a lot of experience. Everyone goes to him when they are in trouble, and his advice is to their advantage, for he is well versed in magic and cunning. He is also a thief, and the thieves come to him at night. Therefore, I repeat: go to his lodging and hide yourself from your enemies so you may hear what they say unseen by them. You will see that he tells them which party got the best of a deal and which got the worst. Then you can make your own plans when you overhear their conversations."

So he went to the place she mentioned and hid himself near the blind man. Before long, the four men who were his adversaries appeared and sat down next to the sheikh, who set some food before them, and they ate. Then each began to tell what had happened to him during the day, and after the man who had bought the sandalwood and had agreed to pay the asking price told his story, the old man said, "Your opponent has gotten the better of you.'

"How can that be?" he asked.

"What if he says," said the sheikh, "I shall take everything in gold or silver? Will you give it to him?"

"Yes," he said. "I shall give it to him because I shall buy it below the price of the wood."

"But what if he says," added the old man, "that he wants to be paid in fleas, half male and half female, what will you do?"

So the thief knew that he was in a bad position. Then the one-eyed man came forth and said, "Oh sheikh, I met a blue-eyed stranger in town. So I picked a quarrel with him and grabbed hold of him and said, 'You were the one who robbed me of my eye!' And I did not let go until some people guaranteed that he would return tomorrow and pay for my eye."

"If he does, he may get the better of you," said the sheikh.

"How so?" asked the thief.

"He may say to you, 'Pluck out your eye, and I shall pluck out one of mine. Then we will weigh them both, and if your eye is the same weight as mine, you have spoken the truth, and I shall pay you.' But you will probably owe him the legal price of his eye and be stone blind, and he will be able to see with his one eye."

So the thief knew that the merchant might baffle him with this proposal. Then came the cobbler, who said, "Oh sheikh, a man brought me a sandal today and asked me to mend it. I asked him what he would give me, and he answered that I could have whatever I wanted. Now nothing will content me except all the wealth that he has."

"But he will take the sandal from you and give you nothing," said the old man.

"How so?" asked the cobbler.

The sheikh replied, "He only has to say to you, 'The sultan's enemies have been put to rout. His foes have grown weak and his children and helpers have multiplied. Are you content or not?' If you say, 'I am content,' he will take his sandal and go away. If you say, 'I am not content,' he will take his sandal and beat you with it because you are not content for the sake of the sultan.''

So the cobbler admitted that he did not have a leg to stand on. Then the gambler came forward and said, "I played a game of forfeits with a man today and beat him. Then I said to him, 'If you drink all the water in the sea, I shall give you all my wealth. If not, I shall take all of yours.' ''

"He has gotten the better of you," said the old man. "How so?" asked the thief.

And the sheikh responded, "He only has to say, 'Hold the mouth of the sea in your hand, and I shall drink it.' But if you can't do this, he will baffle you with his proposal.''

When the merchant heard all this, he knew how to deal with his enemies. Then the thieves left the sheikh, and the merchant returned to his lodging. The next morning the gambler came to him and demanded that he drink the sea. So the merchant said to him, "Hold the mouth of the sea in your hand, and I shall drink from it.''

Thereupon the gambler confessed that he had been beaten and gave the merchant one hundred gold pieces. Then the cobbler came and asked for whatever would make him content. But the merchant said, "The sultan has overcome his foes and has destroyed his enemies, and his children have multiplied. Are you content or not?''

"I am content," replied the cobbler, and he returned the sandal without receiving any money.

Next came the one-eyed man and demanded the legal price of his eye, but the merchant said, "Pluck out your eye, and I shall pluck out mine. Then we shall weigh them, and if they are the same weight, I shall admit that you have told the truth and will pay you the price of your eye. But if they are different, and you have lied, I shall sue you for the legal price of my eye."

"Give me time to think about this," said the one-eyed man.

But the merchant said, "I am a stranger here and I shall grant time to nobody. Nor shall I part until you pay."

So the thief saved his eye by paying the merchant one hundred ducats and went away.

Finally the buyer of the sandalwood arrived and said, "Name the price of your wood."

"What will you give me?" asked the merchant.

"We agreed that I would pay you whatever you desire," he said. "So I will give it to you in gold and silver."

"No," replied the merchant. "I want to be paid in fleas, half male and half female."

"I can't do this," said the thief, and when he realized that he had been beaten, he returned the sandalwood and paid him one hundred gold pieces so he wouldn't be sued. Then the merchant sold the sandalwood at his own price and left the city of thieves to return to his own land.

"But this tale," continued the prince, "is really not more marvelous than the one about the three-year-old child."

"What might that be?" asked the king.

And the prince answered, "I have heard tell this tale of

The Womanizer and the Three-Year-Old Child

There was once a certain profligate man, who was a womanizer, and when he heard of a beautiful woman who lived in another city, he journeyed there with a present. When he arrived he wrote a note and described how long he had been longing for her and suffering because of his great passion for her and how his passion had driven him to forsake his native land and come to her. He ended the note by begging for a rendez-vous. She gave him permission to visit her, and when he entered the room, she stood up and received him with honor. She kissed his hands and entertained him with the best of food and drink.

Now, she had a little son, who was but three years old, whom she left in the chamber and went off to cook some rice. Soon the man said to her, "Come, let us go and lie together."

But she replied, "My son is sitting and looking at us."

"He is a little child," he said, "and he does not understand anything or know how to speak."

"You wouldn't speak this way if you knew his intelligence," she responded.

When the boy saw that the rice was done, he began weeping, and his mother asked him, "Why are you weeping?"

"Ladle me out some rice," he said, and put pure butter into it. And the child ate a little, and then he began to weep again.

"What's the matter now, my son?" the mother asked.

"Oh Mother," he said, "I want some sugar with my rice."

Upon hearing this, the man, who was angry by now, burst out, "You are nothing but a cursed child!"

"Curse yourself, by Allah," answered the boy. "You wear yourself out by traveling from city to city to commit some adulterous act. As for me, I wept because I had something in my eye, and my tears brought it out. Now I have eaten rice with butter and sugar and am content. So which one of us two is cursed?"

The man was confounded by this rebuke from a little child, and he felt grace enter him and was redeemed. Therefore he did not lay a finger on the woman but left and returned to his own country, where lived a contrite life until he died.

"As for the story of the five-year-old," continued the prince, "I have heard tell, oh king, of the following tale called

The Stolen Purse

Four merchants once owned a thousand gold pieces in common, and they put them in one purse and set out to buy some merchandise with the money. They came across a beautiful garden on their way, and they decided to leave the purse with a woman who was in charge of the garden.

"Mind you," they said, "you are not to give this purse back unless all four of us are together and demand it from you in person."

She agreed to this, and they entered the garden and strolled along the walks. Then they ate and drank and entertained themselves until one of them said to the others, "I have a clay jug with me. So let's wash our heads in this running water."

"But we need a comb," said another.

"Let us ask the caretaker," said the third merchant. "Perhaps she has a comb."

Thereupon one of them arose, went to the caretaker, and said, "Give me the purse."

"Not until all of you are present," she said.

Then he called to his companions, who could see him but not hear him, and said, "She will not give it to me."

And they yelled to her, "Give it to him!" But they thought he meant the comb.

When the three others grew tired of waiting, they went to the keeper and asked her, "Why wouldn't you give him the comb?"

"He only demanded the purse, and I gave it to him with your consent," she said. "Then he went on his way."

When they heard her words, they slapped their faces, grabbed her, and said, "We authorized you only to give him the comb."

"He did not say anything about a comb to me," she replied.

Then they took her to the kazi and stated their claim. He sentenced her to make good the purse and ordered some of her debtors to be responsible for her. So she left the kazi's office and had no idea what she should do. Soon she met a five-year-old boy, and when he saw that she was very troubled, he asked her, "What's the matter, mother?"

But she did not reply, shunning him because of his tender age, and he repeated his question two more times until, at last, she told him everything that had happened.

"Give me a dirham to buy some sweetmeats, and I shall tell you how you can solve this predicament," he said.

So she gave him a piece of silver and said to him, "What do you suggest that I do?"

"Return to the kazi," the boy advised, "and say to him, 'The four merchants and I had agreed that I should not give them the purse unless all four were present. Let all four of them come back, and I shall give them the purse, as we agreed.' "

So she went back to the kazi and told him what the boy had advised. Then he asked the merchants, "Was this what was agreed between you and this woman?"

"Yes," they answered.

"Then bring me your comrade," he said, "and you can take the purse."

So they went in quest of their comrade, while the caretaker got off scot-free and went her way without having to pay a thing. And Allah is omniscient.

When the viziers and all those present in the assembly heard the prince's words, they said to his father, the king, "Truly, your son is the most accomplished man of his time." Then they blessed the king and the prince, while the king drew his son to his bosom, kissed him between the eyes, and questioned him about what had happened between him and his favorite concubine. The prince swore to him by Allah and by His Holy Prophet that it was she who had demanded that they make love and that he had refused her.

"Moreover," he added, "she promised me that she

would give you poison to drink and kill you. Then the throne would be mine. But I grew furious and indicated to her, 'Oh cursed one, once I can speak, I shall reward you!' So she was afraid of me and did what she did."

The king believed his words, and while he sent for his favorite concubine, he asked the others present, "How shall we put this lady to death?"

Some advised him to cut out her tongue, and others to burn her alive. But when she came before the king, she said to him, "My situation is like the one in the tale of the fox and the folk."

"How so?" he asked.

And she answered, "I have heard tell, oh king, a tale about

The Fox and the Folk

A fox once made his way into a city by the wall and entered a currier's storehouse. There he caused havoc and damaged all the owner's skins. One day the currier set a trap for him, and after catching him, he beat the fox with the hides until he fell down and lost consciousness. The man thought that he was dead and threw him out onto the road by the city gate. Soon an old woman came by, and upon seeing the fox, she said, "I have heard that a fox's eye hung around a child's neck will keep it from weeping." So she plucked out his right eye and went away.

Then a boy passed by, and he said, "What good is this tail on the fox?" So he cut off the tail and departed.

After a while, a man came and said, "The fox's gall is supposed to help against blindness." So he took out his knife and slit open the fox's paunch.

But Reynard said to himself, "I have put up with the plucking out of my eye and the cutting off of my tail, but I shall not put up with the slitting of my paunch!"

Upon saying this, he sprang up and ran through the city gate and could hardly believe that he had escaped.

"I pardon you," said the king, "and your fate is now in my son's hands. If he wants, he may torture or kill you."

"Pardon is better than vengeance, and mercy is the quality of the noble," the prince said.

"It is for you to decide, my son," repeated the king.

So the prince set her free and said, "You are to leave our realm, and may Allah pardon what has passed!"

Thereupon the king rose from his throne and seated his son on it. He crowned him with his crown and asked the nobles of his realm to swear loyalty to him and commanded them to do homage to him. Then he said, "My folk, to tell the truth, I have led a full life and desire now to retire and devote myself to the service of my Lord. I call upon you to witness that I am divesting myself of my crown and am having it set on my son's head."

So the troops and officers swore loyalty to the prince, and his father devoted himself to the worship of his Lord, while his son now ruled as king with a just and fair hand. His power grew and his sultanate became stronger, and he lived in happiness until the time came for his certain departure.

Abdullah the Fisherman
and Abdullah the Merman

There was once a fisherman named Abdullah, who had a large family of nine children. Since he owned nothing but his net, he was very poor. Every day he used to go to the sea and fish. If his catch was small, he sold the fish and spent the money on his children for provisions, and if he caught a lot, he would cook a good deal of it, buy fruit, and spend money without stinting until nothing was left. "Tomorrow will bring whatever it brings," he would say to himself.

Soon his wife gave birth to another child, making a total of ten, and it so happened on this day that he had nothing at all. So his wife said to him, "Oh my lord, see to it that you find something so that I may nourish myself."

"I shall go to the sea and fish, and perhaps our new born child will bring us some luck," he replied.

"Put your trust in Allah," she said.

Then he took his net and went down to the seashore, where he cast it, hoping that his little one would bring him luck, and he cried out, "Oh my God, may you grant my son a life of comfort without hardship and with plenty to eat!"

He waited awhile and drew in the net, which came up full of rubbish, sand, pebbles, and weeds. There were no signs of fish, big or little. He cast it again and waited, then drew it in, but found nothing. He threw the net a third, fourth, and fifth time. Still not a single fish came up. So he moved to another place and implored Allah Almighty to provide him with his daily bread. He kept working this way until the end of the day, but he did not catch as much as a minnow. So he began to wonder and ask himself, "Has Allah created this newborn child without providing for him? This can never be, for Almighty Allah has pledged himself to all his children and provides for everyone!"

Upon saying this, he swung his net over his shoulder and headed home with a broken spirit and heavy heart, worried about his family, especially since he had left them without food and his wife had just given birth. As he continued trudging along and saying to himself, "What shall I do, and what shall I say to the children tonight?" he came to a baker's oven and saw a crowd of people standing around it. There was widespread famine at this time, and food was scarce. So people were offering the baker lots of money, but he paid no attention to them, because there were too many. The fisherman stood looking and sniffing the smell of the hot bread (and indeed, his soul longed for it because he was so hungry) until the baker caught sight of him and cried out to him, "Come here, oh fisherman!"

So, he went up to him, and the baker said, "Do you want bread?"

But he was silent.

"Speak up," said the baker, "and don't be ashamed, for Allah is bountiful. If you do not have any money, I shall give you bread and shall be patient until fortune shines upon you."

"By Allah, oh master," replied the fisherman, "it is true. I have no money. But give me bread enough for my family, and I shall leave this net as pawn until tomorrow when I hope to repay you."

"No, my poor fellow," said the baker. "This net is the door to your shop, and it opens the way for you to provide for your family. So, if you pawn it, how will you be able to fish? Tell me how much you need."

"Ten half-dirhams' worth."

So the baker gave him ten nusfs' worth of bread and ten in silver currency, saying, "Take these ten nusfs and buy and cook all the meat you need. Altogether you will owe me twenty nusfs, and you can pay me back with the fish you catch tomorrow. But if you don't catch any fish again, I want you to come and take your bread and ten nusfs, and I shall be patient until you have better luck."

"May Almighty Allah reward you," said the fisherman, "and may he repay you for all the good that you have done." Then he took the bread and the coins and went away happily. After he bought what he needed, he returned to his wife, whom he found sitting up and soothing the children, who were weeping for hunger. "Your father will be here soon," she kept saying, "and then you will have something to eat."

Indeed, once he arrived, he set the bread before them, and they ate while he told them what had happened, and she said, "Allah is bountiful."

The next day, he picked up his net and went out of the house saying, "I implore you, oh Lord. Grant me a good catch so that I can pay back the baker."

When he came to the seashore, he proceeded to cast his net and pull it in, but there were no fish to be seen. He continued to toil this way until the end of the day, but he caught nothing. Then he set out for home in great concern, and the way to his house went by the baker's oven. So he asked himself, "How shall I go home? When I reach the baker's place, I had better walk fast so he won't see me." When he reached the shop, he saw a large crowd around it and walked faster because he was ashamed to face his creditor. But the baker caught sight of him and cried out, "Ho, fisherman! Come and take your bread and spending money. You seem to have forgotten it."

"By Allah," said Abdullah, "I had not forgotten, but I was ashamed to face you, because I did not catch any fish today."

"Don't be ashamed," responded the baker. "Didn't I tell you that I would be patient until you have better luck?"

Then he gave him the bread and the ten nusfs, and the fisherman returned and told his wife, who said, "Allah is bountiful. Your luck will turn, and you will give the baker his due."

For the next forty days Abdullah kept going daily to the seashore and remained from dawn to dusk. Each day

he returned home without fish, and each day he received
bread and spending money from the baker, who never
once mentioned the fish or neglected him. He never kept
him waiting as he did other people. Rather he gave him
bread and the ten half-dirhams without delay. Whenever
the fisherman said to him, "Oh my brother, let me settle
my debt somehow," the baker would say, "Stop this
nonsense! This is no time to settle debts. Wait until you
have better luck, and then I shall settle accounts with
you."

And the fisherman would bless him and go away
thanking him. On the forty-first day, he said to his wife,
"I have a good mind to tear up this net and stop fishing forever."

"Why do you want to do this?" she asked.

"It seems that I can no longer earn our daily bread
from the sea. How long will this last? By Allah, I burn
with shame whenever I walk by the baker's shop. I don't
want to go to the sea anymore because I have to pass
his oven along the way. And each time I return home,
he calls me and gives me bread and the ten silver coins.
How much longer shall I go into debt with him!"

His wife replied, "Praise the Lord, for He has moved
the baker's heart so that he gives us our daily bread.
Why do you dislike this?'

"I owe him now a great sum of dirhams, and there is
no doubt but that he will demand his due," the fisherman stated.

"Has he been bothering you and asking you for the
money?" his wife asked.

"On the contrary," Abdullah replied, "he still refuses
to settle my debt and keeps insisting that I should wait
until my luck turns."

"Well then, if he presses you for the money, you
should say to him, 'Wait until the good luck comes that
you and I are hoping for,' " his wife advised.

"And when will this good luck come that we hope
for?" the fisherman asked.

"Allah is bountiful."

"You speak the truth."

Upon saying this, the fisherman lifted his net on to

his shoulder and went down to the seashore, praying, "Oh Lord, please provide me with just one fish that I can give to the baker."

And he cast his net into the sea, and as he pulled it in, he found that it was heavy. So he tugged at it until he was tired and sore from all the work. But when he got the net ashore, he found a dead donkey swollen and stinking. Repulsed by the dead animal, he freed it from the net and remarked, "May Allah's might be praised! I can't go on like this. I've told that wife of mine that I can no longer earn a living from fishing and that I want to abandon this profession. But she answers me that Allah is bountiful and something good will happen to me soon. Is this dead ass the good thing that she meant?" And he grieved with all his heart. Then he moved to another place to get away from the stench of the dead donkey, and he cast his net there and waited a full hour before drawing it in and finding it heavy. "Well, it seems," he remarked, "that I am hauling up all the dead donkeys in the sea and ridding it of its rubbish." However, he had to keep tugging until blood came from the palms of his hands, and when he got the net ashore, he saw a man in it and took him for one of the ifrits of the Lord Solomon, who used to imprison them in vessels of brass and cast them into the sea. The fisherman thought that the vessel had burst after lying in the sea for many years and that the ifrit had come out and become entangled in the net. So he fled from him, crying out, "Mercy, mercy, oh ifrit of Solomon!"

But the creature called to him from the net and said, "Come here, fisherman, and don't flee from me. I am human just like you. Release me so that I may give you your just reward from Allah."

When the fisherman heard these words, he took heart, and approaching the creature in the net, he said, "Aren't you an ifrit of the jinn?"

"No," the stranger replied. "I am a mortal and a believer in Allah and his Apostle."

"Who threw you into the sea?" asked Abdullah.

"I am one of the children of the sea," the man stated. "I was swimming in the sea when I was caught by your net. We are people who obey Allah's commandments and show loving-kindness to the creatures of the Almighty. Since I fear and dread to be disobedient, I could not tear your net. Rather I accepted the fate that Allah decreed for me. Now, by setting me free, you have become my owner and I your captive. Will you now set me free for the love of Almighty Allah and agree to become my comrade? I shall come to you every day at this spot, and you are to come to me and bring me a gift of the fruits of the land such as grapes, figs, watermelons, peaches, pomegranates, and so forth. Anything you bring will be acceptable to me. In the sea, we have coral, pearls, chrysalides, emeralds, rubies, and other gems, and I shall fill the basket in which you carry the fruit with all the precious stones and jewels of the sea. What do you say to this, my brother?"

"Let us swear an oath on the opening chapter of the Koran!" replied the fisherman.

So they recited the Fatihah together. Then the fisherman set the merman loose from the net and asked him, "What is your name?"

"My name is Abdullah of the Sea," he answered, "and if you come here and do not see me, call out and say, 'Where are you, oh Abdullah, oh merman?' and I shall come to you. But what is your name?"

"My name is also Abdullah," the fisherman stated.

"You are Abdullah of the Land, and I am Abdullah of the Sea," the merman remarked. "But wait here until I go and fetch you a present."

Now the fisherman regretted that he had set the merman free and said to himself, "How do I know that he will come back to me? Indeed, he beguiled me so that I would set him free, and now he will laugh at me. If I had kept him, I might have used him in a show to amuse the cityfolk and collected money and gone with him to the houses of the great people." And he continued to regret that he had set him free and said, "You have let your prey slip out of your hands!" But as he was lamenting his folly of letting the prisoner escape, lo and behold, Abdullah the Merman returned to him with both hands full of pearls, coral, emeralds, rubies, and other gems.

"Take these, my brother," he said, "and excuse me. If I had had a fish basket, I would have filled it for you."

Abdullah the Fisherman rejoiced and took the jewels from the merman, who said to him, "Come here every day before sunrise." Then he wished the fisherman farewell and went down into the sea, while the other returned to the city full of joy. As soon as he reached the baker's oven, he cried out, "Oh my brother, good luck has come to us at last, and I want to settle my debt."

"It's not necessary for us to settle accounts," said the baker. "If you have something, give it to me. If you have nothing, take your bread and spending money and be gone, unless you have had some luck."

"Oh my friend, luck has indeed allowed me to partake of Allah's bounty, and I owe you a great deal of money. But take this first," and he took a handful of the pearls, coral, rubies, and other jewels, about half of his treasure, and gave them to him. "Now I want you to lend me some money to spend this day until I sell the rest of these jewels."

So the baker gave him all the money he had on hand and all the bread in his basket. He rejoiced in receiving the jewels and said, "I am your slave and servant." Then he placed all the bread on his head and followed the fisherman to his home, where he gave it to his wife and children. Afterward the baker went to the market and bought meat, vegetables, and all kinds of fruit. Indeed, he abandoned his oven for the day and spent his time with Abdullah attending his affairs. But the fisherman said, "Oh my brother, I'm afraid that you're wearing yourself out."

"This is my duty," said the baker, "for I have become your servant, and you have overwhelmed me with your presents."

"It was you who was my benefactor in days of need and distress," replied the fisherman.

And the baker spent that night with him enjoying good cheer and became a faithful friend to him. Then the fisherman told his wife what had happened with the merman, and she was glad and said, "Keep all this a secret. Otherwise, the government will come down on you."

"You are right," he said. "I shall keep this a secret from everyone, but I shall not hide it from the baker."

The next morning he rose early and took with him a basket which he had filled the evening before with all kinds of fruit. He went straight to the seashore before sunrise and set the basket down on the water's edge, where he cried out, "Where are you, Abdullah, oh Merman?"

"Here I am at your service," came the reply. Then the merman came forth, and the fisherman gave him the fruit. Upon taking it he plunged into the sea and was absent a full hour, after which time he reappeared with the fish basket full of all kinds of gems and jewels. The fisherman set it on his head and went away. When he came to the oven, the baker said to him, "Oh my lord, I have baked forty buns for you and have sent them to your house. Now I shall bake you some more bread, and as soon as all is done, I shall bring them to your house and then go and fetch the vegetables and meat."

Abdullah gave him three handfuls of jewels out of the fish basket. Then he returned home, set the basket down, and took a valuable gem of each sort, and went to the jewel bazaar, where he stopped at the jeweler's shop. "I have some precious stones to sell," he said.

"Show them to me," said the sheikh.

So the fisherman showed them to the jeweler, who asked, "Do you have any more of these?"

"I have a basketful at home," Abdullah replied.

"Where is your house?" the jeweler asked.

As soon as the fisherman told him, the sheikh took the jewels from him and said to his followers, "Grab him! He's the thief who stole the queen's jewelry."

He ordered his men to beat the fisherman, and they hit him and tied him up. Then the jeweler and all the people from the jewel market set out for the palace and told everyone along the way that they had caught the thief of the queen's jewels.

"We have the villain," said one man.

"It was he who has been robbing our homes!" said another.

Many other things were said about poor Abdullah. Meanwhile he remained silent and did not reply to their charges. After they reached the king's palace, the jeweler began speaking: "Oh king, when the queen's necklace was stolen, you asked us to help find the culprit. So I did the best I could, more than anyone else, and I have caught the thief for you. Here he stands before you, and these are the jewels that we have recovered."

Thereupon the king said to the chief eunuch, "Carry these jewels to the queen and ask her whether they are the ones that she lost."

So the eunuch took the jewels and went to the queen, who marveled at their luster, but she sent a message to the king saying, "I have found my necklace in my own place, and these jewels are not my property. Indeed, these gems are finer than those on my necklace. So do not punish this man. But if he will sell them, buy them for your daughter Umm al-Su'ud so that we can make her a necklace with them."

When the eunuch returned and told the king what the queen had said, he condemned the jeweler and his followers, and they said to him, "Your majesty, we thought this man was a poor fisherman and could not imagine how he came upon the jewels. So we thought that he had stolen them."

"Oh you filthy villains, do you begrudge a true believer good fortune? Why didn't you make certain that your accusations were true? Fortunately, Allah has blessed him with these things from a source that he did not expect. Why did you make a thief out of him and disgrace him among the folk? Begone, and may Allah never bless you!"

So they left full of fear, and the king said to Abdullah, "May Allah bless you and all that he has bestowed upon you. No harm shall come to you, but tell me truthfully, where did you get these jewels? I am a king, and nevertheless, I have never seen such precious jewels as these."

"Your majesty," the fisherman replied, "I have a fish basket full of them at home, and I shall tell you the story of how I came upon them." So he told the king about his friendship with the merman and added, "We have formed a pact. I am to bring him a basket full of fruit every day, and he will fill my basket with these jewels."

"You have been most fortunate," said the king, "but wealth needs rank for protection. For the time being I shall defend you against other powerful men, but if I should unfortunately be deposed or die and another king rules in my place, he might slay you because of his greed and desire for wealth. Therefore, I intend to wed you to my daughter, make you my vizier, and bequeath the kingdom to you so that nobody can hanker for your riches when I am gone." Whereupon the king turned to his servants and said, "Take this man to the Hammam bath."

So they took him to the baths, cleaned his body, dressed him in royal robes, and brought him back to the king, who appointed him his vizier. Then he sent couriers and soldiers of his guard and all the wives of the notables, who clad his wife and children in kingly costume. The woman was placed in a horse litter with a little child in her lap, and the couriers, officers, and soldiers escorted her to the palace. They also brought her elder children to the king, who was very glad to see them. He took them in his lap and seated them by his side. There were nine boys altogether, and the king had no son and heir and had been blessed only with one daughter called Umm al-Su'ud. Meanwhile the queen treated Abdullah's wife with honor by bestowing favors on her and making her an adviser. Then the king had the marriage contract between his daughter and Abdullah of the Land drawn up, and Abdullah assigned all the gems and precious stones in his possession to her as her dowry. Then the king proclaimed that the gates be opened for the festival and that the city be decorated in honor of his daughter's wedding. Then Abdullah went in to the princess and took her maidenhead.

Early the next morning the king looked out his window and saw Abdullah carrying a fish basket full of fruit on his head. So he called to him, "What do you have there, my son-in-law? Where are you going?"

"To my friend Abdullah the Merman," he replied.

"But this is no time to go to your comrade," said the king.

"To tell the truth," Abdullah responded, "I am afraid to break our agreement. Otherwise he might think me a liar and say, 'Worldly matters have made you forget me.'"

"You are right," stated the king. "Go to your friend, and may God be with you."

So Abdullah went through the city on his way to his companion, and as he walked, he heard the folk who knew him say, "There goes the king's son-in-law to exchange fruit for gems."

Other people who did not know him remarked, "Hey, fellow, how much for a pound? Sell some of your fruit to me."

And he answered, "Wait until I come back." He did not want to hurt the feelings of any man. So he kept walking until he came to the seashore and met with his friend Abdullah the Merman, who gave him gems in return for the fruit. He continued doing this until, one day, when he passed the baker's shop, he found it closed. Indeed, the shop remained closed during the next ten days, and he saw nothing of the baker. So he said to himself, "This is a strange thing! I wonder where the baker has gone." Then he asked a neighbor, "Do you happen to know where the baker has gone and what Allah has done with him?"

And the man replied, "Oh my lord, he is sick and does not leave his house."

"Where is his house?" asked Abdullah, and the neighbor told him where he lived. So, Abdullah went there and made inquiries about him. When he knocked at the door, the baker looked out of a window, and seeing his friend the fisherman with a basket on his head, he came down and opened the door. Abdullah entered and threw his arms around the baker and wept. "What is going on, my friend? Every day I pass your shop and it is closed. So I asked your neighbor, who told me that you were sick. Finally I made inquiries and found your house so I could see you."

"May Allah bless you for your kindness," the baker replied. "I am not sick, but I learned that the king had taken you prisoner because the people had lied about you and accused you of being a robber. Therefore I feared for my life, closed the shop, and hid myself."

"It's true that the king took me," said Abdullah, but then he told him all that happened. "In the end, the king gave me his daughter to wed and made me his vizier. Now I want you to take what is in this fish basket for your share and not to be afraid of anything."

After assuaging the baker's fear, he left him and returned to the king with an empty basket. Thereupon the king said to him, "Oh my son-in-law, it would seem that you did not meet with your friend the merman today."

"On the contrary," Abdullah replied. "I went to him, but I gave away everything to my friend the baker, who has been most kind to me."

"Who is this baker?" asked the king.

And the fisherman answered, "He is a benevolent man, who treated me generously when I was poor, and he never neglected me a single day or hurt my feelings."

"What is his name?" the king inquired.

"His name is Abdullah the Baker, and my name is Abdullah of the Land and that of my friend the merman Abdullah of the Sea."

"And my name is also Abdullah, and the servants of Allah are all brothers. So send for your friend the baker so that I may make him my vizier of the left."

So the fisherman sent for the baker, who came to the palace right away, and the king appointed him vizier of the left while Abdullah of the Land was given the title of vizier of the right. During the next year, the fisherman enjoyed this office, and every day he continued to carry a basket of fruit to the merman, who would then fill his basket with jewels. When the fruit crops failed in the gardens, Abdullah carried him raisins, almonds, filberts, walnuts, figs, and so forth. The merman always accepted whatever he brought him and returned the fish basket full of gems according to their agreement.

Now it happened one day that the fisherman carried him the basket full of dry fruit as was his wont, and his friend took them from him. Then they sat down to talk, Abdullah the Fisherman on the beach and Abdullah the Merman in the water near the shore. As they discussed many different things, they hit upon the subject of sepulchers, whereupon the merman said, "Oh my brother, they say that the Prophet is buried with you on land. Do you know where his tomb is?"

"Yes, it is in a city called Yathrib," replied Abdullah.

"And do the people of the land visit it?" the merman asked again.

"Yes," answered the fisherman.

Then the merman said, "How fortunate you people of the land are to be able to visit that noble and compassionate Prophet! Whoever journeys to him deserves his intercession. Have you ever visited him, oh brother?"

"No," replied the fisherman. "I was poor and did not have the necessary amount of money to spend for the journey. It is only since I met you and you bestowed this good fortune on me that I have been in a position to make such a journey. Indeed, I intend to make this journey after I have made the pilgrimage to the Holy House of Allah, and nothing keeps me from this pilgrimage except my love for you, because I cannot leave you for one day."

"Do you set your love for me above a pilgrimage to the tomb of Mohammed, who will intercede for you on the Day of Review before Allah and will save you from the fire and enable you to enter paradise?" the merman asked. "And are you neglecting this out of the love of the world to visit the tomb of your Prophet Mohammed? May God bless and preserve him!"

"No, by Allah," responded the fisherman. "I place the pilgrimage to the Prophet's tomb above everything, and I beg your permission to take the journey and pray before it this year."

"I grant you this permission," said the merman, "provided that when you stand by his sepulcher, you will salute him for me with the salaam. In addition, there is something I want to give you in trust. Therefore, come with me into the sea so that I may carry you to my city and entertain you in my house and give you something to deposit before the Prophet's tomb. When you are there, I want you to lay it on the ground and say, 'Oh Apostle of Allah, Abdullah the Merman salutes you and sends you this present, imploring your intercession to save him from the Fire.' "

"Oh my brother, you were created in the water," said the fisherman, "and water is your dwelling place and does no harm to you. But if you should come onto the land, would you be hurt in any way?"

"Yes," replied the merman. "My body would dry up, and the breezes of the land would blow upon me, causing me to die."

"And I in like manner was created on land," the fisherman stated, "and the land is my dwelling place. So if I went down into the sea, the water would enter my belly and choke me, causing my death."

"Have no fear," the merman said. "I shall bring you an ointment, and after you have spread this ointment on your body, the water will not harm you even though you will enter deep waters and swim to the bottom of the sea and rise with the waves."

"Well, if this is the case, well and good," answered the fisherman. "But bring me the ointment so I can test it."

"So be it," said the merman, and he took the fish basket and disappeared into the depths of the sea. After a brief absence, he returned with an unguent that seemed to be made from the fat of beef. It was yellow as gold and had a sweet smell to it.

"What is this, my brother?" the fisherman asked.

"It is the liver fat of a kind of fish called the Dandan, which is the largest of all the fish in the sea and our fiercest foe," replied the merman. "He is larger than any beast of the land, and if he were to meet a camel or an elephant, he would swallow it with a single bite."

Abdullah was curious and said, "What does this terrible beast do?"

"He eats beasts of the sea," the merman responded.

"Haven't you ever heard the saying 'Like the fish of the sea, the mighty eat the feeble'?"

"True, but do you have many of these Dandans in the sea?"

"Yes, there are many. No one lives to tell anything about them except the Almighty Allah."

"To tell the truth," the fisherman said, "I'm afraid to go down with you into the depths of the sea. Surely if I meet a creature like this it will devour me."

"Have no fear," the merman assured him. "When he sees you, he will recognize you as a son of Adam and will fear you and flee. The only thing that he dreads in the sea is a son of Adam. If he should eat a man, he will die right away, because human fat is a deadly poison for this kind of creature. The only way we can collect its liver fat is by means of a man after he has fallen into the sea and drowns. Then the man's shape is changed, and often his flesh is torn. So the Dandan eats him, thinking that it is one of the fish of the deep, and it dies. Then we approach our dead enemy and take the fat of his liver and grease ourselves so that we can wander through the waters in safety. Also, wherever there is a son of Adam, even if there are a hundred, two hundred, or a thousand of these beasts in the same spot, they will die right away if they but hear him. Moreover, they cannot move from their spot. So whenever a son of Adam falls into the sea, we take him and anoint him with this fat and go around the depths with him. Whenever we see a Dandan or two, we tell him to cry out, and they all die instantaneously because of a single cry."

"I shall place my trust in Allah," said the fisherman, and he took off his clothes and buried them in a hole which he dug in the beach. After doing this, he rubbed his body from head to toe with the ointment. Then he dove into the water and opened his eyes, and the brine did not hurt him. So he walked left and right, and whenever he wanted, he rose to the surface of the sea or sank to the bottom. Indeed, the water was like a tent over his head and caused him no harm. Then the merman said to him, "What do you see, my brother?"

"I see nothing but wonderful things," the fisherman

answered. "You were absolutely right. The water is not hurting me."

"Follow me," said the merman.

So the fisherman followed him, and they moved from place to place while Abdullah discovered mountains of water on his right and left and was content to gaze at various sorts of fish, some large and some small, that scattered as he approached. Some of them looked like buffaloes, others like oxen and dogs. Some even looked like human beings. But whenever they drew near them, the fish fled, especially when they spied the fisherman, who said to the merman, "My brother, why is it that the fish flee as soon as we approach them?"

"Because they are afraid of you. Every creature that Allah has made fears the son of Adam."

The fisherman was continually astounded by the marvels of the deep as they swam by a high mountain. Suddenly he heard a mighty roar, and when he turned around, he saw some black thing, the size of a camel or larger, coming down upon him from the liquid mountain and crying out. So he asked his friend, "What is this, my brother?"

"It's the Dandan," the merman answered. "He's coming after me and wants to devour me. So cry out at him, my brother, before he reaches us, or else he will snatch and gobble me up."

Without hesitating, Abdullah cried out at the beast, and it immediately fell down dead. When he saw it, he exclaimed, "Glory be to God! I killed it without using a sword or knife. How is it possible that such a huge creature could not bear my cry?"

"Don't be astonished, my brother," replied the merman. "By Allah, even if there were a thousand or two thousand of these creatures, they would not be able to endure the cry of a son of Adam."

Then they continued to walk on the bottom of the sea until they reached a city whose inhabitants the fisherman realized were all women, and so he asked his companion, "What city is this, my brother, and what are these women?"

"This is the city of women, for its inhabitants are the women of the sea."

"Aren't there any men among them?"

"No!"

"Then how do they conceive and bear young without any males?" the fisherman wondered.

"The king of the sea has banished them here, and they can neither conceive nor bear children," the merman told him. "He sends all the women of the sea with whom he is angry to this spot, and they cannot leave it. If any of them should try to leave, the beasts of the sea who saw them would eat them right away."

"Are there other cities than this in the sea?" the fisherman asked.

"There are many," replied his companion.

"And is there a sultan who rules over you?"

"Yes."

"Oh my brother, I have indeed seen many marvels in this sea."

But the merman said, "And what have you seen of its marvels? Haven't you heard the saying 'The marvels of the sea are more manifold than the marvels of the land'?"

"True," replied the fisherman and began gazing at the women whom he saw. They had faces like moons and hair like women's hair, but their hands and feet were in their middle, and they had tails like fish. Now, when the merman had shown him the people of the city, he walked with him to another city, which he found full of men and women. They, too, were shaped like the women of the other city and had tails. But there was neither selling nor buying among them as with the people of the land. None of them wore clothes and simply went about their daily chores naked.

"Oh my brother," said Abdullah, "I see men and women totally nude."

"This is because the folk of the sea have no clothes," remarked the merman.

"And what do they do when they marry?"

"They don't marry," answered the merman, "but

every man who takes a liking to a female takes his will of her."

"This is unlawful," replied the fisherman. "Why doesn't he ask her hand in marriage with a dowry and make her a wedding festival in accordance to the laws of Allah and His Apostle?"

"We are not all of one religion," responded the merman. "Some of us are Moslems, believers in the Unity, others are Nazarenes and members of different religions. Each marries in accordance with the laws of his creed, but those of us who marry are mostly Moslems."

"You are naked, and there is neither buying nor selling among you," said the fisherman. "What then makes up your wives' dowry? Do you give them jewels and precious stones?"

"For us gems are only stones without worth," the merman responded. "But if a Moslem wants to marry, they impose a dowry of a certain number of fish of various kinds that he must catch, a thousand or two thousand, more or less, according to the agreement reached between himself and the bride's father. As soon as he brings the amount required, the families of the bride and the bridegroom assemble and eat the fish at the marriage banquet. After this, they bring him in to his bride, and he catches fish and feeds her. If he is unable to do this, she catches the fish and feeds him."

"And what if a woman commits adultery?" asked the fisherman.

"If a woman is convicted of adultery," the merman stated, "they banish her to the city of women. If she is pregnant, they leave her until she gives birth. If she gives birth to a girl, they banish her with the child, calling her adulteress and one child daughter of adulteress, and one child must remain a maid until she dies. But if she gives birth to a boy, they carry him to the Sultan of the Sea, who puts the baby to death."

Abdullah was astounded by this. Then the merman carried him to another city and from there to another and yet another until he had shown Abdullah eighty cities. And in each city the people were completely different from the people of the other cities. Then he said to the merman, "Are there other cities in the sea?"

"Haven't you seen enough of the cities of the sea and its wondrous spectacles?" the merman replied. "If I were to show you every day a thousand cities for a thousand years and in each city a thousand marvels, I would have shown you only one carat of the twenty-four carats of the cities of the sea and its miracles! I have merely shown you our own province and nothing more."

The fisherman continued, "Oh brother, since this is the situation, what I have seen is sufficient for me. I am now tired of eating fish, and the past eighty days that I have been in your company, you have fed me nothing but raw fish night and day. And none of it was broiled or boiled."

"And what is broiled and boiled?"

"We broil fish with fire and boil it in water. We also dress it in various ways and make many dishes out of it."

"And how are we to obtain fire in the sea? We know nothing about broiling and boiling or anything else of this kind."

"We also fry fish in olive and sesame oil."

"How can we obtain olive and sesame oil in the sea? We know nothing about all these things."

"True, but, my brother, you have shown me many cities, but you have not shown me your own."

"Well, we actually passed my own city a long time ago, for it is near the land from where we came, and I left it and came with you here because I wanted to entertain you by showing you the greater cities of the sea."

"I have seen enough of them," the fisherman said, "and I would now like you to show me your own city."

"So be it," answered the merman, and he carried his friend back to his own city.

Abdullah of the Land looked and saw a city which was small by comparison with those that he had seen. Then they entered and continued on their way until they came to a cave.

"This is my house," said the merman. "All the houses in the city are either small or large caverns, and this is true of all the houses in the other cities of the sea. Whoever wishes to have a house must go to the king and say to him, 'I wish to make a house in such and such a place.' Thereupon the king sends with him a band of the fish called Peckers, which have beaks that crumble the hardest rock. They receive a certain sum of fish for their work, and they go to the mountain chosen by the owner and pierce the mountain while the owner catches fish and feeds them until the cave is finished. Then they go their own way, and the owner takes possession of the house. This is what all the people of the sea do. They only trade with one another or serve each other by means of fish. Their food is fish, and they themselves are a kind of fish." Then he said to his friend, "Enter!"

So Abdullah entered, and the merman cried out, "Ho, daughter!'

Just then a damsel appeared, and she had a face that glittered like the moon, long hair, big hips, black eyes, and a slender waist. But she was naked and had a tail. When she saw Abdullah of the Land, she said to her sire, "Oh my father, what is this no-tail that you have brought with you?"

"Daughter, this is my friend of the land from whom I have brought you the fruits of the ground. Come here and greet him with the salaam."

So she came forward and greeted the fisherman with eloquent tongue and elegant speech, and her father said to her, "Bring meat for our guest, for he blesses our house with his visit."

So she brought him two large fish, each the size of a lamb, and the merman said to him, "Eat."

Despite the fact that they only served fish, he ate it because he was so hungry. Before long the merman's wife came in, and she was beautiful and graceful and had two children with her, each with a young fish in his hand. When she saw the fisherman with her husband, she said, "What is this no-tail?"

She and her sons and daughter approached the fisherman and began examining the back part of Abdullah of the Land.

"By Allah," they laughed at him, "he is tailless!"

"My brother," the fisherman responded, "have you

brought me here to make me a butt and laughingstock for your wife and children?"

"Pardon, my friend," said the merman. "Those who have no tails are rare among us, and whenever one is found, the sultan takes him to make fun of him, and he is like a marvelous thing among us, and all who see him laugh at him. But, my brother, please excuse my wife and children, for they lack common courtesy." Then he cried out to his family, "Silence!"

They were scared by the merman and immediately became quiet, while he continued to soothe Abdullah's hurt feelings. As they were talking, ten tall and strong mermen entered and said to him, "Oh Abdullah, the king has learned that you have a no-tail of the no-tails of the earth with you."

"Yes," he responded. "Here he is, but he is not of us or of the children of the sea. He is my friend of the land and has come to me as a guest, and I intend to carry him back to the land."

"We must take him with us," they said. "If you have something to say about this, then arise and come with him to the king. Whatever you might want to say to us, you should say to the king."

"Oh my brother," said the merman, "please accept my profound apology, but we cannot disobey the king. I shall go with you and do my best do deliver you from him. May God help us! Fear not, for he thinks that you are of the children of the sea. When he sees you, he will know that you are of the children of the land. Then he will surely treat you honorably and let you return to the land."

And Abdullah of the Land replied, "It is your decision. I shall trust in Allah and go with you."

So the merman took him and carried him to the king, who, when he saw the fisherman, laughed at him and said, "Welcome, no-tail!"

And all those people who were standing around the king began to laugh at him and say, "By Allah, he is tailless!"

Then Abdullah of the Sea stepped forward and told the king all about the fisherman and reported, "This man is of the children of the land, and he is my comrade and cannot live among us, especially since he does not like to eat fish unless it is boiled or broiled. Therefore, I request that you permit me to return him to the land."

"Since the case is so," the king responded, "and he cannot live among us, I give you permission to return him to his place after due entertainment. Now, bring him the guest meal!"

So they brought him a variety of fish, and he ate in obedience to the royal command. Then the king said to him, "Ask a favor of me."

"I request that you give me jewels," the fisherman said.

"Carry him to the jewel house," the king commanded, "and let him choose whatever he needs."

So the merman carried him to the jewel house, and the fisherman picked out whatever he wanted. Afterward his friend carried him back to his own cave, where he pulled out a purse and said, "Take this deposit, and lay it on the tomb of the Prophet for the grace of Allah."

The fisherman took the purse, not knowing what was inside. Then the merman went forth with him to bring him back to land, and along the way they heard singing and merrymaking and saw a table spread with fish. People were eating and enjoying a large festival. So Abdullah of the Land said to his friend, "Why are these people celebrating like this? Is there a wedding?"

"No," replied the merman. "One of them is dead."

"Do you celebrate and sing and eat when one of you dies?"

"Yes, and what do you of the land do?"

"When one of us dies, we weep and mourn for him, and the women beat their faces and tear the bosoms of their raiment in a gesture of mourning for the dead."

Abdullah the merman stared at him with wide eyes and said to him, "Give me my purse!"

So he gave it to him. Then he set him ashore and said to him, "I am terminating our agreement and ending our friendship. From this day on, you will no longer see me, nor shall I see you."

"Why are you saying this?" cried the fisherman.

"Aren't you folk of the land Allah's creation like a deposit?"

"Yes."

"Why then," asked the Merman, "is it so bad that Allah should take back his creation, and why do you weep over it? How can I trust you with my deposit for the Prophet when I see that you rejoice in the birth of a child in which the Almighty places a soul as a deposit, and then you weep and mourn and consider it bad when he takes it away? Since it is hard for you to give up the deposit of Allah, how can it be easy for you to give up the deposit of the Prophet? Now you see why we do not need your companionship."

Upon saying this, the merman left him and disappeared into the sea. So Abdullah of the Land put on his clothes, picked up the jewels, and went to the king, who was glad to see him again and said, "How are you, my son-in-law, and what caused you to be absent so long?"

Thereupon the fisherman told him his tale and recounted all the marvels of the sea and thus astounded the king. In addition, he told him what Abdullah the merman had said, and the king replied, "Indeed, you should not have told him about our mourning."

Nevertheless, the fisherman continued for some time to go down to the shore and call for Abdullah of the Sea, but he never received an answer. At last, he gave up all hope of ever seeing him again. Meanwhile, the fisherman, the king, his father-in-law, and their families lived happily and devoutly followed all the proper customs until the Destroyer of Delights and the Severer of Societies came to them, and they all died.

The Tale of Zayn al-Asnam

There was once a powerful king who ruled the city of Bassorah. He was exceedingly rich and possessed everything imaginable. However, he did not have a child to whom he could bequeath his wealth and land. So, in hope that he might somehow change this tragic situation, he began to give a huge amount of alms to the poor, the fakirs, and other holy men. In return, he asked them to pray to Allah Almighty to bless him with an heir. Finally, in his compassion for the unfortunate king, Allah granted his petition, and on a certain night after the king lay with his wife, she informed him that she was going to conceive a child.

Now as soon as the sultan heard that his wife was pregnant, he rejoiced with all his heart, and when the day of the delivery approached, he called together all the astrologers and sages who drew charts of the stars.

"Before my child is born this month," he said to them, "I want you to tell me whether it will be male or female, what will happen to the child in the course of time, and what the child will accomplish."

Thereupon the astrologers drew their charts and the sages traced the lines. Together they prepared the horoscope of the unborn babe. Then the astrologers said to the sovereign, "Oh mighty king, the queen will soon give birth to a boy, and it will be best if you name him Zayn al-Asnam—Zayn of the images."

Afterward the sages spoke up and said, "Oh king, this little one will prove himself to be valiant and intelligent when he becomes a man. But during the course of time he will experience various trials and tribulations, and only if he bravely struggles to overcome certain obstacles will he become one of the richest kings of the world."

"If the child demonstrates his valor, as you have stated," said the king, "then the toil and suffering that will be his lot will mean nothing. Indeed, calamities only serve to strengthen the mettle of the sons of kings."

Shortly after this, the queen gave birth to a son, and may glory be to the Lord who endowed the babe with such peerless beauty and loveliness! The king named his son Zayn al-Asnam, and in time he became a handsome young man. When he reached his fifteenth year, the sultan appointed a tutor, versed in science and philosophy, who was to instruct him until he became familiar with every branch of knowledge by the time he reached adulthood.

Then the sultan summoned his son and heir to him and addressed him in the presence of all the lords of his lands.

"Oh, my son, Zayn al-Asnam," he said, "I feel that the time has come and I shall soon be swept away by a sickness that will happily end my days in this world. Thus, it is time for you to take my place, and I command you to observe my advice and fulfill my legacy. Beware, my son, and never do harm to any person, and be sure not to give the poor any reason to complain. But do justice to the oppressed according to the power vested in you. Furthermore, be wary when the great lords speak to you, and pay attention to the words of the people. Indeed, your lords will surely betray you because they seek only what suits their needs, not what suits the needs of your subjects."

A few days later, the old sultan's sickness became worse, and he fulfilled his term on earth. Upon his death his son, Zayn al-Asnam, arose and wore the mourning dress for his father during the next six days. On the seventh he went forth to the divan and took the seat upon his father's throne. He also held a meeting attended by all the defenders of the realm, and the ministers and the lords came forward and consoled him for the loss of his father. They wished him good fortune and rejoiced in his kingship. Finally, they wished him long-lasting honor and permanent prosperity.

But Zayn al-Asnam was young in years and lacked experience. So when he realized how much honor he had and how wealthy he was, he immediately began to spend his money lavishly and to associate with other young men like him. Indeed, he wasted immense sums on his own pleasure, neglected the government of his country, and paid scant attention to the welfare of his subjects. Consequently, the queen mother intervened with her counsel and forbade him to lead such a way-ward life. She advised him to abandon his perverse urges and dedicate himself to ruling the country and setting good policies for his kingdom. Otherwise, the liege lords would reject him and would certainly rise up against him and depose him. But he would not listen to a single word and persisted in his folly. In the meantime the folk muttered and complained because the lords of the land had begun to oppress and tyrannize the people when they saw the king was neglecting his subjects. Soon the common people rose up against Zayn al-Asnam and would have dealt harshly with him if his mother had not been wise and resourceful and had not been held in high esteem by the people. So she satisfied the malcontents and promised that they would be treated in a fair and just way. Then she summoned her son, Zayn al-Asnam, to her and said, "Behold, my son, everything that I told you has come true. You have ruined your realm and your own life to boot by ignoring my words. You have placed the governance of the kingdom in the hands of inexperienced youth, have neglected the elders, and have dissipated all your own money and the treasures of the monarchy just because you wanted to indulge yourself in wanton and carnal pleasure."

Shocked by his mother's words, Zayn al-Asnam awoke from the slumber of negligence and accepted his mother's advice. He went straight to the divan and placed the governance of the monarchy in the hands of some old officers—men of intelligence and experience. Unfortunately he did all this only after Bassorah had been ruined by his foolish and decadent ways. He had wasted away all the wealth of the sultanate and had become utterly impoverished. Consequently, the prince repented all that he had done, and he was so sorrowful that he could not sleep and shunned meat and drink. Finally, one night, when he had been steeped in grief and vain regret, his eyelids closed a little as dawn drew near. All at once an old and venerable sheikh appeared to him in a vision and said, "Oh Zayn al-Asnam, do not grieve, for after grief, no matter how bitter it may be, there will be nothing but joy. So if you want to be rid of your woes, you must travel to Egypt, where you will find hoards of wealth that will replace whatever you have wasted away and more than double your former treasures."

Now, when the prince was aroused from his sleep, he recounted to his mother all that he had seen in his dream, but she began to laugh at him.

"Do not mock me, Mother," he replied. "I have no choice but to travel to Egypt."

"Do not believe in such visions," she said. "They may be merely confused dreams and fantasies that will mislead you."

"But," he retorted, "I believe that my vision is true, and the man whom I saw in them is one of the saints of Allah, and his words are true."

On the following night, he mounted his horse alone, and he secretly abandoned his kingdom and set off for Egypt. He rode day and night until he reached Cairo. When he entered the city, he was impressed by what he saw. Upon tethering his steed, he found shelter in one of the cathedral mosques, for he had become exhausted from his long journey. However, when he had rested a little, he went out and bought himself some food. After he had eaten his meal, his excessive fatigue caused him to fall asleep in the mosque. He had not slept long before the sheikh appeared to him a second time in a vision and said, "Oh Zayn al-Asnam, you have obeyed my instructions, and I have tested you to see whether you are valiant or cowardly. Now I know your mettle insofar as you accepted my words and have taken my advice. So I want you to return immediately to your capital, and

I shall make you a wealthy ruler. Indeed, there will be no king comparable to you in your time and in the time to come."

At this point Zayn al-Asnam awoke and cried out, "In the name of Allah the Compassionate, who is this sheikh who compelled me to travel to Cairo? Why did I have faith in him and think that he was either the apostle or one of the righteous saints of God? Thank the Lord that I was smart enough not to relate my dream to anyone except my mother or to tell anyone that I was departing for Cairo. I had full faith in this old man, but now it seems to me that the man is not one of those who know the truth. So, by Allah, I shall no longer trust this sheikh and his acts."

Upon making this decision, the prince spent the night in the mosque, and on the next day he mounted his horse and returned to Bassorah after a few days of a strenuous journey. It was night when he entered the city, and he went straight to his mother, who asked him, "Have you discovered what the sheikh promised you?"

He responded by telling her about his adventure, and in turn, she began consoling and comforting him.

"Grieve not, my son," she said. "If Almighty Allah has determined that you are to receive something, you will obtain it without any trouble. What's past is past, and what is written is written and shall come to pass. But I hope that you will become wiser and more sensible and abandon those ways that have landed you in poverty. You must stop listening to the seductive songs of tempting women and stop associating with loose-living people. All of these wanton pleasures are for the sons of the ne'er-do-well, not for the scions of kings, your peers."

Upon hearing this, Zayn al-Asnam swore that he would bear in mind all that she had said to him, and never go against her commandments nor deviate from them in the least. He promised to abandon his old ways and to concentrate on governing his kingdom. Then he went to sleep, and as he slumbered, the sheikh appeared to him a third time in a vision and said, "Oh Zayn al-Asnam, you valorous prince, I shall fulfill my agreement with you this very day, as soon as you awake from your slumber. You will take a pickax and go to the grave of your sire. Once you are there, you are to dig up the ground in a certain spot, where you will find something that will enrich you."

As soon as the prince awoke, he rushed to his mother with great joy and told her his tale. But she broke out laughing at him again and said, "Oh, my son, this old man is mocking you, and nothing else. So keep away from him."

But Zayn al-Asnam replied, "Mother, I believe this sheikh is telling the truth. He's not a liar. The first time he tested me. Now he wants to fulfill his promise."

"At any rate, the work will not hurt you," the mother said. "So do whatever you want. Do his bidding and let him test you, and God willing, you will return to me with a joyful heart. But I fear that you will suffer and come back to me saying, 'Your words were true, Mother!'"

However, Zayn al-Asnam took a pickax and descended to that part of the palace where his father lay entombed. He began to dig and explore, and he had not worked long before—lo and behold!—he noticed a ring embedded in a marble slab. He removed the stone and saw a flight of stairs like a ladder. Down the stairs he went until he found a huge subterranean cave supported by pillars of marble and alabaster. When he entered the inner recesses, he saw a pavilion that dazzled his mind, and in the pavilion stood eight large clay jars made of green jasper. Then he said to himself, "I wonder what these jars are and what may be inside them."

So he went over to them, and after he took off their lids, he found antique golden coins in each one of them. So he took a few in his hand, rushed to his mother, and gave them to her.

"What do you say to this, Mother?" he asked.

She was astonished and replied, "Beware, my son, that you do not waste this treasure as you dissipated your wealth before this."

Thereupon he swore an oath and said, "Don't worry,

Mother. You can rest assured that I want you to be satisfied with my actions."

Then she arose and went forth with him, and the two descended into the subterranean cave and entered the pavilion, where the queen was astonished by what she saw. Indeed, she made certain with her own eyes that the jars were full of gold, and while they were enjoying the spectacle of the treasure, they caught sight of a small jar that was marvelously wrought in green jasper. So Zayn al-Asnam opened it and found a golden key inside.

"My son," said the queen, "this key must be able to unlock some door."

Accordingly they searched all about the cave and the pavilion to see if there were a door or something like one, and after a while they came upon a wooden lock and realized that the key would fit it. Therefore the prince stuck the key into the lock, and the door opened into a palace. When the two entered, they found it more spacious than the first pavilion, and it was illuminated by a light that dazzled their eyes. Since there were no wax candles or places for lamps, they believed that it was a miracle of some kind. Then they discovered eight images like statues made of precious stones, all seated upon golden thrones. Each and every one was cut from the same solid piece, and all the stones were pure and precious. Zayn al-Asnam was puzzled by this and said to his mother, "Where could my father have obtained all these rare things?"

The two of them took pleasure in gazing at the images and inspecting them, and both wondered why the ninth throne was unoccupied. All of a sudden the queen caught sight of a silken tapestry with an inscription that read: "My son, do not be astounded by this great wealth that I acquired through pain and suffering. Know that there is also a ninth statue whose value is twentyfold greater than those that you have seen. If you want to obtain it, you must return to Cairo. There you will find a former slave of mine named Mubárak, and he will take you and guide you to the statue. You need not worry about how you will find him when you enter Cairo. The first person you will encounter will point out the house to you, for Mubárak is well known there."

When Zayn al-Asnam had read this inscription, he cried out, "Mother, I want to return to Cairo and search for this image. What do you say now about my vision? Is it real or false? Do you think that this is a confused dream? At any rate, Mother, there is nothing that can stop me. I must travel to Cairo."

"Oh my son," she replied, "seeing that you are under the protection of the Apostle of Allah, I bid you farewell. Your vizier and I shall maintain order in your kingdom until you return."

Accordingly the prince went forth, mounted his horse, and rode until he reached Cairo, where he asked for Mubárak's house. Some people told him, "My lord, this is the wealthiest man here, and there is no one who does greater deeds. His home is always open to strangers."

Then they showed him the way, and he followed them until he came to Mubárak's mansion, where he knocked at the door, and a slave opened it and asked, "Who are you, and what do you want?"

"I am a foreigner from a distant country, and I have heard that Mubárak, your lord, is famous for his kindness and generosity. So I have come here with the purpose of becoming his guest."

Thereupon the slave went to this lord, and after reporting the matter to him, he came out and said to Zayn al-Asnam, "My lord, your presence is a blessing for this house. Please enter. My master Mubárak awaits you."

The prince went into a very spacious court lined with beautiful trees and fountains, and the slave led him to the pavilion where Mubárak was seated. As the guest entered, the host rose up immediately and met him with a cordial greeting: "Your arrival makes this an auspicious occasion, and this night is the most blessed of nights because you have come! Who are you, young man? Where do you come from, and what do you seek?"

"I am Zayn al-Asnam," he replied, "and I seek a man named Mubárak, former slave of the sultan of Bassorah, who died a year ago, for I am his son."

"What did you say?" responded Mubárak. "You are the son of the king of Bassorah?"

"Yes, truly I am his son," the prince stated.

"To be honest," Mubárak said, "my late lord the king of Bassorah left no son known to me. But how old are you, young man?"

"About twenty," the prince replied and then added, "But how long has it been since you left my sire?"

"I left him eighteen years ago," said Mubárak. "But can you give me some sort of sign to assure me that you are the son of my old master, the king of Bassorah?"

"You are the only person," the prince remarked, "who knew that my father laid out a subterranean cave beneath his palace, where he placed forty jars of the finest green jasper filled with coins of antique gold. You also know that he built a second palace within a pavilion and placed these eight images of precious stones, each one made of a single gem and all seated upon royal seats of plated gold. Finally, he wrote a message on a silken tapestry which I read and which told me to come here, for it said you would inform me where I might find the ninth statue that is supposed to be worth all the eight together."

Now, when Mubárak heard these words, he fell at the feet of Zayn al-Asnam and kissed them. "Pardon me, my lord!" he exclaimed. "In truth you are the son of my old master, and since I have prepared a feast for all the nobles of Cairo, I would like your highness to honor it by your presence."

Thereupon Mubárak arose and guided Zayn al-Asnam into the salon that was filled with the lords of the land who had gathered there. After giving Zayn al-Asnam the place of honor, he seated himself. Then he ordered the servants to begin the feast and bring out the food. Moreover, he waited upon the prince himself with arms crossed behind his back and at times falling upon his knees. The nobles of Cairo were greatly astounded to see Mubárak, one of the great men of the city, serving this young man, for they had no idea who the stranger was. But they ate and drank well and were entertained until at last Mubárak turned toward them and said, "My friends, do not be astonished to see me wait upon this young man with dedication and honor, for he is the son of my old lord, the sultan of Bassorah, who bought me with his money and who died without legally severing my ties to him. I am, therefore, obliged to serve his son, my young lord. All my possessions and supplies belong to him, and all that I have is his."

When the nobles of Cairo heard these words, they stood up before Zayn al-Asnam and bowed to him with great respect, treated him with high regard, and blessed him.

"My lords," said the prince, "I am in the presence of noble men, and you are my witnesses. So I say to you, oh Mubárak, that you are now free, and all the goods, gold, and supplies that once belonged to your sire and are my entitlement are henceforth yours for the keeping, each and every article. Also, you may ask whatsoever you want of me, and I shall grant all your requests."

Upon hearing this, Mubárak arose and kissed the hand of Zayn al-Asnam and thanked him for his favors. "Oh, my lord," he replied, "my only wish is for your welfare, but the wealth that I own exceeds my own needs."

Then the prince resided with Mubárak, the free man, for four days. During this time all the nobles of Cairo came to visit and offered their respects as soon as they heard men say, "This is the master of Mubárak and the king of Bassorah."

Finally, on the fourth day, Zayn al-Asnam said to his host, "I have been staying with you too long."

"You know," responded Mubárak, "that your quest and the matter at hand are extraordinary, but I am not sure you know that it also involves the risk of death. Nor do I know whether you have the valor to accomplish a certain task."

"Know, oh Mubárak, that opulence is obtained only by blood. Whatever happens to a man is predetermined by the Creator, may He be praised. So, concern yourself with your own courage, and do not worry about me."

Thereupon Mubárak commanded his slaves to get everything ready for a journey, and they obeyed him right away and prepared their horses for travel. Then they rode night and day through the wildest regions, and every day they saw marvelous things that dazzled their minds. Finally, they arrived at a certain place, where the party dismounted. Mubárak commanded the slaves and eunuchs to stay at that spot and said to them, "Keep watch and guard the beasts of burden and horses until we return."

After this the two set out by foot, and Mubárak said to the prince, "Oh my lord, here is where you will need all your valor, for we are in the land of the image that you have been seeking."

They continued walking until they came to a lake that was long and wide, and Mubárak said to his companion, "Let me tell you, my lord, that a little boat bearing a blue banner will come to us before long, and all its planks are made of chander wood and lign aloes of Comorin, the most precious of woods. Now I must command you to do as I say."

"What is this command?" Zayn al-Asnam asked.

Mubárak answered, "You will see a rower in the boat, and his features are not at all like those of a human being. But beware, for if you utter one word about this, he will drown us. You should also know that this place belongs to the king of the jinn, and everything that you see is the work of the jinn."

When the boat arrived, Zayn al-Asnam saw that the ferryman had the head of an elephant while the rest of his body resembled that of a lion. As the creature approached them, he wound his trunk around them and lifted them both into the boat and seated them beside him. Then he began rowing until he passed the middle of the lake, and he continued rowing until he landed at the bank on the other side of the lake. Here Zayn al-Asnam and Mubárak stepped ashore and walked straight ahead, gazing at the trees of ambergris and lign aloes, sandal, cloves, and jasmine. There were flowers and fruits everywhere that filled them with joy and excited their spirits. The birds warbled with various voices. Their songs were ravishing, and their melodies captivated their hearts. So Mubárak turned to the prince and asked him, "What do you think about this place, my lord?"

"I think, oh Mubárak," he replied, "that this is truly the paradise promised to us by the Prophet."

Then they continued walking until they came upon a magnificent palace built of emeralds and rubies with gates and doors made of refined gold. There was a bridge out front, one hundred and fifty cubits long and fifty wide, and the whole thing was constructed from the single rib of a fish. At the far end stood numerous hosts of the jinn, all with frightful and awesome features. Each one held a steel javelin in his hand that sparkled like the sun. Upon seeing them, the prince said to his companion, "This spectacle is overwhelming my senses!"

"We had better stand still and not move one inch further," Mubárak advised. "Otherwise, something might happen to us, and may Allah grant us safety!"

As he said this, he took out four strips of a yellow silken stuff from his pocket, and after forming a circle with one, he draped another over his shoulder. Then he gave the two remaining pieces to the prince so that he would do the same. Next he spread a vast shawl of white silk on the ground and pulled out of his pocket various precious stones, scents, ambergris, and sandalwood. Finally, each sat down on his sash, and when both were ready, Mubárak repeated the following words to the prince and taught him how he was to pronounce them in front of the king of the jinn: "Oh my Lord, sovereign of the spirits, we stand here within your realm, and we seek to be under your protection." Whereupon Zayn al-Asnam added, "And I sincerely implore you to accept us." But Mubárak exclaimed, "Oh, my Lord Allah, I am terribly afraid. Pay attention to my words, prince. Before he decides to accept us without harming us, he will approach us in the semblance of a man who is extraordinarily handsome. But he may also assume the form of a frightful and terrifying creature. Now, if you see him in a more favorable human shape, you must not forget to rise right away and bow to him. Above all, beware that you do not step beyond the circle of this cloth."

The prince replied, "To hear is to obey."

Meanwhile Mubárak continued: "And let us bow to him before you say, 'Oh king of the spirits and sovereign of the jinn and lord of earth, my sire, the former sultan of Bassorah, whom the angel of death has carried off, was always under your protection, and I, like him, have come to you to request the same safeguard.' Then, if he greets us with a glad face of welcome, he will undoubtedly say, 'Ask whatever you want of me!' And the moment he gives you his word, you should submit your petition at once and say, 'Oh my lord, I should like your highness to give me the ninth statue, which is the most precious thing in the world, for you promised my father to keep it safe for me.' "

And after this Mubárak continued to instruct his master how to address the king, how to make the request, and how to use pleasant speech. Then he began to conjure, fumigate, adjure, and recite words that were incomprehensible. Shortly thereafter, cold rain poured down on them. Lightning flashed. Thunder roared. Darkness veiled the earth's face. A mighty wind gushed by, and a voice like an earthquake, the quake of earth on Judgment Day, could be heard. When the prince saw all these horrors, things that he had never seen before in his life, every bone in his body trembled with fear, but Mubárak burst into laughter and said, "Fear not, my lord. That which you are dreading is exactly what we've been seeking. To us it is a sign of glad tidings and success. So you can be content and feel safe."

After this the skies grew clear and serene, while crisp winds and the purest scents breathed upon them. Before long the king of the jinn presented himself in the shape of a handsome man who was incomparable in his looks except for the Almighty, who has no likeness in all His honor and glory. The king gazed at Zayn al-Asnam with a pleasant aspect and a smile, whereas the prince immediately stood up and recited the string of benedictions taught to him by his companion. In turn, the king said to him with a pleasant demeanor, "Oh Zayn al-Asnam, it is true that I used to love your sire, the sultan of Bassorah, and whenever he visited me I was accustomed to giving him an image of those you saw, each cut from a single gem. Soon you, too, will become as honored by me as your father was, and even more so. Before he died, I commanded him to write those words you read on the silken tapestry. I also promised him and agreed to take you under my protection as a parent and to bestow a gift of an image on you. In this case it is the ninth, which is worth much more than all the eight that you have seen thus far. So now it is my desire to keep my word and to take you under my protection. The sheikh that you saw in your dreams was none other than I myself, and it was I who told you to dig under your palace down to the subterranean cave where you found the jars of gold and the statues of fine gems. Moreover, I know full well where you have come from, and it is I who have caused you to come here, and I shall give you what you are seeking. But there is one condition: you must bring back to me a maiden, fifteen years of age, who is unrivaled in beauty and loveliness. Furthermore, she must be a pure virgin and a clean maiden who has never lusted for a man or ever been solicited by any man. Lastly, you must be faithful to me and keep the girl safe when you return with her here. Beware that you don't betray me while you are bringing her back to me."

In response, the prince swore a firm oath and added, "Oh my lord, you have indeed honored me by requesting such a service from me, but to be honest, it will be most difficult for me to find such a fair maiden as you have described. Even if I do find one as perfect and beautiful as you have required, how shall I know whether she has ever longed for another man, or that another man ever lusted for her?"

"Right you are, oh Zayn al-Asnam," the king replied. "This kind of knowledge is impossible for the sons of men to attain. However, I shall give you a mirror of my own that has a special virtue. Whenever you catch sight of a young lady whose beauty and loveliness please you, you are to open the glass, and if you see that her image is clear and distinct in it, you will know right away that she is a clean maid without any defect and endowed with praiseworthy qualities. On the other hand, if you see a darkened figure or one dressed in dirty garments, you will know right away that the maiden is sullied by the soil of sex. Should you find that she is pure and talented, you are to bring her to me. But beware that you do not offend her and commit sinful acts. If you are not faithful to me and do not keep your promise, you will lose your life."

After these words were spoken, the prince made a solemn and solid pact with the king, a covenant that the sons of sultans may never violate. Then the king gave Zayn al-Asnam his mirror and ordered him to depart right away. So the prince and Mubárak arose and made the return journey to the lake, where they had to wait only a short time before the boat that had brought them appeared. Once again, the ferryman was the jinnee with the elephant's head and the lion's body, and he was standing up and ready to row. After crossing the lake, the prince and his companion set out for Cairo, and upon reaching their quarters, they rested from the long and exhausting trip. Once they had recuperated, Zayn al-Asnam went to Mubárak and said, "Come with me to Baghdad so we can look for the maiden that the king described."

But Mubárak replied, "My lord, we are in Cairo, a city of the cities, a wonder of the world, and there is no doubt in my mind that we shall be able to find the right maiden here. So there is no need to travel to a distant country."

"You are right, Mubárak," Zayn al-Asnam said. "But how are we going to find such a girl, and who is going to help us find her?"

"Don't be troubled by such difficulties, my lord," his companion said to calm him. "There is an old woman in my palace who arranges marriages and is unrivaled in her profession. There is no obstacle that she can't overcome."

Upon saying this, he sent for the old lady and informed her that he wanted a maiden who was to be the perfection of beauty and not more than fifteen. This girl was to marry the son of his lord, he told her, and he promised her sumptuous rewards and riches if she would do her very best.

"Oh my lord," she responded, "rest assured that I shall not only satisfy your requirements, but I shall exceed them. I have young damsels under my control who are unsurpassable in beauty and loveliness, and they are all the daughters of honorable men."

But the old woman did not know that Zayn al-Asnam had the mirror. So she went forth to wander about the city and conduct her business in the wily ways she knew. Whenever she found a remarkable beauty, she brought her to Mubárak, but when he looked at her reflection in the mirror it showed an exceedingly dark and dim figure. So he would dismiss the girl. This lasted until the crone had brought him all the damsels in Cairo, and not one was found whose reflection was clearly reflected in the mirror and whose honor was pure and clean just as the king of the jinn had demanded. Since Mubárak realized that he would not find one maiden in Cairo to please him or one who proved pure and clean as the king of the jinn had ordered, he decided to visit Baghdad with the prince. So they set out on their journey, and in due time they reached the city of peace, where they rented a mighty fine mansion in the center of the capital. Then they furnished the rooms with articles of such comfort and luxury that the lords of the land would come daily to dine at their table. What remained of the meat was distributed to the poor and the miserable. Also, every poor stranger lodging in the mosques would come to the house and find a meal. Therefore, Zayn al-Asnam and Mubárak became known for their generosity and charity throughout the city. Their reputation and fame grew so much that the people continually spoke about their wealth and honored names.

Now it so happened that there was an imam named Abu Bakr in one of the cathedral mosques. He was a ghastly man, very jealous and loathsome, who dwelled near the mansion in which the prince and Mubárak were living. When he learned about their lavish gifts, charity, and honorable reputations, he was smitten by envy, malice, and hatred. So he began to devise a scheme of how he might bring about their downfall so that they could not enjoy their good fortunes and reputations. Indeed, it is the custom of envy to fall only upon the fortunate. So one day, as Abu Bakr lingered in the mosque after the noon prayer had been concluded, he went forward among the people and cried out, "Hear me, my brothers of the true faith, I want you to know that there are two strangers living in our quarter who lavish and waste immense sums of money, in fact, extravagant sums. For my part I cannot help but suspect that they are thieves and crooks who commit robbery in their own country and come here to enjoy their spoils. Oh, believers of Mohammed, I advise you in Allah's name to guard yourselves against such cursed men. Fortunately, the caliph will soon hear about these two, and you will share in whatever punishment they receive. I have hastened to warn you, and having done this, I wash my hands of your business. After this, you do as you judge fit."

All those present replied unanimously, "We shall do whatever you wish us to do, oh Abu Bakr!"

When the imam heard this, he arose and took out pen, ink, and a sheet of paper and began writing a letter to the Commander of the Faithful, recounting all that he could to indict the two strangers. By chance, however, Mubárak happened to be among the crowd in the mosque when he heard the speech of the vile imam and saw how he meant to incriminate him and the prince with a letter to the caliph. So he rushed home right away and took a hundred dinars, packed them in a parcel of costly clothes, all made in silver, went back quickly to the imam's lodgings, and knocked at the door. The preacher came and opened it, but when he saw Mubárak, he asked him in anger, "What do you want, and who are you?"

"I am Mubárak and am at your service, oh my master Imam Abu Bakr. I have come to see you in behalf of my lord the emir Zayn al-Asnam. He has heard and learned about your knowledge in religious affairs and your fair reputation in this city. Therefore, he would like to make your acquaintance and should like to help you in any way he can. He has also asked me to give you these garments and this spending money. He hopes you will excuse him for such minor gifts that cannot do justice to your reputation. But after this, he will not fail to give you what you deserve."

As soon as Abu Bakr saw the gold coins and the clothes, he answered Mubárak by saying, "I beg your lord the emir's pardon that I have not paid my respects. Indeed, I repent for failing to do my duty, and I hope that you will be my deputy and ask him to pardon my fault. God willing, I shall go to him tomorrow and offer my services in the appropriate manner."

"My master's main purpose," Mubárak replied, "is to see your worship and be exalted by your presence and thereby to win your blessing."

After saying all this, Mubárak kissed the imam's hand and returned to his own place. On the next day, as Abu Bakr was leading Friday's dawn prayer, he took his place among the folk in the middle of the mosque and exclaimed, "Oh, my Moslem brothers, great and small, folk of Mohammed one and all, I want you to know that envy only falls upon the wealthy and praiseworthy and not upon the mean and miserable. With regard to the two strangers about whom I spoke yesterday, I have discovered that I was wrong. One of them is an emir high in honor and son of most reputable parents and not a thief and crook as I was informed by the person who envied him. I have found out that the report about this stranger was a lie. So beware if any of you speak evil about the emir. Otherwise you will get yourself and me into trouble with the Prince of True Believers. A man of such exalted reputation cannot possibly set up residence in our city without the caliph's knowledge."

When he had ended the congregational prayers and returned to his home, the imam put on his long gaberdine robe and went straight to the mansion of the prince. When he went in to see the stranger, he stood up before him and did him the highest honors. Now Zayn al-Asnam was by nature conscious of what was to be done, even though he was young in years. So he returned the imam Abu Bakr's civilities with great courtesy. He had him seated next to him upon the high raised divan and ordered ambergris coffee for him. Then the tables were prepared for breakfast, and the two ate and drank to their content. Afterward they began chatting like boon companions. Soon the imam asked the prince, "Oh my lord Zayn al-Asnam, do you intend to stay long in our city of Baghdad?"

"Yes, indeed," the prince replied. "I intend to stay here until my task is completed."

The imam inquired further: "And what task may this be? I hope that I might devote my life to help you fulfill it when I hear what you must do."

"My goal is to marry a maiden who must be extraordinarily beautiful, fifteen years of age, pure, chaste, and virginal. She must be unsoiled and must never have lusted after a man. Finally, she must be completely unique in her beauty and loveliness."

"Oh my lord," replied the imam, "it will be extremely difficult to find a maiden like this. But I happen to know a damsel of that age who meets your demands. Her father, a vizier, who resigned his position of his own free will, is now living in his own mansion and jealously guards his daughter and oversees her education. I'm of the opinion that this maiden will suit your fancy, while she will rejoice in an emir like yourself. Even her parents will be pleased."

"By Allah," responded the prince. "I believe this damsel will suit me and fulfill my needs. I shall leave the matter in your hands. But, my lord imam, I wish first of all to look at her and see if she be pure. With regard to her unique beauty, your word suffices, and your guarantee is truth for me. However, even you cannot be certain about her purity."

"But how will it be possible for you, my lord," said the imam, "to learn anything from her face about her honor and whether she is pure? Indeed, if you can discover this, you must be an expert in physiognomy. However, if your highness is willing to accompany me, I shall take you to the mansion of her sire. Once you make his acquaintance, he will allow you to see her."

So Imam Abu Bakr took the prince to the mansion of the vizier, and when they entered, both bowed to the master of the house, whereupon he arose and received them with greetings, especially when he learned that an emir was visiting him and was inclined to wed his daughter. So he summoned her to his presence, and once she was there, he asked her to raise her veil. When she did his bidding, the prince gazed upon her and was amazed and startled by her beauty and loveliness. Indeed, he had never seen a young woman as bright and brilliant as she was. So he said to himself, "If only heaven would enable me to win a damsel like this! Unfortunately, I am not permitted to have this one." As he was contemplating such thoughts, he drew the mirror from his pocket and looked at her reflection carefully. Lo and behold, the crystal was bright and clean as virgin silver. When he glanced at her reflection in the glass, he saw that it was as pure as the white of a dove. So he immediately sent for the kazi and witnesses, and they tied the knot and signed the appropriate papers, and the bride was duly crowned.

Soon thereafter the prince led the vizier, his father-in-law, to his own mansion. At the same time he sent a present of costly jewels to the young lady. The marriage celebration itself was a notable event. None like it had ever been seen before. Zayn al-Asnam made sure that numerous noble people were invited, and he honored Abu Bakr the imam by giving him plenty of gifts. In addition, he sent the bride's father an abundance of rare and precious articles. As soon as the celebration ended, Mubárak said to the prince, "Oh my lord, let us rise and begin our journey before we relax too much. Indeed, we have found what we sought."

"You are right," responded the prince, and he arose with his companion. The two began preparing for the journey, and once they had arranged for a covered litter to be carried by camels for the bride, they set out. Meanwhile, Mubárak knew quite well that the prince was deeply in love with the young lady. So he took him aside and said to him, "Oh my lord Zayn al-Asnam, I want to warn you and plead with you to keep watch and control over your desires and feelings and to observe the pledge that you made to the king of the jinn."

"Oh, Mubárak," replied the prince, "if you knew the love, the longing, and the ecstasy that I feel for this young lady, you would feel pity for me! Indeed, I can think of nothing else but taking her to Bassorah and sleeping with her."

"Oh my lord," Mubárak said, "remain true and keep your pact! Otherwise you will suffer great harm, and you will not only lose your life but the life of the young lady as well. Remember the oath that you swore. Don't let your lust get in the way of your reason and deprive you of all that you have achieved and your honor and life."

"Oh, Mubárak," exclaimed the prince. "You must help me and be her guardian! Do not allow me to look at her again."

And so it happened. Mubárak prevented the prince from looking at his bride again. They traveled along the road toward the island of the jinn. But when the young lady became bored during the journey and was concerned that she had not seen her bridegroom since the wedding celebration, she turned to Mubárak and said, "May Allah be with you. Please tell me, oh Mubárak, have we traveled such a long distance by order of my bridegroom Prince Zayn al-Asnam?"

"Oh my lady," he responded, "your situation is a difficult one, but I must disclose the secret to you. You think that Zayn al-Asnam, the king of Bassorah, is your bridegroom. But, alas! This is not true. He is not your husband. The deed that he drafted in front of your parents and your people was a mere pretext. You are now going to be the bride of the king of the jinn, who demanded you from the prince."

When the young lady heard these words, she burst into tears, and Zayn al-Asnam wept bitter tears for her because of his great love and affection for her. Then the young lady spoke earnestly: "You have no pity in you, nor feeling for me. Don't you fear Allah's wrath? What will he do when he sees how you have cast a maiden into such a calamitous situation? What answer shall you give the Lord on the Day of Reckoning for the treacherous way you have dealt with me?"

However, her words and weeping were in vain, for

they continued traveling with her until they reached the king of the jinn. As soon as they were settled, they brought her to him right away. When he had examined the damsel, he was very pleased and turned to Zayn al-Asnam and said. "Truly, the bride that you have brought me is exceedingly beautiful and lovely. Yet lovelier and more beautiful to me are your loyalty and the mastery of your own passions as well as your marvelous purity and valorous heart. So I want you to return home, and you will find the ninth statue that you requested next to the other images, for I shall send it with one of my slaves of the jinn."

Thereupon Zayn al-Asnam kissed his hand and returned with Mubárak to Cairo. But he did not stay long with his companion because he was anxious to see the ninth statue. So after a brief rest, he hastened home. All the time, however, he could not stop thinking about his bride and how lovely and beautiful she was. He was filled with such great sorrow that he would often groan and cry out, "Lost is all the joy in life which you were! How could I have taken you away from your parents and carried you to the king of the jinn, you who are so unique in all ways? Alas! How I regret that day!"

When he finally reached Bassorah, he entered his palace, and after greeting his mother, he informed her of what had happened.

"Arise, my son," she replied. "Let us go and regard the ninth statue, for I am most happy that we now have it in our possession."

So they both descended into the pavilion where the eight images of precious gems were standing, and here they discovered a great miracle. Instead of seeing the ninth statue upon the golden throne, they found the young lady, who glittered like the sun. Zayn al-Asnam recognized her at first glance, and she spoke to him right away: "Do not be surprised to find me in place of the statue you had been seeking. Nor do I think that you will regret it or repent when you accept me instead of what you requested."

"No, by Allah, oh lifeblood of my heart," he said, "you are truly the goal of all my wishes, and I would not exchange you for all the gems of the universe. If only you knew how terribly sad I was because of our separation and because of the way I deceived your parents and took you to the king of the jinn as a present. Indeed, I had almost decided to forfeit the treasure of the ninth statue and to take you away to Bassorah as my own bride when my comrade and councillor dissuaded me from doing so because I might have brought about your death and mine."

No sooner did Zayn al-Asnam end his words than they heard the roar of thundering that might split a mountain in two and shake the earth, and it caused the queen to be seized by fright and terror. But all at once the king of the jinn appeared, and he said to her, "Oh my lady, fear not. It is I, the protector of your son. I have a strong affection for him thanks to the devotion that his sire showed me. It was also I who appeared to him in his sleep, and my purpose was to test his valor and to learn whether he could keep a promise and control his passions and whether he would be tempted by the beauty of this lady to betray me. Indeed, Zayn al-Asnam has not been entirely faithful and has not kept his promise exactly as we agreed with regard to the young lady insofar as he longed for her to become his wife. However, I am sure that this lapse occurred because of man's natural weakness. To be sure, I had to command him repeatedly to defend and protect her until he concealed his face from her. I am now convinced of this man's valor and bestow her upon him as his wife, for she is the ninth statue that I promised him, and she is fairer than all these jeweled images, and there is no damsel in the entire world who can match her beauty and loveliness."

Then the king of the jinn turned to the prince and said to him, "Oh Emir Zayn al-Asnam, this is your bride. You may take her and enjoy her with the condition that you love only her and you do not choose another woman in addition to her. And I shall pledge myself that she will be most faithful to you."

Thereupon the king of the jinn disappeared, and the prince, who was overcome with joy went forth with the maiden. That same night, out of his love and affection for her, he paid her the first ceremonial visit. The following day he ordered feasts and banquets to be held throughout his realm, and in due time he formally wedded her and went in to her. Then he established himself on the throne and ruled the kingdom, granting favors and keeping the law, and his wife became the queen of Bassorah. His mother left this life a short while after, and they both lamented and mourned her departure. Finally he lived with his wife in complete joy until the Destroyer of Delights came to separate them from earth and took them away.

The Ten Viziers, or the Story of King Azadbakht and His Son

In olden days there was once a king of kings whose name was Azadbakht. His capital was called Kunnaym Madud, and his kingdom extended to the borders of Persia and from the borders of Hindostan to the Indian Ocean. He had ten viziers, who tended his kingship and dominion, and he was most just and wise.

One day he went forth with some of his guards on a hunt, and he encountered a eunuch riding a mare and holding the halter of a mule which he led along. On the mule's back was a covered litter made of brocade, lined with gold and girded with an embroidered band set with pearls and gems. Surrounding the litter was a company of knights. When King Azadbakht saw this, he left his guards and headed for the mule and the company of knights. As he approached them, he asked, "Whose litter is this, and what's inside?"

The eunuch, not knowing that he was speaking to King Azadbakht, replied, "This litter belongs to Isfahand, vizier to King Azadbakht, and his daughter is inside. She is intended to wed King Zád Sháh."

As the eunuch was speaking with the king, the maiden suddenly raised a corner of the curtain so that she could look upon the speaker and see the king. When Azadbakht beheld her and saw how lovely she was (and indeed, he had never seen any woman like her), he was ravished by her sight. His soul went out to her, and she captivated his heart. So he said to the eunuch, "Turn the mule's head and return, for I am King Azadbakht, and truly I shall marry her myself, since Isfahand, her sire, is my vizier, and he will accept what I do. It won't be hard for him."

"Oh king, may Allah grant you a long life, I beg that you have patience until I inform my lord, and then you shall wed her with his consent, for it is not proper, nor is it fitting, for you to seize her this way. It will be an affront to her father if you take her without his knowledge."

"I have no patience to wait until you go to her father and then return to me," Azadbakht said. "He will not be shamed in any way if I marry her."

"Oh, my lord," replied the eunuch, "nothing that is done in haste will endure long, nor does the heart rejoice in things like that. Indeed, it behooves you not to take her in this unseemly way. Whatever happens, don't destroy yourself with haste, for I know that her sire will be upset by this affair. Your actions will not bring about what you wish."

But the king said, "Verily, Isfahand is my mameluke and a slave of my slaves, and I do not care whether her father be pleased or displeased."

Upon saying this, he drew the reins of the mule and took the maiden, whose name was Bahrjaur, to his house, where he married her. Meanwhile the eunuch and the knights went to her father and said to him, "Oh my lord, you have served the king loyally for many years and have never failed him. Now he has taken your daughter without your consent and permission." And he related what had happened and how the king had seized Bahrjaur by force.

When Isfahand heard the eunuch's words, he became furious, and after assembling many troops, he said to them, "When the king was occupied with his women, we took no heed of him, but now he interferes with our harem, and it is my advice that we find a place which can be our sanctuary."

Then he wrote a letter to King Azadbakht stating, "I am a mameluke of your mamelukes and a slave of your slaves, and my daughter at your service is a handmaid. May Almighty Allah prolong your days and bring you joy and happiness! Indeed, I always was armed to serve and preserve your dominion and to protect you from all your enemies. But now my zeal has become even greater

and I have become even more watchful because you have taken my daughter as your wife."

And he sent a courier to the king with the letter and a present. When the messenger delivered the letter and the present to Azadbakht, the king read the letter and rejoiced. Then he spent hours eating and drinking, but the chief vizier of his viziers came to him and said, "Oh king, you should know that Isfahand the vizier is your enemy, for he does not like what you have done with him, and this message that he has sent is a trick. So do not rejoice about it. Don't be misled by his sweet words and gentle speech."

The king listened to his vizier's words but soon made light of the matter and continued to enjoy himself with eating and drinking. Meanwhile, Isfahand wrote a letter and sent it to all the emirs and informed them how he had been treated by King Azadbakht, and how the king had forcefully taken his daughter to become his wife. "Indeed," he added in the letter, "he will do even worse things to you than he has done to me."

After all the chiefs had received the letter, they gathered together at Isfahand's domicile and asked him to tell them all about this affair. Accordingly, he related everything that had happened to his daughter, and they agreed wholeheartedly to murder the king. So they mounted their horses and departed with their troops to search for the king. Azadbakht knew nothing about their plans until the revolt reached the capital city.

"What shall we do?" he asked his wife Bahrjaur.

"You know best, and I am at your command," she replied.

So he ordered his servants to fetch two swift horses, which he and his wife mounted. Then they took as much gold as they could carry and flew through the night to the desert of Karman. Meanwhile, Isfahand entered the city and made himself king.

During their flight, King Azadbakht and his wife had to slow down when they reached the foot of the mountains because she was pregnant and about to give birth. So they stopped by a spring, and she gave birth to a boy as handsome as the moon. Bahrjaur took off a coat of gold-woven brocade and wrapped the child in it, and they spent the night at that place, where she breast-fed him until morning. Then the king said to her, "We are hampered by this child and cannot stay here or carry him with us. So I think we had better leave him here and continue on our way, for Allah will look after him and send someone to take him and rear him."

So they wept bitter tears over him and left him next to the spring wrapped in the coat of brocade. Then they laid a thousand gold pieces in a bag at his head and fled on their horses. Now, it so happened that a group of highway robbers fell upon a caravan near that mountain and took all their goods and merchandise. Then they headed for the mountain so that they could share their loot. When they reached the foot of the mountain, they spotted the coat of brocade. So they went to see what it was, and they found the boy and the gold. Astonished, they said, "Praise be Allah! What misfortune brought this child here?"

Thereupon they divided the money between them, and the captain of the highwaymen took the boy as his son and fed him sweet milk and dates until he arrived at his house, where he appointed a nurse to rear him. Meanwhile, King Azadbakht and his wife continued their flight until they came to the court of the king of Fars, whose name was Kisra. When they presented themselves to him, he bestowed great honors on them and entertained them in regal fashion. When Azadbakht told him his tale from beginning to end, King Kisra promised to aid him with powerful troops and vast amounts of money. So Azadbakht rested for several days until he was ready to depart with his soldiers, and when he arrived at his own dominions, he waged war with Isfahand, and once he gained entrance to the capital, he defeated his former minister and slew him. Then he sat down upon his throne, and after he was rested and his kingdom was restored to peace, he sent messengers to the mountain in search of his son. But they returned and informed the king that they had not found him.

As time went on, the boy grew up and began waylaying travelers with the bandits because they used to take him with them when they went out to rob people. One day they attacked a caravan in the land of Sistan, but there were strong and valiant men in the caravan, which was carrying rich merchandise. Indeed, they had heard that there were many bandits in the land of Sistan. So they had prepared themselves with many weapons and had sent out spies who had returned and brought them news of the plunderers. So they were totally prepared for battle when the robbers drew near the caravan. The result was a fierce battle between the two, and at last the caravan people overcame the robbers by dint of numbers and slew some of them, while the others fled. They also took the son of King Azadbakht prisoner, and seeing that he was like the moon, handsome and lovely, graceful and bright, they asked him, "Who is your father, and how did you come to be with these bandits?"

"I am the son of the captain of the highwaymen," he responded.

So they seized him and took him to their destination, the capital of King Azadbakht. When they reached the city, the king heard of their arrival and commanded that they should show him their merchandise. Therefore they presented themselves before him and brought the boy with them. When the king saw the boy, he asked them, "Who is this boy?"

"Oh king," they answered, "on our way to your city, we were attacked by robbers, and this boy was among them. After we fought and beat them off, we took the boy prisoner. Then we questioned him and asked him, 'Who is your sire?' and he replied, 'I am the son of the captain of the robbers.'"

"I would like to have this boy," said the king.

"By Allah, you shall have the boy as a gift," responded the captain of the caravan, "and we shall remain your servants."

Then the king, who was not aware that the boy was his own son, dismissed the people of the caravan and commanded that the boy be brought into his palace and trained as a page. As the days rolled on, the king observed that the boy had good breeding, understanding, and ability. He was so pleased with him that he placed the boy in charge of his treasury and thus took the authority away from the viziers. In fact, he ordered that nothing could be taken from the treasury without the permission of the boy.

Some years went by like this, and the king saw that

the boy was honest and trustworthy. Now, until the boy
had arrived at the palace, the treasury had been in the
hands of the viziers, who could do with it whatever they
liked, and when the treasury was placed in the youth's
charge, the ministers could no longer exercise their will.
At the same time, the boy became dearer than a son to
the king, who could not bear being separated from him.
Gradually, the viziers became jealous of him and tried
through various means to oust him from the king's favor.
But it was to no avail.

Finally, however, the fateful hour arrived, for it happened one day that the boy drank some wine and became so drunk and dizzy that he meandered aimlessly
around the king's palace, until destiny led him to the
lodging of the women, in which there was a sleeping
chamber where the king lay with his wife. It was there
that the young man found a couch, upon which he threw
himself and stared with wonder at the paintings that
were in the chamber and lit by one wax candle. Soon
he fell asleep and remained sound asleep until the evening, when a handmaid came, as was her custom, and
brought all the desserts usually made for the king and
his wife. Upon seeing the young man lying on his back,
she thought that it was the king asleep on his couch, for
no one knew about his condition, and he in his drunken
stupor did not know where he was. So she set the vessels
and perfumes by the bedside, shut the door, and went
her way. Soon after this the king came from the wine
chamber and took his wife by her hand to go to the
chamber in which he slept. When he opened the door
and entered, he was surprised to find the young man
lying on the bed. Immediately he turned to his wife and
asked, "What is this young man doing here? He
wouldn't be here if it were not for you."

"I have no idea why he is here," she replied.

Suddenly the young man awoke, and upon noticing
the king, he jumped up and prostrated himself before
him, and Azadbakht said to him, "You vile thing! Un-
worthy traitor, what has driven you to my chamber?"

And Azadbakht ordered him to be imprisoned in one
place and the queen in another. When the next day ar-

rived, the king sat on his throne and summoned his grand vizier, the premier of his ministers, and asked him, "What do you think about the deed that this young robber has committed? He entered my harem and lay down on my couch, and I fear that something must be going on between him and my wife. What do you think of this affair?"

"May Allah preserve your highness," replied the vizier. "What did you ever see in this young man? Isn't he lowborn, the son of thieves? A thief must always revert to his vile ways, and whoever rears the serpent's brood shall get nothing from them but poison bites. As for your wife, she is not at fault, since he has always exhibited good breeding and modest bearing up to the present. If the king permits me, I shall go to her and question her so I may learn more about the affair and tell you everything."

The king gave him permission, and the vizier went to her and said, "I've come to you because of some grave shame, and I would like you to be truthful with me and tell me how the young man happened to be in the sleeping chamber."

"I know nothing about this whatsoever. Nothing at all," she said, and swore an oath to him so that he knew that the woman had no inkling about the affair, nor was she to blame.

"I shall show you a means to acquit yourself of this matter before the king so he will know that you are innocent," he stated.

"What is it?" she asked.

"When the king calls you and asks you about this affair," he answered, "you are to say to him, the young man saw you in the boudoir chamber and sent you a message saying that he would give you a hundred grams of the most priceless gem if you would allow him to enjoy you. However, you laughed at him and his proposal and rebuffed him. But he sent another message to you, saying that if you would not consent, he would come one night drunken, and enter and lie down in the sleeping chamber, and the king would see him and slay him. Then the king would put you to shame, and you would be dishonored. Now, I recommend that you go to the king right now and repeat to him what I have just told you."

"I shall say all this," stated the queen.

So the minister returned to the king and said to him, "Truly, this young man deserves to be punished severely after the way you have treated him so generously. Indeed, no kernel which is bitter from the beginning can ever grow sweet. As for the woman, I am certain that she is not to blame."

Thereupon he repeated to the king the story that he had taught the queen, and when Azadbakht heard it, he tore his garments and commanded that the young man be brought to him. So they fetched him and set him down before the king, who summoned the executioner. And all the people gazed at the young man to see what the king would do with him. Then Azadbakht said to him with great anger, "I bought you with my money and expected you to be loyal, especially when I chose you over all my grandees and pages and made you keeper of my treasury. Why, then, have you outraged my honor, betrayed me in my own house, and disrespected all that I have done for you?"

"Oh king," replied the young man with great reverence, "I did not do this out of choice and free will, and I had no business being there. Thanks to my bad luck I was driven to your chamber. Fate was contrary, and good fortune abandoned me. Indeed, I have endeavored with all my might not to commit a foul deed, and I have kept watch over myself in case I might lose control and show some faults. But no one can withstand misfortune, nor can one use money to ward off adverse destiny, as in the example of the merchant who was struck by bad luck. All his efforts were to no avail, and fate caused his downfall."

"What is the story of this merchant, and how was he doomed by bad luck?"

"May Allah grant the king long life," the young man answered, and he began

The Story of the Merchant Who Lost His Luck

There was once a merchant who prospered in trade, and at one time every dirham he earned won him an additional fifty. However, soon his luck turned against him, and he did not know it. He said to himself, "I have wealth galore, but I toil and travel from country to country. It would be better if I stay in my own land and rest from all this travail and trouble. I can remain in my own house and sell and buy at home." So he divided his money into two parts, and with one he bought wheat in the summer and said, "When winter comes, I shall sell it at a great profit." But when the cold set in, wheat fell to half the price for which he had purchased it. Deeply concerned about the situation, he decided to leave everything until the next year. However, the price fell even lower, and one of his close associates said to him, "You have no luck with wheat. So I suggest that you sell it for whatever price you can get."

"Ah, since I have always made profits, I can afford to lose this time. Allah is all-knowing! Even if the wheat must stay in my granary for ten years, I shall not sell it unless I make some money."

Then, in his anger, he walled up the granary door with clay, and a great rain came and fell on the terrace roofs of the house in which the wheat was stored, and the grain rotted. Consequently, the merchant had to pay porters five hundred dirhams to carry it away and dump it outside the city because the stench had become so bad. Then his friend said to him, "How often did I tell you that you would have no luck with wheat? But you would not listen to me, and now you had better go to the astrologer and ask him about your constellation."

Accordingly, the merchant went to the astrologer and asked him about his stars.

"Your rising line is adverse. Do not try your hand at business right now, for you will not prosper."

However, the merchant did not pay any heed to the astrologer's words and said to himself, "If I take care of my business, I'm not afraid of anything." So he took the other half of his money and built a ship, which he loaded with a cargo of whatever goods seemed profitable and everything that he owned. He planned to embark on a voyage in search of markets where he might gain a profit. The ship remained in port several days so that he could determine where he should go, and he said, "I'll ask some other traders what this merchandise might be worth and what countries might be interested in it and how much I can gain." They advised him to sail to a far country where his dirham could bring him a hundredfold gain. So he set sail for this particular land, but while he was on this voyage, a furious gale arose, and the ship foundered. The merchant saved himself on a plank, and the wind cast him, naked as he was, on the seashore where there was a town nearby. He praised Allah and thanked Him for saving his life. Then, upon seeing the village, he headed there and saw a very old man seated there, and he told this man what had happened to him. When he heard the tale, the sheikh was sorry for him and set food before him. The merchant ate it, and the old man said to him, "Stay here with me so I can make you the overseer and administrator of my farm, and I shall give you five dirhams a day."

"May Allah reward you and bring you great profit," replied the merchant.

So he remained in the old man's employ until he had sowed, reaped, threshed, and winnowed, and everything worked out well in his hands. The sheikh did not need to appoint either an agent or an inspector but relied utterly on him. Then the merchant thought to himself and said, "I doubt whether the owner of this grain will ever give me my due. So the best thing to do would be to take what I think I deserve as my wage. Later, if he gives me my rightful wage, I shall return whatever I have taken."

So he took the grain that he maintained was his due

and hid it in a secret place. Then he carried the rest and meted it out to the old man, who said to him, "Come take your wage that I promised you, and sell the grain. Then buy some clothes and whatever else you need with it. As long as you stay with me, I shall always give you this salary, and you shall always receive it this way."

The merchant said to himself, "I see now that I've committed a crime by taking the wheat without his permission." Then he went to fetch the grain that he had hidden, but he could not find it and returned perplexed and sorrowful to the sheikh, who asked him, "What's troubling you?"

"I thought you would not pay me my due," answered the merchant. "So I took a certain amount of grain that matched my wages. But when you paid me my due, I went to bring the grain that I had hidden back to you, but I found it gone. Someone must have stolen it."

The sheikh was angry when he heard these words and said to the merchant, "There is no way to counter bad luck! I had given you this position and these wages only because I was sorry for the way fate had treated you. But now you have committed this crime, oh oppressor of your own self! You thought that I would not give you your proper wages, and now, by Allah, I shall never give anything to you!"

Then he drove him away, and the merchant went forth. Woeful, grieving, teary-eyed, he wandered along the seashore until he came upon some men diving for pearls in the sea. When they saw him weeping and wailing, they asked him, "What's the matter? What has caused you to shed these tears?"

So he told them what had happened to him from the beginning to the end. As it turned out, the divers had heard all about him and were familiar with his story. So they consoled him and said, "Stay here while we dive and seek your luck. Whatever we find this next time, we shall divide between you and us."

Thereupon they dived and brought up ten oyster shells, and in each one they found two pearls. Astonished, they said to him, "By Allah, your luck has reappeared, and your good star is rising!" Then the divers gave him ten pearls and told him to sell two of them and make them his stock in trade. They also advised him to hide the rest, which he might be able to use in times of scarcity.

So the merchant took them with great joy and happiness, and he set about sewing eight of them in his gown and kept the two others in his mouth. But a thief saw him and ran to tell his comrades about all of this. So they attacked the merchant, took his gown, and abandoned him. When they were gone, he arose and said, "The two pearls that I have in my mouth will suffice," and he headed for the nearest city, where he placed his pearls in the hands of a broker who was to offer them for sale. Now, as destiny would have it, a certain jeweler of the town had been robbed of ten pearls like those which the broker was offering for sale. So when he saw the two pearls in the broker's hand, he asked him, "Who owns these pearls?"

"That man over there," the broker replied and pointed to the merchant.

When the jeweler saw the merchant in tattered clothes, he suspected him and said, "Where are the other eight pearls?"

The merchant thought he was asking him about the eight that he had sewn in his gown, whereas the jeweler had intended only to trick him into a confession, and so he responded, "The thieves stole them from me."

When the jeweler heard his reply, he was certain that the merchant was the man who had robbed him. Therefore he seized him, took him before the chief of police, and said, "This is the man who stole my pearls. I have found two of them on him, and he confessed to stealing the other eight."

Now the wali had known about the theft of the pearls. So he had the merchant thrown into jail, where they whipped him, and he lay in prison for an entire year until, by the grace of Allah, the chief of police arrested one of the divers who had originally found the pearls and put him into the prison where the merchant was jailed. When the diver saw him and asked him why he was there, the merchant told him what had happened, and the diver was surprised to hear about his misfortune. So when the diver was released from prison, he went to the sultan and told him all about the merchant's bad luck and how the diver was the one who found the pearls. Then the sultan ordered that the merchant be brought before him and asked the merchant to tell his story, which he did. When the sultan heard everything, he took pity on him and gave him a place of lodging in his own palace along with a salary and certain allowances. Now the lodging in question was right next to the king's house, and the merchant rejoiced and said, "Truly, my luck has returned, and I shall live in the shadow of this king for the rest of my life." As he was saying this, he noticed an opening in the wall of clay and stones, and so he cleared the opening to see what was behind it, and behold, it was a window that gave him access to the lodging of the king's women. When he saw this, he was startled and frightened. So he stood up, fetched some clay, and stuffed the opening with the clay. But one of the eunuchs saw him and went to the sultan and told him what he had seen. So the sultan went to the merchant and saw that the stones had been pulled out. He was furious with the merchant and said to him, "Is this the reward I get for helping you? Do you intend to cast your eyes on my harem?"

Thereupon the sultan ordered that the merchant's eyes be plucked out, and his servants did as he commanded. The merchant took his eyes in his hand and said, "How long, oh my bad star, will you torture me? First my wealth and now my life!" And he bemoaned his fate and said, "No matter how much I strive, it does not benefit me in the least, nor does it protect me from bad luck. The Compassionate does not help me, and all my efforts are in vain."

"Likewise, oh king," the youth concluded his story, "when fortune shone upon me, everything that I did turned to good. But now that fortune is against me, everything turns bad."

Upon hearing the youth's story, the king's anger subsided a little, and he said, "Return him to the prison, for the sun is setting, and tomorrow we shall look into his affair and punish him for his misdeeds."

When the next day came, the second of the king's viziers, whose name was Baharun, came in and said, "May Allah help the king! This deed which the young man has committed is a grave matter and an insult to the king's household."

After hearing the vizier's accusations, Azadbakht had the young man fetched again, and when he arrived, the king said to him, "Woe to you, young man! Nothing can help you, and I sentence you to death, for you have committed a grave crime, and I shall make your death a warning to the folk!"

"Oh king," replied the young man, "do not be so hasty, for a king who looks into all the causes builds a strong foundation for his kingdom and will assure the preservation of his realm. Whoever does not examine the causes of actions will pay for it the way the merchant had to pay, and whoever examines the consequences of his actions will be rewarded with the joy that the merchant's sons received."

"And what is the story of the merchant and his sons?" the king asked.

So the young man replied, "Hear, oh king,

The Tale of the Merchant and His Sons

There was once a merchant who had great wealth and a wife to boot. He set out one day on a business trip, leaving his pregnant wife at home, and he said to her, "Never fear. God willing, I shall return to you before the birth of the babe." Then he bade her farewell and traveled from country to country until he came to the court of one of the kings who needed someone like him to order his affairs and those of his kingdom. Seeing that the merchant was so well-bred and intelligent, he insisted that he stay at his court and treated him honorably.

After some years, the merchant asked the king's permission to return to his own home for good, but the king would not consent. Thereupon the merchant said to him, "Oh king, please let me go and see my children, and I promise to return to you."

So he granted him permission for this and gave him a purse with a thousand gold dinars. Then the merchant embarked in a ship and set sail for his motherland.

In the meantime his wife had much different experiences. After some years had passed, the news had eventually reached her that her husband had accepted service with the king. So she arose, took her two sons (for she had given birth to twins in his absence), and set out to join him. As fate would have it, they landed on an island, and her husband also arrived there that very night on the ship. So the woman said to her children, "That ship has come from the country where your father is working. Go to the seashore so you can ask about him."

When they went to the ship at the seashore, they began playing near the ship until evening. Now the merchant, their father, lay asleep in the ship, and after a while he became upset by the noise of the boys at play. So he got up, went to the side of the ship, and cried out to them, "Silence!"

As he did this, the purse with the thousand dinars fell among the bales of merchandise. When he realized that it was missing, he looked for it and racked his head until he realized that it must be the boys who had taken it. So he seized them and said, "No one could have taken the purse but you. You were playing around the bales so you could steal something. Nobody else was in the area."

Then he took his staff and began to beat and flog the children, who broke into tears. Then the crew gathered around them and said, "The boys of this island are all rogues and robbers."

Now the merchant was so angry that he swore that unless they produced the purse, he would drown them in the sea. When the boys denied taking the purse, he took the two boys, tied them each to a bundle of reeds, and cast them into the water. Some time after this their mother realized that the boys had not returned, and she went in search of them. When she reached the ship, she asked whether anyone had seen her boys and described their size and age. The sailors responded that her description fit the two boys who had just been drowned at sea. Upon hearing this, she began calling them and crying out, "Alas, my sons! Where was your father? If only he could have seen you!"

Then one of the sailors asked her, "Whose wife are you?"

And she told him that she was the wife of the merchant who had left her some years ago. "I was on my way to see him," she said, "and now this calamity has struck me."

When the merchant, who was nearby, heard this, he recognized her and stood up while he beat himself and tore his clothes. "By Allah!" he cried. "I have destroyed my children with my own hand! This is what happens to those who do not look into all the causes of an affair. This is the reward for those who do not take time to reflect."

Then he continued to weep and wail, as did his wife, and he said to his shipmates, "By Allah, I shall never enjoy my life until I receive news of what happened to them."

And he began to sail about the sea in quest of his sons, but he did not find them. Meanwhile, the wind had carried the two children toward the land and cast them upon the seashore. One of them was found by a company of the king's guards, and they carried him to their lord, who admired him so much that he adopted him and treated him as his own son, pretending that he had kept him hidden for some time out of love for him. So the folk rejoiced for their lord's sake, and the king appointed him as his heir apparent of his kingdom. After some years passed, the king died, and the people crowned the young man in his place. When he took over the reign of the kingdom, his estate flourished, and his affairs prospered with all regularity.

Meanwhile, during this entire time, his father and mother had searched for him and his brother on all the islands of the sea, hoping that the tide might have cast them on the seashore, but they found no trace of them. Finally, they gave up in despair and made their home on one of the islands. One day, when the merchant went to the market, he saw a broker who was selling a boy, and he said to himself, "I'm going to buy that boy, and perhaps he will be able to compensate me for my loss." So he bought him and took him to his house. When his wife saw the boy, she cried out, "By Allah, this is our son!"

Naturally, his father and mother rejoiced and were excited. When they asked him what had happened to his brother, he replied, "The waves parted us, and I don't know what became of him."

Thereafter his father and mother consoled themselves with him, and they lived this way for many years.

Now, the merchant and his wife had made their home in a city in the country that was ruled by the other son as king, and when the boy they had recovered had grown up, his father placed him in charge of all his merchandise that his son was to sell on his travels through the land. One time he took the goods and traveled to the city where his brother was ruling, and soon news reached the king that a merchant had arrived with merchandise suitable for royalty. So the king sent for the merchant, who obeyed the summons. When he came before the king and sat down, neither of the young men recognized the other, but blood was stirred between them, and the king said to the merchant, "I would like you to stay with me, and I shall offer you a high position and give you whatever you desire and crave."

So the merchant stayed with him for a while and never left his side. And when he saw that the king would never let him go, he sent for his mother and father, and they decided to join him. After they arrived, their son continued to reap honors from the king, who still did not know that he was his brother. Now, it so happened one night that the king left his palace to go drinking, and the wine got the better of him and he became drunk. Fearing for the king's safety, the young merchant said, "I myself will watch over this king tonight. This is the least I can do for all that he has done for me." So he arose right away and stationed himself with a drawn sword in front of the king's pavilion. But one of the royal pages saw him standing there with the drawn sword in his hand, and he was one of those who was jealous of him because the king favored him so much. Therefore, he said to him, "What are you doing there with your drawn sword at this time of night?"

"I'm watching over the king in gratitude for everything that he has done for me," the young man replied.

The page did not ask him any more questions. However, when morning came, he told a number of the king's servants what had happened, and they said, "This is our opportunity. Come, let us go together and inform the king so that the young merchant will fall out of favor. Then we'll be rid of the merchant and no longer have to bother about him."

So they all went to the king and said, "We should like to warn you about something, your highness."

"And what is your warning?" they asked.

"You know the young man, the merchant, whom you have promoted above the greatest of your chiefs," they said. "Well, we saw him bare his sword last night. He was planning to slay you."

When the king heard this, his color changed, and he asked them, "Do you have proof of this?"

"What proof do you need?" they rejoined. "If you need some, then pretend to be drunk again tonight and lie down as if you were asleep. Then watch him secretly, and you will see with your own eyes what we have just described to you."

Then they went to the young man and said to him, "We want to tell you that the king is grateful for the way you acted last night, and he commends your good deed." And they encouraged him to continue to do this.

Accordingly, when night arrived, the king pretended to be drunk and fall asleep. However, he kept on the alert for the young man and watched him as the merchant went to the door of the pavilion, unsheathed his scimitar, and stood in the doorway. When the king saw him do this, he was greatly upset and commanded that the merchant be seized.

"Is this the reward that I get from you?" the king exclaimed. " I showed you more favor than anyone else, and you wanted to commit such an abominable crime!"

Then two of the king's pages arose and said to him, "Oh king, if it is your will, we shall cut off his head."

But the king said, "Haste in killing is a vile thing, for it is a grave matter to kill a man. The living can kill time quickly, the killed cannot be quickened with time. Therefore, we must look into all the causes of this affair. We can slay this young man whenever we want."

Thereupon he ordered that the merchant be imprisoned, while he himself went back to the city. After he performed his duties, he went on a hunt. Then he returned to town and forgot all about the young man. So the pages went to him and said, "Oh king, if you keep silent and do not do anything to the young man who intended to slay you, all your servants will take advantage of the king's majesty, and indeed, the folk are talking about this affair."

Upon hearing this, the king became mad and cried, "Fetch him here! I want his head cut off."

So they brought the young man and tied a cloth around his eyes. And the executioner stood at his head and said to the king, "When you give the order, my lord, I shall cut off his head."

But the king cried, "Wait. I must look into this affair. If I have to put him to death, I can do it whenever I want."

Then the king had the young man sent back to prison, and he was to stay there until the king decided whether he was going to put him to death. Soon the merchant's parents heard about this affair, and the father wrote a letter and brought it to the king, who read it, and he came across the words "Have pity on me, so may Allah have pity on you, and do not be hasty in slaying my son. Indeed, I once acted hastily in a certain affair and drowned his brother in the sea, and to this day, I mourn him. If you need to kill him, kill me in his stead."

At this point, the old merchant prostrated himself before the king, who said to him, "Tell me your tale."

"Oh my lord," said the merchant, "my son had a

brother, and I in my haste threw the two into the sea."
And he related the entire story until the king cried
loudly with joy, jumped from the throne, embraced his
father and brother, and said to the merchant, "By Allah,
you are my very own father, and this is my brother, and
your wife is our mother."

And they stood there weeping, all three of them. Then
the king informed his people all about the past history
and said to them, "Oh folk, what do you think now
about my looking into all the causes of this matter?"

And they all admired his wisdom and foresight. Then
he turned to his father and said to him, "If you had
looked into the causes of your concern and taken your
time to investigate everything, then you would not have
had to repent and experience all the sorrow that you
experienced all this time."

Thereupon he sent for his mother, and they rejoiced
in their reunion and lived the rest of their days in joy
and gladness.

"What can be more grievous," continued the young
man, "than haste and not investigating the causes of all
events? Therefore, do not rush to slay me. You may be
sorry and repent for your actions."

When the king heard this, he said, "Return him to the
prison until tomorrow so that we can look into his affair.
It is advisable, I think, to do things in all due deliberation, and we can slay him whenever we want."

When the third day arrived, the third vizier came to
the king and said to him, "Oh king, do not delay dealing
with the case of this young man. His deed has caused
rumors to spread among the folk, and it behooves you
to slay him soon so that the talk may not spread and it
not be said that the king saw a man with his wife on his
bed and spared him."

The king was troubled by these words and commanded that the young man be brought before him. So
they fetched him in fetters, and indeed, the king's anger
was inflamed by the minister's speech, and he was upset.
So he said to the young man, "You vile lowlife, you

have dishonored us and marred our name, and I must do away with your life."

"Oh king," replied the young man, "if you make use of patience in all your affairs, you will succeed in everything that you wish for. Allah Almighty has blessed those who suffer long with all things good, and indeed, it was due to patience that Abu Sabir rose from the lower depths to ascend a throne."

"Who was Abu Sabir," asked the king, "and what is his tale?"

And the young man answered, "Listen, oh king, to

The Story of Abu Sabir

There was once a man, a village chief, called Abu Sabir, and he had many black cattle and a buxom wife, who had provided him with two sons. They lived in a little village, and a lion used to come there often and attack and devour Abu Sabir's herd so that most of his cattle had been devastated. Well, one day his wife said to him, "This lion has destroyed most of our cattle. Get going and mount your horse and take your men to kill him so we shall no longer be pestered by him."

But Abu Sabir said, "Have patience, my wife, for those who are patient will win the Lord's praise. It is the lion that commits crimes against us, and it is Allah Almighty who must destroy the criminal. Indeed, it is our long suffering that will slay him, and whoever does evil will suffer an evil end."

A few days later the king went forth one morning to hunt and encountered the lion. The king and his company pursued the beast and did not stop until they slew it. When the news reached Abu Sabir, he went to his wife and said, "Didn't I tell you, woman, that whoever does evil will suffer evil? If I had tried to slay the lion, I would not have prevailed. This is the result of patience."

It so happened that, after this, a man was killed in Abu Sabir's village. Consequently, the sultan ordered that the village be plundered, and his soldiers ruined everything, including Abu Sabir's possessions. Then his wife said to him, "All the king's officers know you. So why don't you complain to the sultan so that he will give you compensation for the beasts that you have lost?"

But he said to her, "Oh, woman, didn't I tell you that he who wrongs others will always be punished in some way? Indeed, the king has done evil, and soon he will suffer the consequences of his crime, for whoever takes the possessions of the folk will have his possessions taken from him."

One of his neighbors heard him talking to his wife, and since this neighbor had always envied Abu Sabir, he went to the sultan and told the king what Abu Sabir had said. So the king sent more soldiers, who destroyed every last thing that Abu Sabir owned and drove him and his entire family from the village. So they wandered about the desert beyond the village, and Abu Sabir's wife said to him, "If you weren't slow in responding to things and so helpless, all this would not have happened."

But he said, "Have patience, for the result of patience is good."

Then they walked on a little way, and thieves met them and robbed them of whatever they still possessed. Not only did they strip them of their clothes, they took their two children, causing the woman to weep and say, "Listen, my good man, stop being so foolish and let us pursue the thieves and beg them to have compassion on us and restore our children to us."

"Oh woman," he replied, "have patience, for he who does evil will be repaid with evil, and his perversity will doom him. If I were to follow them, one of them would most likely take his sword and kill me. But have patience, for the outcome of patience is laudable."

Then they continued traveling until they reached a village in the land of Kirman and stopped by a river.

"Stay here," said the man to his wife, "while I enter

the village and look for a place where we can set up our home."

And he left her by the river and entered the village. Soon thereafter a horseman arrived to water his horse, and he noticed the woman. Since he found her attractive, he said to her, "Get up and mount my horse. You will become my wife, and I shall treat you kindly."

"Spare me, and Allah will spare you!" she responded. "To tell the truth, I have a husband."

But he drew his sword and said, "If you do not obey me, I shall slay you."

When she saw his evil intention, she wrote on the ground in the sand with her finger, "Oh Abu Sabir, you have not ceased to be patient. But after all your goods were taken, your children and wife, who were more precious to you than all your possessions, are now gone. Indeed, may you remain sorrowful for the rest of your life, so you will learn the benefits of patience."

Then the horseman set her on the horse and took her away.

When Abu Sabir returned, he soon discovered that his wife had disappeared, and he read what she had written on the ground, whereupon he wept and bemoaned his fate for some time. Then he said to himself, "Oh Abu Sabir, it behooves you to be patient, for perhaps something worse and more grievous will happen to you." And he went forth and wandered haphazardly, as if he were distraught by love or simply mad. At one point he came across a group of men who were working on the palace of the king as forced laborers. When the overseers saw him, they seized him and said, "You had better work with these men at the king's palace, or else we shall have you imprisoned for life."

So Abu Sabir began working with them as a laborer, and every day he received a hunk of bread. He continued doing this for a month until one of the laborers mounted a ladder and accidentally fell and broke his leg. As he lay on the ground, he cried, and Abu Sabir said to him, "Have patience, and don't weep, for you shall find consolation in your endurance."

But the man said, "How long must I be patient?"

And he answered, "He who suffers a long time shall rise from the bottom of the pit and sit on the throne of the kingdom."

It so happened that the king was seated at a nearby window and heard their talk. Abu Sabir's words angered him, and he ordered that the man be brought before him. Now there was an underground dungeon and a vast cell in the king's palace, and the king commanded that Abu Sabir be brought there and said to him, "You witless fellow, Abu Sabir, I shall never see you come forth from this pit and sit on the throne of the kingdom."

And the king would continually visit him and stand at the mouth of the pit and say, "You witless fellow, Abu Sabir, I shall never see you come forth from this pit and sit on the king's throne!"

The king allowed him to have two hunks of bread a day, and Abu Sabir kept silent and patiently bore this treatment. Now the king had a brother whom he had imprisoned in that pit some time before this, and the brother had died. However, the folk of the realm thought he was still alive. As time passed, the courtiers of the king continued to talk about the brother and the tyranny of their lord. Word spread abroad that the sultan was a tyrant, and the people eventually attacked him and killed him. Then they went down to the cell of the dark dungeon and brought out Abu Sabir, thinking that he was the king's brother, for he had been down in the pit a long time and there was nobody else there. So they did not doubt that he was the prince and said to him, "It is now your turn to reign in your brother's palace, for we have slain him, and you are to replace him as our sovereign."

Abu Sabir was silent and did not say a word, but he knew that this was the result of his patience. Then he left the pit and went to sit down on the king's throne, donned the royal dress, and was just and fair in his dealings with the people so that all his affairs prospered. Consequently, the liege lords obeyed him, the people were kindly disposed toward him, and many became his soldiers.

Now the king who had long ago plundered Abu Sabir's goods and had driven him from his village had an enemy, and this foe mounted a campaign against him, defeated him, and captured his capital. So this king took flight and came to Abu Sabir's city, requesting his support and seeking safety. He did not know that the king of the city was the village chief whom he had once ruined. So he approached himself before Abu Sabir and presented his case. But Abu Sabir knew him and said to him, "This is somewhat the outcome of patience. Allah the most High has given me power over you."

Then he commanded his guards to take all the unjust king's possessions. So they did this and stripped him of his clothes and banished him from the country. When Abu Sabir's troops saw this, they were surprised and said, "Why is the king doing this? Another king comes to him and requests protection. Instead he ruins him and banishes him. This is not the way kings usually act."

But they did not dare to talk about this openly. Soon news came to the king that there were some robbers in his land. So he set out in search of them and did not stop pursuing them until he had captured them all. To his astonishment, he discovered that they were the very thieves who had plundered him and his wife and had carried off their children. Naturally, he commanded that the thieves be brought before him, and when they were in his presence, he questioned them about the boys.

"They are with us," they said, "and we shall present them to our lord the king as mamelukes to serve you, and we shall give you wealth galore that we have seized and doff all we own and repent from lawlessness and fight in your service."

Abu Sabir, however, did not pay attention to their words. He had all their goods seized and ordered them all put to death. Furthermore, he took his two boys and rejoiced immensely in having them once more by his side. However, his troops murmured among themselves and said, "Truly, this man is a greater tyrant than his brother! He captures a gang of thieves and they seek to repent and give him two boys as a peace offering. Then he takes the two lads and everything that the thieves own, and he has the thieves slain. Indeed, this is violent oppression!"

Some time after this, the horseman who had seized Abu Sabir's wife came and complained to the king that she would not give her body to him even though she was his wife. The king ordered that she be brought before him so that he might hear her plea and pronounce judgment upon her. So the horseman returned with her, and when the king saw her, he recognized his wife. So he took her from her ravisher and ordered that he be put to death. At this point he became aware that his troops were murmuring against him and talked about him as though he were a tyrant. So he turned to his courtiers and ministers and said to them, "As for me, by Allah the Almighty, I am not the king's brother! No, I am just a man whom the king had imprisoned because he had heard me speaking some words that offended him. He used to come and taunt me every day with those words. You thought I was the king's brother, but I am Abu Sabir, and the Lord gave me the kingship as a reward for my patience. As for the king who sought my protection and whom I plundered, it was he who first wronged me, for he plundered me some time ago and drove me from my native land and banished me without due cause. So I returned his treatment by way of lawful retribution. As for the robbers who showed repentance, there was no repentance for them with me because they waylaid me and took all my possessions and my sons, the two boys that I took from them. Indeed, those boys who you think are mamelukes are my very sons. So I avenged myself on the thieves and did to them what they did to me with strict justice. As for the horseman whom I slew, he had taken my wife from me by force. Indeed, this woman you see before you is my wife, and Allah the Most High has restored her to me. So this was my right, and the deed that I have done was correct. To be sure, since you all were not familiar with the events of my life, you thought that I was acting in a tyrannical way."

When the folk heard these words, they were astonished and prostrated themselves before him. Their esteem for him doubled; their affection increased; and they begged his pardon and admired all that Allah had done with him and how Allah had given him the kingship because of his long-suffering and his patience. They marveled at how Abu Sabir raised himself by his endurance from the bottom of the pit to the throne of the kingdom, while Allah threw the late king from the throne into the pit. Then Abu Sabir drew his wife close to him and said, "What do you think now about the fruit of patience and its sweetness and the fruit of haste and its bitterness? Truly, all the good and evil that a man does will surely come back to him."

"Likewise, oh king," said the young man, "you would do well to be patient whenever it is possible for you to do so, for noble people are those who know how to endure suffering, and patience is their greatest quality, especially kings."

When the king heard this from the young man, his anger subsided, and he ordered the young man returned to the prison, and the folk dispersed that day.

When the fourth day arrived, the fourth vizier, whose name was Zushad, appeared and prostrated himself before his liege lord and said to him, "Oh king, do not let the talk of that young man deceive you, for he does not tell the truth. As long as he remains alive, the folk will not stop talking, nor will your heart be relieved."

"By Allah," said the king, "what you say is true, and I shall have him fetched today and slay him with my own hands."

Then he commanded that the young man be brought before him. So they fetched him in fetters, and the king said to him, "Woe to you! Do you think you can appease my heart with your chatter and pass time with empty talk? I intend to put you to death this day!"

"Oh king," replied the young man, "it is entirely within your power to make an end of my life whenever you want, but haste is the way of the ignoble and patience the sign of the noble. If you put me to death, you will repent it, and then if you change your mind and want to restore me to life, you will be unable to do this.

Indeed, whoever acts hastily in an affair will receive what Bihzad, the son of the king, received."

"And what is this tale?"

"Listen, oh king, to

The Story of Prince Bihzad

In olden days there was once a king who had a son called Bihzad, and nobody was more handsome than he. Now Bihzad loved the company of the folk, and he often mixed with merchants and sat and talked with them. One day, as he was seated with a group of men, he heard them talking about him. One of the men said, "I've never seen anyone more handsome than he."

But one of the company said, "I've seen the daughter of a certain king who is definitely more beautiful than he is handsome."

When Bihzad heard this, he was thunderstruck, and his heart was stirred. He immediately called the last speaker and said to him, "Repeat to me what you just said and tell me the truth about this princess whom you believe to be more comely than I am. Whose daughter is she?"

"She is the daughter of King Suka," said the man, and after hearing more about this maiden, Bihzad was totally enamored, and he became lovesick. Soon the news reached his father, who said to him, "Oh my son, this maiden who has captured your heart can be at your command, for I have strong ties to her father. So wait until I demand her in wedlock for you."

But the prince said, "I can't wait."

So the king made haste to take care of the matter and sent a message to her father demanding his daughter in marriage. Thereupon the father responded by asking for a hundred thousand dinars paid to his daughter's dowry.

"So be it," said Bihzad's father and weighed out the money that was in his treasury, but there was not enough for the dowry. So he said, "Have patience, my son, until we gather together the rest of the money and send to fetch the princess for you. Indeed, she has become yours."

In reaction, the prince became exceedingly angry and cried, "I shall not be patient!"

So he took his sword and lance, mounted his horse, and went forth to become a highwayman in order to collect money for completing the dowry. Then one day it so happened he attacked some people who overcame him by dint of numbers, and they took him prisoner. After they tied and bound him, they carried him to the lord of that land where he was active as a highwayman. When the king saw how handsome and well-mannered he was, he could not believe he was a robber.

"You are not a highwayman," the king said. "Tell me truly, young man, who you are."

Bihzad was ashamed to tell him who he was and preferred to die. Therefore he answered, "I am nothing but a thief and bandit."

"Well," responded the king, "I am not obliged to act rashly in this matter. I shall look further into this affair, for impatience engenders penitence."

So the king had Bihzad imprisoned in his palace and assigned him a servant. Meanwhile, news spread that Bihzad the prince was lost, and his father sent letters in quest of him to all the kings in the neighboring area. When the letter reached the king who held Bihzad prisoner, this king praised Almighty Allah for endowing him with patience, and he summoned Bihzad to appear before him.

"Do you want to destroy your life?" the king asked the young man.

"I did this out of shame," responded Bihzad.

"If you fear shame, then you should not be hasty in what you do," stated the king. "Don't you know that the fruit of impatience is repentance? Had I acted hastily, I, too, like you, would have repented."

Then he conferred on him a robe of honor, gave him money to complete his dowry, and sent the good and comforting news to his father that his son was safe. Afterward he said to Bihzad, "Arise, my son, and go to your father."

"Oh king," responded the prince, "please be so kind as to let me go to my wife first. If I go back to my father, it will take a long time for him to send a messenger to my bride's father and for the messenger to return with an answer."

The king laughed and was surprised by him. "I fear that you may be somewhat precipitate," said the king. "You may shame yourself and not achieve your wish."

Nevertheless, he gave him a great deal of money and letters commending him to the father of the princess and sent him on his way to see the princess and her father. When the prince approached their country, the king came forth to meet him with the people of his realm. He provided the prince with fine lodgings and hastened in making the arrangements for his daughter's wedding in compliance with the other king's letter. He also sent a message to the prince's father about the wedding, and all the people occupied themselves with the affair of the young lady. When the day of the wedding arrived, the impetuous Bihzad lost patience and went to the wall between his lodging and her chamber. There was a hole in the wall, and he hastily looked through it so that he could see his bride. But her mother spotted him, and she was so enraged that she took two red-hot iron spits from one of the pages and thrust them into the hole through which the prince was looking. The spits ran into his eyes and put them out, and he fell to the ground in a swoon. The wedding festival was thus changed into a day of mourning and grief.

"Oh king," continued the young man, "you see what happened to the prince because of his haste and lack of deliberation. Indeed, he was made to repent for his impatience, and his joy turned to grief. Likewise, the woman who rushed to poke out his eyes and did not think about the consequences of her actions suffered greatly. All this was caused by haste. Therefore, it behooves the king not to be hasty in putting me to death, for I am under your power. Whenever you wish to slaughter me, you can easily do so."

When the king heard this, his anger subsided, and he said, "Return him to the prison until tomorrow so that I may investigate his case."

When it was the fifth day, the fifth vizier, whose name was Jahrbaur, came to the king and prostrated himself before him. "Oh king," he said, "it behooves you, if anyone casts an eye on your harem, that you must have this person's eyes plucked out. What are you going to do with him who saw the most intimate place of your palace and lay on your royal bed? He is suspected of mingling with your harem, and he is not of your lineage and kith and kin. You must do away with this shame by putting him to death. Indeed, I am urging you to do this to guarantee the safety of your empire and because of my zeal to provide counsel and because of my affection for you. How can you legally allow this young man to live for a single hour?"

Upon hearing this, the king was filled with fury and cried, "Bring him here immediately!"

So his servants fetched the young man, whom they set before him in fetters, and the king said to him, "Woe to you! You have committed a great sin, and your life has been unduly prolonged. The time has come for your execution, because I shall have no peace and comfort until I take your life."

"I want you to know, oh king," responded the young man, "that I, by Allah, am innocent, and because of this I hope for life. Indeed, he who is innocent of all offense does not go in fear of pain and punishment, nor do his worries and concerns increase. But he who has sinned must have his sin expiated upon him, though his life be prolonged. His sin will overtake him just as it overtook Dadbin the king and his vizier."

"How did that happen?" asked Azadbakht.

"Hear, oh king, and may Allah grant you long life," the young man said,

The Story of King Dadbin and His Viziers

There was once a king in the land of Tabaristan by the name of Dadbin, and he had two viziers, one called Zorkhan and the other Kardan. The minister Zorkhan had a daughter named Awra, and in her day none was fairer than she, nor could any maiden match her chastity and piety, for she honored Allah greatly in her fasting, prayers, and adoration. Now Dadbin, the king, heard tell of her praises. So his heart went out to her, and he called her father the vizier to him and said, "I request the hand of your daughter."

"Oh my lord," responded Zorkhan, "please let me consult with her, and if she consents, she will be your wife."

"See to it soon," said the king.

So the minister went to his daughter and said to her, "Oh my daughter, the king has requested your hand in marriage."

"Oh my father," she replied, "I don't desire a husband, but if you want to wed me, I ask you only to wed me to a man who will be inferior in rank and less noble than I am so that he may not turn to anyone other than myself nor look down upon me with eyes of contempt. Please don't marry me to one who is nobler than I, for he would then treat me as a slave and servant."

Accordingly, the vizier returned to the king and told him what his daughter had said, but this only caused the king's desire and longing to grow, and he said to the vizier, "If you do not marry me to her in good grace, then I shall take her in spite of you and by force."

The minister returned to his daughter and repeated the king's words, but she replied, "I do not want a husband."

Thereupon he went back to the king and told him what she had said, and the king was furious and threatened him. Consequently, the vizier fetched his daughter and fled. When the king learned about this, he dispatched troops in pursuit of Zorkhan. They managed to overtake him and detain him until the king arrived and slew him with his scepter. Then he took the daughter by force, and upon returning to his place, he had sex with her and married her. Awra resigned herself with patience to all that had happened to her, and she placed her fate in the hands of Allah Almighty. Indeed, it became her custom to serve Him night and day with proper worship in the house of King Dadbin her husband.

Now, one day, it so happened that the king had to make a journey. So he called his second vizier, Kardan, to him and said, "While I am absent, I want you to take charge of my wife, and I want you personally to keep her and guard her, because there is nothing in the world dearer to me than she."

"In truth," Kardan thought to himself, "this is a great honor to have the king entrust me with this lady," and he answered, "I shall gladly do this."

When the king had departed on his journey, Kardan said to himself, "I must look upon this lady whom the king loves with all his might."

So he hid himself in a place so that he might watch her. And he was stunned by her beauty, which surpassed all description. Consequently, he was confused and bewildered, and love overwhelmed him so that he sent a message to her saying, "Have pity on me, for I am desperately in love with you."

She sent a message back to him and replied, "Oh vizier, you've been placed in a position of trust and confidence. So don't betray this trust, and fulfill your duties as you are supposed to do. Take care of your wife and everything that duly belongs to you. As for your affections for me, it is mere lust, and women are all of one and the same taste. And if you don't heed what I am writing, I'll make this known to everyone, and you will live in shame."

When the minister heard her answer, he knew that she was chaste of soul and body. Therefore, he repented and became afraid of what the king would do when he learned about his feelings for his wife. So he said to himself, "I must devise a scheme to destroy her. Otherwise I shall be disgraced before the king."

Now, when the king returned from his journey, he questioned Kardan about the affairs of his kingdom, and the vizier answered, "All is well, oh king, except for a vile matter which I observed here. But I'm afraid to tell my sovereign about this. On the other hand, if I hold my peace, I fear that others might discover it, and I shall have neglected my duty by not warning the king. As a result, I shall have betrayed his trust."

"Speak openly," said Dadbin, "for you have always told the truth and have been a loyal and trustworthy counselor."

And the minister said, "Oh king, this woman, to whom your heart clings and whose piety you admire, is all craft and guile, and I can prove it to you."

Of course, the king was troubled and remarked, "I want you to tell me all you know."

The vizier replied, "Well, some days after your departure, someone came to me and said, 'Come, oh vizier, and look.' So I went to the door of the queen's sleeping chamber, and behold, she was sitting with Abu al-Khary, her father's page, whom she favors, and she did with him what she does with you, and that is what I saw and heard."

When Dadbin heard this, he burst with rage and said to one of his eunuchs, "Go and slay her in her chamber."

But the eunuch said to him, "Oh king, may Allah prolong your life! Believe me, it is unwise to have her killed like this. Instead, I suggest that you order one of your castratos to take her on a camel, lead her deep into the woods, and abandon her there. If she is guilty, Allah will let her perish. If she is innocent, Allah will deliver her, and the king will be free of committing a crime against her. After all, this lady is dear to you, and you slew her father just so you could marry her."

"By Allah," responded the king, "what you say is true!"

Then he ordered one of his eunuchs to carry her on

a camel to a desolate forest and to leave her there. Then he was to return without caring for her. So the eunuch fetched her and went into the wilderness with her. He left her there without provisions or water and returned. Thereupon she headed for one of the hills and arranged stones before her in the form of a prayer niche and began to pray. Now it so happened that a camel driver who served a king named Kisra had lost some camels, and King Kisra had threatened him that if he did not find them, he would be slain. So the camel driver had set out and gone into the wilderness, until he arrived at the place where the lady was praying. Upon seeing her standing and praying utterly alone, he waited until she had finished. Then he went up to her and saluted her with the salaam and asked her who she was.

"I am a handmaid of the Almighty," she said.

"What are you doing in this desolate place?"

"I serve Allah the Most High."

When he saw her beauty and loveliness, he fell in love with her and said, "Listen, take me as your husband, and I shall be tender to you and treat you with great care. I shall look after you in obedience to Allah Almighty!"

"I have no need for wedlock, and I desire to dwell here alone with my Lord and to worship Him. But if you want to treat me with great care and look after me in obedience of Allah the Most High, take me to a place where there is water, and you will have done me a great kindness."

Thereupon he took her to a place that had running water, and after setting her down on the ground, he left her and went his way with great admiration for her. After he left her, he found his camels and knew that it was due to her blessing. When he returned to the palace, King Kisra asked him, "Have you found the camels?"

He answered yes and told him about the incident with the lady and described her beauty and loveliness to him in great detail. Upon hearing these words, the king's heart went out to her, and he mounted his horse, took some men with him, and went to the place, where he found the lady, and he was amazed because she surpassed the camel driver's description. As he approached her, he said, "I am King Kisra, greatest of the kings. Will you have me for your husband?"

"What will you do with me, oh king?" she asked. "I am a woman abandoned in the wilderness."

"This need not be the case," he replied. "If I cannot have your consent, I shall make this spot my abode and devote myself to Allah's service and your service, and I shall worship the Almighty with you."

Then he ordered his servants to set up a tent for the lady and one for himself facing her so he might adore Allah with her. He also began sending her food, and she said to herself, "This is a king, and it is not right for me that I make him abandon his subjects and his land for my sake." Presently she said to the serving woman who brought her the food. "Speak to the king and get him to return to his subjects, for he has no need of me, and I desire to dwell in this place so that I may worship Allah the Most High."

The slave girl returned to the king and told him this, whereupon he sent the girl back and told her to say to Awra that he had no need of the kingship, and he desired to stay there and worship Allah with her in this wilderness.

When she saw how earnest he was, she complied with his wishes and said, "Oh king, I shall consent to what you desire and shall become your wife, but only on the condition that you take me to Dadbin the king and his vizier Kardan and his chamberlain the chief eunuch. They must all be assembled so that I may say something to them in your presence and thus win your affection even more."

"Why is it that you want to do all this?" Kisra asked.

So she related her story to him from first to last, how she was the wife of Dadbin the king, and how the vizier Kardan had disgraced her honor. When King Kisra heard this, his love and affection for her doubled, and he said to her, "I shall do whatever you want."

Then he had a litter brought to her, and she was carried on it to his palace, where he treated her with the utmost honor and married her. Soon he assembled a great army and sent the troops to King Dadbin. In short order they returned with Dadbin, his vizier, and the eunuch, who appeared before King Kisra, and they had no idea why he had done all that he had done. In the meantime, the king had a large tent set up as a pavilion in the courtyard of his palace for Awra, and she entered it and let down the curtain in front of her. When the servants had set up their seats, and everyone was seated, Awra raised a corner of the curtain and said, "Oh Kardan, stand up, for it is not fitting that you sit in the like of this assembly before the mighty King Kisra."

When the vizier heard these words, his heart fluttered and his joints trembled and he rose to his feet in fear. Then she said to him, "By virtue of Him who has made you, stand and be judged. I command you to speak the truth and reveal what caused you to lie against me, to humiliate me, and to drive me from my home and from the land of my husband. What made you lie about Abu al-Khary, man and Moslem, so that my husband had him executed after I left? This is no place where lying and deceit may help you."

When the vizier realized that she was Awra and heard her speech, he knew that he could not lie and that nothing would save him except the truth. So he bowed his head to the ground and wept and said, "Whoever does evil will incur it. By Allah, it was I who sinned and committed a crime, and it was nothing but fear that prompted me and my desires that overcame me. Indeed, this woman is pure and chaste and entirely without fault."

When King Dadbin heard this, he beat his face and said to Kardan, "May Allah slay you! It is you who have wronged me and caused me to drive my wife away!"

But Kisra the king said to him, "Allah will most assuredly slay you because you acted with haste and did not look into your affairs. Therefore, you couldn't tell the guilty from the innocent. If you had thought things through deliberately, you would have been able to distinguish wrong from right. When this deceitful vizier sought to undermine you, where was your judgment and why couldn't you see what was going on?"

Then he asked Awra, "What do you want me to do with them?"

"Follow the divine ordinance of Almighty Allah," she said. "Let the slayer be slain, and the criminal be punished according to the crime he committed. Let the man who did good deeds for us be rewarded accordingly."

So she gave her officers the orders, and they slew Dadbin with a scepter. And she said, "This is for the slaughter of my father."

Then she ordered the vizier set on a camel and taken to the desert where he had previously commanded her to be taken without provisions or water. And she said to him, "If you are guilty, you will suffer the punishment of your guilt and die in the desert of hunger and thirst. But if you are innocent, you will be saved just as I was saved."

As for the eunuch who had advised King Dadbin not to slay her but to have her taken to the desert, she bestowed a costly robe of honor on him and said to him, "People like you should be held in high honor by kings and should be promoted to high places, for you spoke loyally and well, and a man is rewarded according to his deeds."

And King Kisra made him a wali in a certain province of his empire.

"You should know, oh king," the young man continued, "that whoever performs a good deed will be rewarded with good, and he who is innocent will never fear the outcome of his affairs. I, my liege lord, am innocent and place my hope in Allah so that He will let the truth shine for my king and guarantee me victory over my enemies and those who are envious of me."

When the king heard this, his wrath subsided, and he said, "Return him to the prison until tomorrow so that we may investigate his case."

When the sixth day arrived, the anger of the viziers grew in intensity because they had not been able to have their way with the young man, and they feared for their lives. So three of them went to him and prostrated themselves before him.

"Oh king," they cried out, "we are loyal counselors and concerned about your welfare. Truly, if you persist much longer in letting this young man live, you will not benefit from this at all. Each day he continues to live, the folk become ever more suspicious and continue to talk about you. Therefore, we urge you to kill him so that you can kill all this talk."

When the king heard this speech, he said, "By Allah, you are right and speak the truth!"

Then he commanded them to bring the young treasurer, and when the young man appeared before him, he said, "How long shall I investigate your case? No one has come forth to help you, and everyone is thirsting for your blood."

The young man answered, "Oh king, I hope for help only from Allah, not from mortals. If He aids me, no one will have the power to harm me, and if He is with me and on my side because I am truthful, whom shall I have to fear because of their lies? Indeed, my dedication to Allah is pure and sincere, and I have given up all hope for help from fellow mortals. Indeed, whoever truly seeks the aid of Allah finds that which Bakhtzaman found."

"Who was this Bakhtzaman," the king asked, "and what is his story?"

"Hear, oh king," said the young man,

The Story of King Bakhtzaman

There was once a king of kings whose name was Bakhtzaman, and he was a great eater, drinker, and carouser. Now it came to pass that some of his enemies appeared in certain parts of his realm which they coveted, and one of his friends said to him, "Oh king, your foes are plotting against you. Be on your guard against them."

"I'm not concerned about them," said Bakhtzaman.

"I have weapons, wealth, and warriors and am afraid
of nothing."

Then his friends said to him, "Ask Allah for help, oh
king, for He will help you more than wealth, weapons,
and warriors."

But he turned a deaf ear to the advice of his loyal
counselors, and soon the enemies attacked, waged war

against him, and were victorious, for he had no trust in Allah. So Bakhtzaman fled to one of the nearby sovereigns and said to him, "I come to you and beg for refuge and provisions so that you may help me against my foes."

This king gave him money, men, and a mighty force, and Bakhtzaman said to himself, "Now I am strengthened by these troops and I should easily be able to conquer my foes with such warriors." But he did not say, "with the help of Allah Almighty."

So his enemy met him and defeated him again. Put to rout, his troops were dispersed, and he lost all his money. Since his enemy pursued him, he took to the sea, and when he had crossed it, he saw a great city on the other side and asked some people its name. When they informed him that it belonged to King Khadidan, Bakhtzaman continued on his way until he came to the royal palace, where he disguised himself and passed himself off as a horseman and sought service with King Khadidan, who hired him and treated him with honor. Nevertheless, Bakhtzaman still missed his homeland.

Some time thereafter an enemy declared war on King Khadidan, who sent his troops into the field with Bakhtzaman as head of the host. Khadidan also took part in the campaign with his lance and fought a fierce battle. Eventually he overcame his foe, who fled ignominiously with his troops. When the king and his army returned in triumph, Bakhtzaman said to him, "Listen, my king, I find this very strange that you are surrounded by a great and mighty army, and yet you engage in the battle yourself and risk your life."

"Do you call yourself a knight and an intelligent fellow and think that victory is simply due to the number of men you have?" responded the king.

"Yes," said Bakhtzaman, "this is what I believe."

"By Allah, then, you are wrong in your belief," stated the king. "Woe to him who does not place his complete trust in Allah! Indeed, I have gathered together this army only to gratify my imagination and majesty. Victory is due to Allah alone. I, too, oh Bakhtzaman, believed at one time that victory was due to the number of men I had in my army, and an enemy came against me with eight hundred men, while I had eight hundred thousand. I trusted in the power of my troops, while my foe trusted in Allah. So he defeated me and put me and my troops to a shameful flight, and I hid myself in one of the mountains where I met with a religious hermit who had withdrawn from the world. So I stayed with him, bemoaned my situation, and revealed to him what had happened to me. Then the hermit said, 'Do you want to know why this happened to you and why you were defeated?' 'I have no idea how this came about,' I responded, and he said, 'It was all because you put your trust in the might and number of your troops and did not rely upon Allah the Most High. If you had placed your trust in Allah and believed that it is He alone who will help and protect you, your foe would have never been able to cope with you. Return to Allah.' So I returned to my right senses and repented, thanks to the hermit, who said to me, 'Go back to what remains of your troops and engage your foe again. If your enemy's intent has changed and has turned away from Allah, you will overcome him, even if you are alone.' When I heard the hermit's words, I put my trust in Allah the Almighty, gathered together the remainder of my troops, and attacked my enemy by surprise during the night. They thought I had many men and fled in shame, whereupon I entered my city and took over my place once again, thanks to the power of Almighty Allah. And now, whenever I fight, it is only by placing my trust in His aid."

When Bakhtzaman heard these words, he awoke from his decadent ways and cried, "Praise be the perfection of God the Great! Oh king, I want you to hear about my affairs and my story, for I am King Bakhtzaman, and you will learn all about what happened to me, and then I shall seek the gate of Allah's mercy and repent."

So Bakhtzaman revealed his past and then went forth to one of the mountains and worshiped Allah for a while until one night, as he slept, a person appeared to him in a dream and said to him, "Oh Bakhtzaman, Allah has accepted your repentance and has opened the door of succor and will help you against your foe."

When he was assured of this in a dream, he arose and headed toward his own city. When he approached the city, he met a company of the king's men, who said to him, "Where are you coming from? We see that you're a foreigner and fear for your life, for every stranger who enters this city is killed by the king because he dreads the return of King Bakhtzaman."

"Only Allah the Most High can determine whether this king will have his way and profit," replied Bakhtzaman.

"But this king has a vast army," they said. "The enormous number of troops gives him courage."

When King Bakhtzaman heard this, he was comforted and said to himself, "I place my trust in Allah. If he wills it, I shall overcome my enemy thanks to the Lord of Omnipotence." Then, turning to the men standing near him, he said, "Don't you know who I am?" and they replied immediately, "By Allah, we don't."

"I am King Bakhtzaman!" he cried.

When they heard this and knew that it was indeed the king, they dismounted from their horses and kissed his stirrup to do him honor and said to him, "Oh king, why are you risking your life?"

"My life is a light matter to me, and I place my trust in Almighty Allah and look to Him for protection," Bakhtzaman stated.

"May that be sufficient for you," they said. "We shall do all in our power to help you and provide you with all that you deserve. Don't worry, for we will aid you with our lives. We are the king's chief officers and are popular with the folk. So we shall take you with us and encourage the people to follow you because they are inclined to be loyal to you, all of them."

"Do whatever Allah Almighty enables you to do," Bakhtzaman responded.

So they carried him into the city and hid him with them. Then they met with a company of the king's chief officers who had formerly served Bakhtzaman and told them what they had done. Upon hearing this, these officers rejoiced. Together they went to Bakhtzaman and made a pact of loyalty to serve him. Then they attacked the king, slew him, and seated Bakhtzaman on his throne again. Gradually, his affairs prospered, and Allah improved his estate and restored His bounty to him. And Bakhtzaman ruled his subjects justly and dwelled in the obedience of the Almighty.

"In this way, oh king," continued the young treasurer, "he who is aided by Allah and whose intentions are pure will have only good things happen to him. As for me, I have no helper other than the Almighty, and I am content to submit myself to His commands, for He knows the purity of my intentions."

Upon hearing this, the king's wrath subsided, and he said, "Return him to the prison until tomorrow so that we may look into his case."

When the seventh day arrived, the seventh vizier, whose name was Bihkamal, came to the king, prostrated himself before him, and said, "Oh king, why are you torturing yourself so much with this young man? What are you going to get out of all this? Indeed, the people keep gossiping about you and him. So why do you keep postponing his execution?"

The minister's words aroused the anger of the king, and he ordered the young man to be brought before him. So his guards fetched him in fetters as before, and Azadbakht said to him, "Woe to you! By Allah, you can expect no salvation from my hand after this day, for you have damaged my honor, and there can be no pardon for you."

"Oh king," the young man replied, "there is no great pardon unless there is a great fault. Indeed, only if the offense is great can mercy be magnified, and there can be no grace for the likes of you to spare the likes of me. Truly, Allah knows that there is no crime in me, and indeed, He commands clemency, and there is no greater clemency than that which spares a man from slaughter. Hence, your pardon of the man whom you propose to put to death is like reviving a dead man, and whoever does evil shall find it before him, as was the case with King Bihzard."

"And what is the story of this King Bihzard?" asked the king.

So the young man answered, "Listen, my king, to

The Story of King Bihzard

There was once a king named Bihzard, and he had great wealth and many troops. However, his deeds were evil, and he would punish anyone for a slight offense, and he never forgave any offender. Now, one day he went hunting, and one of his pages shot an arrow which hit the king's ear and cut it off. Bihzard cried, "Who shot that arrow?"

So the guards quickly seized a young man named Yatru, and out of fear this page fell to the ground and started trembling. Then the king commanded, "Slay him!"

But Yatru cried out, "Oh king, I didn't intend to shoot you, nor did I have any control over what happened. So I beg you to pardon me in the hour of your power over me, for mercy is the best of deeds, and as such it will be your provision in this world and a good work for which you will be repaid one of these days. Indeed, it will be a treasure that will be taken into account with Allah in the world to come. Therefore, pardon me, and keep evil away from me, and Allah will do likewise and keep evil from you."

When the king heard this, he was pleased and pardoned the page, even though he had never pardoned anyone before this. Now this page happened to be the son of a king who had fled his sire because of a sin he had committed. This is why he had entered the service of King Bihzard and how things had come about. After a while, a man happened to recognize the page and went and told his father, who sent him a letter in which he forgave his son and asked him to return home. Accordingly, the page went back to his father, who came forth to meet him and rejoiced in the reunion, and the prince's affairs were set right with his sire.

Some time later, King Bihzard decided to go fishing in a ship, and while he was at sea, the wind became so strong that a storm arose and sank the ship. Fortunately for the king, he grabbed a plank and landed on a coast mother-naked, and it so happened that he landed exactly in the country ruled by his former page's father. During the night Bihzard came to the gate of the king's capital, and finding it shut, he slept in a burial place nearby. When the sun rose the next morning and the people went forth from the city, they found a man who had been murdered and thrown into a corner of the burial ground. At the same time, they noticed Bihzard and were certain that it was he who had committed the crime. So they seized him, took him to the king, and said, "This man has murdered someone."

The king sent Bihzard to prison, and while he was in jail, Bihzard kept repeating to himself, "All this is due to my many sins and tyrannical ways, for I have slain many people unjustly, and this is the punishment for my evil deeds and for all the oppression that I have caused."

As he was pondering his fate, a bird came and landed on the pinnacle of the prison. Out of habit from hunting, Bihzard took a stone and threw it at the bird. By chance, the king's son was playing in a nearby field with a ball and bat, and the stone hit him on his ear and cut it off, causing the prince to fall down in a fit. The guards then inquired who had thrown the stone, and after discovering that it was Bihzard, they took him before the king's son, who ordered him to die. Accordingly, the guards took the turban from Bihzard's head and were about to blindfold him when the prince noticed that an ear was missing from the man about to be executed. So he said to Bihzard, "I see that you have already had an ear cut off for your crimes."

"This is not true, by Allah," said Bihzard. "I lost this ear because of an accident some years ago, and I pardoned the young man who caused me to lose this ear after he had shot an arrow at me by mistake."

When the prince heard this, he looked Bihzard in the face and recognized him.

"Aren't you Bihzard the king?" the prince exclaimed.

"Yes," Bihzard replied.

"Well, what bad luck brought you here?" the prince asked.

Thereupon Bihzard told him all that had happened, and the people were so astonished that they cried out, "Praise the Lord Almighty!"

Then the prince stood up, embraced Bihzard, kissed him, and treated him with respect. He seated the king in a chair and bestowed the robe of honor on him, and then he turned to his father and said, "This is the king who pardoned me, and this is his ear which I cut off with an arrow. Indeed, he deserves my pardon for having pardoned me."

Then the prince turned to Bihzard and said, "Truly, the mercy that you showed me a long time ago has stood you in good stead."

Afterward, they treated Bihzard with utmost kindness and sent him back to his country in honor.

"So you see, my king," the young man continued, "there is no greater quality than mercy, and all that you do in the name of clemency will reap you benefits."

When the king heard this, his wrath subsided, and he said, "Return him to the prison until tomorrow, when we shall look into his case."

When the eighth day arrived, the viziers all assembled for a discussion and said, "What shall we do with this young man who is undermining us with his talk? Indeed, if he is saved, he will certainly cause our destruction. So we must all go to the king and strengthen our efforts to have this young man executed. Otherwise he will be declared innocent and get the better of us."

Accordingly, they all went to the king, prostrated themselves before him, and said, "Oh king, be on your guard or else this young man will ensnare you with his sorcery and enchant you with his charms. If you heard what we heard, you wouldn't let him live, not even for a single day. Therefore, don't listen to his talk, for we are your ministers, who seek to keep you in permanent power, and if you do not listen to our words, whose words will you heed? You see, we are ten viziers who claim that this young man is guilty, and we are convinced that he entered your sleeping chamber with evil intentions to put your highness to shame and to damage your honor. If you don't want to slay him, then at least you should banish him from your realm so that the people stop wagging their tongues."

When the king heard the words of his ministers, he became enraged and ordered that the young man be brought before him. When the young man appeared, the viziers all cried out with one voice and declared, "Oh, you numbskull, do you think you can save yourself from execution by deception and deceit? Do you really think that you can charm the king with your talk and think he will pardon you for the great crime that you have committed?"

Then the king commanded that the executioner be brought forth to chop off the young man's head, whereupon the viziers began arguing among themselves, and each one cried out, "I want to slay him!" and rushed toward him.

Thereupon the young man said, "Oh king, just look at your ministers and see how eager they are to do away with me! Don't you think this is envy? They want to bring about a separation between you and me so that they can continue to plunder you as they have done in the past."

"But I must consider their charges against you," stated the king.

"How can they charge me with something, oh king, when they were not present?" responded the young man. "They are acting out of envy and malice, and if you slay me, you will miss me and regret your action. Indeed, I fear that you will repent and experience the same thing that happened to Aylan Shah because of the malice of his viziers."

"And what is his story?" the king asked.

"Hear, oh king,

The Story of Aylan Shah
and Abu Tammam

Once there was a merchant named Abu Tammam, and he was a clever man who was well-bred, quick-witted, and honest in all his affairs. In addition, he was very wealthy. Now in this land there was a king as unjust as he was jealous, and Abu Tammam was afraid that the king might take all his money, and so he said, "I'm going to move to another place where I shall not have to live in dread."

Soon thereafter he moved to the city ruled by Aylan Shah, and after building a palace, he took up his residence there and transported all his wealth to his new abode. After a while the King Aylan Shah heard about him and invited him to his palace. When Abu Tammam arrived, the king said, "I recently was told about your arrival and your new allegiance to our city, and indeed, I have also heard about your excellent character, wit, and generosity. So I welcome you to my kingdom. The land is your land, and I am at your disposal, and whatever you need from me, consider it already accomplished. I desire to have you near me and a part of my gatherings."

Then Abu Tammam began serving the king with great dedication and generously sent the king all sorts of presents. In the course of time, the king saw that Abu Tammam was intelligent, well-bred, and wise. So he became particularly fond of him, and the king asked him to take charge of his affairs and gave him the power to administer everything. Now Aylan Shah had three viziers, who were accustomed to looking after the king's affairs and were always with him day and night. But they became excluded from the king's life because of Abu Tammam, who had become the king's favorite. Therefore, the ministers discussed the matter together and said, "What shall we do? The king neglects us because of Abu Tammam, and he even bestows more honor on him than on us. We must devise some plan to separate him from the king."

So each of them said what was on his mind, and one of them said, "The king of the Turks has a daughter, who is the most beautiful maiden in the word, and all the messengers who have been sent to him to demand her in marriage have been slaughtered by her father. Now our king doesn't know about this. So let us meet with him and mention her. When his heart is taken with her, we shall advise him to send Abu Tammam to seek her hand in marriage. Then her father will slay him, and we shall be rid of him for good."

Accordingly, they went to the king one day while Abu Tammam himself was present, and they mentioned the daughter of the king of the Turks. They talked about her charms so much that the king's heart was taken by her, and he said to them, "We shall send someone to demand her to be my wife. But who will be my messenger?"

"No one is better suited for this business," the viziers said, "than Abu Tammam. He has great wit and good breeding."

"Indeed," the king said, "I agree. No one is better suited for this affair than Abu Tammam."

So he turned to Abu Tammam and said, "Would you please deliver my message and seek the hand of the daughter of the king of the Turks for me?"

"To hear is to obey, my sovereign," responded Abu Tammam.

So they prepared him for the trip, and the king gave him a royal robe of honor. In addition, Abu Tammam took a present and a letter written in the king's hand, and soon he departed and did not stop until he came to the capital city of Turkistan. As soon as the king of the Turks heard about his arrival, he dispatched his officers to receive him and treated him with honor by lodging him as befitted his rank. After entertaining him as his guest for three days, the king summoned Abu Tammam, who prostrated himself before him and delivered the present and the letter.

The king read the letter and said to Abu Tammam, "We shall do what this matter demands, but Abu Tammam must interview my daughter, and she must interview you. You must hear what she has to say, and she must hear your speech."

Upon saying this, he sent him to the lodging of the princess, who had been informed about all of this. Indeed, for this special occasion, the king had adorned her sitting room with the costliest gems and vessels of gold and silver, and she seated herself on a chair of gold, clad in the richest of royal robes and ornaments. When Abu Tammam entered the room, he became pensive and said to himself, "The wise declare that whoever controls his sight shall suffer nothing unjust, and he who guards his tongue shall hear nothing to taunt him, and whoever keeps watch over his hand will find his hand lengthened and not shortened."

So he entered, and after seating himself on the floor, he cast his eyes down and covered his hands and feet with his garment,

"Raise your hand, oh Abu Tammam," said the king's daughter. "Look at me and speak with me."

But he did not speak, nor did he raise his head, and she continued, "They sent you only to interview me and talk with me, and yet, behold, you have not uttered a peep. Now, take these pearls that are around you and some of these jewels and gold and silver."

But he did not extend his hand or touch anything, and when she saw that he paid no attention to anything she became angry and cried, "They have sent me a messenger who is blind, dumb, and deaf!"

Then she related to her father what had happened, and the king called Abu Tammam to him and said, "You came to interview my daughter. Why then did you not look at her?"

"I saw everything," said Abu Tammam.

"Why didn't you take some of the jewels and the other things that you saw?" asked the king. "Indeed, they were set out for you."

But he answered, "It is not right for me to extend my hand and take what does not belong to me."

When the king heard his words, he gave him a sumptuous robe of honor and became very fond of him.

"Come, look at this well," he said to Abu Tammam.

So Abu Tammam went to the well and looked, and behold, it was full of heads of many men, and the king said to him, "These are the heads of the envoys whom I slew because I saw they were not loyal. Whenever I met an envoy without manners, I believed that he who sent him must have worse manners than the messenger because the messenger is the tongue of the lord who sends him, and his breeding is of his master's breeding. Whoever is raised this way is therefore not fit to be my kin. For this reason I used to put the envoys to death. But you have passed the test and have won my daughter because of your excellent manners. So now may your heart rejoice, for my daughter belongs to your lord."

Then he sent him back to King Aylan Shah with presents and rare items as well as a letter that said, "All this is in your honor and that of your envoy."

When Abu Tammam returned after accomplishing his mission and brought the presents and the letter, King Aylan Shah was overwhelmed with joy and showed him even more favor and bestowed the highest honors on him. Some days later, the king of Turkistan sent his daughter, and she went to meet King Aylan Shah, who was exceedingly pleased, and his esteem for Abu Tammam grew even greater. When the viziers saw this, their envy and spite increased, and they said, "If we do not come up with a plan to get rid of this man, we shall die of rage." So they thought and thought until they agreed upon a plan that they would put into practice.

Soon thereafter they went to two young pages who served the king and lay at his head in his bedchamber. He would often place his head on their laps before he fell asleep. So the ministers gave them each a thousand dinars of gold and said, "We are going to ask you to do something, and we want you to have this gold for your time of need."

"What would you like us to do?" asked the pages.

"When you are alone with the king," they said, "and he leans back as if he were asleep, one of you is to say to the other, 'Verily, the king has graced Abu Tammam with his favor and has promoted him to a high rank. However, he has betrayed the king's honor and is a cursed traitor.' Then let the other of you ask: 'What crime did he commit?' Then the first should answer, 'He disgraces the king's honor and says that the king of Turkistan was accustomed to slay all the messengers who were sent to seek his daughter in marriage, but he did not slay him because the king's daughter took a liking to him. The only reason why the princess came here, according to him, was to be near him.' Then let the other say, 'Do you know that this is really the truth?' Let the first reply again, 'By Allah, all the people know this, but because they fear the king, they dare not divulge it to him. Indeed, whenever the king goes hunting or takes a trip, Abu Tammam goes to her, and they spend time together alone.' "

After hearing all this, the pages said, "We shall do your bidding."

Accordingly, one night when they were alone with the king and he leaned back as if he were asleep, they spoke these words. The king heard everything and felt as if he were going to die of fury and spite and said to himself, "These are young boys who know no better. They're not old enough to mix with anyone else, and therefore I'm certain that they are speaking the truth."

When it was morning, he was so overcome with anger that he summoned Abu Tammam immediately, took him aside, and said, "What do you think that someone who does not guard the honor of his liege lord deserves as a punishment?"

"His lord should not guard his honor," replied Abu Tammam.

"And whoever enters the king's house and does treacherous things," Aylan Shah continued, "what does he deserve?"

"He should be put to death," answered Abu Tammam.

Thereupon the king spat in his face and said to him, "You are the one who has done both these deeds."

Then the king quickly drew his dagger and stabbed

him in the belly, and Abu Tammam died on the spot.
Then Aylan Shah dragged him to a well in his palace
and threw him into the water. After everything had been
done, he began to repent his hasty act, and his mourning
and sorrow increased and weighed heavily on his heart.
But he would not confide in anyone and reveal the cause
of his sadness. Nor could his love for his wife prevail
upon him to tell her why he grieved.

When the viziers learned about Abu Tammam's death,
they were overcome with joy and knew that the king's
sorrow was due to the loss of his friend. As for Aylan
Shah, he began going to the sleeping chamber of the
two pages to spy on them and to hear what else they
might have to say about his wife. As he stood one night
outside the door of their chamber, he saw them spread
out gold between their hands and play with it. As they
were doing this, he heard one of them say, "Woe to us!
What's the use of all this gold? We cannot buy anything
with it or spend any of it on ourselves. We have sinned
against Abu Tammam and caused an unjust death."

"If we had known that the king would slay him on
the spot," said the other, "we would not have done what
we did."

When the king heard this, he could not contain himself. Immediately he rushed into their chamber and said,
"Woe to you! What did you do? Tell me!"

And they cried, "Mercy, oh king!"

"If you want pardon from Allah and me," the king
responded, "you had better tell me the truth, for nothing
will save you from me but honesty!"

Hearing this, the two pages prostrated themselves before him and said, "By Allah, oh king, the three viziers
gave us this gold and taught us to lie about Abu Tammam so that you would kill him. What we said to you
that night were words that they put into our mouths."

When the king heard this, he plucked his beard until
he almost tore it out by the roots, and he bit his fingers
until he almost cut them in two. He deeply regretted
that he had acted so rashly and had not taken time to
consider Abu Tammam's case. Then he sent for his ministers and said to them, "I have discovered how sinister

you are! You thought that Allah had paid no attention to your evil deeds, but your wickedness will be turned against you. Don't you know that whoever digs a pit for his brother shall himself fall into it? From me you will receive the punishment of this world, and tomorrow you will receive the punishment of the next world and requital from Allah."

Then he ordered them to be put to death. So the executioner chopped off their heads before the king, and he went to his wife and informed her about his mistreatment of Abu Tammam. Thereupon she grieved for him with great sorrow, and the king and his household wept and repented for the rest of their lives. Moreover, they fetched Abu Tammam's body from the well, and the king built him a domed tomb in his palace and buried him in there.

"You see, then, my auspicious king," the young man continued, "what sorrow is caused by jealousy and injustice, and how Allah caused the viziers' malice to turn against them and cause them to lose their heads. I trust in the power of the Almighty, who will enable me to triumph over all who are jealous about the favor that my king has shown me. Allah will bring forth the truth. Indeed, I am not afraid of dying. I only fear that the king will repent my slaughter, for I am innocent, and may I be struck dumb if I am guilty of any offense against you whatsoever."

When the king heard all this, he bowed his head toward the ground and was very confused and perplexed. "Take this young man back to the prison until tomorrow," he said, "so that we can look into his case."

Now when the ninth day arrived, the viziers met and began discussing the situation among themselves. "Truly, this young man is baffling us. Just as soon as the king gets set to kill him, the young man charms him and bewitches him with a story. What can we do to slay him? How can we finally get rid of him and have our peace?"

After discussing the situation for many hours, they decided to go to the king's wife, and when they appeared before her, they said, "You are unaware of the dangerous situation in which you are, and your ignorance might be to your disadvantage. While the king is occupied with eating, drinking, and entertaining himself, he forgets that the people are beating their tambourines and singing about you and spreading rumors that the wife of the king loves the young man. Well, as long as this young man remains alive, the talk will increase and not diminish."

"By Allah, it was you who egged me on against him," she replied. "What shall I do now?"

"Go to the king," they said, "and weep and say to him, 'Truly, the women come to me and tell me that I am being disgraced throughout the city. What is there for you to gain by sparing the life of this young man? If you will not slay him, then slay me so that all this talk can be put to an end.' "

So the queen arose, tore her garments, and went to see the king in the company of the viziers. When she arrived, she cast herself upon him and said, "Oh king, hasn't my shame touched you, or don't you fear shame? Indeed, this is not the way of kings, who are usually quick to avenge themselves when it comes to jealousy about their women. Aren't you aware that all the men and women of your realm are talking about you? Either slay the young man so that the talk will stop, or slay me if your soul will not consent to his slaughter."

Upon hearing her words, the king was enraged and said to her, "I take no pleasure in preserving his life, and I shall have him slain this very day. So return to your palace, and console your heart."

Then he ordered the young man to be fetched, and when he stood before the king, the viziers said, "You vile creature, fie upon you! Your life is about to end, and the earth hungers for your flesh and wants to make a meal out of it."

But he said to them, "Death cannot be brought about by your words, nor by your envy. No, it is a destiny written upon the forehead. Therefore, if it is written on my own forehead, there is nothing I can do about it. There are no precautions that I can take, no ideas to stop it. Nothing will be able to save me from death. This is exactly what happened to King Ibrahim and his son."

"Well, who was this King Ibrahim, and who was his son?" he king asked.

"Listen, oh king," the young man said, "to

The Story of King Ibrahim and His Son

There was once a king of the kings called Sultan Ibrahim, and all the other sovereigns prostrated themselves before him and obeyed his laws. But he had no son and was saddened by the thought that he might not be able to pass on his reign to his own heir. He continued to long for a son, and so he bought slave girls and lay with them until one of them became pregnant. Upon hearing this news he was overwhelmed by joy and distributed great gifts with utmost generosity. When the ninth month drew near and the girl was about to give birth, the king summoned the astrologers, and they watched for the hour of the birth, raised their astrolabes, and carefully noted the time. The slave girl gave birth to a boy, and the king rejoiced. Outside the palace the people celebrated when they heard the glad news. Then the astrologers drew their charts, and when they looked into his birth and rising star, their color changed, and they were confounded. Then the king said to them, "Tell me his horoscope, and you will always have my pardon and have nothing to fear."

"Oh king," they replied, "we can see from the birth of the young prince that in his seventh year, he will be in dreadful danger from a lion that will attempt to tear him apart. If he is saved from the lion, there will be another danger more dreadful and more terrifying than the first."

"What is it?" asked the king.

"We shall not speak," they said, "unless the king commands us to do so and guarantees our safety."

"By Allah, I assure you that nothing will happen to you," responded the king.

Then they said, "If he is saved from the lion, the king will then be destroyed by his hand."

When the king heard this, his complexion changed, and he became extremely downcast. But he said to himself, "I shall be watchful and do my best to make sure that the lion does not eat him. It is not certain that he will kill me, and indeed, I think the astrologers lied."

Then the king had his son reared by wet nurses and noble matrons. Meanwhile, he continued to think about the prediction of the astrologers, and truly, his life was troubled. So he went to the top of a high mountain and had his slaves dig a deep cave with many dwelling places and rooms, and he filled the entire dwelling with all the rations and clothes that were necessary and whatever else was needed. Then he had pipes and conduits of water constructed in the mountain, and the boy was taken there to live with a nurse who was to rear him. At the first of the month the king would go to the mountain and stand at the mouth of the cave. Then he would let down a rope he had with him and draw the boy up to him. Taking him to his bosom, he would kiss him and play with him awhile. Then he would let him down again to his place and return to the palace.

The king was accustomed to counting the days until his son would turn seven. Ten days before the predicted fate that was engraved on his son's forehead approached, some hunters who were chasing wild beasts came to the mountain, and upon seeing a lion, they attacked him. The lion fled from them and took refuge in the mountain, and he fell into the cave. The nurse saw the lion right away and escaped into one of the chambers. Thereupon the lion made for the boy, seized him, and tore his shoulder. Then the lion sought the room in which the nurse was hidden, and after the lion found her, he devoured her while the boy lay in a swoon. Meanwhile, when the hunters saw that the lion had fallen into the cave, they came to the mouth and heard the boy's and woman's shrieks. After a while the cries died away, and they knew that the lion had slain them. As they stood at the mouth of the cave, behold, the lion came scrambling up the sides and would have escaped, but whenever he showed his head, they pelted him with stones until he was beaten down and fell. Then one of the hunters descended into the cave, killed the lion, and saw the wounded boy. Afterward he went to the chamber where the woman lay dead, and indeed, the lion had eaten his fill of her. Upon noticing all her clothes and other items, he informed his fellow hunters and began passing the stuff up to them. Finally, he sent the boy up and out of the cave, and the hunters carried him to their dwelling place, where they dressed his wounds. He grew up with them but did not tell them about his background. Indeed, when they questioned him, he did not know what he should say, because his father had sent him down into the cave when he was but an infant. The hunters marveled at his speech and loved him very much, and one of them adopted him as his son. This hunter always kept him at his side and trained him in hunting and horseback riding until he reached the age of twelve, when he was then allowed to participate in the hunt with the rest of the men.

Now it so happened one day when they sallied forth that they encountered a caravan, which they attacked. But the members of the caravan, were strong and on their guard, and they defeated the hunters. The boy fell wounded and lay on that spot until the next day, when he opened his eyes. There he found his comrades slain, and he lifted himself up and began walking along the road. Soon he met a treasure seeker, who asked him, "Where are you heading, my boy?"

So he told the man what had happened, and the treasure seeker said, "Don't be discouraged. Your good fortune has come, and Allah is going to bring you joy and happiness. I am searching for a hidden treasure which contains a huge amount of wealth. So come with me and help me, and I'll give you so much money that you will never have to worry about a thing for the rest of your life."

Then he took the young boy to his dwelling and dressed his wounds, and he rested with the boy for some

time until his wounds had healed. Then the treasure
seeker took him and two beasts and all the provisions
they needed, and they journeyed until they came to the
mountains. Here the man took out a book, and after
reading something in it, he dug in the crest of the mountain five cubic meters deep and discovered a stone. He
pulled it up, and behold, it was a trapdoor covering the
mouth of a pit. So he waited until the foul air came out
of the pit, and then he took a rope, tied it around the
boy's waist, and let him down bucket-wise to the bottom.
Then the boy lit a candle that he had been carrying with
him, and at the upper end of the pit he saw a great deal
of money and jewels. So the treasure seeker let down a
rope and a basket, and the boy began filling the basket,
and the man kept drawing up the basket until he had
all he wanted. Afterward the man loaded his beasts and
stopped working, while the boy called to him to let down
the rope and pull him up. Instead, the treasure seeker
rolled a stone over the mouth of the pit and went on
his way.

When the boy realized what the treasure seeker had
done to him, he called upon Allah to help him out of
his predicament. "This will be a bitter death," he said.
Indeed, his situation was gloomy, and there was no way
out of the gloomy pit. So he began weeping and saying,
"I escaped the lion and the robbers, and now I shall find
my slow death in this pit." And there was nothing he
could do but wait for death to arrive in that dark pit.
But as he stood there pondering, he suddenly heard a
sound of rushing water. So he stood up and walked in
the pit following the sound until he came to a corner
and heard the mighty rushing of water. Then he placed
his ear to the sound of the current, and hearing it rushing strongly, he said to himself, "This is the flowing of
a mighty river, and if I have to surrender my life in this
place, be it today or tomorrow, I shall throw myself into
the stream and not die a slow death in this pit." Thereupon he summoned his courage and threw himself into
the water, and it carried him along with force under the
earth. The river flowed outside and took him to a deep
lake, and there he was cast ashore. When he found him-

self on the face of the earth, he was in a daze all that day. When he finally came to himself, he stood up and journeyed into the valley. He praised Almighty Allah along the way until he came to an inhabited land and a large village in the realm of his sire. So he entered, and the villagers gathered around him and asked him what had happened. In response, he told them his tale, and they admired how Allah had delivered him from all those dangers. Then he took up his abode with them, and they became very fond of him.

This is all that had happened to him up to this point in time. But with regard to the king his father, when he went to the pit, as was his custom, and called to the nurse, there was no answer. He became despondent and ordered a man to be let down into the cave, where he found the woman dead and the boy gone. When the man informed the king what had happened, the king pulled his hair and wept. Then he descended into the cave to see what had happened. There he saw the slain nurse and dead lion, but he did not find the boy. So he returned to his palace and told the astrologers that they had predicted the truth.

"Oh king," they said, "the lion has eaten him. He has found his destiny, and you are delivered from his hand. If he had been saved from the lion, we would have been afraid for your life because the king's destruction would have been by his hand."

So the king stopped being sorry for what had happened, and the days passed, and the affair was soon forgotten. Meanwhile, the boy grew up and dwelled with the people of the village, who occasionally went out to raid and rob caravans. When the time arrived for the inevitable to happen and for Allah's decrees to be fulfilled, the young boy became a leader in the raids on caravans. But people began complaining to King Ibrahim, his father, about the villagers and their attacks on caravans, and the king went out with a company of his soldiers and surrounded the highwaymen from the village. Now, since the boy happened to be with them and wanted to protect them, he shot an arrow that hit the king and wounded him in a mortal place. So his men carried him to his palace, and afterward they seized the boy and his comrades and brought them before the king and asked, "What would you like us to do with them?"

"I am on the brink of death right now," he said. "So bring me the astrologers."

Accordingly, they brought the astrologers before him, and he said to them, "You told me that my death would be brought about by the hand of my son. How is it possible then that I have been wounded mortally by these thieves?"

The astrologers were astonished and said to him, "It is not beyond the teaching of the stars and the will of Allah that he who has wounded you may be your son."

When King Ibrahim heard this, he had his guards fetch the thieves and said to them, "Tell me truly, which one of you shot the arrow that wounded me."

"It was this young man who is with us," they said.

Thereupon the king began interrogating him and said, "Young man, tell me about your past. Tell me who your father was, and I assure you, by Allah, that you will be safe from harm."

"Oh my lord," replied the young man, "I never knew my father. He lodged me in a cave with a nurse to rear me. And one day, a lion attacked, and he tore my shoulder. Then he seized the nurse and devoured her. Thanks to Allah, I was saved by a hunter who carried me out of the cave."

Then the young man told the king all that had happened to him from the first to the last incident. When he was done, King Ibrahim cried out and said, "By Allah, this is my son! Now show me your shoulder."

So the young man uncovered it, and behold, it was scarred. Then the king assembled his lords and the astrologers and said to them, "Take note that what Allah has written upon the forehead, be it fair fortune or misfortune, no one can efface it, and everything that is decreed will come about. Indeed, all the precautions that I took and all my endeavors were to no avail. What Allah decreed for my son has come to pass, and what He has decreed for me I have endured. Nevertheless, I praise Allah and thank Him because my death was by my son's hand, and not by the hand of another. Praise the Lord, for my son will assume the kingship."

And he reached out and took the young man to his bosom and embraced him and kissed him. "Oh, my son, I placed you in that cave because I sought to avoid fate and to protect you, but it was to no avail." Then he took the crown, set it on his son's head, and had the lords and people do homage to him. Then he commended the subjects to his care and advised him to treat them with justice and equity. That night the king died, and his son reigned in his stead.

"So it is with you, too, oh king," the young man continued. "If Allah has written anything on my forehead, this is what must happen to me, and nothing that I say to you will help me. Nor will my examples that I have been using help against Allah's will. And so it is with these viziers. All their eagerness and endeavors to bring about my destruction will not benefit them. If Allah decides to save me, He will provide me with the victory over them."

When the king heard these words, he came perplexed and said, "Return him to the prison until tomorrow, so we may look into his affair. The day is drawing to a close, and I intend to have him put to a terrible death. Tomorrow I shall dole out the punishment that he deserves."

When the tenth day arrived—now this day was called Al-Mihrjan, and it was the day when the gentle and simple folk came to the king to salute him and give him joy—the viziers agreed that they should speak with a company of the city notables. So they said to them, "When you go to visit the king today and to salute him, say to him, 'Oh king, your policies are praiseworthy, and all your actions are just for your subjects. But with regard to this young man whom you have favored, and who has nevertheless shown his base origin and done this foul deed, what purpose could you have in preserving his life? Indeed, you have imprisoned him in your palace, and every day you listen to his palaver, and you pay no attention to what the folk say.'"

And the notables responded, "Hearing is obeying."

Accordingly, when they entered with the folk and had prostrated themselves before the king and congratulated his majesty, he gave them promotions. Now it was the custom of the folk to salute and go forth. Instead, they took their seats, and the king knew that they had something on their minds and would like to address him. So, in the presence of the viziers, he turned to them and said, "Tell me what is on your minds."

Therefore they repeated to him everything that the viziers had taught them, and the viziers also spoke their piece. In response Azadbakht said to them, "My people, I want you to know that there is no doubt in my mind that your words come from your love for me and your loyal counsel. You know that if I were to inclined to kill half the folk on these premises, I could bring about their deaths, and it would not be difficult for me to arrange all this. So what is to prevent me from slaying this young man? He is in my power and within reach. Indeed, his crime is manifest, and this has incurred the death penalty. I have deferred it only because his offense is so great. If I defer his death and my proof against him is strengthened, my heart will be healed as well as the heart of my whole folk. If I don't slay him today, then he will not escape his death tomorrow."

Then he had his guards fetch the young man, who prostrated himself before the king and blessed him. Thereupon the king said, "Woe is to you! How long shall my folk reprimand me because of you? I have become a laughingstock among them, and indeed, they come to me and reproach me for not putting you to death. How long shall I delay this? Indeed, I intend to put you to death this very day so I can stop the prattling of my folk."

The young man replied, "Oh king, if rumors have been spread about you among the folk because of me, by Allah and again by Allah the Great, those who have spread the rumors are none but these wicked viziers, who chatter with the crowd and tell them foul tales and evil things about the king's house. But I have placed my hope in the Most High that He will cause their malice to recoil upon their own heads. As for the king's threat to slay me, I am completely in your power. So it is not necessary for the king to worry about my execution, because I am like the sparrow in the grasp of the fowler who can cut the bird's throat at will and let him go at will. As for the delaying of my death, this is not determined by the king but by Him in whose hands my destiny lies. By Allah, oh king, if the Almighty decided that I should die, you could not postpone it, not even for a single hour. And indeed, a person can try to fend off evil from himself, as was the case with the son of King Sulayman Shah, whose anxiety and care with regard to the newborn child brought him nothing. His last hour was deferred many times, and Allah saved him until his life had been fulfilled according to Allah's decrees."

"Fie upon you!" cried the king. "You have a great gift of storytelling and speech! So now tell me their tale."

And the young man said, "Listen, oh king, to

The Story of King Sulayman Shah and His Niece

There was once a king named Sulayman Shah, who was good and wise, and he had a brother who died and left a daughter behind him. So Sulayman Shah gave her the very best education, and the girl became a model of reason and perfection. Moreover, she was the most beautiful maiden in her time. Now the king had two sons, one of whom he intended in his mind to become her husband, while the other intended to have her for his own. The elder son's name was Bahluwan, and the younger Malik Shah. The girl was called Shah Khatun. One day King Sulayman Shah went to his brother's daughter and, kissing her head, he said, "You are my daughter and as dear to me as my own child because of the love I bear for your late father, who has found mercy. Therefore I propose to marry you to one of my sons and to appoint him my heir apparent so he may become king after me. Decide, then, which of my sons you will have, for you have been reared with them and know them."

The maiden arose, kissed his hand, and said to him, "Oh my lord, I am your handmaid, and you are the ruler over me. So whatever you decide will be fine with me, especially since your wish is higher, more honorable, and more venerable than mine, and if you would want me to serve as your handmaid for the rest of my life, it would be fairer to me than any mate."

The king commended her speech, bestowed a robe of honor on her, and gave her magnificent gifts. After doing this, he made his choice known, and he decided to wed her to his younger son, Malik Shah, who became his heir apparent, and King Sulayman Shah called upon his people to swear loyalty to him. When the news of this wedding reached Bahluwan, he realized that his younger brother had been preferred over him, and he became extremely upset and was filled with envy and hate. But he concealed all this in his heart.

Meanwhile Shah Khatun went to the king's son in all her bridal splendor and soon became pregnant. Nine months later she gave birth to a son who was as illuminating as the moon. When Bahluwan saw what was happening with his brother, envy and jealousy overcame him. So one night he went to his father's palace and entered his brother's chamber, where he saw the nurse sleeping at the door with the cradle before her and his brother's child asleep in it. Bahluwan stood by the cradle and looked at the face of his nephew, whose radiance was like that of the moon, and Satan crept into his heart and caused him to think, "Why can't this baby be mine? Indeed, I am more worthy of him than my brother. Yes, I am also more worthy of the maiden and the entire realm." He became obsessed by this idea, and his anger kept driving him so that he took out a knife, placed it to the child's gullet, cut his throat, and almost severed his windpipe. Then he left him for dead and entered his brother's chamber, where he saw Malik Shah asleep with the princess by his side, and he thought about slaying her but said to himself, "I shall leave this maiden for myself." Then he went up to his brother and cut his throat, and after taking his head from his body, he went away.

Now nothing mattered to him anymore, and his life was a light matter. So he sought the lodging of his sire, Sulayman Shah, to slay him as well, but he could not gain entrance. Consequently, he left the palace and hid himself in the city until the next day, when he fled to one of his father's fortresses and took precautions to protect himself.

This is what happened to Bahluwan. But as far as the nurse is concerned, she soon awoke to suckle the child, and upon seeing the cradle overflowing with blood, she cried out. Then everyone who was sleeping awoke, and the king was aroused. He went straight to his son's chamber, where he found the child with his throat cut and the cradle running over with blood. He also found his son dead from a knife wound. They examined the child and fortunately found life in him. His windpipe was whole, and they sewed up the place of the wound. Then the king sought his son Bahluwan, and when he did not find him, he realized that he had fled. So he knew that it was his son who had done this deed, and this caused great grief for the king, the people of his realm, and the lady Shah Khatun. In his grief the king laid out his son Malik Shah, buried him, and made him a splendid funeral. All the people mourned him greatly, and afterward the king set to rearing the infant.

As for Bahluwan, when he fled and fortified himself, his power began to grow. In the following years he declared war against his father, who had become extremely fond of his grandson and used to hold him on his knees and beg Almighty Allah that he might live long enough to bestow his kingdom upon his grandson. When the child became five, the king mounted him on horseback, and the people of the city rejoiced when they saw him and prayed that he would live a long life so that he might take vengeance for his father and heal his grandfather's heart.

Meanwhile, Bahluwan the rebel went to pay court to Caesar, king of Roum, and he requested aid from him to do battle with his father. And Caesar was kindly disposed toward him and gave him a large army. When Bahluwan's father heard about this, he sent a message to Caesar saying, "Oh glorious and mighty king, do not aid an evildoer. This is my son, and he cut his own brother's throat and that of his brother's son in the cradle." But he did not tell the king of Roum that the child had recovered and was alive.

When Caesar heard the truth of the matter, he was extremely disturbed, and he sent a message back to King Sulayman Shah saying, "If it be your wish, oh king, I shall cut off his head and send it to you." But Sulayman Shah answered and said, "I don't care anything about him. Surely he will receive a reward for his deed, and his crimes will overtake him, if not today, then tomorrow." And from that date on he continued to exchange letters and presents with Caesar.

Now the king of Roum heard tell of the widowed princess and of her beauty and loveliness, and he sent a messenger to seek her hand in wedlock. In this case, Sulayman Shah could not refuse him. So he arose and went to Shah Khatun and said to her, "Oh my daughter, the king of Roum has asked for your hand in marriage. What do you say to this?"

She wept and replied, "Oh king, how can you find it in your heart to speak to me about such a matter? Can I really think of another husband after what happened to my former husband, your son?"

"Oh my daughter, the situation is exactly as you describe it," said the king, "but let us look at all of the issues involved here. I must now take into consideration that I may die soon, for I have become old and weak, and the only things that concern me and cause me to worry are you and your little son. Indeed, I have written to the king of Roum and other kings and have said that his uncle slew him and did not reveal that your son had recovered and is living. Instead, I have concealed all this. Now the king of Roum has asked for your hand in marriage, and this is something we cannot refuse, since it would be important to have our position strengthened with his assistance."

Since Shah Khatun was silent and did not speak, King Sulayman Shah sent an answer to Caesar that said "To hear is to obey." Then he arose and sent Shah Khatun to him, and when Caesar met her, he found that she fit the description that he had been given, and therefore his love for her increased every day, and he preferred her over all his women. But Shah Khatun's heart remained with her son, and she could say nothing.

As for the rebel Bahluwan, when he saw that Shah Khatun had married the king of Roum, he became upset and depressed. Meanwhile, his father, Sulayman Shah, watched over the child and cherished him and named him Malik Shah after his dead son. When Malik Shah reached the age of ten, King Sulayman Shah made the folk do homage to him and named him his heir apparent. After some days, the old king's time for paying his debt to nature drew near, and he died.

Now a group of the troops in Sulayman Shah's realm had always remained loyal to Bahluwan. So they sent a message to him, and he secretly returned to the kingdom. Then the soldiers went to little Malik Shah, seized him, and seated his uncle Bahluwan on the throne, proclaiming him king and doing homage to him.

"We want you," they said, "and we have placed you on the throne of this kingdom. But we don't want you to slay your brother's son, because we re still bound by the oaths we swore to his sire and his grandsire, and we are still bound by the covenants that we made with them."

So Bahluwan consented, and he imprisoned the boy in an underground dungeon. Soon the disturbing news reached his mother, and it reopened old wounds. However, she could not speak to anyone about it and placed her trust in Allah Almighty. In particular, she could not confide in King Caesar, her husband, for otherwise she would make her uncle, King Sulayman, into a liar. As for Bahluwan the rebel, he remained king in his father's place, and his affairs prospered while young Malik Shah lay in the underground dungeon four years until he lost his looks and his charm. It was then that Allah, praise be to the Almighty, determined to relieve him and bring him out of the prison.

On this day Bahluwan sat with his chief officers and the lords of his land and were discussing the story of his sire, King Sulayman Shah, and what was in his heart. Several worthy viziers were present, and they said to him, "Oh king, truly Allah has been generous to you and has brought about your wishes so that you have become king in your father's place and have won whatever you have desired. But as for this young boy, he is not guilty of anything. From the day of his birth he has had neither comfort nor pleasure, and indeed, his looks have faded and his charm is gone. What crime has he committed that he deserves such pain and punishment? Indeed, others were to blame, not him, and Allah has allowed you to triumph over them. This boy is innocent."

"Indeed," answered Bahluwan, "it is exactly as you say. But I fear his machinations, and I am not safe from his mischief. I am convinced that most of the folk will favor and support him."

"Oh king," they replied, "what is this boy, and what power does he have? If you fear him, send him to one of the frontiers."

And Bahluwan said, "This is good advice. I shall send him as a captain of war to take over one of the outlying stations."

Now the place in question was occupied by fierce enemies, and Bahluwan thought that they would probably kill the young boy. So he had him fetched from the underground dungeon, allowed him to approach, and saw how he had changed. Then he gave him garments, and the people rejoiced. Afterward, he gave him his assignment and many troops and sent him to the frontier. Accordingly, Malik Shah journeyed there with his men, and one night the enemy attacked, whereupon some of his men fled, and the rest the enemy captured. They also seized Malik Shah and threw him into a pit with a company of his men. His soldiers mourned that he had lost his handsome features and charm, and there he remained for twelve months in a terrible plight.

At the beginning of each year it was the enemy's custom to bring forth their prisoners and throw them down from the top of the citadel to the bottom. So at the accustomed time, they brought them out and threw them down, and Malik Shah was with them. However, he fell upon the other men, and his body did not touch the ground, for Allah had not ordained that this was the time for his death. But all the others who were thrown down died on the spot, and their bodies lay there until wild beasts ate them and the winds scattered their bones. As for Malik Shah, he remained there in a swoon the entire day, and that night, when he regained consciousness and found himself safe and sound, he thanked Allah the Most High for saving him and departed from that spot.

For days he kept wandering about, lost, and living off the leaves of trees. By day he hid himself wherever he could, and at night he traveled at risk. Finally he reached a place inhabited by people, and he told them how he had been imprisoned in a fortress and how his captors had thrown him from the citadel, but Almighty Allah had saved him and enabled him to escape alive. The people took pity on him and gave him something to eat and drink, and he remained with them for several days. Finally he asked them which way led to the kingdom of his uncle, Bahluwan, but he did not tell them that Bahluwan was his father's brother. So they showed him the road, and he walked barefoot until he drew near his uncle's capital. He was practically naked and hungry, and, indeed his limbs were lean, and the complexion of his skin had changed. When he sat down at the city gate, a company of King Bahluwan's chief officers appeared. They had been out hunting and wanted to water their horses. After they sat down to rest, the young boy approached them and said, "I would appreciate it if you would tell me something."

"Ask what you will," they replied.

"Is King Bahluwan well?" he asked.

"What a fool you are, boy!" they derided him. "You

are a stranger and a beggar, and what concern could you have about the king's health?"

"In truth," he cried, "he is my uncle."

In their astonishment they responded, "Your first question was a puzzle, and now you dazzle us with your second! We think that the jinn have driven you mad. How can you possibly claim kinship with the king? Indeed, his only kin is his nephew, a brother's son, who was imprisoned and then sent to wage war on the infidels, but they killed him."

"I am the person you are talking about," said Malik Shah. "But they did not slay me."

And after he revealed what had happened to him, they recognized him right away. Immediately, they stood up, kissed his hands, and rejoiced in his salvation.

"Oh our lord," they said, "you are indeed a king and the son of a king, and we desire nothing but good for you, and we pray for your welfare. Look how Allah has rescued you from this wicked uncle who sent you to a place from which nobody has ever returned safe and sound. The only purpose that he had in doing this was to make sure you would be killed. Indeed, you were almost destroyed, but Allah saved you. Why do you now want to return to your foe and place your life in his hands? By Allah, save yourself and don't return to him this second time. Chances are that you will live upon the face of the earth until it pleases Almighty Allah to welcome you into his kingdom. But if you fall into the hands of your uncle again, he will not let you live a single hour."

The prince thanked them and said, "Allah reward you with health and prosperity, for you have indeed given me good advice. But where do you think I should go?"

"To the land of Roum," they said, "where your mother lives."

"I don't think I can do this," he said. "When my grandfather, Sulayman Shah, sent my mother to the king of Roum, he concealed my existence from him, and my mother has done the same. I cannot make a liar out of her."

"You speak the truth," they responded. "Still, if you

were to go there, you could become part of the people and not reveal your identity. This would be a way for you to save your life."

Then each one of them gave him some money and clothes, and after feeding him, they took him far from the city. Then they let him know that he was safe and left him alone. In the meantime, Malik Shah kept traveling until he entered the realm of the king of Roum. When he reached a village, he stopped and made this place his abode. After a while he began working in the fields.

As for his mother, Shah Khatun, her longing for her son was great, and she constantly thought of him. However, since she was cut off from news of him, her life was troubled, and she could not sleep nor could she talk about him in front of King Caesar, her husband. Now she had a castrato, who had come with her from the court of her uncle, King Sulayman Shah, and he was intelligent, quick-witted, and wise. So she took him aside one day, and with tears in her eyes, she said, "You have been my eunuch from my childhood to this day, and you know that I cannot speak about my son before the king. Therefore, I ask you to go out and search for news of my son."

"Oh my lady," he replied, "you have kept your son's existence a secret from the beginning, and so even if your son were here right now, you wouldn't be able to entertain him because your honor would be besmirched before the king. Nor would they ever believe you, because the news that circulated many years ago was that your son was slain by his uncle."

"You are right," she said, "and you speak the truth. But if I can find my son alive, I could let him live in this region looking after sheep, and I need not see him, nor does he need to see me."

"How shall I manage this affair?" he asked.

"Here is some money," she replied. "Take all you need and bring me my son or else news of him."

Then they conceived a plan and pretended that they had some business in their own country, namely that she had some buried wealth there from the time of her husband Malik Shah, and nobody knew about it except this eunuch, who had been with her. So it was necessary for him to return and fetch it. Accordingly she told her current husband all about this and asked permission for the eunuch to return to the kingdom of Bahluwan. The king granted him permission to take this journey, and he advised him to make plans to protect himself in case there was trouble. Therefore, the castrato disguised himself in a merchant's outfit and returned to Bahluwan's city, where he made inquiries about the queen's son. Soon he learned that Malik Shah had been imprisoned in an underground dungeon, and that his uncle had released him and sent him to the frontier, where he had been slain by infidels. The eunuch was very upset when he heard about the boy's misfortune. Indeed, he became depressed and did not know what to do. It so happened that one day one of the officers who had helped Malik Shah and had given him money and clothes saw the eunuch in the city clad as a merchant and recognized him. So he approached him and asked him what he was doing in the city.

"I've come to sell merchandise," he said.

"Well, I'll tell you a secret if you can keep it," responded the officer.

"That I can!" answered the eunuch. "What is it?"

"We met the king's nephew, Malik Shah," the officer revealed. "I was with a group of officers and horsemen, and we came across him outside the city gate when we went to water our horses. Then we gave him some money and clothes and sent him in the direction of the land of Roum to be near his mother. We did not want him to be slain by his uncle, Bahluwan."

Upon hearing all this and more, the countenance of the eunuch changed, and he said to the officer, "Your secret is safe with me."

The officer replied, "And you are also safe with me, even though you have come in search of him."

"Indeed, that is my mission," said the eunuch. "His mother will never be able to rest until she has news of him."

"Go in safety," said the officer, "for he is certainly

somewhere in the land of Roum, as I've explained to you."

The castrato thanked him and blessed him, and after mounting his horse, he traveled with the officer a certain distance on the way to Roum.

"This is where we left him," said the officer, and he turned and headed back toward the city. In the meantime the eunuch continued along the road and inquired in every village he entered about the young boy, using the description that the officer had given him. Finally, he came to the village that Malik Shah had made his home. So he entered, dismounted, and asked after the prince, but nobody knew anything about him. Again he was distressed and got ready to depart. Accordingly he mounted his horse, but as he passed through the village, he saw a cow bound with a rope and a young boy asleep by her side holding the halter in his hand. So he looked at him, moved on, and forgot about him. But soon he halted and said to himself, "If the young boy I am searching has become like that sleeping boy whom I just passed, how shall I know him? Alas, all this traveling and work, and it may be for nothing! How can I search for somebody I don't know? Even if I met him face to face, I wouldn't know him."

Upon saying this, he turned around, and after coming to the sleeping boy again, he dismounted and sat down by his side. Since the boy was still sleeping, the eunuch stared at him for a while and said to himself, "For all I know, this young boy may be Malik Shah." Then he began speaking louder and woke the boy.

"Who is your father in this village?" the eunuch asked. "And where do you live?"

The boy sighed and replied, "I am a stranger here."

"Where do you come from and who is your sire?" the castrato continued to ask.

The boy kept answering the questions, and the eunuch kept inquiring until he was certain that he knew him. So he arose and embraced him, kissed him, and wept for joy. He also told him that he had been searching for him and informed hm that he had come in secret and that his mother would be content to know that he was alive and well, even if she could not see him. Then the eunuch reentered the village, and after he bought the prince a horse, they traveled together until they came to the frontier of their own country, where they were attacked by robbers, who took all they had and tied them with rope. Afterward the robbers threw them into a nearby pit and went on their way. The robbers had left them to die, and indeed, they had thrown many people into that pit, all of whom had perished. The eunuch began weeping in that pit, and the boy said to him, "Why are you weeping? What's the use of all your weeping?"

"I'm not weeping because I fear death," the castrato said. "I'm weeping for you and because you have been cursed so badly and because of your mother's heart and all the horrors that you have suffered. I am weeping because your death will be so ignoble after you have endured so much distress."

But Malik Shah responded, "All that has happened to me was preordained and written on my forehead, and whatever is written, nobody has the power to efface. If the term of my life is up, then nobody may defer it."

Then the two of them passed that night and the following day and the next night and the next day in the pit until they were weak with hunger and on the brink of death. All they could do was to groan feebly. Now it so happened that, by the decree of Almighty Allah, King Caesar went forth hunting that morning. He flushed a head of game, and he and his company chased it until they came to the pit. One of the hunters dismounted to slaughter the animal, which had been caught right near the mouth of the pit. All of a sudden he heard a sound of low moaning from the bottom of the pit. So he got up and mounted his horse and waited for the rest of the company to arrive. Then he told the king what he had heard, and Caesar ordered one of his servants to descend into the pit. So the man climbed down and brought out the young man and the eunuch, who had almost lost consciousness. The men cut their bonds and poured wine down their throats until they came to themselves. When the king looked at the eunuch, he recognized him and asked, "Aren't you the one who serves my wife?"

"Yes, my lord," replied the castrato, who prostrated himself before the king.

The king was somewhat astonished and continued to question him.

"How did you happen to come to this place? What happened?'

The eunuch answered, "I went and found the treasure, and I took it this far. But the evil eye was on me, and I was unaware. So some thieves attacked us, seized the money, and threw us into this pit so that we would die, just as they had done with others. But Allah the Most High took pity on us and sent you to rescue us."

The king and his company were flabbergasted by this story, and they praised the Lord for having sent them there. Then the king turned to the castrato and said, "Who is this boy you have with you?"

"Oh king," replied the eunuch, "this is the son of a nurse who belonged to us, and we had left him when he was a little one. I saw him today, and his mother said to me, 'Take him with you.' So this morning I brought him so that he might be a servant to the king. Indeed, he is adroit and clever."

Then the king and his company set about their return to the capital city, and along the way the king questioned the boy about Bahluwan and about how he dealt with his subjects, and the boy responded, "Believe me, oh king, the people are not satisfied with him. Nobody wishes to see him be they high or low."

When the king returned to the palace, he went to see his wife and said to her, "I bring you good news about your eunuch's return." And he told her what had happened and about the young boy whom he had brought with him. When she heard this, she almost went out of her mind, and she would have screamed, but her reason restrained her, and the king said to her, "What is this? Are you overcome with grief because you have lost your treasure or because the eunuch suffered so much?"

"No," she responded quickly. "Believe me, women are just weaklings."

Then the castrato came and told her what had happened to him, and he also informed her about her son, and as he recounted all the perilous adventures of her son, she could do nothing but weep. Then she asked him, "When the king saw him and asked you about him, what did you say?"

"I said to him that this was the son of a nurse who had belonged to us. We had left him as a little one, and he grew up. So I brought him with me to serve the king."

"You did well," she exclaimed and asked him to become the prince's loyal servant.

As for the king, he treated the castrato with even greater kindness and gave the young boy a liberal allowance, and he was allowed to live in the king's palace, to come and go as he pleased and to serve the king. And every day, his situation improved. As for Shah Khatun, she began stationing herself at places where she could watch for him. She gazed upon him from the windows and the balconies. It was like sitting on coals of fire, and yet she could not speak. This is the way things went for a long time, and indeed, her yearning for him was killing her. So she stood and watched for him one day at the door of her chamber. As he came by, she reached out, took him to her bosom, and kissed him on both cheeks. Just at this moment, the majordomo of the king's household suddenly appeared, and he was amazed to see her embrace the young boy. Then he inquired about whose chamber it was where he had seen the incident, and he was told that it belonged to Shah Khatun, the wife of the king. Upon hearing this, he turned around as if he had been struck by lightning, and when the king saw him in such a tremor, he asked, "Out with it! What's the matter?"

"Oh king," he said, "nothing could be more distressing than what I've just seen!"

"What did you see?" asked the king.

And the officer answered, "I saw and now I see that the young boy who came with the eunuch was only brought with him for Shah Khatun. Just now I passed by her chamber door, and she was standing and watching. When the boy came up, she stretched out her arms, took him to her, and kissed him on both cheeks."

When the king heard this, he bowed his head. Amazed and perplexed, he sank into his seat, clutched his beard, and tore at it until he almost plucked it out. Immediately he stood up, went and seized the young boy, and sent him to jail. He also took the eunuch and cast him into an underground dungeon in his palace. After this he went to see Shah Khatun and said to her, "Bravo, by Allah, oh daughter of nobles. Oh you whom kings desired to wed because of your reputation for purity and your famous beauty! How deceiving your appearance is! Now may Allah curse you for having such a different inner character in contrast to your outer appearance. What foul deeds are brought about by such a beautiful exterior! Indeed, I intend to make an example of you and your spineless boy for my liege lords. You did not send your eunuch to search for treasures but for this boy so that he would come into my palace and disgrace me. You have been exceedingly bold, but you will see what I shall do with you all!"

Upon saying this, he spat in her face and left her. Shah Khatun could say nothing, because she knew that if she spoke at that time, he would not have believed one word. Then she humbled herself and beseeched Allah Almighty to come to her aid: "Oh God the Great, You know all about the secrets and what can be sealed and revealed."

This was how she passed the next several days, while the king became utterly despondent. He stopped eating meat and drinking and sleeping and did not know what he should do. "If I slay the eunuch and the young boy," he said to himself, "I shall not be consoled, for they are not to blame. She was the one who sent the castrato to fetch the boy, and my heart does not want to kill all three of them. I had better not be too hasty in order their deaths, for I fear I might repent my actions."

So he kept them in confinement in order to look into the affair.

Now the king had a nurse, a foster mother, on whose knees he had been reared, and she was a woman of understanding and suspected that he was plagued by something terrible, but she did not dare question him. So she went in to see Shah Khatun, and finding her even more despondent than he, she asked what had happened. But the queen refused to answer. However, the nurse continued to coax and question her until the queen made her promise not to say anything if she revealed her secret. Accordingly, the old woman took an oath that she would keep everything secret that the queen told her. Thereupon the queen related her history, first and last, and told her that the young boy was her son. Upon hearing this the old woman prostrated herself before her and said, "This is a right easy matter to fix."

But the queen replied, "By Allah, oh my mother, I prefer my destruction and that of my son than to defend myself with a story that they will not believe, for they will say she has invented this and is pleading only so that she can save herself from shame. Nothing will help me except more suffering."

The old woman was moved by her speech and her wisdom, and she said to her, "Indeed, my daughter, everything you say is true, and I place my faith in Allah that he will allow the truth to shine forth. Have patience. I shall go now to the king and listen to his words and try to do something. May God be with you!"

Thereupon the old woman arose, and when she entered the king's chamber, she found him with his head between his knees in deep pain and sorrow. She sat down by him for a while and talked to him softly.

"Indeed, my son, you are troubling me a great deal," she said. "It's been many days now since you have mounted a horse. You are grieving about something, and I don't know what it is."

"Oh my mother," he replied, "it is all due to that cursed woman, whom I have held in high esteem, and who has deceived me."

Then he related to her the entire story from beginning to end, and she exclaimed, "So your sorrow is due to a woman who is no better than she should be!"

"I was only considering what kind of death they

should have so that the folk will take warning and repent," he said.

"Oh my son," she replied, "beware of doing things precipitate, for it may cause you to repent. You have plenty of time to slay them. When you are certain that they have done wrong, then you can do whatever you want."

"But mother," he said, "I don't need to be assured of anything about the boy who was fetched by the eunuch in her behalf."

"There is, however, something we can use to make her confess everything that is in her heart," she stated, "and then you will know everything."

"What is that?" asked the king.

"I shall bring you the heart of a hoopoe," she replied, "and when the queen goes to sleep, you are to place it on her bosom and ask her everything that you want to know, and she will reveal everything to you. Then you will know the truth."

The king was happy about this and said to his nurse, "Do this quickly, and make sure that nobody knows about it."

So she arose, went straight to the queen, and said, "I have done my business, and it is as follows. Tonight the king will come to you, and you are to pretend that you are sleeping. If he begins asking you questions, you are to answer him as if you were still asleep."

The queen thanked her, and the old lady went away to fetch the bird's heart, which she gave to the king. As soon as night arrived, he went to his wife's chamber and found her on her back asleep. So he sat down by her side and placed the hoopoe's heart on her bosom. Then after waiting awhile to make sure that she was asleep, he said, "Shah Khatun, Shah Khatun, is this how you reward my love for you?"

"What offense have I committed?" she responded.

"What offense can be greater than the one you have committed?" he stated. "You sent for the young boy and brought him here because you lust after him and want to enjoy him."

"I know nothing about carnal desire," she replied.

"Among your pages there are many more who are handsomer and more charming than he is. Yet I have never desired any one of them."

"Why, then, did you embrace him and kiss him?" the king asked.

"This young boy is my son and a piece of my very own flesh," she admitted. "And since I have longed to see him for many years and love him, I could not contain myself and sprang upon him and kissed him."

When the king heard this, he was dazed and amazed and said to her, "Do you have proof that this young man is your son? Indeed, I have a letter from your uncle, King Sulayman Shah, who informed me that your son's uncle, Bahluwan, had cut his throat."

"Yes," she said, "he did cut his throat, but he did not sever the windpipe. So my uncle had the wound sewn and reared him during the time allotted for him to live."

When the king heard this, he said, "This is proof enough for me."

So he got up, and in the middle of the night he sent for the young boy and the eunuch. Then he examined Malik Shah's throat with a candle and saw the scar that extended from ear to ear. It had healed so nicely that it looked like a long thread that had been stretched. Then the king fell to the ground and prostrated himself before Allah, who had delivered the prince from numerous perils and from the distress that he had suffered. He was especially happy because he had delayed the execution and had not been too hasty to slay the boy and the eunuch. Otherwise, he might have sorely regretted his action.

"As for Malik Shah," the young man continued, "he was saved only because his lifetime had been deferred, and this is my situation as well, oh king. I, too, have a deferred term which I shall attain, and I trust in Almighty Allah, who will enable me to triumph over these sinister viziers." After the young man had come to the end of his tale, the king said, "Return him to his prison." When the guards had done this, he turned to his ministers and said, "That young man charmed me once again with his tongue, but I know how much you care about the welfare of my empire, and I appreciate your loyal counsel. Therefore, do not worry, for I shall do everything that you advise me to do." The king's ministers were very pleased when they heard these words, and each one of them had his say. Then the king remarked, "I only deferred his execution so that I might hear his words and talk. Yet, now he will be slain without delay, Therefore, I want you to go and set up a scaffold outside the city and have the crier announce among the folk that they should come and fetch the young man and carry him in a procession to the gallows. You are to instruct the crier to say: 'This is the reward for the man whom the king favored and who has betrayed his majesty!'"

The viziers rejoiced when they heard this, and they could not sleep that night out of joy. Indeed, they made sure that the proclamation would be made and the gallows set up. When the eleventh day arrived, the viziers gathered early in the morning at the king's gate and said to him, "Oh king, the people have assembled from the portals of the palace to the gallows so that they may see the king's order carried out."

So Azadbakht had the prisoner fetched, and when he stood before the king and the ministers, the viziers said to him, "You vile thing, do you still have a desire to live? Can you possibly hope for salvation after this day?"

"Oh wicked viziers," he responded, "shall a man of understanding renounce all hope in Almighty Allah? No matter how much a man may be oppressed, deliverance can come to him in the midst of distress and life from in the midst of death, just as it was in the case of the prisoner who was saved by Allah."

"What is this story?" asked the king.

And the youth answered, "Oh king, they tell

The Story of the Prisoner and How Allah Granted Him Relief

There was once a king of the kings who had a high and mighty palace that overlooked his prison, and during the night he used to hear one of the prisoners say, "Oh my savior, oh you whose salvation is always present, I beg of you to relieve me!"

One day the king grew mad and said to his officers, "That fool of a prisoner is looking for relief from the pain and punishment of his crime. Just who is he?"

"He's only some man who was caught red-handed," they said.

Upon hearing this, the king commanded them to bring the man before him, and when he was present, the king said to him, "Oh fool, you nitwit, how can you be saved when you know you have committed a mortal crime?"

Then he ordered his guards to take him outside the city and crucify him within the sight of the folk. Now it was nighttime, and the soldiers carried him outside the city with the intention of crucifying him. All of a sudden, they were attacked by robbers, who fell upon them with swords and other weapons. Consequently the guards left the man they were supposed to slay and fled. At the same time, the prisoner also took flight and plunged deep into the desert. He had no idea where he was going, and before long he found himself in a thicket. To his surprise, a terrifying lion came at him, and the beast snatched him and threw him down without killing him. Then the lion went up to a tree, uprooted it, covered the man with the tree, and went into the thicket in search of the lioness. As for the man, he knew that only Allah the Most High could save him, and relying upon him for salvation, he said to himself, "What is all this about?" Then he removed the leaves from himself and stood up. There he saw numerous human bones of the people that the lion had devoured, and as he continued to look, behold, he saw a heap of gold lying beside a money belt. Astonished, he gathered up the gold and filled his pockets and fled the thicket. He ran haphazardly because he was afraid that the lion might come after him, and he did not stop running until he came to a village and threw himself down on the ground as if he were dead. He lay there until sunrise, and after he recovered from his travail, he buried the gold and entered the village. Thus Allah provided him with relief, and he got the gold.

"How long are you going to beguile me with your stories?" the king asked. "Your time has run out. The hour of your execution has arrived."

So he ordered the young man to be crucified on the cross. But as the guards were about to hoist him up, behold, the captain of the thieves who had found him and reared him came out of the crowd at that moment and asked, "What is going on here? Why are all the people gathered?"

They informed him that one of the king's pages had committed a great crime and was about to be executed. So the captain of the thieves moved forward, and when he gazed at the prisoner, he recognized him immediately. Without hesitating, he rushed up to him, drew him to his bosom, threw his arms around his neck, and began kissing him on his mouth. Then he began telling his story.

"I found this young man as a baby wrapped in a gown of brocade in the mountains, and I reared him as my son. And he learned our ways. One day we attacked a caravan, but they put us to flight and wounded some of us and took the boy away from us. From that day to this very moment I have searched for him, and now I have finally found him. To be sure, it is him!"

When the king heard this story, he was certain that the young man was his very own son. So he cried out at the top of his voice and rushed toward him. After he embraced the young man, kissed him, and shed tears, he said, "If I had put you to death as was my intention, I would have died of remorse."

Then the king cut the ropes that bound the young

man, and after taking the crown from his head, he put it on the head of his son, whereupon the people burst forth with cries of joy. Trumpets blared. The kettledrums beat. The people rejoiced loud and clear. They decorated the city, and it was a glorious day. Even the birds stopped in their flight to hear the great cries of joy and the clamor of the crying. The army and the folk carried the prince to the palace in a splendid process, and news came to his mother, Bahrjaur, who went out to meet him and embrace him. Finally the king commanded that the prison doors be opened, and he granted amnesty to all who were confined there. For seven days and seven nights they held a huge festival and celebrated with great joy.

This is what happened to the young man. But with regard to the ministers, they were overcome by terror and silence, shame and fright, and they gave themselves up for lost. When the time came, the king sat with his son by his side, and the viziers were on their knees before him. After the king summoned his chief officers and the subjects of the city, the prince turned to the ministers and said to them, "Now you see, you sinister viziers, that Allah can provide speedy relief."

But they did not utter a word, and the king said, "I am content that everything alive rejoices with me this day, even the birds in the sky. But you must be despondent. Indeed, you have shown great hostility toward me. If I had listened to you, I would have certainly have died of sorrow and remorse."

"Oh my father," said the prince, "you have achieved this day of great joy because you were fair, perspicacious, and wise in the deliberation of your affairs. If you had slain me in haste, you would have deeply repented your action. Indeed, whoever prefers haste shall live to regret it."

Soon the king sent for the captain of the robbers and bestowed a robe of honor on him. Then he commanded that all who loved the king should take off their garments and throw them on him. So many robes of honor fell upon the captain that he was weighed down by the clothes. Then Azadbakht appointed him the chief of police of his city. Afterward, the king ordered that nine other posts be set up alongside the first one and said to his son, "You are innocent, and yet these sinister viziers sought to have you slaughtered."

The prince replied, "Oh my sire, my only fault was that I was your loyal counselor and kept watch over your wealth and kept their hands from your treasury. Therefore they became jealous and plotted against me with the intention of slaying me.'

"The time of retribution is at hand, my son," said the king. "What do you think we should do to pay them back for what they have done to you? Indeed, they have schemed to kill you and managed to disgrace you and besmirch my honor among kings."

Then he turned to the viziers and said to them, "Woe to you! What liars you are! Do you have anything to say that will excuse your actions?"

"Oh king," they said, "we have no excuse. We are being tortured by our own sins. Indeed, we planned to kill this young man, and everything turned against us. We plotted evil things, and the tables have been turned against us. Yes, we dug a pit for him, and we ourselves have fallen into it."

So the king commanded that the viziers be hoisted on the posts and crucified, because Allah is just and decrees everyone receive his just due. Then Azadbakht, his wife, and his son lived in joy and happiness until the Destroyer of Delights came to them, and they died. And praise be the Living One, who does not die, and glory to Him whose mercy be with us for ever and ever!

The Tale of Al-Malik al-Nasir and the Three Chiefs of Police

Once upon a time Al-Malik al-Nasir sent for the chiefs of police of Cairo, Bulak, and Forstat and said to them, "I want each one of you to recount the most marvelous thing that has happened to him during his term of office."

They all responded that they would be pleased to recount their adventures, and then the chief of police of Cairo said, "Here is the most wonderful thing that ever happened to me," and he began

The Story of the Chief of Police of Cairo

There were two men in Cairo who had excellent reputations as jurists and who often acted as kazis in cases of murder and injury. But they were both secretly addicted to intrigues with dissolute women, wine, and decadent living. No matter what I did, I was never successful in booking them. As time went by, I began to despair of success. So I ordered the tavern keepers, fruitsellers, merchants, and owners of brothels to inform me whenever these two good men should be engaged in drinking or some other kind of debauchery. It did not matter to me whether I found them alone or together, and I also stated that if either one bought something for their partying, the vendors should tell me. And they all replied, "We shall do your bidding."

Soon a man came to me one night and said, "Oh my

master, I want you to know that these two men are in a nearby house and are doing something wicked."

So I disguised myself, and I and my bodyguard went to the house and knocked on the door. In response, a slave girl came, opened the door, and said, "Who àre you?"

I entered without answering her and saw the two kazis and the master of the house sitting with lewd women by their side and plenty of wine before them. When they saw me, they arose to greet me, and after they gave me the place of honor, they said, "Welcome! You are our illustrious guest, and we hope that you will be a pleasant drinking companion."

This was the way they treated me, without showing a sign of alarm or trouble. Soon the master of the house arose, went out, and returned after a while with three hundred dinars. Then the men said to me without the least bit of fear, "We know, our great lord the wali, it is in your power to disgrace and punish us, but this will bring you nothing in return but trouble and exhaustion. So we believe that it would be better for you if you were to take this money and protect us, for Almighty Allah is named the Protector and loves those among His servants who protect their Moslem neighbors. So you will have your reward in this world and due compensation in the world to come."

Then I said to myself, "I shall take the money and protect them this one time. But if ever again I have them in my power, I shall arrest them." Indeed, the money had tempted me, and I took it and went away, thinking that no one would ever know. But next day, all of a sudden, one of the kazis' messengers came to me and said, "Oh wali, be good enough to answer the summons of the kazis, who expect you to come to their court."

So I arose and accompanied him, even though I did not know the reason why they had summoned me. But when I came into the judge's presence, I saw the two kazis and the master of the house, who had given me money. And it was this man who rose and sued me for three hundred dinars, and I could not deny the debt, for he produced a written obligation, and the kazis testified against me that I owed the amount. Their evidence satisfied the judge, and he ordered me to pay the sum, and I could not leave the court until I had returned the three hundred gold pieces. So I went away in great anger and shame, vowing to cause them trouble and gain vengeance on them. To be sure, I repented that I had not punished them when I had them in my power. Such then is the most remarkable event that happened to me during my term of office.

Thereupon the chief of the Bulak police arose and said, "As for me, oh sultan, the most marvelous thing that happened to me since I became wali was as follows," and he began

The Tale of the Chief of the Bulak Police

I was once in debt to the full amount of three hundred thousand gold pieces, and since I was so distressed by this, I sold all my possessions, but I could only collect a hundred thousand dinars for everything. The result was that I was at a complete loss about what I should do. Then, one night, as I sat alone at my home, I heard a knocking at my door. I told one of my servants to go and see who was at the door, and he returned with a pale face and his muscles quivering. So I asked him, "What's the matter?"

"There is a man at the door," he replied, "and he is half naked, clad in skins, with a sword in his hand and a knife in his belt. With him are some other men who have the same appearance, and they have asked for you."

Well, I took my sword and went out to see who they were, and lo and behold, they were exactly as my servant had described them.

"What do you want?" I asked.

"To tell the truth," they answered, "we are thieves and have just finished doing a job and have come away with a nice haul. So we have decided to give it all to you so that you can pay the debts that sadden and distress you so much."

"Where is the loot?" I asked.

Then they brought in a great chest filled with vessels of gold and silver. When I saw all this, I rejoiced and said to myself, "I can use all this to pay off my debts, and there will be plenty left over for me." So I took the treasure, and after going inside, I thought it would be ignoble of me to let them go away empty-handed. Thereupon I took out the hundred thousand dinars that I had stored away, and I gave the money to them, thanking them for their kindness. They pocketed the money and went their way under the cover of night so that they would not be noticed. But when morning dawned and I examined the contents of the chest, I found the money to be copper and tin and merely plated with gold worth five hundred dirhams at the most. This was a disaster for me, because I had lost all the money I had saved, and my troubles doubled. Such, then, is the most remarkable event that happened to me during my term of office.

Then the chief of police of Forstat rose and said, "Oh my lord, the most marvelous thing that happened to me when I became wali is as follows," and he began

The Story of the Chief of the Forstat Police

I once hanged ten thieves, each on his own gallows, and I commanded the guards to watch over them and to prevent the folk from taking down any of the bodies.

Next morning, when I went to look at them, I found two bodies hanging from one gallows and said to the guards, "Who did this? Where is the tenth gallows?"

But they knew nothing about the matter, and I was about to beat them when they confessed and said, "Oh emir, we fell asleep last night, and when we awoke, we found that someone had stolen one of the bodies, gallows and all. So we were alarmed and were afraid that you would be very angry with us. Just then a peasant came by, and he was driving an ass before him. So we grabbed him, killed him, and hung his body on the gallows in place of the thief who had been stolen."

Now, when I heard this, I was astonished and asked them, "What was he carrying with him?"

"He had a pair of saddlebags on the ass," they said.

"What was in them?" I inquired.

"We don't know," they replied.

So I said, "Bring them here," and when they brought them to me, I ordered them to open them, and behold, there was the body of a murdered man, cut into pieces. Now as soon as I saw this, I was stunned and said to myself, "Glory be to God! The peasant paid for his crime through our hanging. The Lord is not unjust toward His servants!"

And people also tell the tale of

The Thief and the Money-Changer

There was once a money changer, who was carrying a bag of gold coins, and he passed a company of thieves. One of these fellows said to the others, "I, and only I, have the power to steal that man's purse."

"How will you do it?" his friends asked.

"Just watch!" he said, and he followed the money changer, who went into his house and threw the bag on a shelf. Since he had diabetes, he went straight to the toilet to relieve himself, and he called to the slave girl, "Bring me a pitcher of water."

She took the pitcher and followed him into the toilet, leaving the door to the house open. So the thief entered, seized the bag, returned to his companions, and told them what had happened.

"By Allah," they said, "you have played a clever trick. It's not everyone who could have done it. But soon the money changer will come out of the toilet, notice the missing bag of money, and beat and torture the slave. So there's nothing to praise for what you have done. If you really are as clever as you say you are, let's see if you can return and save the girl from being questioned and beaten."

Then the thief went back to the money changer's house and found him punishing the girl because of the missing purse. So he knocked at the door, and the man said, "Who's there?"

"I am the servant of your neighbor in the exchange office," cried the thief.

So the man came out and said, "What do you want?"

"My master sends his greetings and wants to know whether you are deranged, for you left this bag of money at the door of your shop and went away without taking it. If a stranger had come upon it, he would have made off with it. Fortunately, my master saw this and took care of the bag, otherwise you would have certainly lost it for good."

Upon saying this, the thief pulled out the purse and showed it to the money changer, who exclaimed, "Yes, that is my purse," and he put out his hand to take it, but the thief said, "By Allah, I shall not give you this purse until you write a receipt declaring that you have received it. I fear that my master will not believe that you have recovered the purse unless I bring him some writing to that effect with your seal on it."

The money changer went in to write out a receipt, and in the meantime, the thief made off with the bag of money and was thus able to save the slave girl from her beating.

And people also tell the tale of

The Chief of the Kus Police and the Highwayman

One night Ala al-Din, chief of police at Kus, was sitting in his house when all at once a handsome and dignified man came to his door. He was accompanied by a servant carrying a chest on his head, and when he stood at the door, he said to one of the wali's young men, "Go in and tell the emir that I would like to talk to him about some private business."

So the servant went in and told his master, who gave his permission to allow the visitor to enter. Since this man was so handsome and well-dressed, the emir received him with honor and had him seated next to himself.

"What is your wish?" he asked the visitor.

"I am a highwayman," replied the stranger, "and I should like to repent and place myself in your hands. Indeed, I want to turn to Almighty Allah, but I need your help, for I am in your district and under your jurisdiction. Now, I have here a chest with some forty thousand dinars, and nobody is entitled to it but you. So please take it, and give me a thousand dinars of your own money that you have legally earned in exchange so that I may have a little capital to help me in my repentance and to save me from resorting to sinful thievery for my subsistence. And may Allah Almighty reward you!"

After saying all this, he opened the chest and showed the wali that it was full of trinkets, jewels, bullion, gems, and pearls. Of course, the chief of police was amazed and rejoiced at the sight. So he called to his treasurer, "Bring me a purse with a thousand dinars in it!" Then he gave it to the highwayman, who thanked him and went his way into the night. Now, when morning arrived, the emir sent for a goldsmith and showed him the chest and everything in it, but the goldsmith revealed to him that it was nothing but tin, brass, and glass jewels. Upon hearing this news, the wali became enraged and sent his men in search of the highwayman, but no one ever found him.

Fables

The Mouse and the Cat

A cat went out one night to a garden in search of something to devour, but she found nothing and became weak from the cold and rain that had prevailed that night. So she sought for some means to save herself, and as she prowled about in search of prey, she noticed a nest at the foot of a tree. As she drew near it, she sniffed and purred until she smelled a mouse inside and went around the tree to find a place to enter and seize the mouse. When the mouse smelled the cat, he turned his back to her and scraped some dirt to block the nest door. Seeing this, the cat pretended to have a weak voice and cried out, "Why are you doing that, my brother? I've come to seek refuge with you and hope you will take pity on me and harbor me in your nest tonight. I am very weak because of my old age. I can hardly move because I have lost my strength. I am exhausted from venturing into your garden tonight, and you can't imagine how many times I have called upon death to relieve me of my pain! Look, here I am at your door, flat on my back because of the cold and rain, and I implore you, by Allah, to show your charity and give me shelter in the vestibule of your nest. I am but a wretched stranger, and it is said, 'Whoever shelters a wretched stranger in one's home will have paradise as his shelter on Doomsday.' And you, my brother, it will benefit you, and you will earn eternal reward by saving me and allowing me to stay with you this night until morning, when I shall go my own way."

Upon hearing these words, the mouse replied, "Why should I let you enter my nest when you are my natural enemy and your food is my body? Indeed, I am afraid because you might be lying to me, for that is your nature, and there can be no trust in you. There is a proverb that says, 'It is smart not to trust a lecher with a fair woman, nor a penniless man with money, nor fire with fuel.' So it would not be smart for me to trust myself with you."

The cat responded in an extremely faint voice as if she were in a pitiful condition and said, "All these examples are perfectly true, and I cannot deny my offenses against you and your kind. But I implore you to pardon the hostilities of the past between you and me. It is said that 'whoever forgives a creature like himself, his Creator will forgive him his sins.' It is true that I was your foe in the past, but now I am courting your friendship, and they say, 'If you want your foe to become your friend, treat him kindly.' Oh my brother, I swear to you by Allah that I shall bind myself with an oath and that I shall never hurt you again. Indeed, there is a very good reason why I won't: I don't have the power to harm you. So place your trust in Allah, do good, and accept my word of honor."

"How can I accept the word of honor of somebody who is my most treacherous enemy?" the mouse asked. "If the feud between you and me were only one of blood, I wouldn't worry. But it is a clash of the souls, and it is said, 'Whoever trusts his foe might as well stick his hand into a serpent's mouth.'"

"You have cut me to the core," said the cat angrily. "I feel faint. Here I am dying at your doorstep, and you say all this. My blood will be on your hands, for you have it in your power to save me, and these will be my last words to you."

Now the fear of Allah Almighty overcame the mouse, and compassion moved his heart, and he said to himself, "Whoever seeks the help of Allah the Most High against his foe should show compassion and kindness to this foe. I shall rely upon the Almighty in this affair and save the cat from her predicament and earn a divine reward." So he went out and dragged the cat into his nest, where the cat lived until she was well rested and regained her strength. As she was recuperating, she continued to bewail her lack of strength and weakness, and the mouse treated her in a friendly fashion, comforted her, and went about his business. Soon the cat familiarized herself with the nest and took command of it and blocked the exit so the mouse could not escape. Indeed, when the mouse wanted to go out as was his custom, he had to approach the cat, who seized him by her claws and began to bite him. Then she shook him, took him in her mouth, lifted him up and down, and threw him on the ground and ran after him and tortured him. The mouse cried out for help to Allah and began to scold the cat.

"What has happened to the word of honor that you gave me?" he cried. "Is this my reward? I brought you into my nest and trusted you, but now I know 'Whoever relies on his enemy's promise does not deserve salvation for himself.' And, 'Whoever trusts a foe deserves his own destruction.' But I do trust the Creator, for He will save me from you."

Now, just as the cat was about to pounce on him and devour him, a hunter appeared with hunting dogs trained for the chase. One of the hounds passed by the mouth of the nest and heard a great scuffle. He thought it might be a fox, and so he crept into the hole to fetch it, and when he came upon the cat, he seized her, and she was forced to try to save herself. So she dropped the mouse, who managed to escape alive and without a scratch. But the dog broke the cat's neck, dragged her from the nest, and threw her down on the ground dead as a doormat. In the end her death exemplified the saying, "Whoever has compassion will find compassion in the end. Whoever oppresses will learn what it is to be oppressed."

The Fish and the Crab

There was once a pond with a great deal of fish, and it so happened that the water soon began to evaporate, shrink, and dwindle, until there was little water left and the fish were on the verge of death.

"What will become of us?" they cried. "What shall we do? Who can tell us how we can save ourselves?"

Thereupon one of the fish, who was among the oldest and smartest, arose and said, "There is nothing that we can do but ask Allah for salvation. But let us first consult the crab and ask his advice. Come with me and let us listen to his advice, for he is the wisest of us all and knows how to determine the truth."

They all approved of this fish's words and went as a whole to the crab, whom they found squatting in his hole and unaware of their predicament. So they saluted him with the salaam and said, "Oh lord, doesn't our predicament concern you? After all, you are our ruler and the head of the pond."

The crab returned their salutation and replied, "Peace be with you! Tell me exactly what is happening and what you want."

So they told him their situation and how the pond was drying up and that they would be devastated if the water evaporated completely. Then they added, "We've come to you in hope of advice and salvation. You are our chief and the most experienced in the pond."

The crab bowed his head for a while and then said, "Obviously, you fail to understand the workings of the world, because you have given up hope for the mercy of Allah Almighty. But He is the one who provides for all creatures. Don't you know that Allah takes care of all his creatures and that He determined their daily food before their creation and that He appointed each of His creatures a fixed term of life and certain provisions? Why then should we burden ourselves with a concern for something when we can never know His secret purpose? Therefore, it is my advice that you had better seek Allah Almighty's aid, and you had better clear your conscience with the Lord in public and private and pray to Him to deliver us from our predicament. Indeed, Allah the Most High does not disappoint the expectations of those who put their trust in Him and does not reject the petitions of those who revere Him. When we have mended our ways, our affairs will be set, and all will be well. When winter comes and our land is deluged through the prayers of the just, He will not destroy the good that He has built up. So it is my counsel that we be patient and wait to see what Allah will do with us. If death comes as it does, we shall be at peace with ourselves, and if something happens that will cause our flight, we shall flee and leave our land to go wherever Allah wants us to go."

"You speak the truth," said all the fish with one voice. "May Allah bless you and keep you well."

Then they all returned to their places in the pond, and in a few days the Almighty brought about a violent storm, and when the rain came, the pond was fuller than it ever had been before.

The Crow and the Serpent

A crow once dwelt in a tree with his wife, and they were both content with their lives. When the time came for the hatching of their young in midsummer, a serpent came out of its hole, crawled up the tree, and wriggled around the branches until it came to the crow's nest, where it coiled itself up, and it lived there for the rest of the summer. So the crow and his wife were driven away and could not have any offspring because they had no place to live.

When the hot days of summer went by, the serpent went back to its own place, and the crow said to his wife, "Let us thank Almighty Allah, who has saved us from the serpent even though we were not able to have little ones this year. But the Lord will not cut off all our hope. So let us express our gratitude to Him for having kept us safe and sound. Indeed, we have nobody other to trust, and if He wills it, we shall live to see next year and have young ones at that time."

Next summer, when the hatching season came around, the serpent sallied forth from its place and made for the crows' nest. But as it was coiling itself on a branch, a hawk swooped down, struck its claws into it, and tore it apart so that it fell to the ground, where the ants came and made a feast out of it. So the crow and his wife lived in peace and quiet. Indeed, they bred a large brood and thanked Allah for their safety and for the young that were born to them.

The Wild Ass and the Jackal

There was once a jackal that used to leave his lair every day and search for his daily bread. Now one day when he was roaming around a certain mountain, and when the day was done, he set out to return to his lair and met another jackal. Then they began to tell each other of the quarry they had caught.

"The other day I came upon a wild ass," said one of them, "and I was starving because I had not eaten for three days. I rejoiced in this and thanked Almighty Allah for bringing him into my power. Then I tore out his heart and ate it until I was full, and returned home. That was three days ago, and since then I've had nothing to eat. But I'm still full of the meat from the ass."

When the other jackal heard his story, he was envious and said to himself, "I must eat the heart of a wild ass."

So he stopped eating for some days until he became emaciated and near death. He did not stir or try to get food, but lay in his lair. And while he was lying there, two hunters appeared one day in quest of quarry, and they came upon the trail of a wild ass. They followed him and tracked him all day. Finally, one of them shot an arrow at him which pierced his vitals and reached his heart so that he fell dead in front of the jackal's hole. Then the two hunters went up to him, and when they found the ass, they pulled out the shaft from his heart, but only the wood came out, and the sharp tip of the arrow remained in the ass's heart. So they left him lying there and expected other wild beasts would flock to it. But when evening arrived and no animals appeared, they returned to their dwelling.

In the meantime, the jackal had heard the commotion in front of his cave and decided to lie quiet until nightfall. Then he came out of his lair, groaning from weakness and hunger. When he saw the dead ass at his door, he rejoiced so much that he almost soared into the air. "Praise be to Allah," he cried. "He has brought me what I wished without having me work for it! Truly, I had lost hope of coming across a wild ass or anything else. Surely the Almighty has sent him to me and driven him to my homestead."

Then he sprang onto the body of the ass, tore open its belly, and thrust his head and nose into the entrails until he found the heart and swallowed it. But as soon as he had done so, the arrow struck deep into his gullet, and he could neither get it down into his belly or regurgitate it. So he prepared himself for death and said, "Truly, it is not fitting for any creature to seek things over and beyond that which Allah has allotted him. If I had been content with what Allah had provided me, I would not be about to die."

The Crows and the Hawk

There was once a large oasis in a certain desert, and it was full of rills, trees, fruit, and birds singing the praises of Allah Almighty day and night. Among the inhabitants was a flock of crows that led the happiest of lives. Now they were governed by a crow, who ruled them with mildness and benevolence so they lived with him in peace and contentment. Since they ordered their affairs in a wise way, none of the other birds could do anything against the crows. Soon, however, it so happened that their chief had to go the way all creatures have to go, and he died. Thereupon the other crows went into deep mourning, and their grief was made all the greater because there was no one among them who could fill his place. So they all assembled and took counsel and discussed who would be the best and most pious among them to become their new leader. And a group of them chose one crow and asserted he would be the most appropriate to become king, while another group objected to him and wanted nothing to do with him. Soon the dissension and division led to heated debate and strife. But finally they agreed among themselves that they would gather in one place the following morning and see who would fly into the sky the highest, and whoever soared the highest would be appointed ruler and king."

The next day, they did as they agreed and took flight, but each one of them thought that he had flown higher than his comrade and cried out, "I am higher." Then another said, "No, I am higher." Finally, the lowest among them said, "Just look above you, and whoever is the highest will be our chief."

So they all raised their eyes, and they saw a hawk soaring above them.

"We all agreed," they said, "that whichever bird flies the highest would be made king. Behold, the hawk is the highest."

So they all accepted him as their king and summoned him to their assembly and said, "Oh father of good, we have chosen you to be our ruler so that you may govern our affairs."

The hawk consented and said, "By Allah, you shall prosper under my rule."

So they rejoiced and made him king. But after a while, he began taking a group of them every day and flying far off to a cave where he struck them down, then ate their eyes and brains and threw their bodies into the river. And he intended to continue doing this until they were all destroyed. When the crows saw their numbers diminish, they flocked to him and said, "Oh king, we have come to you because we are troubled. Ever since we made you king, there are groups of us that appear to have disappeared, and we do not know why. We are especially disturbed because most of them were of high rank and were your personal attendants. Now we are concerned about our own safety."

Upon hearing this, the hawk became furious and said to them, "Truly, you are the murderers, and yet you are accusing me!"

Immediately, he pounced upon them and tore ten of their chiefs to pieces in front of the rest, threatened them, and drove them out with a beating. So they repented for what they had done and said, "We have not had one good day since the death of our first king, especially since this stranger has become our ruler. But we deserve our sufferings even if he were to destroy every last one of us. Indeed, there is a saying that serves as a good example for us: 'Whoever foolishly allows a stranger to rule over him will soon feel the domination of his foe.' And now there is nothing for us to do but to flee for our lives, or else we shall perish."

So they took flight, spread out, and settled in various places.

The Spider and the Wind

A spider once attached herself to a high gate, spun her web there, and dwelled in peace. She gave her thanks to the Almighty, who had made this place comfortable and safe from noxious reptiles. She lived this way a long time and continued to give thanks to Allah for her comfort and regular supply of daily bread until the Creator decided to test her and see how grateful and patient she was. So he sent her a strong East Wind that carried her away, web and all, and cast her into the water. The waves washed her ashore, and she thanked the Lord for saving her and began to scold the wind. "Oh Wind," she cried, "why have you treated me like this, and what good is it to you that you've carried me far from my dwelling where I was safe and secure on top of that gate?'

"Oh spider," said the Wind, "haven't you learned that this world is a house of calamities? Tell me, who can boast of lasting happiness so that you can make a portion of it yours? Don't you know that Allah tempts all His creatures in order to test their powers of patience? How dare you scold me when I've saved you from the vast ocean?"

"Your words are true, oh Wind," replied the spider. "But I still want to escape from this strange land to which you have carried me."

"Stop your complaining," said the Wind, "for I shall soon restore you to your place on the gate."

So the spider waited patiently for the Northeast Wind to stop blowing, and there arose a Southwest Wind, which gently swept the spider up and flew her toward her dwelling place. When the spider reached her abode, she recognized it and clung to it with all her life.

The Jackals and the Wolf

A pack of jackals went out one day to seek food, and as they were prowling about, they came upon a dead camel and began talking among themselves. "Truly, we have found something that will furnish us food for some time. But we are afraid that one of the stronger will take advantage of the weak and cause them to die. Therefore, we had best choose one of us to judge among ourselves and assign each one his portion so the strong may not dominate the weak."

As they were consulting about this matter, a wolf suddenly appeared, and one of the jackals said to the others, "This is a good idea, but let us make the wolf our judge, for he is the strongest of beasts, and his father was our sultan in the past. So let us hope in Allah's name that he will bring about justice."

Accordingly, they approached the wolf and told him what they had decided and said, "We want to make you our judge so you may give each one of us our daily portion of the meat according to each one's need. Otherwise the strong might dominate the weak, and some of us might be destroyed."

The wolf accepted and told them he would govern their affairs and allotted to each one that same day what he thought was fair, but he said to himself, "If I divide this camel among these weaklings, I shall receive nothing but the small part they will assign me, and if I eat it alone, they cannot harm me because I and my house have always preyed upon them. Who, then, is to hinder me from taking it all for myself? Surely, it is Allah who has brought me this meat as my provision without any obligation to them. So it's best that I keep the meat for myself, and from tomorrow on, I shall not give them anything."

So, the next morning, when the jackals came to him, as was their custom, they sought their food and said, "Oh lord, give us our daily provisions."

"I have nothing left to give you," he responded.

Therefore they went away and were very troubled.

"Truly, Allah has placed us in a terrible predicament because of this foul traitor," they said. "He has no regard for Allah, nor does he fear Him. But we have neither the power nor any ideas of how to overcome him."

"Perhaps," added one of them, "it was hunger that drove him to do this today. So let him eat his fill, and tomorrow we shall go to him again."

Accordingly, the next day, they went to the wolf and said, "Oh lord, we gave you authority over us so that you would divide each day's meat among us and provide justice for the weak against the strong. We also expected that when these provisions were finished, you would try to get us more so that we would always be under your governance. Now we are suffering from hunger because we have not eaten these past two days, and we would like our daily ration. Naturally you are free to dispose of all the rest as you want."

But the wolf did not deign to give them an answer and remained hard, and when they tried to change his mind, he would not listen. Then one of the jackals said to the others, "There is nothing we can do but go to the lion and place ourselves under his protection and give him the camel. If he guarantees us some part of the camel, we shall be fortunate, and if not, he still deserves to have the camel more than the scurvy rascal of a wolf."

So they went to the lion and told him all about what had happened with the wolf. "We are your slaves," they said, "and we have come to seek your protection so you may save us from this wolf, and we will be your thralls."

When the lion heard their story, he was jealous and went with them to the wolf, who fled when he saw the lion approaching. But the lion ran after him, seized him, tore him to pieces, and restored the camel to the jackals.

Such is what happens when a king neglects the affairs of his subjects.

The Partridge and the Tortoises

Some tortoises lived on an island that was full of trees, fruit, and rills, and it happened one day that a partridge was passing over the island and was overcome by the heat and fatigue. Therefore he decided to stop there and went looking about for a cool place. Soon he spotted the abode of the tortoises and landed near their home.

Now they chanced to be away from their dwelling place, foraging for food. When they returned, they found the partridge there, and his beauty pleased them. Indeed, he was so lovely that they extolled the Creator for bringing him to them, and they began to dote on him.

"To be sure," they said, "this is the godliest of birds," and they all began to caress him and treat him with great kindness.

When he saw that they looked at him affectionately, he returned their feelings and decided to dwell with them. He would fly away in the morning to go wherever he wanted and return in the evening to pass the night with them. He continued to do this for a long time, until the tortoises, who were desolate because he was gone most of the day and they only saw him during the night, said to each other, "Indeed, we love this partridge, and he has become our true friend, but we cannot bear to part from him during the day. So how can we find some way to keep him with us always?"

"Don't worry, my sisters," said one of them. "I shall manage to get him to stay with us all the time."

"If you do this," they said, " we will always be indebted to you."

So when the partridge came back from his feeding place and sat down among them, the wily tortoise drew near him and began blessing him and said, "Oh my lord, Allah has witnessed our love for you just as He has moved you to love us. As a result you have become a friend and comrade in this desert. Now the best of times for those who love one another is when they are together, and the worst of times is when they are separated and absent. Now you part from us at the peep of day and do not return to us until sundown. During the day, we are desolate without your company. Indeed, this is very troublesome for us, and we would like to know the reason for your leaving us."

"Indeed," replied the partridge, "I love you, too, and yearn for you even more than you can yearn for me. Nor is it easy for me to leave you. But I have little to say about this, for I am a fowl with wings and may not always dwell with you because that is not my nature. As a bird with wings, I cannot remain still except when I sleep at night. But as soon as it is day, a bird is accustomed to fly off and seek his morning meal wherever he wants."

"You have spoken the truth," said the tortoise. "Nevertheless, he who has wings never has any rest during all the seasons. Whatever good he gets from all this also brings him harm, and the highest aims in life are rest and comfort. Now, Allah has fostered love and friendship between us, and we are afraid that some of your enemies might catch and kill you, and we would be denied the sight of your countenance."

"True!" said the partridge. "But what advice do you have for me?"

"My advice," stated the tortoise, "is that you pluck out the feathers on your wings that enable you to fly, and stay with us in tranquillity. You can eat our meat and drink our drink and enjoy all the fruit in this area. We shall rest in this fruitful place and enjoy each other's company."

The partridge was persuaded by her speech and wanted to have a restful life. So he plucked out the feathers on his wings, one by one, as the tortoise had suggested. Then he set up his dwelling with them and contented himself with the pleasant and peaceful life they led. Soon, however, a weasel appeared, and when he noticed that the partridge's wings were plucked so that he could not fly, he rejoiced and said to himself, "Truly, that partridge over there has a good deal of fat and not many feathers." So he went up to him and seized him, whereupon the partridge called out to the tortoises for help. But when they saw the weasel take him, they drew back and huddled together, and as they watched how the beast tortured the bird, they wept and choked from their sobbing.

"Is that all you can do, weep?" asked the partridge.

"Oh brother," they replied, "we have neither the power nor the resources to fight a weasel."

Upon hearing this the partridge was distressed, lost all hope for his life, and cried out to them, "It's not your fault but my own. I shouldn't have listened to you and plucked out the feathers that I used for flying. Indeed, I deserve this death for having listened you. Sometimes best friends can inadvertently help one's best enemies."

Afterword

No other work of oriental literature has had such a profound influence on the western world as *The Thousand and One Nights*. Translated first into French between 1704 and 1717 by Antoine Galland (1646–1715), a gifted orientalist, the *Nights* spread quickly throughout Europe and then to North America. The amazing success of the *Nights* was due largely to the remarkable literary style of Galland's work, which was essentially an adaptation of an Arabic manuscript of Syrian origins and oral tales that he recorded in Paris from a Maronite Christian Arab from Aleppo named Youhenna Diab or Hanna Diab.

Galland was born in Picardy and studied at the Collège du Plessus in Paris. His major field of study was classical Greek and Latin, and in 1670, thanks to his command of these languages, he was called upon to assist the French ambassador in Greece, Syria, and Palestine. After a brief return to Paris in 1674, he worked with the ambassador in Constantinople from 1677 to 1688, during which time he perfected his knowledge of Turkish, modern Greek, Arabic, and Persian. In addition he collected valuable manuscripts and coins for the ambassador. Back in Paris, he devoted the rest of his life to oriental studies and published historical and philological works such as *Paroles remarquables, bons mots et maximes des Orientaux* ("Remarkable Words, Sayings and Maxims of the Orientals," 1694).

One of his great achievements was to assist Barthélemy d'Herbelot in compiling the *Bibliothèque orientale*, which was the first major encyclopedia of Islam, with more than eight thousand entries about Middle Eastern people, places, and things. When d'Herbelot died in 1695, Galland continued his work, and he published the completed dictionary in 1697. But, by far, Galland's major contribution to European and oriental literature was his translation or, one could say, "creation" of the *Nights*, which began during the 1690s when he obtained a manuscript of "The Voyages of Sinbad"; he published the Sinbad stories in 1701. Because of the success of this work, he began translating and adapting a four-volume Arabic manuscript in French and added such stories as "Prince Ahmed and the Fairy Pari-Banou," "Aladdin," "Ali Baba," and "Prince Ahmed and His Two Sisters." By the time the last volume of his *Nights* was published posthumously in 1717, he had fostered a vogue for oriental literature and had altered the nature of the literary fairy tale in Europe and North America.

In addition to this literary vogue, the enormous European interest in and curiosity about the Orient, stimulated through trade and travel reports, contributed to the popularity of the *Nights*. At first the tales were famous chiefly among the literate classes, who had direct access to the different English, German, Italian, and Spanish translations of Galland's work. However, because of their exotic appeal, there were many cheap and bowderlized editions of the *Nights* in the eighteenth century that enabled the tales to be diffused among the common people and to become part of their oral tradition. Moreover, they were also sanitized and adapted for children. By the end of the nineteenth century, the *Arabian Nights* had become a household name in most middle-class families in Europe and North America, were an important source of knowledge about Arabic culture for intellectuals, and were known by word of mouth among the great majority of the people.

The development of the *Nights* from the secular oriental imagination of the Middle Ages into a classical work for western readers is a fascinating one. The tales in the collection can be traced to three ancient oral cultures, Indian, Persian, and Arab, and they probably circulated in the vernacular hundreds of years before they were written down some time between the ninth and fourteenth centuries. The apparent model for the literary versions of the tales was a Persian book entitled *Hazar Afsaneh* ("A Thousand Tales"), translated into Arabic in the ninth century, for it provided the framework story of a caliph who for three years slays a new wife each night after taking her maidenhead, and who is finally diverted from this cruel custom by a vizier's daughter, assisted by her slave girl. During the next seven centuries, various storytellers, scribes, and scholars began to record the tales from this collection and others and to shape them either independently or within the framework of the Scheherazade Shahryar narrative. The tellers and authors of the tales were anonymous, and their styles and language differed greatly; the only common distinguishing feature was that they were written in a colloquial language called Middle Arabic that had its own peculiar grammar and syntax.

By the fifteenth century there were three distinct layers that could be detected in the collection of those tales that came to form the nucleus of what became known as *The Thousand and One Nights*: (1) Persian tales that had some Indian elements and had been adapted into Arabic by the tenth century; (2) tales recorded in Baghdad between the tenth and twelfth centuries; and (3) stories written down in Egypt between the eleventh and fourteenth centuries. By the nineteenth century, at the time of Richard Burton's unexpurgated translation, *The Book of the Thousand Nights and a Night* (1885–86), there were four "authoritative" Arabic editions, more than a dozen manuscripts in Arabic, and the Galland work that one could draw from and include as part of the tradition of the *Nights*. The important Arabic editions are as follows:

Calcutta I, 1814–18, 2 vols. (also called ed. Shirwanee)
Bulak, 1835, 2 vols. (also called the Cairo edition)
Calcutta II, 1839–42, 4 vols. (also called ed. W. H. Macnaghten)
Breslau, 1825–38, 8 vols., ed. Maximilian Habicht

In English, the Burton translation became the basis for numerous books for adults and children in the twentieth century. Considered one of the greatest scholar-explorers of the nineteenth century, Burton (1821–90) was the son of a retired lieutenant colonel and was educated in France and Italy during his youth. By the time he enrolled at Trinity College, Oxford, in 1840, he could speak French and Italian fluently, along with the Béarnais and Neapolitan dialects, and he had an excellent command of Greek and Latin. In fact, he had such an extraordinary gift that he eventually learned twenty-five other languages and fifteen dialects. Yet, this ability was not enough to help him adapt to life and the proscriptions at Oxford. He soon encountered difficulties with the Oxford administration and was expelled in 1842. His troubles there may have been due to the fact that he was raised on the Continent and never felt at home in England. Following in his father's footsteps, he enlisted in the British army and served eight years in India as a subaltern officer. During his time there, he learned Arabic, Hindi, Marathi, Sindhi, Punjabi, Teugu, Pashto, and Miltani, which enabled him to carry out some important intelligence assignments, but he was eventually forced to resign from the army because some of his espionage work became too controversial.

After a brief respite (1850–52) with his mother in Boulogne, France, during which time he published four books on India, Burton explored the Nile Valley and was the first westerner to visit forbidden Moslem cities and shrines. He participated in the Crimean War in 1855, then explored the Nile again (1857–58), and in 1860 he took a trip to Salt Lake City, Utah, to do research for a biography of Brigham Young. In 1861, Burton married Isabel Arundell, the daughter of an aristocratic family, and accepted a position as consul in Fernando Po, a Spanish island off the coast of West Africa, where he remained until 1864. Thereafter, he was British consul in Santos, Brazil (1864–68), Damascus, Syria (1868–71), and finally Trieste, Italy, until his death in 1890. Wherever he went, Burton wrote informative anthropological and ethnological studies such as *Sindh, and the Races*

That Inhabit the Valley of the Indus (1851) and *Pilgrimage to El-Medinah and Mecca* (1855–56), composed his own poetry such as *The Kasidah* (1880), and translated unusual works of erotica such as *Kama Sutra of Vatsyayana* (1883) and significant collections of fairy tales such as Basile's *The Pentamerone* (1893). Altogether he published forty-three volumes about his explorations and travels, more than a hundred articles, and thirty volumes of translations.

Burton's *Nights* is generally recognized as one of the finest *unexpurgated* translations of William Hay Macnaghten's Calcutta II edition (1839–42). The fact is, however, that Burton took over and plagiarized part of John Payne's *The Book of the Thousand Nights and One Night* (1882–84) so that he could publish his translation quickly and acquire the private subscribers to Payne's edition. Payne (1842–1916), a remarkable translator and scholar of independent means, had printed only five hundred copies of his excellent unexpurgated edition, for he had not expected much of a demand for the expensive nine-volume set. However, there were a thousand more subscribers who wanted his work, and since he was indifferent with regard to publishing a second edition, Payne gave Burton permission to offer his "new" translation to these subscribers about a year after Payne's work had appeared. Moreover, Burton profited a great deal from Payne's spadework (apparently with Payne's knowledge). This is not to say that Burton's translation (which has copious anthropological notes and an important "Terminal Essay") should not be considered his work. He did most of the translation by himself, and only toward the end of his ten volumes did he apparently plagiarize, most likely without even realizing what he was doing. In contrast to Payne, Burton was more meticulous in respecting word order and the exact phrasing of the original; he included the division into nights with the constant intervention of Scheherazade and was more competent in translating the verse. In addition, he was more insistent on emphasizing the erotic and bawdy aspects of the *Nights*. As he remarked in his introduction, his object was "to show what *The Thousand Nights and a Night* really is. Not, however, for reasons to be more fully stated in the Terminal Essay, by straining *verbum reddere verbo*, but by writing as the Arab would have written in English."

The result was a quaint, if not bizarre and somewhat stilted, English that makes for difficult reading today. Even in his own day his language was obsolete, archaic, and convoluted. Although Burton and John Payne, whose translation preceded Burton's, relied on the Calcutta II and Breslau editions for their translations, neither these two nor the other editions can be considered canonical or definitive. There was never a so-called finished text by an identifiable author or editor. In fact, there were never 1,001 nights or stories, and the title was originally *One Thousand Nights*. When and why the tales came to be called *The Thousand and One Nights* is unclear. The change in the title may stem from the fact that an odd number in Arabic culture is associated with luck and fortune, and it also indicates an exceedingly large number. The editions vary with regard to content and style, and though there is a common nucleus, the versions of the same tale are often different. Nevertheless, together the various editions, along with the manuscripts and Galland's work, can be considered to constitute what has become accepted in the West as *The Thousand and One Nights*. In sum, as Robert Irwin as pointed out in the most informative scholarly study of the tales to date, *The Arabian Nights: A Companion*, "the *Nights* are really more like the New Testament, where one cannot assume a single manuscript source, nor can one posit a fixed canon. Stories may have been added and dropped in each generation," including today's.

As already mentioned, the tales of the *Nights* have been published in all western languages either separately or in collections of different kinds ever since the eighteenth century. The anonymous editors of the *Nights* consistently and purposely chose a core of forty-two tales that continually reappeared in the four different Arabic editions and Galland's work. Without disregarding the entertaining and humorous aspects of these stories, they are primarily *lessons* in etiquette, aesthetics, decorum, religion, government, history, and sex. Though there are many sea adventures, mysterious caves, and deserts, the action of the tales is primarily in cities where criminals, confidence men, police chiefs, wily women, and members of the wealthy classes mix and seek their fortunes. Together the tales represent a compendium of the religious beliefs and superstitions of the time, and they also convey the aspirations and wishes of a strong middle class, for most of the tales concern merchants and artisans, who continually take risks to make their fortune. Since they are daring and adventurous, they can survive only through cunning, faith in Allah, and mastery of words. That is, there is an artistic side to them. Like Scheherazade, most of the protagonists are creative types, who save themselves and fulfill their destiny because they can weave the threads of their lives together in narratives that bring their desires in harmony with divine and social laws. Narration is raised to an art *par excellence*, for the nights are paradoxically moments of light, epiphanies, through which the listeners gain insight into the mysteries and predicaments that might otherwise overwhelm them and keep them in darkness.

In the tales that concern the Caliph Harun al-Rashid, who actually existed, the king's curiosity is always rewarded, for when he goes out among the people he learns the most astonishing things about his subjects and also about strangers. Their stories in "The Caliph's Night Adventure" and "The Sleeper and the Waker" enable him to grasp the difficulties that the common folk are encountering, and he will use the experiences that he gains to rule more wisely. But not only does storytelling pass on wisdom; the very art itself is apparently necessary for survival. The framework story of the *Nights* depends on the ability of Scheherazade to weave a tale filled with suspense and a pertinent message so adroitly that it will move the listener to act in a manner that the storyteller seeks. In this respect the storyteller casts a spell and demonstrates the power of a story to change a life and to save a life. In "The Porter and the Three Ladies of Baghdad," "The Craft and Malice of Women," and "The Ten Viziers," there are a series of fascinating tales that are intended to persuade a powerful ruler to save the lives of people who are unjustly accused of crimes that they did not commit. In some instances, a sultan is challenged to kill his own son despite the fact that the regent's fame depends on the survival of his son. In other stories such as "The Tale of Zayn al-Asnam," the father leaves a mysterious bequest that tests the son's fidelity. Nothing is whatever it seems to be in the *Nights*, because jinnees are likely to appear at any moment, and they may be good or evil depending on whether their allegiance is to Allah. Thieves and highwaymen are everywhere, and in "The Tale of Al-Malik al-Nasir and the Three Chiefs of Police," we learn that con men are very rarely caught, and their victims are often the police, who may have been thieves themselves at one point in their lives. The tales told by and about the police are intended to warn readers about deception, while the fables reflect upon power relations in the animal kingdom and demonstrate how the weak must be constantly on their guard against their more powerful superiors. Cunning is always necessary for survival as well as fortune. In "Abdullah the Fisherman and Abdullah the Merman," one of the rare science-fiction tales in the *Nights*, Abdullah the fisherman is blessed by his friendship with the baker and by his chance discovery of Abdullah the merman, who leads him into a futuristic world. Abdullah the fisherman's fortune depends, however, on his faith in Allah, and neither he nor any of the protagonists in the *Nights* can ever succeed without Allah's aid.

The constant appeal to Allah in all the tales indicates that the characters have little faith in the temporal order, which is either unjust or breaks down. Despite the long period of congestion and the different authors/editors, the tales are consistent in the way they derive their force from the tension between individual desire and social law. As Burton recognized, despite the fantastical elements, the tales tell life as it is, and they expose hypocrisy, deceit, and, most of all, despotism. In fact, in the figure of Scheherazade, they empower the oppressed, who fulfill their deepest desires in ways they had thought were unimaginable. Yet, everything is imaginable in the *Nights*, and it is no doubt the miraculous realization of the unimaginable in the tales that drew readers and still draws them to the *Nights* today.

In regard to the development of the fairy tale as genre in the West, *The Thousand and One Nights* played and continues to play a unique role. From the moment Galland translated and invented his *Nights*, the format, style, and motifs of the so-called Arabian tales had a profound effect on how other European writers were to define and conceive fairy tales. In some respects, the *Nights* are more important and famous in the West than they are in the Orient. Robert Irwin discusses this point in his chapter on the European and American "children of the nights" in his critical study, and he shows how numerous authors were clearly influenced by *The Thousand and One Nights*: in France, Voltaire, Anthony Hamilton, Thomas Simon Guellette, Crébilon fils, Denis Diderot, and Jacques Cazotte; in England, Joseph Addison, Samuel Johnson, William Beckford, Horace Walpole, Robert Southey, Samuel Coleridge, Thomas De Quincey, George Meredith, and Robert Louis Stevenson; in Germany, Wilhelm Heinrich Wackenroder, Friedrich Schiller, Wilhelm Hauff, and Hugo von Hofmannsthal; in America, Washington Irving, Edgar Allan Poe, and Herman Melville. In recent times such gifted writers as John Barth, Jorge Luis Borges, Steven Millhauser, and Salman Rushdie have given evidence of their debt to the *Nights*. In particular it was Borges who, in his essay "The Translators of the 1001 Nights," superbly summed up the ironic significance that the Arabian tales had and will continue to have for the literary fairy tale and readers of fairy tales in the West: "Enno Littmann observes that *The 1001 Nights* is, more than anything, a collection of marvels. The universal imposition of that sense of the marvels. The universal imposition of that sense of the marvelous on all Occidental minds is the work of Galland. Let there be no doubt of that. Less happy than we, the Arabs say they have little regard for the original: they know already the men, the customs, the talismans, the deserts, and the demons that those histories reveal to us."

—Jack Zipes

Glossary

Abbas   uncle of Mohammed, died 653; he was a
   wealthy merchant and chief supporter of Islam; his
   descendants founded the Abbasid dynasty of caliphs
   (750–1258).
abd   servant of
abu   father of
bastinado   beating, punishment, also used to make
   someone confess to a crime
bint   daughter of
calender   a member of the Sufistic order of wandering
   mendicant dervishes. Sufism was a system of Moham-
   medan mysticism developed in Persia.
Copt   a descendant of the ancient Egyptians
dervish   a member of a Moslem order who takes vows
   of poverty and austerity
divan   a royal court where a council is held, or a large
   reception room.
emir   a chieftain or military commander, a title given
   to descendants of Mohammed through his daughter
   Fatima
fakih   a doctor of law and religion
fakir   a religious mendicant
Fatihah   the opening chapter of the Koran
Ghusl ablution   complete ablution, washing of hands
gobbo   a hunchback
Hammam bath   bath for convalescence and relaxation,
   a necessity and a luxury
ibn   son of
ifrit   jinnee, usually an evil one
ifritah   female ifrit
imam   the leader at the prayer niche

jinn collective name for jinnees and jinneyahs

jinnee suspernatural being; genie

jinneyah female jinnee

kasidah ode, elegy

kazi a chief justice, judge in religious matters, the great legal authority of a country

khan a place of lodging, caravanserai, "hotel"

lign aloes the soft resinous wood of an East Indian tree, used for making nadd, a perfume

lisam veil mouth band

mameluke a white slave trained to arms

marid jinnee

nabob a viceroy, governor, or man of great wealth

olema the learned in the law

sheikh an old man, elder, chief

vizier minister of state

Wuzu ablution a kind of ablution necessary before joining in prayers

Selected Bibliography

Major English Translations

Burton, Richard F. *The Book of the Thousand Nights and a Night. A Plain and Literal Translation of the Arabian Nights Entertainment.* 10 vols. Stoke Newington: Kamashastra Society, 1885–86.

——. *Supplemental Nights to the Book of the Thousand Nights and a Night, with notes anthropological and explanatory.* 6 vols. Stoke Newington: Kamashastra Society, 1886–88.

Lane, Edward William. *A New Translation of the Tales of a Thousand and One Nights; Known in England as the Arabian Nights' Entertainments.* London: Charles Knight & Co., 1838–40.

Payne, John. *The Book of the Thousand Nights and One Night.* 9 vols. London: Villon Society, 1882–84.

——. *Tales from the Arabic of the Breslau and Calcutta Editions of the Book of the Thousand and One Nights.* 3 vols. London: Villon Society, 1884.

——. *Alaeddin and the Enchanted Lamp; Zein ul Asnam and the King of the Jinn.* London: Villon Society, 1889.

Secondary Literature

Ali, Muhsin Jassin. *Scheherazade in England: A Study of Nineteenth-Century English Criticism of the Arabian Nights.* Washington, D.C.: Three Continents Press, 1981.

Bencheikh, Jamel Eddine. *Les Mille et une Nuits ou la parole prisonnière.* Paris: Gallimard, 1988.

419

Burton, Richard F. "Terminal Essay" in *The Book of the Thousand Nights and a Night. A Plain and Literal Translation of the Arabian Nights Entertainment.* Vols. 5–6. New York: Heritage Press, 1934. Pp. 3653–3870.

Caracciolo, Peter L., ed. *The Arabian Nights in English Literature: Studies in the Reception of "The Thousand and One Nights" into British Culture.* New York: St. Martin's Press, 1988.

Clinton, Jerome W. "Madness and Cure in the 1001 Nights." *Studia Islamica* 61 (1985): 107–25.

Conant, Martha Pike. *The Oriental Tale in England in the Eighteenth Century.* New York: Columbia University Press, 1908.

Gerhardt, Mia A. *The Art of Story-Telling: A Literary Study of the Thousand and One Nights.* Leiden: Brill, 1963.

Ghazoul, Ferial J. *The Arabian Nights: A Structural Analysis.* Cairo: Cairo Associated Institution for the Study and Presentation of Arab Values, 1980.

Grossman, Judith. "Infidelity and Fiction: The Discovery of Women's Subjectivity in the *Arabian Nights*." *Georgia Review* 34 (1980): 113–26.

Hovannisian, Richard G., and Georges Sabagh, eds. *"The Thousand and One Nights" in Arabic Literature and Society.* Cambridge: Cambridge University Press, 1997.

Irwin, Robert. *The Arabian Nights: A Companion.* London: Penguin, 1994.

Kabbani, Rana. *Europe's Myths of the Orient.* New York: Macmillan, 1986.

Kelen, Jacqueline. *Les nuits de Schéhérazade.* Paris: Albin Michel, 1986.

Lahy-Hollebecque, Marie. *Le féminisme de Schéhérazade.* Paris: Radot, 1927.

Macdonald, D. B. "A Bibliographical and Literary Study of the First Appearance of the Arabian Nights in Europe." *Literary Quarterly* 2 (1932): 387–420.

Malti-Douglas, Fedwa. *Woman's Body, Woman's Word:*

Gender and Discourse in Arabo-Islamic Writing. Princeton: Princeton University Press, 1991.

Mahdi, Mushin. "Remarks on the 1001 Nights." *Interpretation* 2 (Winter):157–68.

Marzoph, Ulrich, ed. *The Arabian Nights: An Encyclopedia.* Santa Barbara, CA: ABC-CLIO, 2004.

——. *The Arabian Nights Reader.* Detroit: Wayne State University Press, 2006.

Saadawi, Nawal El. *The Hidden Face of Eve.* London: Zed Press, 1980.

Timeless Allegories
to Entertain and Delight

Arabian Nights
edited by Jack Zipes
These beautiful tales are not only the stories told to the
brooding prince by the beautiful Scheherazade, they are also
the story of her survival. This edition contains 40 of the most
popular tales adapted directly from the unexpurgated 1886
10-volume translation by Sir Richard F. Burton.

The Canterbury Tales: A Selection
by Geoffrey Chaucer
edited by Donald Howard and with a new
Foreword by Frank Grady
This unique edition maintains much of the middle English
text, while at the same time incorporating normalized
contemporary spellings to produce a text which is both easy
to read and faithful to the sound and sense of Chaucer's
original.

READ THE TOP 20
SIGNET CLASSICS

1984 BY GEORGE ORWELL

ANIMAL FARM BY GEORGE ORWELL

FRANKENSTEIN BY MARY SHELLEY

THE INFERNO BY DANTE

BEOWULF (BURTON RAFFEL, TRANSLATOR)

HAMLET BY WILLIAM SHAKESPEARE

HEART OF DARKNESS & THE SECRET SHARER
   BY JOSEPH CONRAD

NARRATIVE OF THE LIFE OF FREDERICK DOUGLASS
   BY FREDERICK DOUGLASS

THE SCARLET LETTER BY NATHANIEL HAWTHORNE

NECTAR IN A SIEVE BY KAMALA MARKANDAYA

A TALE OF TWO CITIES BY CHARLES DICKENS

ALICE'S ADVENTURES IN WONDERLAND &
      THROUGH THE LOOKING GLASS BY LEWIS CARROLL

ROMEO AND JULIET BY WILLIAM SHAKESPEARE

ETHAN FROME BY EDITH WHARTON

A MIDSUMMER NIGHT'S DREAM BY WILLIAM SHAKESPEARE

MACBETH BY WILLIAM SHAKESPEARE

OTHELLO BY WILLIAM SHAKESPEARE

THE ADVENTURES OF HUCKLEBERRY FINN BY MARK TWAIN

ONE DAY IN THE LIFE OF IVAN DENISOVICH
   BY ALEXANDER SOLZHENITSYN

JANE EYRE BY CHARLOTTE BRONTË